PRAISE FOR SARAH BETH DURST

New York Times, USA Today, and Indie Bestselling Author

"Durst consistently defies expectations."

—*Publishers Weekly* (starred review)

"Elements of fantasy and magical realism provide an intriguing framework for exploring the ideas of complicated grief and whether not telling the truth can leave real remnants that affect the world around us."

—*Booklist*

"*The Lies Among Us* is a wonderfully inventive novel, beautifully written, with a cast of characters that is fantastic in every sense of the word . . . a marvelous read!"

—Louisa Morgan, author of *A Secret History of Witches*

"This book is full of lies (and that's exactly why you should read it). *The Lies Among Us* is an engrossing and wildly inventive story that takes a magic wand to the lies we tell ourselves and each other and imagines a world in which the line between truth and fiction is a curtain that could be pulled back at any moment."

—Ruth Emmie Lang, author of *Beasts of Extraordinary Circumstance*

"An incredibly fun and inspiring read."

—Katherine Arden, *New York Times* bestselling author of *The Bear and the Nightingale*

THE
WARBLER

OTHER TITLES BY SARAH BETH DURST

Books for Kids

Spy Ring

The Shelterlings

Even and Odd

Catalyst

Spark

The Stone Girl's Story

Journey Across the Hidden Islands

The Girl Who Could Not Dream

Out of the Wild

Into the Wild

THE
WARBLER

A NOVEL

SARAH BETH DURST

LAKE UNION
PUBLISHING

Published by Lake Union Publishing, Seattle

www.apub.com

Amazon, the Amazon logo, and Lake Union Publishing are trademarks of Amazon.com, Inc., or its affiliates.

ISBN-13: 9781662524110 (paperback)
ISBN-13: 9781662524103 (digital)

Cover design by Laywan Kwan
Cover image: © rolandtopor / Shutterstock; © enot-poloskun / Getty

Printed in the United States of America

To Becca and Noah
Whatever path you choose to follow,
Wherever life takes you,
I will always love you.

Fly free and root deep!

CHAPTER ONE

ELISA

Now

My mother is a willow.

She stands by a stream that burbles like a toddler's kisses, and her leaves dip into the water whenever the wind blows, to be nibbled by fish who don't know any better.

Everyone believes I am being so poetic when at last I tell them, when I say goodbye.

I am not.

If I stay, then one day, beneath the watchful blue sky, I too will grow roots, my skin will harden to bark, and the strands of my hair will blossom.

Perhaps I will be a pear tree.

I'm packed before I'm ready to leave—socks rolled, underwear efficiently tucked into my bra cups, extra cash wedged into sneakers at the bottom of my backpack, a half dozen granola bars stashed in the outer pocket with my toothbrush and floss.

I am an expert at packing the stuff I don't care whether I lose.

Everything else I can't bring anyway.

Sitting on the edge of the bed, I look at our—at *his*—bedroom. There are photos of us tucked into the edge of the mirror. I'd meant to buy frames. I wish I had. Not to hang on the wall, because that would be too permanent and whoever comes next won't appreciate my face smiling so determinedly at them. But to sit on the dresser, to be tucked into a drawer, to be *kept*. Unframed photos are too easy to toss. I don't want to be tossed. I'd rather be gradually forgotten, like a sunny afternoon indistinct from other summer days. The ones where I sipped iced coffee that was more sugar than bean and he haphazardly weeded the flower bed, randomly assigning "weed" and "flower" status to the indistinguishable green shoots.

I'd love to take just one memento with me: A shell from the beach where the breeze blew my hat into the surf. He waded in after it even though the water was frigid. Or the lucky dime I found the day I realized he'd memorized my favorite kind of pizza (with ricotta), my favorite ice cream flavor (black raspberry), and my favorite cheese (Havarti, melted on pita bread). Or even just his old headphones—a practical theft—but I'd know they were his every time I used them, which is exactly why I can't take them. I don't dare.

Only leave with what you brought, or what's exclusively yours— that's safest. Only keep what doesn't matter.

I stayed ten and a half months this time, half a month longer than I've ever stayed in any one place. I let Tyler distract me. He was a lovely distraction.

When I was a kid, ten months was the max we'd live anywhere, no exceptions. Mom would enroll me in school from September to June, and then we'd use the summer to disappear. Another school in another state would take me as its new kid the next September. Sometimes, Mom even let me keep my name.

Elisa.

She told me it means "wanderer."

Sometimes I just vary the spelling when I uproot myself: Elissa, Alissa, Alyssa, Lyssa, Lissa, Liss, Lise. But I've also been Beatrix, Wanda, Gitana, and Barbara—all of which mean "traveler" or "stranger." Once, I introduced myself as Journey, but that felt too on the nose.

To Tyler, I've been Lyssa. I liked being her. Lyssa had ticklish feet, a fondness for slightly-too-violent nineties cartoons, and an unholy love of cheese.

Who will I be next?

I haven't decided yet, or even let myself think about it. That's for the bus, which is leaving in—I check the clock beside the bed, his bed—fifteen minutes.

I heave my backpack onto my back and hop so the straps settle evenly on my shoulders. Last night, I told Tyler the truth. He didn't believe me, of course, but at least he didn't yell like Kevin did—the last boy I'd loved and left. So that was nice. Tyler said we'd talk more when he got home from work, even though I knew I'd be halfway to . . . well, not halfway *to* anywhere. Halfway *from* here.

I say a silent goodbye to the tiny slip of a house—formerly his parents'; he'd bought it from them when they moved to Florida—and let myself out the front gate. Above, a crow scolds me. Inside a neighbor's house, a dog barks. I walk briskly past all the other houses, with my head down. I always walk with purpose. Tyler used to tease me about it, and I never tried to explain. He wouldn't have understood. But there is a simple reason: when you can't control *when* you go, it's nice to at least control *how*.

As I reach the end of the street, I realize I'm already doing it: thinking of Tyler in the past tense, as if he's died. I don't cry as I walk toward the bus stop. There's no point in that. I'm moving forward now, not backward. Away to my next life, my next self.

When the bus comes, I board and don't look back.

Never look back.

This bus smells like stale coffee and peanut butter, mixed with the familiar odors of exhaust and urine that have seeped into the plastic upholstery of every bus I've ever been on. I have a window seat, which is the way I like it. I watch the houses flicker by and imagine the lives of the people who live in them. Mothers, fathers, sisters, brothers, friends. I try to guess who is lonely and who wishes they were, based on only a glimpse:

Manicured bushes and mulched flower beds? They have either something to prove to the neighbors (*Look, I belong!*) or something to prove to themselves (*Look, I belong!*). Or they don't want to prove anything to anyone; they just want to be left alone to play in the dirt.

Shades down? They want to either shut the world out or keep their own world in.

Junk in the yard? Perhaps they never learned to let go.

I could teach them about that.

With each mile, I shed who I was and gather who I will be. I know the drill. This isn't my first bus ride. In fact, I can't remember what number bus ride it is, and that unsettles me. When did I forget what I've forgotten?

What do I remember? My first real goodbye was to Emma Sanchez. She'd shared her green crayon the first week of kindergarten and was terrified of puppets. She came to my birthday party, the first to arrive and the last to leave. While our mothers talked, Emma and I hid in a closet and ate all the leftover cupcakes. I knew I couldn't pack them.

My first goodbye kiss was Jasper Andrews. I was thirteen and had decided that a constant state of impermanence meant no consequences. I knew I'd be leaving; therefore there was no reason not to kiss him. It would have been a sweet moment, except he surprised me by shoving his tongue between my teeth, and I surprised *him* by instinctively biting down. I'm confident it was memorable for both of us.

There were a few years where I tried not to make any friends. And a few years where I tried to make every friend, as if quantity could make up for quality. With Tyler, I'd chosen quality for the first time in a while: a single intense relationship, all the sweeter for its mortality.

You can cram a lot of living into ten months, if you try.

Tyler didn't understand that—why I was always now, now, now. But he went merrily along with every one of my ideas, from our first kiss at a party I'd crashed (sixteen pizzas delivered to one beach house—how could I resist that lure?) to the next morning, when he said sleepily, "I wish you didn't have to leave." And I said, "I don't. At least, not yet."

He always seemed vaguely surprised I'd chosen him. Equally surprised when it was time for me to leave, even though I'd warned him, obliquely, a thousand times that life is short and joy ephemeral—at least if you're me.

"Goodbye, Tyler," I whisper to the bus window.

And then I let him go.

When the bus squeals to a stop two hours later, I disembark. My ticket is for Springfield, but you don't ever want to go all the way to your destination. You could be tracked and then convinced to return. Safer to have a clean break.

When I approach the ticket counter, I widen my eyes and add a quiver to my voice. "Excuse me? Please? Can I exchange my ticket? I need to change my destination?" Each sentence ends with a question mark. There's an art to being unmemorable, and it begins with leaning into people's expectations of me—*I'm harmless and forgettable,* my rising inflection says.

The extra lilt isn't necessary this time; this woman doesn't give a shit beyond whether I pay and when her lunch break is. She won't remember yet another customer. "Where to?" she asks in a bored drawl.

Perhaps this is an opportunity, given how little she cares. I don't need to choose at random. I pull a list from my pocket, crumpled and stained but still legible. I've kept it for years, ever since I was a kid. It's a list of places that could hold the answers that I so desperately need: where my family came from, why we can never stay anywhere, and how to break the pattern. I've crossed off many places over the years and added many others.

Tyler wasn't on this list. He was a detour.

But it's time to resume my search.

Comparing my list to the bus destination board, I find a match: Greenborough, Massachusetts. I don't remember when I added it or why—perhaps it's the town with the kid who'd miraculously survived a fatal car wreck. Or is it the one with the unexplained deaths that locals blame on a cursed playground? Or where an infertile woman gave birth and insisted it was due to magic water? Regardless, it must have enough unexplained oddities to make it onto my list. One of these places had to be either the place my family's little problem began or the place where it could end. I just need to keep searching. Greenborough will do.

Ticket in hand, I scurry to the bathroom, buy myself a cheese sandwich (with cash—always only cash), and wait to board. I eye the other waiting passengers:

A middle-aged woman with baggy eyes who grips a toddler firmly by the hand.

An older woman with thin hair and headphones that dwarf her head.

A freshly shaved man in an ill-fitting suit.

Two college-age girls, one with an arm draped around the shoulders of the other. The first, an Indian girl with a pixie cut and a nose ring, is glaring at the other passengers-to-be, while the second, a White girl with heavy eye makeup, is absorbed in her phone.

Not the mother. If I were a lot younger, yes. If your cheeks are still squishy, then you can tap into their protect-the-young maternal instincts. But once your cheeks sink closer to your skull, those same mama-bear instincts can work against you if they feel the need to defend their young.

Not the older woman, either, with those don't-talk-to-me headphones.

Definitely not the nervous-looking man in the suit. He's fidgeting too much, adjusting the lapels on his jacket, futzing with his collar. He's on his way to either an interview or a funeral.

So that leaves the young couple, the college-age girls.

I know I can still pass for a college student, even though I never was one. The backpack helps. Clean shorts and T-shirt, hair that's brushed but not styled (a few flyaway pieces), no makeup, simple silver earrings—I'm harmless, that's the snap judgment I want them to make about me, while I'm busy making snap judgments about them.

"Hey," I say to the hostile-looking girl with the nose ring—the other, the one on her phone, is assiduously avoiding eye contact with anyone. "Sorry to interrupt, but any chance you know someone in Greenborough looking for a roommate or to sublet for a few months?"

The pale girl moves her eyes up to me, then back down to her phone. She doesn't speak.

"Nope," the other says.

"Okay, sorry, never mind." I shift away, out of their space, and fix my gaze on the street as if watching for the bus, which I am, but I'm also watching them. Out of the corner of my eye, I see them whisper.

As the bus pulls in, the nose ring girl says, "You don't want to live in Greenborough."

Looking up, the phone girl nods. Her eyes are wide. Solemn. But that could be an effect of her eye makeup, heavy kohl black that makes the whites look startlingly pearlescent.

"Oh?" I say. "Why not?"

They glance at each other.

"It's the kind of place where people get stuck," the wide-eyed one says. Her voice is so soft that I barely catch the words.

A dead-end town.

I've been to those before. Good places to disappear. Not great for what I seek, but it could still serve as a transitional location. I can check out any oddities to see if they relate to my affliction, and I can try to earn as much cash as I can before hitting the next town—I know the drill. "I'll only be there temporarily."

She shrugs. Looks down again and murmurs, "You'll see."

I climb onto the bus and claim a window seat near the back. As we pull away from whatever town this is, I watch the houses again and imagine what it would feel like to call one of them home. And then I squash the thought—there's no point in thinking like that, not when I have a new life to establish.

Greenborough.

What's my story for moving there? A fresh start after a bad breakup? Striking out on my own, away from judgmental family? Lost my job so I'm trying a new town? Just wanted to live somewhere new, without any memories or ties? I like the last one. It lets the listener fill in the blanks. Can't get caught in a lie that way.

It's another hour and a half before the bus pulls off the highway toward the sign to Greenborough. We're somewhere in the middle of Massachusetts; I haven't looked at a map to determine exactly where, mainly because it doesn't matter. Only the details do. I make mental notes of everything we pass. A gas station with a Dunkin' drive-thru, followed by a Burger King, also with a drive-thru, both of which are useless since I won't have a car. Can't afford one. A take-out pizza place with the name A Little Slice of Heaven, followed by an auto repair garage. Then a garden store with flats of impatiens, baskets of petunias, and row after row of flowering shrubs. A particularly baleful garden gnome watches the bus pass, and I maintain eye contact until he's blocked by trees.

The houses are small, old with bikes strewn in driveways, which I take to be a good sign. It's a town that's doing okay, which is the best kind of town for me—not so expensive that I can't stay and not so run down that I shouldn't stay. It also looks like it's an ordinary kind of town, which is a bit disappointing, given that that means it's unlikely to hold the answers I need. *A transitional town isn't terrible,* I remind myself. Worst case, I can use this place to regroup, lick my wounds, and figure out where to search next.

One of the girls, the more talkative one with the nose ring, leans across the aisle and says, "If you're going to stay, you should check the board at Bean Street. It's a coffee shop, block from the bus station on Granchester Street. People post vacancies there."

I flash her a smile. "Thanks!"

"Don't thank me. Trust me. You don't want to stay. It's an unlucky town."

"Oh?"

She doesn't elaborate, just ducks back into her seat. But I think of the crumpled list in my pocket. Maybe, despite initial impressions, this won't be a waste of time. Perhaps Greenborough does have secrets. I am familiar with the flutter I feel inside: *hope.*

After so many bus rides into so many new towns, so many attempts to find answers, it's a ludicrous emotion, but I can't help it. There's a whisper inside me: *Maybe here.*

I don't ask her anything else, even though I have a dozen more questions: Do they know of any job openings? Where's the local laundromat? The cheapest grocery store? In what way is it unlucky? Is there anyone there like me?

Anyone whose family is cursed?

And most importantly: Is there anyone who can reverse a curse?

But it's better not to pepper them with questions, at least not in the beginning.

Better to be unmemorable.

First priority is to find a place to live, fast. It doesn't take many nights of sleeping outside before you don't look so harmless, before you look desperate, before you begin to make mistakes, before you convince yourself that a few nights in a motel will be anonymous enough. It's not. You need to find a place to sleep and shower that can't be easily traced by anyone willing to make a few phone calls. Eventually, I'll be able to ask questions and poke around and uncover whatever secrets this town may or may not be keeping. And in the meantime, I can show the only two family photos I have—one of my mother and one of my grandmother—and see if anyone recognizes them. It's an easy ask. Few people mind looking at a couple photos of lost relatives. I know what I need to do; this isn't the first time I've sailed into a brand-new town. And unless I'm miraculously lucky, it won't be the last. I just need to keep trying—and keep moving.

The bus drives into the heart of town—it still looks ordinary to me, but then again, so do I. There's a post office, a shoe store, a slightly run-down restaurant with picnic tables outside, a few "Space for Rent" empty stores. A laundromat next to a bakery. I spot the coffee shop called Bean Street, my first destination. Next to it, there's a used bookstore with a faded sign that says THE BOOK CELLAR. In the window, curled in front of the book display, is a black-and-white cat. Unlike the garden gnome, the cat doesn't care as we drive past. But I watch it as we round the corner. The bus squeals as it parks.

With my backpack and an unwarranted dose of hope, I step off the bus into a new life.

CHAPTER TWO

I planned to visit the coffee shop first, but the bookstore has a cat.

A bell chimes as I push open the door. Stepping inside, I breathe in the distinctive scent of paper, ink, and dust and feel instantly calmer. I know I've never set foot in here before, but all bookstores have the same kind of familiarity, a comforting sense of *Here you'll find what you need.* Even if all it offers is an illusion that lasts for a few hundred pages.

I'll take the illusion every time.

The two girls on the bus are wrong: any town with a bookstore like this isn't a place you're stuck in; it's a place you *want* to stay. Or at least it's a place I wish I could stay. I breathe in the tastes of dust, paper, cinnamon, and coffee.

The Book Cellar is overflowing with books, exactly as a bookstore should be. Every shelf is stuffed, with volumes wedged horizontally on top of vertical rows and crammed between the top shelf and the ceiling, so many that they look as if they've been quietly breeding for years. Between the shelves, additional books are stacked in precarious towers, knee high to hip high, further narrowing the slender aisles—a labyrinth of books, with handwritten signs to guide: MYSTERY, ROMANCE, FANTASY AND SCIENCE FICTION, COOKBOOKS. I run my fingers over the spines and let the bookstore envelop me. I'm careful to not let my backpack knock into any of the piles.

The best thing about books, at least for me, is that favorites can feel like home. Yet they're portable and replaceable. Any copy will do.

Even more, once you've read them, they're part of you. You don't need the actual book anymore. You can let them go without letting them go. It's a rare and beautiful loophole in the rules that govern my life, and I'm grateful for it.

My mother taught me to love books. Used bookstores were her favorite—every time we came to or left a town, she'd stop to sell the books she'd read and buy a new batch. Sometimes she'd rebuy the same book just to visit the pages again.

It wasn't enough to keep her from wanting more.

But it helped.

Some days, it was all that did. She always viewed our fate as inevitable—"our family inheritance," she called it, as unavoidable and unchangeable as our brown eyes—and that belief was a constant drain on her. I am less fatalistic. Or more foolish.

I was five or six when she first told me about the family curse. *It hits the women in our family,* my mom said, and it's simply this: we always have to leave. If we stay anywhere too long . . . if we even begin to consider a place our home . . . if we start to put down roots . . . then our skin will harden to bark, our blood will turn to sap, and we will never be able to leave.

My mother became a willow tree.

I don't know how to forgive her for that. But I do know I won't let it be my fate.

Being in this store reminds me of her so strongly that I half expect to see her curled in a tattered velvet chair, knees drawn to her chest, a book held out at arm's length because she's lost her reading glasses again, and she doesn't hear—

"Can I help you find anything?"

I jump as if the book spines burned my fingertips.

A man is standing behind the cash register, waist deep in a sea of books. I don't know how I failed to notice him, except that he blends in. He looks a bit like the store: a little rumpled and a little familiar, even though I know we've never met. He's probably in his late twenties or early thirties. His flannel shirt is threadbare at the elbows, his soft brown beard trimmed short, and his warm brown eyes remind me of a cup of tea. His hand rests lightly on an open book, and I wonder if he's the type who reads to consume or be subsumed. I want to ask. Instead, I say, "Just looking." Always the safest reply, especially since it's perpetually true.

"Okay, let me know if you need anything."

Empty words, although he says them as if he means them.

Resisting the temptation to unleash my full list of questions, ranked from practical to existential, I smile vaguely and disappear between the shelves. Later, maybe I can dance around what I really want to know: *Do you know how to save me?*

Unlikely, I know, but somewhere someone must have the answer I need.

And until I find it, I still need to live, which means what I really need is food and a safe place to sleep, neither of which is what the bookseller means. What I need is a little house on a quiet street, with Tyler in the kitchen, smiling at me as if I'm an unexpected gift—*Don't think about Tyler.* Firmly and deliberately, I banish the ball of emotions that Tyler summons. There's a trick to compartmentalizing emotion-laden memories, and I've nearly mastered it.

It's the "nearly" that I have to watch out for. "Nearly" can kill you. It killed my mother.

Wandering the aisles, I touch the books' spines and listen to the piano music that's piped through the shop—it's a soothing run of notes that helps wash away unwanted thoughts. After I find a place to live, I tell myself, I'll dress it up with as many books as I can. Live with them while I'm here. Leave them behind when I go.

Once, when I was younger—eight? ten? the memories bleed together, and I can't sort them into proper order anymore, which is an unsettling realization—when I was eight or ten, I made notes in one of my books, in the margins. It was a book of fairy tales, lots of black-and-white illustrations. I wanted to leave it behind for another person to find, like a letter to a stranger, connecting us through the stories. I added doodles and details about my life: what I liked, what we did on Saturday afternoons, a bird I'd seen, a TV show I'd watched . . . As we took the bus out of town, I told my mother about what I'd done, proud that I'd found a way to leave a piece of me behind. We went back and found the book, and my mother made me tear up every page my pencil had touched. I never wrote in another book again. To this day, I never even bend a corner of a page to mark my place, and I'm always careful not to break the spine. I can read them as many times as I like; I just can't leave any of myself behind.

Maybe I'm too careful.

Maybe my mother was too scared.

But how can you know? It's not as if there's a rule book for curses. There's no way to find out what's truth and what's fear, or even habit, without risking everything. Not worth it—which was always my mother's conclusion too. Every night she was with me, she'd kiss my forehead and say, *Stay safe.* Never *Good night, Sweet dreams, Sleep tight,* or even *I love you.* Always *Stay safe,* her dearest wish for me.

I run my fingers over the spines once more, as if caressing the arm of a lover, and then I sigh and drift back to the front of the store, where the bookstore cat watches me with its yellow eyes. Beside the cat is a sign: **HELP WANTED**. It's curled around the edges, as if it's been there for some time. I stare at it for a moment, feeling hope—my old stubborn friend—rise in me yet again.

Maybe I'm meant to be here.

Sometimes the pieces come together—a job, a bed, access to food—and sometimes they don't, and I have to move on, even if I'd planned to linger. I hope fate is on my side this time.

"He looks wise," I say, stalling while I try to think of the perfect reason for the bookseller to hire me. It's always tricky, without references, without a verifiable work history, and without a permanent address. I have to approach him carefully.

The bookseller snorts. "Two nights ago, he got his head stuck in a tissue box. He thought he could fit himself inside. Ran around yowling until he crashed into the refrigerator and I was finally able to catch him and take it off."

I grin. "Can I pet him?"

He shrugs. "Up to him. You can try. Your fate's in your hands, though. I can tell you he usually doesn't draw blood."

Without moving closer, I hold out a finger. The cat lifts his head to tap his nose against it. I have never met a cat who can resist an outstretched finger. Introduction complete, I rub his cheek with my thumb, and he leans his head against my hand with force, until I'm petting him the way he wants: cheek, neck, back, then cheek again.

"Guess that's a yes," the bookseller says.

Maybe since his cat likes me, he'll give me a job? I wish job interviews were that easy.

"His name's Charlie."

"Hi, Charlie. I'm Elisa." The name slips out before I've decided whether that's what I'll use here. I suppose it won't cause any problems. I haven't used my real name in a while. It's unlikely anyone is still looking for me by that name. I resolve that it will be the only unedited truth that I tell in Greenborough.

"How many cats do you have?" the bookseller asks.

My lips quirk. "I didn't know I gave off a cat-lady vibe."

"Absolutely no offense meant," he backpedals. "It's just that you know how to woo a cat. That's not a skill everyone has."

"No cats of my own. Can't. I move around too much." Charlie's fur is thick, as if he's prepared for an Arctic winter, and he has more whiskers on his eyebrows than a great-great-grandfather. A stately cat who knows his appeal.

"Animals can adjust to new places," the bookseller says. "It's the people that matter to them." He pauses. "Except for Alvin. That's my neighbor's cat. He despises people. Also hates dogs, squirrels, birds, and socks. My neighbor gave up wearing socks because Alvin would pee in his sock drawer."

"Your neighbor could have closed the drawer."

"Alvin can open drawers."

"Clever cat."

Charlie headbutts my hand. Jealous of me talking about another cat, or informing me that I'm not petting him enthusiastically enough. I renew my attention to the fluff on his neck. He purrs as loud as a bus engine. "Does he always—"

"My theory: he ate a lawn mower."

I laugh.

It would be easy to make friends with a man like this—charming, easy to talk to, and clearly loves books. *It's the kind of place where people get stuck.* Or is it the kind of place people want to get stuck? No, I want no involvement this time around. I can't afford more heartbreak. You can only pile up so many regrets before they weigh you down, and I carry enough to rival an Olympic weight lifter. Maybe it would be better *not* to ask him for a job.

"So what brings you to town?" the bookseller asks.

That is a question with a very long answer, and I fully intend to dodge it. "I like to explore new places." Vague but not inaccurate. "I'm thinking of staying here for a while. About ten months . . . or so." I realize "ten months" may seem oddly precise. "You wouldn't happen to know of anyone subletting an apartment in the area or looking for a roommate? Can't do a full-year lease, but if any of your customers are looking for a temporary tenant . . ."

"You should check next door at—"

"Bean Street," I finish. "I will. Thanks."

He leans forward on his desk, which appears to be composed entirely of stacked books. "I have to ask: Why here?"

The question reminds me of the two college girls on the bus, and I wonder again what secrets this town holds. In my experience, people don't usually question why you want to move to their town. It's their home; they expect people will live there. "Why not here? Is there something I should know about this town? Is there anything wrong with it?" *Please say yes.*

He laughs. "It's absolutely normal. So ordinary that we don't get many new arrivals. Really didn't mean to pry. It's none of my business why you came. You just said you move a lot . . . Where from? Is that a better question?"

It's not. But it's one that's easy to dodge. Swallowing my disappointment, I say, "Everywhere. Mostly the US. I've lived in every state except Alaska, Hawaii, and Mississippi. Well, and Rhode Island. Can't trust a state that doesn't know what kind of landmass it is."

He grins.

I wonder if he noticed my dodge. *Possibly.* He's paying more attention than the usual stranger does, and it's nice—when most people small talk, they're either going through the motions or waiting for their turn to monologue. One of the hardest parts about continually starting over is finding new people who see and hear you. Of course, it's safer to be forgettable, but it wears on you, to live like that.

Maybe it would be okay to make *one* friend here. *I can handle another goodbye.* Especially if I don't stay too long this time.

I am a rock skimming the surface of a pond, wanting to make ripples but afraid I'll sink.

"I've never lived anywhere but here," the bookseller says. "Always wanted to. Not Rhode Island—though I think the name is more aspirational than deceptive—but I'd love to live in England. Or Italy. Spain. Greece. Japan. Even California. Montana. Arizona."

Interesting. I can't imagine wanting to ever leave this store. My eyes settle on the **HELP WANTED** sign again. Maybe this is why he wants to hire someone, so he can travel. "Why haven't you?"

"Got ties here," he says lightly, like he's answered that question as often as I've answered his. It's a stock answer. "Plus, can you imagine how many boxes I'd need, to pack up this many books?" He waves his hand at all the shelves. "And of course, there's Charlie."

Didn't he just say pets are portable? *Excuses.*

Everyone has excuses for why they stay or go.

Though, I am the very last person who should pry into anyone's reasons for either. Perhaps the perfect bookstore isn't perfect if it's the only place you ever see.

He leans his elbow on a stack of books. "So, what's your favorite place you've been? And why? Bore me with details, please."

He looks legitimately interested, which makes me feel a twinge of guilt at the half-truths—and lies—I'm about to tell. But then I realize that he has unwittingly handed me the key: "If you hire me for the next few months, I'll tell you about everywhere I've lived."

His brown eyes widen in surprise. "You're looking for a job?"

"Landlords like it if you can pay rent." Thanks to my mother, I have savings, but I refuse to touch it, also thanks to my mother. She wanted to ensure that I never starved, but the cost she paid for that assurance was far too high. If I were to use the money, it would be like saying she did the right thing, and I'll never agree with that.

Maybe someday I'll forgive her. Or maybe I won't. Forgiveness is for people with other things to hold on to.

"You moved here without a job or a place to live? You're brave."

I shrug. "I'm spontaneous." Also desperate, but I try not to dwell on that.

"Do you have any bookstore experience?" he asks.

Yes, but I can't give references. "I've worked more retail jobs than you can possibly imagine, including a couple bookstores and, once, a store that sold only buttons. Plus, I'm excellent at alphabetizing. Never once messed up the location of 'W.'"

He's grinning again. "Quite an achievement."

"I am impressive," I say with a playful wink.

It might be a mistake to stay. This could be exactly as he said: an ordinary town. A dead-end town, where nothing unusual happens or ever has happened.

I'll know for certain soon enough. And then I'll move on.

He hums to himself as he rifles through his desk, then produces a crinkled piece of paper. He skims it before handing it over. "Job application."

Quickly, I fill it out, listing a random assortment of jobs, with zero specifics about their locations, and also leaving both my address and references blank. I hand it back.

He frowns. "Cryptic."

"Once, I lived in a near ghost town that's been on fire since 1962." My mother and I, really, but I'm not ready to talk about her yet. She's been gone for three years, but every time I start anew, it feels like I lost her yesterday. "It's a coal mine fire, underground, and the hills ooze smoke. There are sinkholes hot enough to bake a potato. I tried it. It tasted like rotten eggs. What's left of the town smells like sulfur. You haven't truly smelled a place until you've breathed in a town that stinks like sulfur. More invasive than skunk." I can taste the stench in my memory, even now. Some memories are like that, leaving their residue on your senses. My mother said she deserved the stench; we left because she said I did not. "I heard the fire could burn for another two hundred fifty years, but I moved away after two weeks."

"And the best-smelling place you've ever lived?"

"Above a bakery that made cinnamon rolls the size of Charlie. Had to wake up at four a.m. for that job, but it was worth it for the first roll of the morning, when the frosting was liquid hot and the cinnamon scalded your tongue but you didn't care."

I pet the cat as I talk, and he purrs even louder than before.

"You can start tomorrow, if you'd like," he says. "I'm Owen, by the way."

"Nice to meet you, Owen."

We agree on hours and a wage. Part time, hourly, no health benefits. But it's a job, and there's a cat, as well as a nice man with warm brown eyes and a ton of books.

"Welcome to the Book Cellar," Owen says and holds out his hand.

I stop petting Charlie and shake Owen's hand. Charlie lifts his head, peering from beneath his bushy eye whiskers, a look of absolute betrayal. "I'll be back," I tell the cat. "I promise."

Deal finalized, I walk outside. *I can handle this place.* The greatest lie I've ever told myself.

CHAPTER THREE

The woman who makes a liar of me is in pink: light-pink blouse and magenta pants. Streaks of pink in her hair. And it makes me think of blood on a white linen tablecloth that's been run through a washing machine so many times that the stain has faded to a benign state—Valentine's Day, not war.

Sun in my face, I don't see her at first. I'm looking at the shadows at my feet, cast by a tree onto the sidewalk—a linden tree, special for how symmetrically it grows. There are shadows of blossoms tucked between the leaves, just as delicate and beautiful as the flowers themselves. I am thinking about what a stroke of luck it was to be drawn into that bookstore, with a job that feels made for me, when the woman in pink hurls herself into me.

Her fingernails dig crescent-moon welts into my arms, and I am too shocked to pry her off or push her away. Heavy against me, she sags as if her knees are mush and looks up into my eyes. "Please," she whispers, "help me leave."

Leave? Leave where? "What's wrong? Are you in danger? Are you hurt?" Glancing up, I look for someone who could help. A pickup with lawn equipment rumbles down the street. An older couple strolls out of the coffee shop. They're laughing, arm in arm.

I call to them, "I think this woman needs help!"

The laughter dies.

The couple looks at me. At her. Then looks away.

It's an odd reaction. You don't just ignore someone in obvious distress. Still clinging to me, the woman sinks onto her knees. I can't keep her upright. "Do you need a doctor?" I can't tell what's wrong with her, but clearly something is. Is she having a stroke? A heart attack? "Call 911!"

I can't call. No phone. Tyler never understood that—he tried to buy me one once. But why would I have a phone? I don't want the past to reach me. If he were here now, he'd be saying, "I told you so." Actually, he'd be busy calling 911 himself since he's not a callous monster.

The older couple strolls on.

"Help!" I call after them.

I glance back at the Book Cellar, but I don't see Owen. Only the cat, watching me, the woman, the sky, and the birds. If Owen knew what was happening, he'd help—I'm certain he's that kind of person— but he is deep in the stacks or immersed in a book or just not by the window. "Can you stand?" I ask the woman. My backpack unbalances me, and I brace myself so I don't fall over. I don't think I can carry her. Even if I could, I don't know that I should.

She doesn't answer.

Gently, I try to pry her hands from my arms. Her fingers grip as hard as eagle talons. "Please, tell me what's wrong," I beg. "I don't know how to help you."

She looks directly into my eyes—

She can't see me.

I don't know why I am so certain, but I am. Looking at her feels like standing in a room after the lights have turned off, before your eyes have adjusted to see layers of shadows—you stare and stare but can't make out shapes through the darkness. Only stardust. Her eyes glitter with the reflection of the sun, and I'm reminded of distant galaxies.

My voice feels frozen in my throat. Who is she? What does she want? Chance or choice that she grabbed on to me? She should have chosen someone else. I can't be embroiled in other people's disasters.

I don't have either the time or the strength to care about the fate of strangers when I'm barely able to keep myself afloat. "Let go," I say. "Please." It comes out as a whisper.

She releases.

Half of me wants to flee. Half of me wants to make sure she's okay. She should get help. From someone who isn't me. A doctor. Her family. A friend. I turn toward the Book Cellar—

And she runs.

Before I can react, she darts between two parked cars.

I see a truck, a U-Haul with the Grand Canyon painted on the side, a young driver clutching the steering wheel. He looks like he hasn't driven such a large vehicle before. He's nervous he'll nick the mirror of one of the parked cars. He's focused on the green light up ahead, anxious about whether it will turn yellow and if he can stop before it switches to red. Or he's listening to music and doesn't think to see if a woman is about to burst out from between two parked cars.

I scream.

I think I scream.

I don't hear myself. I hear the tires screech. I hear the thump. It's a terrible sound, a softness to its solidity beneath the shrill cry of the brakes.

The woman collapses to the pavement.

The driver flings the door open and jumps down. He's on his phone already. At last someone calling for help—help that isn't me, because I failed. I was close enough, but I turned away. How could I have known she'd run into the street?

She isn't moving.

A crowd has gathered around her, and I feel as though there's buzzing in my head. People have poured out of the coffee shop and the post office and the other stores, but I didn't see them come, and I don't know why they didn't come earlier. I think of a flock of crows, drawn from the trees. An unkindness of ravens.

Glancing down the sidewalk, I spot the older couple. Even now, they don't look back, and they don't slow. You'd think the screech of the brakes would draw their attention. *What's wrong with these people?*

One of the ravens says, "She's breathing!"

Another: "Don't move her!"

"Did anyone call—"

There are sirens.

I don't know what to do. My hands curl over my arms, caressing the purpling indents she left with her nails. *Help me leave.* Was *this* what she meant? No, it couldn't have been. It was an accident. She didn't seem aware enough to have seen the truck. She was just trying to flee. But flee who? Why?

The driver is leaning against the hood of the U-Haul, and his face looks drained of all blood. A woman is next to him, her hand on his shoulder.

The sirens are closer.

"What happened?" A voice next to me—it takes me a second to place him: the man I was with mere minutes ago, the bookstore owner, my new boss, my possible friend, Owen.

"She just . . . ran. He couldn't have seen her. It wasn't his fault." Was it mine? Could I have stopped her? Yes. Of course, yes, I could have stopped this, if I had known to try. "She didn't give any warning. I didn't think . . ." Except she had. *Help me leave.* If I'd listened. "I should have stopped her."

"You didn't know," he says.

I should have guessed.

I know that kind of galaxy-filled emptiness. I've seen it. In the mirror, years ago, before I decided to reject that my fate is sealed. Many times, in my mother's eyes.

Her body wanted to follow where her heart had already gone.

She believed our curse is unbreakable, and for years, she fought against it, determined that its horrors would never catch us. She followed the rules that she taught me: never stay anywhere long enough

24

for it to feel like home; never return to a place you've been before; never form ties to anyone who could tie you to a place; never let them follow or find you (they could try to force you back); always leave everyone behind. Until the day she stopped fighting.

The ambulance is here. Two EMTs spill out of the front. Another throws open the back doors. The crowd parts to let them through, and my view is blocked.

I want to leave. Walk away from all of this, back to the bus stop, and then far away. This is not what I came here for. I don't need to witness any more tragedy. I've seen enough over the course of my travels. But I feel as frozen to the sidewalk as I did when the woman clung to me. I watch, with Owen beside me, as the stretcher is wheeled quickly to her and she's lifted onto it.

She's visible for the first time: a gash on her cheek, her eyes closed, her head lolled to the side. The paramedics have strapped her to the stretcher for transport.

Beside me, Owen sucks in air.

"You know her?" I ask.

"Allison."

Allison. She has a name. A life. A past. "A friend?"

"Used to be."

We watch as she's loaded into the ambulance. I don't know where the driver has gone, but the U-Haul remains, blocking the street, a line of cars piled behind. There's a police car now, but I don't know when it arrived.

Owen says, "We were engaged."

And I know that this is the moment: if I don't want to be involved, then this is when I walk away, get on a bus, and find a new town. I only know her name; I'm not a part of any of this. There are plenty of other places on my list and a very slim chance that I'll find my salvation here. An hour or two on the bus, and it will be as if I'm a million miles away.

I can leave.

Glancing at the bookstore, I see the cat watching me and remember I promised to return. It shouldn't make a difference in my decision, a promise to a cat. It's absurd.

None of this has anything to do with me. That woman would have grabbed anyone standing on that sidewalk. I'm just passing through, a breeze barely noticed except for a few stirred leaves. I am no one and anyone, searching for something that may not exist. I am the one you don't notice and don't remember. I am the one who always says goodbye.

Yet the cat keeps watching me through the bookstore window.

CHAPTER FOUR

ROSE

1968

Rose flopped onto the grass behind the high school. Breathing in, she appreciated how hard her lungs were working to inhale. The air burned her throat as she gulped in oxygen. Her side ached, her calves burned, and she felt fully alive. Glorious!

Her best friend dropped down next to her with a huff. Her hair had half escaped its ponytail. "You know, Rose, we don't actually have to *run*. All we have to do is finish." She waved her hand toward a pack of girls who were strolling and chattering past the gym teacher. The teacher was clapping her hands, urging them faster, but the pack of girls, no hint of sweat on their gym clothes, ignored her.

"Don't you sometimes feel like you could run forever?" Rose asked dreamily.

"Nope, and you're a weirdo."

"I like the feeling that my feet could take me away." She pictured the road in front of her unending, leading toward the beautiful, unscarred future. "No one can hold me back, because I could always just run . . ."

"Or drive," Cora suggested. "You could always just get in a car and drive."

If only she could! "Someday, I will. Someday, I'll get out of here. We both will." Rose put her hands behind her head and stared up at the sky, imagining she were in a plane crossing the blue, white contrails littering the sky behind her.

Beside her, Cora propped herself up on her elbow. "And go where?"

"Everywhere," Rose breathed. She saw it unfolding in front of her: oceans and rivers and mountains and cities. She'd drink it all in like the sparkling champagne she'd sipped at her cousin's wedding when her parents weren't looking. She felt the unlived moments-to-be bubble up inside her. "Paris first. I want to stroll along the Seine at night. Sip wine in a café. Go to the top of the Eiffel Tower. And then Spain. Barcelona. Madrid. I want to eat an orange in Seville. I want to cross the Strait of Gibraltar and walk through a market in Morocco. Spend a summer on a Grecian island. See the pyramids of Giza and take a boat trip down the Nile."

Cora laughed. "You'd better marry rich."

"I don't want to marry at all," Rose said firmly. She knew that much already, though she'd never said the words out loud before. Speaking them felt like a pronouncement. "You can be the one to have a dozen kids. Teach them all to call me Aunt Rose, and I'll bring them souvenirs from my travels. I'll tell them about my trip to Japan and hitchhiking all the way to California to touch the Pacific."

"You'll change your mind when you meet the right boy," Cora predicted.

"I won't," Rose said. "Because it's not about my mind. It's about my heart." She thumped her chest so hard—for the sake of dramatic emphasis—that she made herself cough.

Cora was neither impressed nor concerned. She stretched like a cat in sunlight. "I want five kids, spaced out nicely so there aren't an unmanageable number of babies at the same time, but close enough in age that they'll be friends—or mortal enemies. Either would be fine."

"Five is a lot." Rose thought of her mother, her days stuffed with chores and errands, the same week after week, endlessly needed by her children, her husband, her parents. No one ever asked Mom what she wanted or what she needed. "You'd never get a moment to yourself."

"Exactly. It'll never be quiet." Softly, Cora said, "I'll never be alone."

That was the horror of it, in Rose's opinion, but she wasn't going to say that out loud. She knew what Cora's house was like, ever since her dad walked out. Quiet as a tomb. Cora didn't have any siblings. It was just her and her mother rattling around in that big old estate, where the plumbing didn't quite work right, the doors were slightly off their frames, and lights flickered whenever they felt like it. "You'll be a great mom," Rose reassured her.

"You think so? I couldn't keep my goldfish alive."

"Goldfish have a three-day lifespan. Don't judge yourself so harshly. Besides, I'm sure you gave that goldfish an incredible three days."

The gym teacher blew her whistle. It was time to change. Geometry was next. Rose didn't move. Beside her, Cora peeled herself off the grass. "Ugh, grass stains. And I know you're making that up about goldfish, but thanks."

"After high school . . . do you want to travel with me?" Rose hadn't planned to ask. She hadn't even known the dream was there, but once the words were out of her mouth, they felt perfect. "It doesn't need to be out of the country. We can take a road trip, straight across America. See everything from the Atlantic to the Pacific, before you have five kids."

Laughing, Cora held her hand out to Rose. "Come on, we'll be late to math."

"We could do it," Rose said, the idea seeding inside her. The more she considered it, the more excited she became. It was doable. They were only sophomores. If they began saving now . . . She could babysit more. Cora had her part-time job at the bakery. They'd need maps, as well as a car. Or they could hitchhike. With two of them, it would be safe enough. They'd watch out for each other, like they always did.

"Your parents would murder you."

"They'll have time to get used to the idea." She began to imagine how she could present it to them. She'd have it all planned out first, with at least a portion of the money they'd need squirreled away. She'd frame it as a broadening experience . . .

The gym teacher's voice cut across the field. "Girls! Inside! Now!"

Cora grabbed Rose's hand and helped her to her feet.

"I'll plan it all out," Rose told Cora. "You don't have to worry about a thing."

Cora looped her arm through Rose's. "Please don't . . ." She sighed heavily and shook her head, as though she thought Rose was some kind of a lost cause.

Rose thought of the champagne fizz of new sights, new places, new experiences! Why shouldn't they have all of that? The whole big beautiful world was out there for them to drink in! "Don't what?"

"Don't pin your hopes on the impossible," Cora said. "I hate seeing you disappointed. Maybe we can take a trip after graduation, if we're clever about it, but all the way to California? You want too much, Rose. It worries me."

"I don't think it's too much to want the world," Rose said. Grinning, she pulled away from her friend and ran toward the gym lockers.

CHAPTER FIVE

LORI

1997

Paris.

City of lights.

City of romance.

And for the first time, it felt like it was.

Lori had been here before, but of course she hadn't told Mark. It was his first visit, and he'd wanted to share it with her, which was sweet and kind and romantic—all the things that Mark was—and she hadn't wanted to ruin it for him. So she'd played wide eyed and breathless when they'd stepped off the train, packs on their backs, hand in hand. It was easy to pretend it was fresh when she saw it with him. Everything with Mark was easy, which was what made this all so impossibly hard.

Opening the window, Lori leaned against the sill. She tried to focus on the moment and not think about the future. Today, this moment, everything was fine. As hostels went, this one wasn't terrible. Yes, everything from the carpet to the bedsheets smelled as if they'd been dipped in old perfume and packed with potpourri, and yes, there were too many bodies per room, but the shared toilet was clean; plus, the room had a view.

Sort of.

If you leaned out far enough and tilted your head to the left, you could see a sliver of the Eiffel Tower between rooftops. It looked a bit like scaffolding set at a forty-five-degree angle.

She told herself she should be grateful, but she just felt tired. It wasn't because of all the snoring in the hostel, although that had kept her up, wondering which bunk would win for loudest snort. It wasn't a tourist kind of tired either, of trying to see too much too fast and love it all, even if what you really wanted was to find a soda and some shade. This was a deeper kind of tired. Soul deep.

This wasn't supposed to be my life.

Lori heard footsteps behind her but didn't turn around.

Arms wrapped around her waist. A chin rested on her shoulder. She felt warm breath against her neck and cheek. "How's the view? Hmm, it's a wall." Mark had an extra-deep voice that made her shiver when it was so close to her ear.

Lori pointed. "Over that way."

Still with his arms wrapped around her, he leaned forward, bending her too, and looked left. "Huh. That's . . . Yeah, that's not anything. Sorry. I promised you a view."

She hated the hint of disappointment in his voice. He was trying so hard to make every day they were together perfect, and it wasn't his fault that she wanted to be a different person in a different place living a different life. She felt a familiar lump in her throat. It never went away, that knot inside her. It only migrated from heart to throat to head. Sometimes the lump of hurt felt heavier to carry than her backpack.

How long will I have to live like this? And how long could she?

Forcing a smile, Lori twisted so that she was facing him, her back against the windowsill. "I do have a view." She slid her arms around his neck and kissed him as if she was never going to see him again, hard and hungry and a little sad. He kissed her back, his breath bright with fresh toothpaste.

A groggy voice from one of the bunks called, "Gah, get a room."

They broke away with a "sorry" that they didn't mean and a laugh they did.

"Breakfast?" Mark suggested, still so close she could taste his breath.

Another of their temporary roommates called, "Egg on toast." A few other orders chimed in, but Lori and Mark ignored them.

"You get the cheese," Lori said. "I'll get the bread. Meet by our bench?"

"Perfect," he said and kissed her again.

His kiss, sweet.

Her kiss, desperate.

She couldn't help wanting to swallow him whole, to savor this moment before it—like every other moment—disappeared.

United, their roommates groaned. One threw a pillow. It skittered across the stained carpet and stopped at their feet. Lori stepped over it. Mark tossed it back. As he pulled on his socks and shoes, she made sure her backpack was secure in her locker and took a smaller bag with essentials: passport, Eurail Pass, umbrella, and what little cash she had left.

She'd need to seek out more cash soon. *After Mark.* She shouldn't waste a second of this illusion of happiness. There was no way of knowing if this kind of gift would ever come her way again.

She certainly wasn't going to jeopardize what they had by letting him see what her life was really like. He thought she was a recent college grad like him, with travel funded by parents and several years of birthday gifts from generous grandparents; he had no idea she was funding her "European vacation" with pickpocketing, shoplifting, and conning rich marks out of whatever gifts she could later pawn. He didn't need to know any of that, and how would she explain it anyway? "It's because I'm cursed," wasn't a sentence she could utter.

They split up on the street, him toward the cheese shop and her toward the bakery. She glanced from the doorway and waved as he rounded the corner. He blew a kiss back at her. Waiting, Lori made sure he wasn't going to pop back and surprise her, before she bypassed the bakery door and stepped into the alley behind.

She spared a glance at the street and then moved quickly, rifling through the trash. Yesterday's bread was tossed at 4:00 a.m. She was later than she would have liked—the best was already claimed by other like-minded scavengers—but she found two short baguettes, one broken but the other whole. The croissants were all crushed, which would have been fine for just her but not for passing off as fresh. She dug deeper and emerged with a prize: a bag of hard rolls. After shoving the baguettes and the rolls into her bag, she strode back to the street. She'd learned not to look furtive. She'd spent a few nights in an Ohio jail once and nearly been arrested several other times before internalizing that lesson.

Lori was at "their" bench well before he was. Pigeons clustered around her feet, and she fed them crumbs from the broken baguette. It was near the Musée de l'Orangerie in the Jardin des Tuileries. A non-descript bench between a path and a road, but they'd sat here on their first day in Paris, before they'd found the hostel, when she wasn't sure if they'd continue traveling together—or if they'd say goodbye.

She couldn't help feeling that, so long as they kept coming back to this bench, everything would be okay. Mark made her feel that way. He was just so optimistic. He walked around with perpetual sunshine beaming over his head. She'd never met anyone like him. When they were together, she wanted to keep traveling and keep seeing new sights. With him, she didn't feel the creeping numbness that made her limbs heavy and her days empty.

The pigeons scattered as Mark jogged up to the bench. "No line?"

"Success." Lori showed off the baguette. The break in it didn't look suspicious since she'd been feeding the pigeons. She wondered what he'd say if he knew she'd rescued it from the trash. Would he be repulsed by it, or by her?

He plopped onto the bench next to her. "So I have an idea . . ."

"Roll or baguette?" she offered. Mark took a roll, and she peeked into the bag with the cheese: Munster. He'd gotten her favorite. He liked the smellier cheeses, like brie and camembert—he'd even experimented with the ones riddled with mold and claimed he'd liked them—but today there was just familiar and tasty Munster. "What's your idea?"

He unwrapped the cheese and broke off a chunk. "Well . . . I thought we could get married."

She nearly dropped the baguette.

He saw the shock on her face and said quickly, "Not right now, obviously. But at the end of the summer, you could come home with me, meet my parents. They're going to love you. Then, whenever you feel ready—no rush—we can get married in the backyard, if you want. Or if you want to do the big reception-hall thing, we can do that. Do you have a dream wedding envisioned? I don't, so whatever you want. I just want to be married to you."

Married.

She was catapulted back to the day three years ago—had it only been three years? It felt like a lifetime or just yesterday, both at once—when she had told her mother that her boyfriend Ryan had proposed. She'd been so elated, especially because of the timing. Her mother was in the hospital again, her cancer had come back, and Lori loved that she'd be able to give her mother good news. Something to look forward to! Ryan had agreed to get married soon so that her mother could be there. He'd even agreed to the hospital chapel, so Mom could be wheeled there with all her tubes and machines. Excited, she'd shown her mother the ring, a princess-cut diamond in a band dotted with tiny diamond shards.

She remembered how her mother had cried. Clutched Lori's hand with her skeleton-thin hands and told her earnestly that she should never tie herself to anyone. Never make herself smaller for another person or for anyone else's expectations. Never allow her dreams to die. You think you need to, she'd said, but you don't—you can say no even when it feels like the entire world is screaming "yes."

"But this *is* my dream," Lori had told her mom. "I want to say yes!"

"You only think you do, because you don't know you have a choice—you think marriage is your only future, the same as I did," Mom had told her. "Don't you worry, though. I'll fix it."

"There's nothing to fix," Lori had said. "You just need to be well enough to come. We can do it soon. Ryan's finding out what paperwork we need to file. Once we have everything ready . . ." But "soon" wasn't soon enough.

And after Mom's death, Lori discovered she had indeed "fixed" things.

Ten months after Mom died, Lori returned the beautiful ring via a padded envelope from a shitty motel in Illinois that she couldn't afford. She cried so hard that she nearly smudged the address. Thanks to Mom, she had no choice. She couldn't stay with Ryan. It had hurt too much when she'd tried. She was cursed, and her life was never going to be the same.

That wasn't a story she'd ever tell Mark. Or anyone. Ever.

"I don't . . ." Lori began.

"If you don't want to marry me, I won't mention it again," Mark said, "but you need to know that you've transformed me. I thought I'd spend a month in Europe, find myself, be spontaneous before law school . . . and instead I found you. And you . . . you're glorious!"

At some point in his speech, he'd slid onto one knee between the pigeons, who were still lurking in hopes of more crumbs. The chunk of cheese lay on Lori's lap, forgotten.

"You're what I think about when I wake up in the morning and when I fall asleep at night," Mark said. "You're the one I want to share things with. Not just cheese and bread, but everything! Everything I see, everything I hear, everything I think. I want to share my life with you."

Lori remembered she should breathe. Inhaling, she felt dizzy. She never let herself think about the future—that was one of her rules, to keep herself sane. How could she? She didn't have a real future. Just a kaleidoscope of days.

Before Mark, Lori had thought she'd spend those days alone. She wondered if maybe it didn't have to be that way. Maybe she didn't have to be alone forever. He could wander the world with her. They could see sights together. They could . . .

"We won't be able to afford a house at first," he said. "But there's married housing at Cornell, and we can save up for an apartment. My grandparents . . . When they died, they left us each money, all the grandkids and step-grandkids, so I won't have loans to pay off after law school. You never talk about what you plan to do after the summer, what you dream about, but whatever career you want to pursue, whatever dream you want to chase—"

Lori cut him off. "I dream about you."

He smiled. "You do?"

"When I think about the future, I dream about you." It was true. But it was a dream she couldn't indulge. Not the life he was describing, living together while he completed law school, in an apartment, then a house. A home. "What if you didn't go to law school? What if we just kept traveling? There's a whole world to see—"

"We can travel," Mark said.

She allowed a sliver of hope to slip into her heart.

"Obviously, we won't be able to take the grandest vacations at first, but eventually. Lori, I can't offer you the moon, but I can offer you my heart. My soul. My everything. Please, marry me?"

Vacations.

He thought that's what this was to her. Of course he did. Why would he think otherwise? She'd intended him to think that. He couldn't imagine she'd want to—*Not "want." Need.* It wasn't a choice whether to stay or go. She always had to go. If she didn't . . . Lori remembered how it had felt, when her throat had sealed and her limbs had slowed. *It's not about* want. *I never get what I want.*

In his mind, traveling forever wasn't what you did. It wasn't practical. Besides, who would even want that? To always be on the move. Never having a place to call home. Surrounded by the world, but alone.

Until she'd met Mark, she hadn't even realized how lonely she was. Since Mom's death, she'd kept people at arm's length, knowing she wouldn't be with them for long. Eventually, she'd move on. Nothing could ever be permanent. But marriage . . . That was a permanent promise. "I want to say yes."

"Then say yes!"

Every part of her, down to her very core, *did* want to say yes. *Maybe there's a way to make it work.* She could convince him to continue traveling. She could talk him into delaying law school.

Except what right did she have to take that from him? He'd been accepted into Cornell Law, an impressive achievement. He'd graduate, join a law firm, build a career. Settle in one place. He had a path and a future, and it wasn't a path she could follow. If she loved him, she couldn't take that from him.

And she did love him. So much.

Lori knew the kindest thing would be to say no right now. She should walk away from their bench, check out of the hostel, and find a new city for a while. Forget about Mark and let him live his life. But he was looking at her with those puppy dog eyes, and she couldn't do it. She couldn't break his heart. Or her own.

Can't I just have this? She'd already lost so much. *Just this, please. I won't ask for more. Give me today. One happy day.*

"Yes," she said.

He hopped back onto the bench, and Lori could feel the joy radiating from him. It was warmer than the sun. They split the rolls and cheese, they talked and laughed, and she imagined what her life could be, if only she could have everything she wanted. She would allow herself to believe it possible, for the space of one day, even while she knew this wish was as ephemeral as a cloud.

At her insistence, they went inside the museum to be absorbed in Monet's water lilies. They curved around the walls, so all you saw was the blue and the pastels. You could get lost in the lilies. She tried to let them soothe her. It wasn't Monet's fault that it failed, any more than it was Mark's fault that she wanted what she couldn't have. *I can have this moment. Maybe it will be enough.* Could one perfect day sustain her for a lifetime?

It has to.

After that, they walked along the Seine. They poked around in an old bookshop that looked as if it had been there since the Middle Ages, and they walked down narrow cobblestone streets in no particular direction. Mark bought them both ice creams, and they laughed when she couldn't lick fast enough. She ended up with hazelnut ice cream drips on her shirt, and when they swung by the hostel so that she could change and soak the shirt, they made the miraculous discovery that they had the room to themselves.

She claimed it as her wedding night.

After the sun set, they strolled through the Paris streets, past the cafés with their outdoor tables crowded together on the sidewalk. They stopped to listen to a street performer with a smoky voice and fingers that flew over guitar strings. And they danced in the street, drunk on happiness and romance and the lights of the most beautiful city in the world. Lori stored every moment in her memory, to be lived and relived later, when she was alone again.

She left in the middle of the night, while everyone in the hostel was asleep and the moon was a slice in the sky. She wanted to leave a letter, to explain everything, but in the end, she didn't. He wouldn't have believed her. Girls didn't turn into trees, not in any view of the world he understood. *He'd never understand.* She left only a short note, written on the paper bag that had held the Munster:

I love you.

And

I'm sorry.

CHAPTER SIX

ELISA

Now

I am still on the sidewalk. The ambulance left; the police took statements; the crowd dispersed like a flock of seagulls when the fish are gone. Yet, I am still on the sidewalk.

Walk away or stay?

I could board the next bus. Let it take me anywhere, away from this drama I've stumbled into. The glory of never staying anyplace long is that there's no time to become embroiled in any ugly history and no responsibility to clean up the aftermath. Whatever happened between Owen and the woman in pink . . . Allison? He said her name was Allison. It's not my problem, and I don't need to let it become my problem. I can continue my search elsewhere. After all, there's zero evidence I'll find what I need here. It's just another place on my haphazard list.

But it *is* on my list.

And Owen is still standing beside me, shaking like it's January in Minnesota instead of Massachusetts in June. I can't leave. Not yet.

I already care.

Shit.

Then: *Oh well.* I've cared before and survived. I can do it again. Really, this is no different from any other pause I've taken in a place. I'll be fine. And who knows? Maybe I'll be lucky and discover the key to my family's curse here. It's been a very long time since I've had even a hint of a clue. I'm due for some luck.

It's an unlucky town, the girl on the bus whispers in my memory.

"You need tea. Chamomile. Or at least berry. No caffeine."

He nods, but I'm not sure he heard me.

Guiding him by the elbow, I lead him into Bean Street. Conversation, which was buzzing, grinds to a halt, and the predominant sound is the ticking of multiple clocks, all slightly out of sync with one another. The barista, a Latina woman with deep circles under her eyes and hair pinned in multiple ponytails, bustles over. "Owen! Are you okay? What happened? Was that Allison?"

"Accident," he says shortly. He thumps into a chair near the window and stares at the flyers taped to the glass. I doubt he sees them.

"Chamomile tea for him?" I say. "Or whatever your most soothing drink is?"

"Yeah, definitely. Are you his new girlfriend? I've been telling Owen for ages that he has to get out there again, at least try. It's not good to be alone."

"New employee." I smile to show I don't think she's being completely intrusive, even though I do. Why do people think it's okay to ask personal questions when all I want is a beverage and some space? "I'll be working part time at the Book Cellar."

"Oh! That's great! He's been saying he's going to hire someone for ages. He's there literally every second, and it's not healthy. He's gotta get out. Travel, like he always talks about. He and Allison used to say they were going to—"

"Tea? Please?" I smile again, even though it makes my cheeks ache.

She looks confused, as if no one has ever cut her off before, but she bobs her head and scurries back behind the counter.

Exhaling, I sit down next to Owen.

I don't know him well enough to guess whether he's the talk-through-it type or the process-it-all-internally-and-hope-not-to-explode type, but given that he spends most of his days in a bookstore with just a cat, I'm guessing he's the latter. Still, I'm here, and I know this dance. "You want to talk about it?"

He doesn't say anything.

That isn't necessarily a no.

The barista brings two mugs of what look like hot chocolate piled with whipped cream and a drizzle of caramel. My opinion of her shoots way up, despite the curious way she's looking at me—*I'm supposed to be the one who asks questions.*

"On the house," she says.

I decide I love her despite her flaws.

"Thanks." I take a sip and suck in a gob of whipped cream and a trickle of velvety chocolate, a hint of dark chocolate bitterness to it—absolute perfection. "Once, I was in Spain. First time there. Barcelona. And I wanted hot chocolate. So I ordered 'chocolate caliente,' which I figured was close enough. The waitress looked at me a moment but didn't say anything, and then she brought over the thickest hot chocolate I've ever had. You could stick a spoon in it, and it would stay upright. Well, I drank it. When in Barcelona, you know. Later, I come to find out that's the sauce you dip churros in. I drank the dip."

His lips quirk.

"Also once ate a wax grape. I thought it was a fruit platter for guests. It was not, but I kept munching because there was no way to gracefully spit it out." Never turn down free food. That was practically Mom's mantra. She taught me the art of dumpster diving. As soon as I was old enough, those lessons expanded into how to crash weddings and other parties with buffets. I always have one cocktail dress stashed in my backpack. Black. Wrinkle-free fabric. It's my most useful outfit: weddings, funerals, graduation parties—all excellent sources of free food and entertainment, even the funerals, if they come with enough family drama. Without that dress, I'd never know the glory of a chocolate-fondue fountain made with Ghirardelli chocolate, which is vastly superior to all other fountains, including both the Trevi and the Bellagio, or the delight of a bacon-wrapped date.

He takes a sip of his hot chocolate. "Allison and I were high school sweethearts. Drifted apart in college, but we reunited when I moved back to Greenborough. She never left."

"And you got engaged?" I keep my voice neutral.

"Yeah." He stares out at the street, and I wonder what he's seeing. Allison, splayed on the road after the truck hit her? Or some memory that I can't imagine? "She wanted an enormous wedding with a huge cupcake-like dress and everyone she'd ever met invited, and she wanted it behind her mother's house. There was this tree she'd picked out—we were going to be married under it, and she was going to string fairy lights in all the branches. She had so many plans . . . She was going to do as much of it herself as she could, and I promised to help with everything. Whatever she wanted, fine with me. I was just happy she'd said yes. She could have hired elephants and circus clowns, and it would have been fine. I'd never seen her happier than when she was planning our wedding."

He falls silent, and I think about asking what happened, but he'll get there when he gets there. I sip my hot chocolate and survey the other customers. I've been in many, many coffee shops in many, many cities and towns. You can tell a lot about an area by who frequents the local coffee shop. You can spot the businesspeople easily—zero smiles, dressed nicely, and on their phones. And the students, with their overflowing backpacks, their hoodies, and their laptops with stickers on them. But Bean Street has a third kind of clientele, my favorite: the oddballs.

I failed to notice when we first came in, but the customers here are decidedly unusual. First there's the table of three blue-haired ladies— sky blue, purple blue, and brilliant peacock blue—each older than the next. Not strange in and of itself—many coffee shops have their "ladies of leisure"—but their behavior is odd. Instead of chatting with one another, they dip biscotti into their coffees in complete silence and watch all the other customers. The one with peacock blue hair is staring at me with such intensity that I have to look away.

In the corner, a twentysomething guy with dark skin, a newsboy cap, and a high-collar seventies shirt is strumming a guitar, but the guitar makes no noise. After a few seconds, I realize it has no strings. He continues playing.

Up by the counter, a silver-haired woman in jeans and a crop top is placing her order. She has a snake curled like a necklace around her neck. Its head rests on her left shoulder, and its tongue flicks out, tasting the air. Absolutely no one reacts.

I feel a fresh whisper of hope as I take all of this in, and I smile before I notice that all three blue-haired women are now staring at me. Suddenly, I am a rabbit in a field, spotted by a hawk—too exposed, too seen. I am not supposed to be noticed.

Looking away quickly, I switch my focus back to Owen.

Questions later. You can't just walk up to a stranger and ask, "Are you cursed, and if not, do you know anyone who might be?" Tried that. Doesn't work. Besides, Owen needs me right now—or at least he needs someone to listen; doesn't matter who.

"After the accident, she just stopped," he says.

I want to ask what kind of accident, but I don't want to interrupt him. He's talking to himself as much as to me. It's as though the words need to pour out of him.

"She threw away her stack of planning papers. I told her we didn't need a big wedding. We could just have a small ceremony. The important thing was to start our lives together. She didn't want to. I told her I'd wait, as long as she needed. But she . . . she changed after that. She . . ."

I reach across the table and touch his hand. "It's okay."

It isn't okay. I know that. He knows that. Probably even the blue-haired ladies know that. I can't help feeling as if everyone in the coffee shop is looking at us now, listening, but I don't check to see. They can eavesdrop if they like. For once, this isn't about me.

"It was years ago," Owen says. "She's moved on. I've moved on. But seeing her like that again . . . It was a car accident before, too, but she was the driver that time. The doctors didn't think she was going to make it. She had internal bleeding. Head injury. She was driving late at night. Freak rainstorm, and she hit a tree. God, what she must be going through . . . Another accident. Another ambulance. Another hospital stay."

He doesn't know. He didn't hear when I made my report to the police. He doesn't know what Allison said before she darted out into the street. *Help me leave.*

I can't tell him that I don't think it was an accident this time, especially since I could be jumping to conclusions—I don't know Allison at all.

Instead, I say, "Head injuries can change people, their personalities."

"Before today, I hadn't seen her in months," he says. "After she called the wedding off . . . She didn't want anything to do with me anymore. So I gave her the space she wanted. I even thought about moving out of Greenborough. Starting over. Making new memories. I should have. But I . . . didn't." He shakes his head. "You're nice to listen, but you really don't need to. Absurd of me to drag you through my old memories when this isn't about me. I'm not the one hurt."

He seems hurt to me. "You can talk to me, if it helps. I've had my share of doomed relationships." All of them, in fact. I wasn't even always the one who left first. Just usually.

"Any broken engagements?"

"None of those, but I once had a date ditch me for a walrus." I tell him about the marine biologist I met in San Francisco who bolted halfway through his chicken parmigiana because he got a text that a walrus he was studying was about to give birth. In fairness, I would have left too, but it would have been nice to have had a redo date, if only so he could show me pictures of a baby walrus. Never seen one, but I imagine they're adorable.

As I hoped, the story does the trick, and he's smiling again. His shoulders relax so they're not up by his ears, and he drinks the hot chocolate with more enthusiasm. He experienced a shock, the kind that dredges up old trauma, but he's going to be okay.

I can handle this. I can stay.

Across the coffee shop, the blue-haired ladies continue watching me, and the guitarist continues playing his silence.

CHAPTER SEVEN

Owen returns to the Book Cellar after finishing the hot chocolate, claiming he'll be fine. *Fine.* We always say that. We rarely mean it. But I don't argue. And I don't follow him. I'm not due to start my new job until tomorrow. I've done all I can for my new friend, so I linger, drinking the dregs of my drink—the chocolate has congealed into a thick sludge at the bottom, and I'm suddenly nostalgic for Barcelona. I was Alissa then. I liked seeing new places, and I promised myself I'd never change. I've always lied to myself just as much as I lie to everyone else. It's easier that way.

Finishing my beverage, I cross to the bulletin board and peruse the flyers.

Lawn mower for sale.

Free kittens.

Acoustic night on Tuesdays at Bean Street.

My neck prickles, and I turn to see the three blue-haired ladies standing in a semicircle behind me, a few inches too close for comfort. "Uh, hi," I say.

The one with the sky blue hair smiles at me, and I notice she has lipstick smeared on her left front tooth, but somehow it feels like part of her whole look. I certainly have no intention of telling her it's there if her friends haven't told her. She looks at least ninety years old, with skin as sun weathered as old leather and a multicolored sweater that is half-unraveled. The loose yarn is wound around her wrist like a bangle.

"New," she says with a smile that sends a shiver through me like an electric shock.

I open my mouth to say yes, I'm new here—

"You're correct, dear one," the second woman says. "She *is* new." She has neon peacock blue hair, and from her pale wrinkles—so pale they remind me of worms—she looks at least one hundred. She reaches out a gnarled hand to pat my hair, and I try not to flinch. She has breath that smells like garlic, which is impressive in a coffee shop with no garlic in sight. "Welcome to Greenborough. Consider us the welcoming committee. Anything you need, my dear, just ask us. We know everyone and everything about this town."

Well, that's . . . nice? Useful? *Creepy.*

"Glad to meet you," I say politely. "I *am* new here and—"

The third woman, sporting purple-blue hair, richly dark skin, and as many wrinkles as her friends, shoos the other two back. "Don't crowd her! You'll scare her off." She then presses even closer to me, pats my cheek, and says, "We might need her."

Before I can respond—and I have at least a dozen questions, beginning with what the hell she means by *that*—the purple-blue-haired woman asks, "Have you just arrived?"

I open my mouth to reply—

"What brings you to Greenborough?"

That's hard to answer, but I have a plausible—

"What are your plans here?"

Okay, I would answer if she'd just—

"Stay or leave?" the one with sky blue hair asks, breathless.

Clarifying, the peacock-haired woman says, "Are you planning to stay long, my dear, or are you only passing through?"

I wait for more questions, but they merely stare at me. "I'm just here for a little while, and then I'll move on." Wow, this is the most awkward conversation I've had in some time. Usually I'm better at this. On the other hand, usually my conversation partners have a sense of personal space. "I'm looking for a place to sublet, ideally as inexpensive as possible. Do you know of anyone looking for a temporary tenant?"

They brighten as if I've gifted them the moon, beaming at me with nearly identical smiles. "'A little while,'" the third woman repeats. "And then you plan to leave?"

"Want to or need to?" the first woman—sky blue hair—asks.

I take a step backward. She's standing very close, so close that I'm inhaling her exhales. It tastes like stale coffee and overripe bananas. "Sorry?"

"Are you certain you're going to leave, dear?" the peacock-haired woman clarifies. "You're only here temporarily?"

"Yes, I'll only be here a few months at most." Maybe they don't want a long-term tenant? There's an intensity to them that's disconcerting, more so than anything they've said. It feels like none of them have blinked. They're staring at me like hawks who've sighted a mouse. "I can't stay."

"You're certain of that?" The purple-blue-haired woman again. She's standing closer now too, though I didn't see her move, and she smells of wilted magnolias, as sour and sweet as cough syrup.

My back is against the bulletin board. "Very."

"Excellent," they say in unison.

Odd. Why would that be excellent?

Before I can ask them another question, they scurry back to their table and proceed to discuss in rapid whispers. Unsure what else to do, I turn back to the bulletin board. There's a yard sale this Sunday . . . oh, that was last Sunday. Also, a flyer about a concert at the Fountain—not sure if that's a bar, restaurant, concert venue, or an actual fountain, but it claims to be free. Maybe I'll go and listen. I love live music. It's something that's actually *supposed* to be ephemeral. You experience it, then move on, carrying it only as an imperfect memory of how it made you feel. It's one of the few things that I can experience exactly like everyone else. I dragged Tyler to every free outdoor concert that I could find, from classical to jazz to retro to who-knows-what-they're-playing, but I also have no problem attending solo.

The blue-haired ladies are back by my side. I didn't see them move.

"One twenty-five East Oak Road," Sky Blue says.

"She's been talking about renting out the old caretaker's house," Purple Blue says. "It's not in the best shape, so she won't be asking much."

"But it's got good bones," Peacock Blue says.

"Good bones," the others agree.

As if that matters when you're renting. Really, the important details are cost (needs to be cheap), location (needs to be close), and safety (can't be a murder house). Also, nice to have running water. Most of this I can ask the landlord, except for the murder part. Question is: How much do I trust these women? *Not at all.* "Why are you telling me about this place?"

They look at one another.

And my curiosity is piqued—there's a story here. I can see it in their eyes. But what kind of story? An unexplainable one? Or just ordinary human drama? Lightly, I ask, "Any chance it's haunted?"

"Hah! No, honey," Peacock Blue says.

"Maybe?" Sky Blue says.

"Aren't most old buildings?" Purple Blue says. She smiles slyly at me, as if we share a secret. It's perhaps the most alarming expression yet, and I have to concentrate not to flinch.

"I like to think so." I keep my voice light, as if I'm only casually interested in the answer, a tourist looking for entertainment. "I love local legends. Does Greenborough have any of those? Anything interesting ever happen here?"

The closest woman, peacock haired, pats my cheek. "Of course not, sugar. You have absolutely nothing to worry about. This is the nicest town you'll ever find."

All of them nod vigorously, as if she's just told the most blatant lie in the world and they expect me to believe it.

That's it. Definitely staying.

"Thank you," I say sincerely. "I'll go check it out."

They smile at me.

◆ ◆ ◆

125 East Oak Road.

Guess this is it.

As the name promises, there are oak trees lining both sides of the road, as well as pine trees, but I'm distracted by the gravel driveway, choked with weeds. A rusted mailbox lists to the left, but that's the only indication that there's a house at the end of the driveway.

I can't help but be a tiny bit optimistic. Or curious, which is practically the same thing. Adjusting my backpack straps so they're more comfortable, I trudge down the driveway. The gravel crunches under my feet. The sounds of cars and the stray truck fall behind me, and I hear birds call to one another—the low two-note coo of a mourning dove, the chitter of a sparrow. As I continue on, the bird chatter amplifies. I crane my neck to spot them in the trees, certain there must be a flock above me, but I see only leaves, woven together in a canopy that blocks out the sun. I am walking in shadows.

The driveway wends to the left. Just when I think it won't end, that I will be perpetually walking through a forest that may swallow me whole, the trees part and the sky opens above like a curtain of blue. Ahead is a dilapidated mansion: three stories, with gingerbread-house-like flourishes adorning every window, door, and eave. The white paint has peeled to show grayed skin beneath, and the unwashed windows are clouded. But that's not the most striking part.

Now I understand why I heard so many birds.

Ornate, antique birdcages fill the wraparound porch. Each holds only a single bird, but what variety! A bright-yellow parakeet gleams brighter than its golden cage. A tiny brown sparrow, flecked with brown and white, huddles in the corner of its massive wooden cage. There's a seagull in one—it caws at me. One looks like a crow.

The birds cry louder as I approach. They flap their wings against their cages and cry, except for the sparrow, who continues to huddle on its perch. I eye it, and it scoots sideways. But then my eye is drawn to the others, birds I can't identify. One with sweeping orange tail feathers, another with a brilliant red beak. One songbird is a perfect pink, like its feathers were dipped in Pepto-Bismol. Another, yellow mixed with tan. Another is bright Christmas red, a cardinal. I've never heard of anyone keeping a cardinal as a pet. Or a seagull.

Is it even legal?

Certainly, it's unusual.

But this could easily be explained as someone's bird obsession, the way someone might own seventeen cats. A bird-watcher gone extreme. It doesn't necessarily mean anything more, or anything that could help me. I brace myself for disappointment as I place my foot on the first step, intending to knock on the front door. Despite the oddities I've seen—the woman in pink with the galaxy-filled eyes, the man playing the guitar with no strings, the three unsettling women with blue hair and piercing stares—Greenborough could turn out to be just as ordinary as any other town I've tried. It's okay to be optimistic, but I can't let myself feel the stab of every disappointment—or I'll leak from all the holes in my heart.

The birds cry louder.

I hear a voice call, from around the side of the house, "Hello!"

Taking my foot off the step, I turn to face who I assume is the homeowner.

In a cheerful voice, she asks, "Can I help you?" She's smiling at me, but I can only stare.

It's her, the woman in pink. *Allison.*

A bandage on her forehead. A scrape on her neck. One arm in a sling. But mostly unscathed and *here*, only an hour after the ambulance carried her away, which should be, if not impossible, then at least very, very unlikely. She smiles as if we've never met, as if she never threw herself into my arms and then tried to shatter her world.

CHAPTER EIGHT

"Ahh . . . ," I say.

"Can I help you?" the woman in pink repeats.

"Ahh . . ." All I can see is the truck hitting her, as if she were a doll tossed against a wall. All I can hear is the soft thump. I'll be hearing it in my nightmares for months. "I saw you get hurt."

Allison shakes her head. "I'm sorry, but you are . . . ?" Her smile hasn't faded, but it has become fixed, as if it were painted between her apple-pink cheeks.

She doesn't remember me. How could she not remember me? Just an hour ago, she threw herself at me and asked me—I take a deep breath. "I'm Elisa. I'm here because . . ." Okay, I really can't discuss my housing situation before addressing her very close brush with death. "I was outside the Book Cellar about an hour ago, when you came up to me. You talked to me. You ran into the street. And then you were hit by a truck and taken away in an ambulance. Are you okay?"

She tilts her head. Wrinkles her nose. "You must have me confused for someone else."

Denial. I wasn't expecting that. "Your arm is in a sling."

"I fell from a ladder."

"You have scrapes on your face."

"Into the brambles." She gestures toward the berry bushes that line the side of her house. "I was attempting to clean leaves out of the gutter. You didn't say why you're here?"

"I saw you." It was clearly her.

"As I told you, you must be mistaking me for someone else."

"You're wearing pink." Can't be the same pink clothes. Similar pink clothes. Same pink hair. Same face. Not the same eyes—they are now alert and focused—but in every other way, she is undeniably the same person. How is she here, mostly unharmed and with no idea of what I'm talking about? She should be in a hospital bed with doctors and nurses hovering and feeding her fluids through tubes, or whatever they do. She was hit by a *truck*.

Wasn't she?

Maybe I'm just projecting what I saw onto her, and she's just an innocent stranger who looks identical, wears the same clothes, and has a few random unconnected injuries? "Sorry. You *weren't* in town earlier today?"

"I've been home all day with my mother." Allison waves her hand in the direction of the house, and I see a figure shuffle past a window. It's too bright outside to see more than her outline, a moving shadow, but she walks as if her joints ache with each step.

Either Allison doesn't remember or is intent on denying what happened, for some unfathomable reason. I make one more attempt: "Do you have a sister? A twin who also likes pink?"

She laughs, a bit strained, although I think it's more in reaction to my questions than anything else. It's clear I'm in danger of scaring her off, and I don't want to do that until I have answers. I have to back off. "Just me," she says. "Can I help you with something?"

Possibly. "Three blue-haired ladies from the coffee shop—they said you have a place to rent." Did they know I'd find Allison here? How is she here, scraped up but memoryless? A thread of excitement worms through my stomach. Could this be exactly the kind of thing I've been searching for? Something inexplicable.

Like me.

Unless there is an explanation. Unless she wasn't injured badly enough for the hospital to keep her but she *did* hit her head hard enough to forget. That would be a reasonable, boring explanation that has zero to do with my problem, or potentially my solution. But if she had a head injury, why would the hospital release her so quickly? Wouldn't they keep her for observation for at least a few more hours? The paperwork alone should have kept her there.

Her expression clears. "Oh! Yes, I was telling the trio about my plans the other day. I asked them to keep an eye out for any prospective tenants. Wow, they work quick. There's a caretaker's cottage on the property—it hasn't been lived in in years. I'm planning on renting it out, as soon as I get it cleaned up. To help with the bills. It's just sitting there, and Mom . . . Well, we could use the extra money. Are you interested?"

Oh yes, I'm very interested. I want to ask her a million questions. Has anything else unusual ever happened to her before? Did she cause this miracle recovery, or was it something else? "Absolutely," I say.

"Great!" Allison strides away from the porch. "Come on. I'll show you the place. Don't expect too much. As I said, I was going to fix it up a bit before I rented it. I can give you a discount on the first month if you help me clean it?"

I follow Allison around the house and wonder how best to handle this, especially since I've already put her on edge with my initial reaction. Over the years, I've learned that if you're too eager with questions, you can scare off someone who might have information you need. You have to be patient.

I can be patient.

As patient as a tree.

Mom taught me that. She was patient, waiting until I was old enough to fend for myself before she secured what she wanted. When she finally acted—well, I never saw her happier than on her wedding day. She glowed in the way that brides are supposed to glow. She didn't stop smiling once from the moment she woke up and brushed her teeth to the moment she waved goodbye with her newly minted husband and went into the house. No one but me understood why she refused to go on a honeymoon. She told everyone she'd had enough of leaving, but she didn't explain.

I should have known then, or at least guessed, what she intended, but I was in denial. She knew the rules—she'd taught them to me, after all. Every rule was designed to keep us safe, to keep us on the move, to keep the consequences of the curse from catching us and condemning us. Don't form ties. Don't take mementos. Don't keep in touch. We changed our names so we wouldn't look back, so we wouldn't be found and drawn back. We started anew in every town, in every school, in every job.

Even on her wedding day, I couldn't imagine she truly meant to stay. We *can't* stay. I didn't guess what she'd planned—what she'd *chosen*—until it was far too late. I trusted her, and I lost her.

She hid so much from him too. He only knew the doctor visits and the lab results. He only knew the shake of her breath, the crack of her cough, the pain at the end.

He only knew her coffin and her grave.

He didn't know her leaves, her branches, her roots.

I wonder if she can feel anything, remember anything, think anything, as she is now. Do trees dream? Or does she only feel the wind through her leaves, the turning of the seasons, the water in the soil? I can't ask her, and I never want to find out for myself. I have learned that there are risks I'll never take and paths I'll never choose. Mom is my cautionary tale.

There's another side porch with even more birdcages. A few are empty, but others hold more songbirds in blue, orange, and brown, as well as birds with golden feathers and black beady eyes that watch as we walk past. Beyond the porch, there's an overgrown vegetable garden and what looks like a sculpture garden. All the statues are buried in vines, and the bench near them is covered in lichen. Craning my neck, I try for a better view—Greek myth themed, maybe? One could be Apollo with his chariot. Beside him, a muse with a lyre?

"Watch your step," Allison cautions.

I look down and step over a hose. A sprinkler soaks a patch of grass that's far greener than the rest, a halfhearted attempt at yardwork. "Thanks."

"This used to be the most beautiful house and grounds in Greenborough," Allison says. "My mother kept everything impeccable. The flower gardens—they were her pride and joy. But she's slowed down, and I just can't keep up." She wiggles her thumb. "No green thumb for me. I try for her sake, but . . ."

"I don't have a green thumb either, but I'm happy to help clean the cottage—that's in my skill set. I've fixed plenty of toilets. Even a few outlets." The fact is that I've done tons of basic maintenance stuff to keep whatever hole I'm living in functioning, but I've never been able to afford a flower garden. I think again of my mother. She started a flower garden the spring she married, even though she knew she'd never see all the flowers bloom. She loved digging in the dirt and planting seeds. I didn't understand it. I like flowers, sure—who doesn't?—but gardening was always a hobby for other people, not for my mother and me. You can only afford to putter over seeds and bulbs for inedible plants when you have food in the fridge and heat in the pipes. Or when you stay in one place for longer than a matter of months.

"We used to have roses climbing over the back of the house." Allison waves her hand in that direction. Turning, I see bare brown vines twisting over the shingles, clinging to the roof as if from memory. "I either overwatered or underwatered them. They haven't bloomed since. But that's not why you're here. This is." She halts as we round a hedge of bushes.

Next to a pond covered in a thin layer of soap-like algae is a cottage as adorable as a dollhouse. It, too, is in disrepair. I see several shingles are askew and the windows are murky. One has a crack running diagonally through it. Gardening equipment is piled next to the front door—a wheelbarrow, many empty pots and trays, a rusted rake, dirt-coated gloves. Ivy creeps over the walls and crowds the front door.

"I know it doesn't look like much," Allison says, "but it's got—"

"—good bones," I finish for her. "It's perfect."

It's a refuge. I can be alone here. There won't be neighbors pressing against the walls, the ceiling, the floor with their voices, their families, their lives. I crave this cottage in a way I didn't expect when I started down the gravel driveway.

This is a place where I can be myself and no one will overhear me. I won't have to pretend to be like anyone else, and even better, I won't constantly be made aware of what I'm missing. Hearing husbands and wives, grandparents, kids, and friends living together and partying together and arguing together and being together, with history behind them—apartments can be torture. But here, I can rest here. Recover. Even if Allison proves a red herring and this town is no different from any other I've lived in . . . *This will do nicely.*

"How much?" I ask.

"Um, I've never rented out a place before. What would you say is fair?"

Oh, sweet summer child. "Can I see inside?"

I don't need to see inside. I already know I'm going to take it, for its proximity to Allison and her mysteries if nothing else, but it's so much more than that. She unlocks the front door. It requires an extra shove to open—one of the hinges is loose, and the door has tilted. It scrapes the floor as it opens, and I see the gouges from where it's been pushed again and again.

A screwdriver and fifteen seconds can fix that.

The air inside smells mildewy, like damp sheets that have been balled up so they never quite dry. Allison opens a window. There's a heavy layer of dust on everything, but it is furnished: a couch, a wood-burning stove—I wonder if that works—and bookshelves with a few paperbacks. There's a kitchen galley in one corner—a small stove, a small fridge, a counter with a stool. The refrigerator is humming, which means the place has electricity, a definite plus. I walk to the sink and turn on the faucet.

It spurts and then runs—the water is brownish tinged at first but then runs clear.

A bed rests in one corner, stripped of sheets and blankets. I could sleep on it bare—I've slept on far worse—but it doesn't hurt to ask if there's an alternative. "Any chance you could throw in a sheet or two? At least until I have a chance to get into town. I didn't pack much." I have a towel in my backpack. Always travel with one. As the famous hitchhiker book says, they have hundreds of uses. Just like a cocktail dress. I could sleep on the towel if I needed to, but I'd rather not.

"Of course," Allison says.

There's a tiny bathroom off the kitchen, with a very narrow shower stall, a miniature sink, and a toilet. It's ringed with yellow and brown, but that can all be scrubbed off. The shower has white streaks on the cracked tile, a buildup of lime. Again, all can be cleaned.

"I can have this place sparkling in a day or two, if you're willing to supply the cleaning stuff," I say. "And, like you said, reduce the rent a bit." I do some quick math and name a monthly figure that is much, much less than what the place is worth but isn't zero—three-quarters of what I'll make at the Book Cellar, which will leave me with enough for food and hopefully allow me to save a bit so that my next landing is smooth.

She counters with a lower amount.

She really doesn't know how to bargain. She doesn't even mention a deposit or a lease or any of that, which is fine by me.

We shake.

This is unprecedented good luck: both a job and a place to live within the same day. If this happened every time I moved someplace new . . . Well, it never happens.

What's the catch? There must be a catch. Again, I hear the soft thunk of Allison's body at the truck's impact. I'm not superstitious, but it's hard not to wonder about the role of luck in my life. So far, since the bus rolled into town, I've witnessed one near tragedy and had two enormous strokes of good luck. Am I due for something bad?

I think of nights on park benches, barely sleeping, aware of how exposed I am. I think of what my mother would do to make sure that I never went hungry . . . That was the point of the nest egg she secured for me—so I'd never have to do what she did, for me.

For a while, I thought she only wanted to marry for the money. It had, of course, been a factor. A very important factor, as she later explained, but not for herself. It was for me. For herself, though . . . she had truly loved planting those flowers.

I still don't know how I feel about any of it.

"I'll, um, leave you to get settled in?" Allison says.

"Actually, if I could get those cleaning supplies, that would be great." I don't want to be alone just yet. Besides, she hasn't answered a single question yet, and if I'm going to get anywhere with her, I need to make her feel comfortable with me.

"Oh! Of course! They're back in the house."

I leave my backpack on the dusty table and follow her through the unloved gardens to the porch. Climbing up the steps, I study the birdcages again. They are massive—each one could hold a dozen parakeets, but there's only one bird to a cage. Maybe there aren't quite as many pet birds as I originally thought. Nah, there are a lot of cages. Any way you slice it, Allison owns far more birds than anyone I've ever met, even including a few zoos.

"You like birds?" It's not my best conversation starter, but it'll do as a soft opening question.

"Oh. Yes. Them. I suppose you have questions."

"A few," I say. But sure, let's talk about the birds.

"They're the only thing that makes my mother happy these days," Allison says. "Ever since my father . . ." Her voice catches. "Ever since we lost my father, she's become obsessed with expanding her collection of birds. I had concerns, at first. I contacted a local veterinarian—he came out to make sure the birds were being well cared for. I didn't want us to become those people with more pets than they can handle. But my mother is diligent about caring for them." She lifts her voice. "Mom? Mom, we have a visitor!"

She opens the back door and steps inside. I follow. After a second, my eyes adjust. There are, impossibly, even more birdcages inside. Surprisingly, the house smells more of rosemary and fresh bread than it does of birds. I would have expected a stronger odor from this many cages. But maybe Allison and her mother are more careful to keep the house clean than they are the caretaker cottage. They must have their hands full already. No wonder Allison's mother doesn't have time for her gardens anymore. "Where did she get them all? Did she catch them?"

"I didn't catch them; I saved them," a woman's voice corrects me.

A moment later, she toddles into view. She has silver-white hair and wrinkles across a tanned face, but she is strikingly beautiful—the kind of old lady that everyone hopes they'll become but only a few ever do. She has grace and dignity, even though she's shaky on her feet. She reaches her finger into a cage and smiles as the parakeet hops on its perch toward her.

"It's true," Allison says. "She rehabilitates them. Anyone who doesn't want to keep their bird, they send to her."

"Lots of people acquire birds without realizing what a commitment it is," Allison's mother says. "Some species can live remarkably long lives. You shouldn't acquire one on a whim. You should only do it with love and foresight." She coos at the parakeet.

"Mom, this is our new tenant," Allison says. "She's renting out the old cottage for a while."

Wait, how is this woman Allison's mom? She looks to be at least eighty, while Allison can't be more than twenty-five or twenty-six. The math doesn't work. Maybe she's her grandmother, and Allison calls her "mom" because she raised her? Or maybe Allison was a miracle baby, born to a mother well past child-birthing age—no medical explanation, just "magic waters" or whatever—and she's why Greenborough was on my list. I can't ask though, and the details don't really matter anyway.

What matters is whether the oddness in Greenborough has anything to do with me—that's what I need to determine.

"Allison, I told you I didn't want it rented. Rental is so impermanent. A renter won't care about the place the way someone who makes it their home will. Now if you could find a nice family who wants to settle here, then we could discuss."

"Mom, we've had this conversation. The cottage is just sitting empty."

"And I disagree with you." She sighs dramatically. "But you choose to disregard my wishes again and again. This is my home. I believe I should have some say."

"If we want to afford your expensive bird feed—"

"Don't you use my birds against me."

Not liking where this is going, I chime in. "I've promised to help fix it up. Make it nice enough to attract a settled family, like you want, after I leave."

She looks at me with more interest. "Oh? And you're certain that won't be you?"

"I'm only here temporarily, until I can resolve a few family matters, but I'm happy to put in the work, in exchange for reduced rent. I've done plenty of home repair and housecleaning in the past. If you have some tools and supplies—"

"Right! The cleaning supplies!" Allison scurries through a doorway, but I don't follow. Her mother has fixed me with her gaze, and I wonder about her. Does she know what just happened to her daughter, in the center of town? I wish I could ask her about the first accident as well, the car accident that Owen said changed her—did her mother think she changed? Which Allison is this now? If I hadn't seen and heard . . . This Allison isn't acting at all like the one from earlier.

As soon as Allison is out of earshot, I ask, "Do you know if your daughter was in town earlier today? I could've sworn I met her before, but she didn't recognize me." It's not the smoothest angle. I don't want to accuse Allison of lying, but—

"What did she tell you?"

"She was here, with you."

"Then she was. Allison never leaves me. She's a good girl." She smiles fondly at the empty doorway. "You said you were here for family matters? Do you have family in the area?"

As much as I want to know more about Allison, *this* is exactly the kind of conversation opener that I wait for. I am not about to let the opportunity slip by. I never know who will hold the answers I need. "I'm looking into my family history. Unfortunately, I have very little to go on." Carefully, I take out a Ziploc with two photos, sealed to protect them from water and dirt—they're the only two photos that I have, and they are more precious to me than the Queen's jewels are to all of England.

We never owned a camera, and Mom never let us keep any photos that other people took. She usually tried to avoid being photographed at all—hid her face, stepped out of the shot. Afraid to leave a trace. Until her wedding day. She didn't seem to mind the hundreds of photos taken that day. I took one right before I left:

Mom in her wedding dress, smiling straight at the camera. She looks so effervescently happy that it sometimes takes me a while to recognize that it's her in the photo. It doesn't match my memories of her. Her worry lines are smoothed out, vanishing against the pull of her smile. "My mother. Imagine her younger."

Allison's mother shakes her head.

I turn the Ziploc over to show the other, older photo. This one is yellowed with age, black and white. It's of a young woman, pregnant, who has my mother's eyes and coiffed brown hair. She's in a summer dress on an immaculate lawn. There are no buildings in the shot. Just lilac bushes in bloom and a weedless expanse of grass. I show both photos without taking them out of the plastic. "And this is my grandmother."

She shakes her head again. "I'm sorry. I don't know them."

It's not a surprise that she doesn't recognize them. It's a long shot every time I try, but someday it's possible. Given how our curse forces us to travel, then I *will* find someone who has seen either my mother or grandmother—someday. It's just a matter of not giving up. "Thanks for looking. Anyway, I'm just passing through."

"A shame you won't be staying more permanently," Allison's mother (or grandmother) says. "You seem to be about my Allison's age. You could be a friend. She could use more friends. Perhaps you'll change your mind after you're here for a bit. Greenborough is a lovely town."

Allison reappears, her arms full with a box piled high with sprays and towels and sponges. "Mom, stop worrying about my social life. I'm fine. You don't have to make friends for me."

Her mother humphs. "If you'd just reach out to the ones you have—like that nice Owen boy. You know he still cares for you."

"He doesn't," Allison says. "Believe me."

"He *was* upset when—" I cut myself off. These are not waters I want to wade into, and I don't know how to explain how he was affected when she was carried off by an ambulance. "That is, he mentioned you earlier today."

Clutching the box of supplies to her chest, Allison takes a step backward. "Did he send you? Because we have nothing more to say. I don't want to keep hurting his feelings, but he has to move on. If that's why you're here—"

"Oh no, I told you the truth: the three blue-haired ladies at the coffee shop recommended your place. They didn't say your name, and I didn't know. He didn't know. Doesn't know. Won't know, if you don't want him to."

One of the birds squawks as if it's been squeezed. It's a blue bird with a bright-orange beak. Allison's mother swivels and stares at me. "You met the trio?"

Allison had called them the "trio" as well. I wonder what it would be like to have friends like that, inseparable friends. Or just a friend who you never had to say goodbye to. I swallow the lump in my throat. I came close to having a friend like that once, Jackie at Quinn High. She latched onto me, and I tried to push her away, but she was persistent . . . I push the memory away. I can't do inseparable. "They didn't actually introduce themselves, but they were the ones who told me that there might be a place for rent here."

"Interesting. I wouldn't expect them to take such a . . ." She trails off as the bird that squawked batters at the bars of its cage. It's frantic, cooing as she reaches into a pocket and withdraws a handful of seeds. She scatters them at the base of the cage. The bird calms, but then another begins to cry and flail, and she forgets that she was midsentence. "Silly. Hush. Ah, that's my pretty. Shh."

As soon as she calms one bird, the next begins to flutter and squawk. I wonder if this is normal bird behavior. I don't know much about birds. Neither Allison nor her mother seem alarmed. I look out the window to see if anything outside could be startling them, but there's nothing.

"Speaking of actual introductions," Allison says, "Mom, this is Elisa. Elisa, this is my mother—Cora." She hefts the box of cleaning supplies onto her hip. "Are you ready?"

I reach out for the box. "I can take that."

"I've got it."

Allison leads the way, and I follow. "Nice to meet you, Cora," I say over my shoulder. But Cora is focused on her frightened birds and doesn't reply.

CHAPTER NINE

ROSE

1971

The fireflies were out when Rose's boyfriend parked his car. "You sure about this, Rosie?" Glenn asked. He peered over the steering wheel at the shadows between the wooded trees.

Cora popped her head between the two front seats. "Rose is always sure. Rarely right, but always sure."

Rose already had the door open, rolling her eyes at both of them.

"Can't we just go to the party?" Cora's date whined behind her.

Rose scooped up her chiffon skirt and climbed out of the car. She slid the corsage off her wrist and left it on the seat—the ribbon had been itching her the entire prom. "It's called 'moonshine' for a reason. You have to find it when the moon is shining."

Glenn shut off the car and got out. "Mmm, that's not the definition, and didn't you tell me it's a bottle of whiskey?"

Ugh, so pedantic. "My point is the party can wait."

"Hey, you have actual whiskey?" Cora's date asked, now mildly interested.

She didn't bother to answer. Rose hadn't wanted to bring him, but when she hinted that they could leave Mr. Boring behind and meet back up with him at Durner's after-prom party, Cora had given her puppy dog eyes and repeated the story of how Mr. Boring had asked her to prom by presenting a half dozen white roses. "I was so surprised," Cora had claimed, even though she'd told his cousin to tell his sister to tell him that white roses were her favorite and wouldn't it be romantic to be asked in front of school on the Thursday before spring break. Good grief. The whole tale forced Rose to invent a story about Glenn asking her with an armful of wild daisies that he'd picked. In reality, he'd asked her with zero fanfare after she'd accidentally shattered a beaker in chemistry class. She'd cut her finger on the glass, and he'd turned green from the drop of blood. She had no idea why he'd picked that moment. It was not a swoon-worthy tale. But he *had* asked her, and he was the handsomest senior at their school. He also had a bright future ahead, as her parents hadn't hesitated to point out—they were thrilled when she said yes and even more so when they started dating. He was going to Yale in the fall and was already working in his daddy's office. And to be fair, he *had* given her a Band-Aid for her finger. It wasn't an armload of daisies, but it was practical and showed that he cared. *Or perhaps he doesn't like blood.*

Either way, she liked him. Or she thought she liked him. She liked the way he adored her; she was certain of that. He made her feel beautiful and daring and wild—it was heady, looking at herself through his eyes. Besides which, there was no reason to say no and every reason to say yes. If she got asked one more time when she was going to get herself a boyfriend—by her parents, her grandparents, her uncle, her neighbor, or the woman on the PTA who brought oranges to all the softball games . . . Well, she had one now, thank you very much, and she was positive that he had a wild side, if she could just nudge it out. After all, he liked her. "Catch me if you can," she told him.

Lifting her chiffon skirt above her knees, she took off into the woods. It wasn't her usual loping stride—she was in heels that squeezed her toes—but she still outran Glenn, Cora, and Mr. Boring. She refused to remember his name. *He won't last.* Cora deserved someone grander who added excitement to her life, or at least knew how to shave his peach fuzz properly.

She galloped over ferns and roots until the headlights from Glenn's daddy's car faded and she was swallowed by delicious darkness. Rose stopped and tilted her head up to see the deep sky between the branches. Clad in her prom dress in the darkness, she felt feral. Raising her arms in the air, she felt as if the shadows were caressing her skin, and she laughed out loud.

"Rose, where are you?" Cora called, her voice somewhere off to Rose's left.

Grinning, Rose crept through the woods, stepping carefully over roots toward the sound of her friends crashing through the underbrush. She saw the light from Cora's flashlight bobbing ahead of her. *Trust Cora to come prepared.*

"Rosie?" Glenn called. "Come out. You're worrying us."

"Yeah, this isn't fun," Mr. Boring complained.

She waited by an oak tree as the flashlight bounced closer. When they were only a few feet away, she leapt in front of them, shouting, "I am the witch of the woods! Suffer my curse for your trespasses!"

Cora shrieked and dropped the flashlight.

Glenn—

Wait, no, it was Glenn who shrieked; Cora was laughing so hard she doubled over. Mr. Boring was spitting out swear words that made him a whole lot less boring.

Gasping in air, Cora said, "I swear you are perpetually six years old."

"Would a six-year-old know how to make our prom night memorable?" Rose countered. "Come on, scaredy-cat." While Cora's date picked up the flashlight, Rose took Glenn's hand and led them deeper into the woods. "You're about to discover the location of the worst-kept secret in Greenborough High."

Glenn's hand closed around hers, engulfing her fingers. She expected him to be embarrassed that she'd made him shriek or angry at her for scaring him, but instead he said, "You mean the Kissing Shack?"

Rose glanced back at Cora. "You told him?"

"He wanted to know." Her prom dress snagged on a twig, and, glaring at the offending branch, she shook her skirt free. She wasn't quite as fond of the woods as Rose, but Rose knew she'd keep up. She always did.

"You pinky swore," Rose said. "I thought you could keep a secret." She'd scolded Cora enough the last time she'd spilled a secret—about her plans for an after-graduation trip, which their parents had collectively squashed before she'd even had a chance to plead.

"Not from the prom king," Cora said blithely. "I owe him my fealty. Besides, we'd already left the car when he asked, so I don't think it truly counts as a broken promise. At what point were you going to tell the boys?"

"When we arrived," Rose said. "It was going to be a whole moment."

"It could have been, if you hadn't taken off to play witch of the woods," Cora said. She was completely unrepentant, which Rose loved about her. When Cora made a decision, she followed through. "I had to convince them you knew where we're going."

Glenn asked, "You *do* know where we're going, don't you?"

"The Kissing Shack," Rose and Cora answered in unison.

Actually, now that he asked . . . She halted. They should have seen the white marks she'd painted on the tree trunks. Follow the deer path twenty paces, and then a left at the first white mark. She'd been on the path when she'd thought to startle them. They couldn't have veered too far. "Can I borrow that?" She took the flashlight from Mr. Boring without waiting for a response.

She swept the area with the light.

In the dark, the trees looked the same. She didn't see the patch of white paint, and she wasn't certain they were on the deer path. The shack, an abandoned hunting cabin, had become a favorite and well-graffitied hangout about a decade ago, but it was lost after a class of seniors refused to give up its location to the juniors. It had taken Rose days of badgering, plus a slight bit of blackmail (she knew which student had been getting "extra help" from the young math teacher) to worm the location out of the last year's graduates. But she'd done it, and she and Cora had made it their own. They'd left it well stocked with supplies that Cora had filched from her parents' liquor cabinet, as well as chocolate chip cookies baked by Cora's grandmother. Rose had supplied the pillows and blankets.

"Ugh, tell me we aren't lost," Mr. Boring said.

"We're not lost," Rose lied. "It's this way."

She led with confidence.

Any minute, she expected to recognize a tree or a boulder. She knew these woods. Occupying the area behind the high school to North Hill Cemetery, these woods were her favorite place to escape the ordinary. She'd been playing in them since fourth grade, when she realized her parents didn't actually care where she was so long as she wasn't underfoot. Back then, this had been her kingdom, and she'd ruled it like a queen, with pollywog servants from the pond, squirrels as sentries (they screeched when anyone approached), and hundreds of nooks and crannies to scamper over. Sometimes she let Cora be queen, so long as Rose could be the brave knight in shining armor who vanquished the dragon—or, even better, she would be the dragon. When they got older, they came to gossip. Sometimes they'd climb a tree and discuss the failings and attributes of every student and teacher at Greenborough High in minute detail. Sometimes they'd plot what they'd do when they escaped this town and were free to see the world—or at least Rose did. She'd even fantasized about traveling with Glenn . . . if she could convince him there was anything of value outside of New England. She'd planned a dozen South American adventures here, a hundred European trips. Asia. Africa. She wasn't that interested in Antarctica, but she'd like to see Australia. So yes, of course, she knew where she was going. Or she would, if it didn't all look different in the dark.

They should have reached the triple boulder by now. If they'd gone straight. Had they walked straight? She'd joined Cora and the boys on the deer path, so that should . . . Unless Cora hadn't followed the deer path?

If we head left, that should correct it.

All she needed was one familiar landmark.

A pond.

A boulder large enough to be recognizable.

A sprawling tree with climbable branches, the one she'd carved her name on. An oak she'd marked with white paint. A stack of stones that someone, not her, had left as a marker.

The trees opened to a clearing, and she exhaled. There were a finite number of clearings in this finite stretch of forest. As soon as she could identify which this was, she'd know where they were and what their direction should be.

She stepped into the open and switched off the flashlight.

"Rose!" Cora yelped.

"Let your eyes adjust," Rose said as Cora took the flashlight from her.

It was the flashlight's fault they were lost. It morphed everything into twisted shadows. If she could just see the shapes clearly . . . She walked forward. With the moon above, the forest was bathed in pale blue. She'd combed through nearly every inch of these woods. It wasn't *that* large an area, and she was certain she'd seen every clearing. As soon as she oriented herself . . .

The flashlight snapped on again.

"What's that?" Mr. Boring asked. He was pointing the flashlight beam at a lumpy rock. *Aha, an odd rock.* Rose strode toward it. Perhaps she'd recognize it.

Her shadow stretched and then warped as her friends moved behind her. She halted in front of the rock and blinked. She'd never seen it before; she was 100 percent positive of that. She'd remember *this*.

It had faces.

She squatted to get a better look, ignoring that she was in a prom dress.

"What is it?" Cora asked.

"Bring the light," Rose ordered.

Her friends came closer, shining the flashlight. "Ooh, creepy," Cora said.

"It's a statue," Mr. Boring said. "A weird statue. Why would someone dump a weird statue in the middle of the woods?"

"I think it's cool," Glenn said. He squatted next to Rose.

It was carved out of gray stone and about the height of a grave. Granite, she guessed, although she didn't know anything about stones, just that granite was gray and the name had gravitas. The rock was carved to look like three women with bodies that fused together into a solid chunk of uncarved rock. Their faces were covered in lichen, their features half-worn by wind and rain—it looked as if it might have been in the woods for decades, which was impossible since Rose had never seen it before. She couldn't have missed something like this.

"Can't believe we've never been here before," Cora said.

Okay, perhaps it was possible that she hadn't combed every inch of the woods.

"I knew we were lost," Mr. Boring said. He swung the flashlight back toward the trees. "If we head back the way we came—"

Rose was *not* about to admit she'd failed. This was just . . . a change in plans, a twist of fate. *Yes, fate!* "We were meant to find this! I called to the witch of the woods, and here she is!"

"Technically, it's three—" Glenn began.

"The three witches of the woods!" Rose jumped to her feet. "Which means we need to dance naked, worship the woods and the wild spirits in the moonlight!"

Cora giggled.

"I don't—" Mr. Boring began.

"Shut up, Jeremy," Glenn said.

"I was promised whiskey," Mr. Boring complained.

"I think you failed to hear the key word," Glenn said. Mouthing "naked" to his friend, he knelt and clasped his hands. "We need to worship the spirits of the woods. Oh, spirits of the woods, hear us!"

Rose laughed so joyously that it startled the birds in a nearby tree. Cawing, they took off in a rustle of branches—a flurry of shadows against the sky.

Mr. Boring began again. "I really don't think—"

"Oh, loosen up," Cora said.

Getting into it, Glenn laid his hands on the statue, on the old woman and the young one. "Oh, spirits of the woods, grant my wish!" He then leaned forward and whispered to the three stone women.

"What did you wish for?" Cora asked.

Glenn released the statue and smiled at Rose. It was her favorite kind of smile—a wicked, wonderful one. "I'll tell you if it comes true." He stood up and held out his hand. "Shall we find the Kissing Shack?"

"And then?" Rose asked, breathless, stepping closer.

He pressed his lips on hers and said, "We see if wishes come true." She knew he had a wild side.

CHAPTER TEN

LORI

1997

Lori lingered near the tampon shelves in the pharmacy and surreptitiously watched the bored cashier in the mirror overhead—while he not so surreptitiously watched her.

I should have picked a busier time.

But the downside of a busier time was that there were too many eyes, a greater chance she'd be seen by someone who liked to report shoplifters.

The pharmacy door opened with a whoosh, and an elderly woman shuffled in. She headed directly for the cashier. Lori could have kissed her as the woman peppered the teen with questions about prints—she needed them in five-by-seven for a graduation party, and did he know how to cut out her grandson since he refused to smile for any shots?

As the teen launched into an explanation, Lori slipped a pregnancy test into the deep pocket of her sweater-coat. She then picked up a package of generic-brand pads, the cheapest on the shelf, and carried it to the checkout. By this time, the cashier was busy at the photo printer. "I'll be with you in just a minute," he called to Lori.

"It's okay. I can come back for this later." Lori propped the package of pads on the counter and strolled out the door. "Got a few more errands to run." She added a hint of a Southern accent, choosing a North Carolina kind of lilt, not a deep Alabama drawl, on the off chance that the cashier described her to anyone later.

She walked across the parking lot, keeping a consistent pace, not glancing over her shoulder. She felt every muscle in her back tense. No matter how many times she'd done it, no matter how easy it was, it still made her feel sick to steal. She imagined what her always-judgmental mother would have said—and she imagined telling her mother what she'd never get the chance to say: *It's your fault. You made me this way.*

Lori crossed the street at the traffic light and only then looked back at the pharmacy. The cashier didn't come charging out, and she didn't hear any sirens. Even if the cashier reviewed the security camera footage later, she never intended to return to this town anyway, much less this pharmacy.

She walked down the broken sidewalk to a gas station convenience store. The bathrooms were at the back, beneath a neon-purple sign that blinked half the letters in "restrooms" and by a puddle on the floor that she hoped was water. She waved to the cashier and ducked into the bathroom.

And then she breathed.

It smelled foul. Stale urine. The scent of gas and oil from the gas station. Body odor that lingered in the air. But she was shaking, and she had to calm down. She breathed as deeply as possible until she could take out the box without feeling like she was about to rattle apart.

Lori unwrapped the test and read the directions twice. It was simple. A single line meant no. A double line, yes. All she had to do was pee on a stick. And not think. That was key. So far, she'd gotten through the day by focusing on the logistics: find a pharmacy, shoplift a test, find a public restroom. And now here she was.

I can't be pregnant. It was the sort of thing that happened to other people, in Lifetime movies and soppy books that were overflowing with feelings and insisted on a moral. *Haven't I had enough heartbreak?*

She'd tried her best to forget Mark since coming back to the United States, and this would make it utterly impossible. *It's impossible already.* If she closed her eyes, she could still feel his arms around her, but the stale smell and the voice outside cut through the memory—a sharp rap on the door shook it in its frame.

"Almost done!" she called.

Quickly, she took the test. Then she opened the window, set the test on the sill, and gently pushed it outside. It had to lie flat for five minutes, the instructions said. She washed her hands and exited the restroom. A lady holding the hand of a teary toddler glared at her before barging inside.

Lori milled around the gas station shop for the five minutes, eyeing chocolate bars she couldn't afford, before circling to the back of the station and picking the test up.

Leaning against a tree, Lori pulled her knees to her chest as if that would keep her new discovery safe. After reclaiming the test, she'd sneaked through a fence into the backyard of a random house—she'd checked for cars in the driveway first, of course, and it seemed safe enough.

She had at least a few minutes alone.

A few minutes to think, to react, to decide.

I'm pregnant.

Lori rolled the word over in her head. It felt as if it belonged to someone else. Yes, she had missed her period, but she'd never been regular. She'd just been grateful she hadn't needed to worry about buying (or stealing) pads yet. And yes, she'd felt queasy off and on, but that wasn't new either. She often ate things that didn't quite agree with her. Not everything that made its way into accessible dumpsters was okay to eat. Mayo could cause problems. Sandwich meat was often suspect. She'd eaten a burger once that . . . Yeah, better not to think about that right now. She swallowed hard and cradled her stomach, unsure if she was feeling morning sickness or nerves.

Could she feel a bump yet? Maybe. Or maybe it was her imagination? She had a very clear guess as to how long it had been: two months, three days, and seventeen hours—the last time she was with Mark, when they found themselves alone in the hostel—before she left him in Paris.

Mark.

She pictured him every time she closed her eyes. Fell asleep thinking of him. Woke up missing him. She'd spent hours wondering where he was, what he'd thought when she left, if he ever thought of her. He must have moved on by now. She liked imagining him in the library of Cornell Law School, bent over leather-bound books, his lips pinched the way they did when he concentrated. His hair would be flopped across his forehead; he wouldn't have remembered to comb it. She could picture him so clearly.

He'd meet someone there, another law student perhaps. Or maybe a girl from the music department who played her guitar in the quad. She wouldn't have enough change for lunch one day, and he'd buy her a sandwich. They'd talk . . . Lori heard his laugh in her head. He'd marry that girl. Bring her home to his parents, and they'd love her. She'd be exactly the daughter-in-law they wanted, and they'd marry in the family's backyard, under a tent, catered by a local bakery. They'd have a three-tier cake—one vanilla layer, one chocolate, and one banana, because it was her favorite.

They'd honeymoon, but not in Europe. Hopefully not Europe. Mark would have memories there, especially Paris. No, they'd go to the Caribbean. Relax in the sand on some island. She'd tan perfectly. He'd burn on his shoulders because he'd forget to put sunscreen there, and she'd rub aloe into his burns so they wouldn't sting. They'd sip piña coladas, and they'd snorkel and come back waterlogged and salty. A week later, they'd be home. He'd get a job at a prestigious law firm, up on the fifth floor—in a cubicle at first, but he'd work his way up—and she'd be . . . a teacher maybe? Or maybe in business. Perhaps a music producer. Wouldn't that be something? She'd start her own record label, and then three years later . . . Or two . . . At the perfect time, when they both agreed they were ready, she'd get pregnant. The baby would have Mark's eyes and, later, his laugh.

My baby could have Mark's eyes.

She knew she couldn't keep it. Of course she couldn't. What sort of selfish monster would bring a baby into a life like hers? Always on the move. Always hungry, tired, dirty, poor. Always lonely.

So very lonely.

There was no way she could have a baby. She thought of mothers on TV, with friends who threw them baby showers, with overinvolved parents and overindulgent grandparents. She didn't even have a doctor, hadn't been to a doctor in years. What about health insurance? Prenatal vitamins? A crib? How was she supposed to afford diapers? Or food? She had to be practical. With a child, you needed to at least be able to offer the stability of a home, and that was the one thing she could never, ever give this baby.

Lori rested her cheek against the tree's bark. It was a catalpa: clusters of white flowers between heart-shaped leaves. One of her favorite trees. This was a nice yard. The flower beds were weeded. She recognized peony bushes and daylilies. She wasn't sure what other kinds of flowers had been planted, but someone had put thought and love into it. They'd planted bulbs in anticipation of seeing them bloom.

I could have had this. If she'd been someone else. If she'd had a different life. She could have had a nice home with a nice garden, with her own catalpa tree. Or maybe this life was always her fate. She certainly hadn't had any choice in it.

But *this*—her hands curved over her stomach—she had a choice right now. She didn't have to be alone. Not ever again. This much she had control over. Maybe she couldn't have her own home, a perfect family, the life of her dreams, the love of her life . . . but she could have this child.

She just hoped someday her child would forgive her.

CHAPTER ELEVEN

ELISA

Now

The bell over the Book Cellar door chimes as I walk in, and Owen jumps to his feet behind his desk. I'm still not certain whether the desk is composed entirely of books. Between the stacks on top and the shelves to the sides, there's no visible wood at all.

"You came!" he says.

That shouldn't be a surprise. "You hired me." Granted, he hadn't told me what time to come, but I figured that since he opened at ten, I'd come a few minutes before.

"Yes, I know, but with yesterday . . ." He looks sheepish, which is an adorable look on him. He reminds me of a golden retriever I met a few towns ago who'd steal burgers off the grill but look too cute to blame. I've forgotten the name of the owner, if I ever knew it, but the dog was Maximus. "I overshared after the accident. You shouldn't have had to console me—that's not in the job description. I mean, I appreciate it, but—"

I cut him off before he spends the entire morning apologizing. "It's fine. Really. Things happen, and you can't always control who they happen around. Glad I was able to—" Not help. I didn't help. But I'd been with him, so he didn't have to process all that alone. "—be there." I'm also glad that, unlike Allison, he remembers the accident. I spent part of last night wondering if I was the only one with any recollection of it.

He runs his fingers through his hair. "Well, I'm embarrassed. What happened with Allison—it was a long time ago, and I'm not mooning over her. I know she's moved on. I respect that. *I've* moved on. It's just . . . You can't just turn off caring about someone, you know? And I'm doing it again. Oversharing. Sorry. You're very easy to talk to."

"Thanks."

We stare at each other for a moment, unsure of what to say, which is a bit ironic. I'm trying to figure out how to tell him that Allison has no idea what happened without having to answer questions that I have no idea how to answer. Luckily, I don't have to.

"She's fine," he says suddenly. "I mean, I heard from a friend that Allison was released from the hospital. She's resting at home."

"Great. That's great." It could have been a head injury that caused her memory lapse. But it doesn't explain why her mother denied it too. Perhaps she also has memory problems. I should stay both skeptical and alert.

Another awkward silence.

"Do you want to show me how this place runs?" I gesture toward the cash register and the various notebooks scattered around it.

"Oh! Yes. Definitely."

He spends the next few minutes showing me how the cash register functions—very similar to how every other cash register works—and how he processes credit cards and smart watches and all of that. Again, very similar to what I've done before. I feign interest while brainstorming how to steer the conversation to what I really want to know, whether he knows anything about curses, anything about my family, or, even better, anything about how to lift a family curse that's passed from mother to daughter. It's not an easy topic to weave into conversation, and I usually fail spectacularly. Perhaps later, when we're more comfortable with each other, I'll have more luck.

I think of when I first witnessed the consequences of the curse. I don't remember how old I was, or even what state we were living in at the time, but I remember it was a Saturday. Our neighbors had a TV the size of a wall, which they watched at top volume as if they were in a movie theater. I liked to open the window and peer at whatever they were watching. There was a cooking show on, and it made me hungry, so I trooped down to the kitchen. Mom was there, on the floor.

Her arm was cradled in front of her, her sleeve pushed up to her shoulder, her skin painted with blood. She had a knife in one hand, and it was covered in red. "I tried to cut it out," she said.

I remember those words so crisply: *I tried to cut it out.*

I don't remember what I said.

"It'll come back," Mom said. "The bark, it'll spread. You'll feel it too."

I tried to get her to stand, to call for help, to find bandages, but she brushed me aside. She moved so slowly—the sap in her blood, she said. She could feel it. She could see it. And I remember I could see it too: white sap in her wound, leaves scattered over the kitchen floor, and a chunk of bark, covered in blood, lying like a dead thing amid the leaves.

We left town that night.

I have dreamed of that memory so often that I'm not certain of the details. Sometimes it's not a TV that I'm watching. Sometimes the kitchen's different. But always the blood, always the leaves, always the lost look in my mother's eyes. And I always remember how I felt.

"I found a place to rent," I say, once Owen runs out of steam explaining how he tracks purchases. "Walking distance, so there's no commute to worry about." It's a two-mile walk, but that's fine by me. Maybe I can find a cheap bike at a yard sale, or maybe Allison has one I can borrow. If not, two miles is pleasant. I once walked seven to a job, every day, there and back, uphill at least one way. "It's a caretaker's cottage for an old house owned by a woman with a lot of birds."

"That's great."

He doesn't seem to draw the connection to Allison. I wonder whether it would be wise to point it out. Does he know where she lives? He must. They were engaged, and this is a small town—he'd know that she lives with her mother. "I've never met anyone with that many birds."

"I'm sure Charlie would love to visit."

We both look at the cat. He's stretched out across several stacks of books. Hearing his name, he pops one eye open and peers at us. When we don't produce food, he closes it and goes back to lounging.

"That said, I've never seen him chase a bird," Owen says. "Or catch a mouse. I don't think he knows he's supposed to be a predator."

"He doesn't look underfed."

"Hmm, maybe if he had to hunt for his food . . ."

The cat opens both eyes this time, as if he knows we're talking about him.

"Just kidding." Owen reaches into a drawer and pulls out a bag of cat treats. He tosses one to Charlie who stretches his neck. His nose reaches within an inch of the treat. He sniffs it but doesn't make any effort to eat it, as if he wants us to know his affection can't be bought. "So does everything make sense?"

Obviously not. I wonder if Allison has had miraculous recoveries before—no, he talked about how injured she was in her last accident. She was in the hospital for weeks. Maybe she was simply not as hurt as she looked? The truck wasn't going *that* fast. She could have just been knocked unconscious, recovered in the hospital, and been sent home— maybe the doctors didn't notice that she had memory loss? Head injuries can mess you up in unusual ways. Maybe she'd blocked out the event, or maybe when I appeared, she didn't want to discuss it. Except that wasn't the impression I got. It had to be her short-term memory.

But he, of course, meant the job.

"Yeah, makes sense," I tell him.

"I'm going to run a few errands," Owen says. "Think you can hold down the fort?"

"Absolutely. Go. Run. Look both ways before you cross the street."

A shadow crosses his face.

"Sorry. My mom—she used to say that all the time," I mutter. I didn't mean to remind him of Allison's accident. It was just habit. *Look both ways. Be careful. Be safe.* Neither of us could ever afford to be injured. Or sick. It happened sometimes. Mom made do as best she could. Once I broke my wrist—I'd been learning how to ride a bike. Our neighbor had offered to teach me. I thought I could go faster than I could. Then a bug flew in my face. And I flew into a hedge. The bike was fine. I would have been fine. Except when I tumbled out of the hedge, I crashed onto the sidewalk and—snap.

As soon as my cast was on, we left town. We couldn't afford the bills. When Mom judged the cast had been on for long enough, she sawed it off herself, with tools she liberated from an unlocked shed in a random neighborhood. I remember how awed I was—my mother, the woman who could do anything. Now, I wonder how she must have felt—was she scared? She must have been. But she didn't let it show, not back then.

"Of course, yeah, I didn't mean to overreact," he says.

"I didn't mean to put my foot in my mouth."

"You didn't. I—"

The cat coughs as if he's about to hack up a hairball.

"Not on the books!" Owen cries. He scoots out from behind the desk faster than I would've thought possible, hoists Charlie off the books, and sets him on the floor. "You okay, buddy?"

Charlie just glares at him. He doesn't hack again.

"All right. I'll . . . be right back, okay?" Owen says, mostly to the cat.

"We'll be fine," I tell him.

The bell over the door rings as he exits, and I watch him hesitate outside as if leaving his toddler with a babysitter for the first time. He glances back, and I smile and wave encouragingly. *You can do it.* At last, he heads off hesitantly, clearly reticent to leave his beloved books. "He doesn't get out much, does he," I murmur to myself. I wonder if

85

I could change that, with a little prodding—sometimes it just takes an invitation for people to leave their comfort zone. It's easier to take a risk when there's someone to catch you. I wonder if he likes outdoor concerts . . . But that's not why I'm here. I push thoughts of Owen from my head. What I need to focus on is if there's anything going on in this town, or anyone that could help me, whether or not they're connected to Allison. I sometimes tend to see only what I want to and to read too much into people's quirks. I've embarrassed myself before, spilling my story to strangers only to have them look at me with *that* look, the one that says I've lost my grip on reality. Concern. Pity.

I've been lucky in Greenborough so far. Now I have to be careful, if I want to stay for any length of time. I'll tread gently with both Allison and Owen, since they control both my housing and my income. But perhaps there are others in town I can talk to. My mind goes to the three blue-haired ladies from the coffee shop. They sent me to Allison. Maybe they know something about her release from the hospital. The timing still bothers me. From what I understand of hospitals, even if you aren't very hurt, there are mountains of paperwork to do, and everything takes a long time. People are always complaining about it. The waiting before a doctor sees you. Longer until you're released. For Allison to go from unconscious in an ambulance to home and perfectly fine so quickly . . . It doesn't add up, as much as I told myself there was a rational explanation. Hospitals just don't move that fast. And the blue-haired ladies, did they know what I'd find when they sent me to her house? I'll pay a visit to the coffee shop on my lunch break. Hopefully the ladies are there. At least I can ask the barista what their usual schedule is so I can—

The bell chimes.

My first customer comes in, and I recognize her instantly: half of the couple from the bus, the hostile girl with the nose ring. "Welcome to the Book Cellar," I say.

She halts just inside the door. "You didn't leave."

"I didn't. Found a job." Widening my arms, I gesture around the bookstore. "I can't resist a bookstore. Or a bookstore cat."

She snorts but pauses to scratch Charlie between the ears. He leans hard against her hand. "Wait," she says. "Does that mean Owen *isn't here*? Huh. He is literally always here."

"He stepped out for a bit."

She glances out the window, as if expecting to see him lurking outside, and I look as well. A car passes by. Across the street, a woman walks into a pharmacy.

Before I can form a question, she ducks in between the stacks. I busy myself neatening books near the desk. A few are out of alphabetical order, probably shoved back by uncareful customers. As I work, I think about what to ask her. You don't get too many chances to ask questions before it starts to feel more like an interrogation than a conversation. I could go the local-legend route, the local-gossip route, the—

She sticks her head back out. "Did Owen leave any books for Emma?"

"Are you Emma? I'm Elisa."

"Emma's my girlfriend. I'm Maddie. He could have labeled them 'For Maddie'?"

He didn't mention any specific customers. "Sorry."

Maddie scowls as if it's my fault. "I buy a book for her every week. She thinks I have good taste. I don't. Owen does. He always recommends the perfect book, and we just don't tell Emma they're his idea. It's the perfect system."

I feel a lump in my throat. It's a sweet tradition and a sweet deception. "Maybe I could help you find a book?"

"Whatever. I'll look myself." She disappears again.

I find I'm thinking about Jackie, for the second time today. Usually, I do a decent job of not reminiscing, but I met Jackie because of a book. Specifically, *Walk Two Moons* by Sharon Creech. I'd found it in the Quinn High School library, where I'd retreated one day instead of going to lunch. I hadn't wanted to face the horrors of the cafeteria. It was about a road trip and a girl who misses her mom. At the time, I couldn't resist road trip books, especially with a mother-daughter story at the core. Anyway, I didn't see the end coming, and when the character finally admits or accepts—I don't remember the exact details—the fact that her mom died . . . I only remember how I felt, as if every bit of oxygen had been stripped out of my blood. I was silently sobbing when Jackie found me, tucked in a corner of the empty library.

"You need a friend," she said.

"I don't. I need a Kleenex."

She gave me one and sat next to me, flipping through a book until I got a grip on myself. "Better?" she asked.

"You don't need to be nice to me," I told her. "We aren't going to be friends."

She shrugged. "That's not entirely up to you."

Jackie wormed her way into my life by simply showing up—at my locker, at lunch, in the library, after school. By midyear, we were inseparable. Even joined yearbook together, the very worst club for someone taught to leave no trace behind. One night, when sleeping over her house, popcorn everywhere and a movie on, I told her the truth. About me. About Mom. About the curse.

She listened and then said, "That's bullshit."

I remember how that felt: like an arrow in my heart. "I shouldn't have told you. I knew you wouldn't understand."

"I understand completely," she said. "It's how your mother controls you."

"It's not like that at all. She's keeping me safe."

"Alyssa"—I was Alyssa that year—"curses aren't real. And people don't turn into trees."

"I've seen the curse trying to take hold. I've seen bark growing on my mother's skin!" I should have known it would be impossible to explain to someone who wasn't there—how pale my mother had been, how hard it was for her to breathe, how afraid she was. My mother, who had sawed off my cast without even a hint of fear—she'd gouged the bark out of her own arm.

"Have you? Or were you just seeing what you expected to? I'm not saying this to be mean. But what your mother's doing isn't right. You need help. *She* needs help."

"Forget I said anything. It was . . . just a joke. A bad joke." But her reaction, her conviction, burrowed inside me.

A month later, she convinced me to talk to the school counselor. And they—Jackie, her parents, the counselor, and my English teacher, who'd raised a concern over an essay I'd written—started to make me think that it wasn't true, that it *couldn't* be true.

Curses don't exist.

I could stay, if I chose.

But, of course, I couldn't. Because *I* felt it that time, the consequences of the curse: the bark in my skin, the thickness of sap in my blood, and the knowledge that my mother would never—and had never—lied to me.

That goodbye hurt a lot.

When Maddie reappears, I muster a smile, but I know it looks as fake as it feels. She reminds me of Jackie, even though they're nothing alike. "Find one?" I ask.

"Yeah. Guess so." She plops down a copy of *Romeo and Juliet* with gilded edges.

"No."

"Excuse me? It's fancy, it's classic, it's romantic."

"It's about two kids who can't use the postal system properly. No. You want . . ." I scan the shelves nearby and settle on *Midnight at the Blackbird Café*. "This one. Small town. Strange happenings. A sprinkling of magic that may or may not be real. Lots of heart. She'll like it."

Maddie studies it. "Fine. I'm returning it if you're wrong."

"Speaking of small towns and strange happenings . . . What's the strangest thing to ever happen in Greenborough?" I keep my tone playful and take my time completing the purchase.

"Right now? You."

"Ha." I don't feel like laughing, but I pretend it's a joke.

Maddie leans her elbows on the counter and looks intently at me. "So, what are you running from?"

My fingers freeze as I reach for the credit card scanner. "I'm not. What makes you . . ." I take a breath, knowing my stammering only sounds suspicious. "I'm looking for someone. My family." I know it's pointless to show her the photos—she's a few years younger than I am. But I reach for the Ziploc anyway.

Maddie glances at the photographs. "Nope. Sorry. Mother and grandmother?"

"Yes." I put the photos away and complete the purchase, tucking the book into a brown bag with the Book Cellar logo—a silhouette of a book and a cat, appropriately.

Taking her bag, Maddie says, "You should show those to the trio. They know everything and everyone." I startle at the word "trio"—the same word Allison used.

"Who are they? Why are they so—" I cycle through adjectives, unable to land on one.

"Creepy? It's just their thing." She pats Charlie one more time and then is out the door. No opportunity for follow-up questions about the blue-haired ladies, Greenborough, or why she and Emma had warned me away from staying.

I'm alone in the bookstore again.

Or not alone—the cat is here. "Any advice?" I ask Charlie.

He lifts his leg into the air and licks without answering me.

CHAPTER TWELVE

Before I've finished re-alphabetizing even a quarter of the shelves, Owen pops back in. "Everything okay? No emergencies? Any customers?"

"One. Maddie. But everything's fine. You didn't have to come back so fast."

"It's lunch time." Bustling over to the desk, he checks over everything, and I try not to take it personally. I'm not certain he's ever had an employee before. In fact, I doubt it. I wonder how long that **HELP WANTED** sign was out there. It's tucked into a drawer now.

Charlie stretches and saunters over to Owen.

He absently pets the cat while studying the purchase I recorded. I wonder if he'll tell me that I should have allowed her to buy *Romeo and Juliet*, but somehow I think he would have vetoed it too. I suddenly want very much for him to approve of my choice.

"She said it was for Emma," I volunteer, hoping he'll express an opinion.

"Good choice," he says, and I feel like I've aced a test, though he doesn't even notice my reaction. He pulls some bills out of a drawer. "Bean Street has good sandwiches. Want to pick us both up some lunch?"

We did not negotiate lunch as part of my pay, but I am not about to say no. I take the money. "What kind would you like?"

"The chicken with green stuff on it."

"Lettuce?"

"Not lettuce."

"Herbs?"

"I know the word. Tip of the tongue . . ."

I smile. "It's okay. I'll figure it out." And I can look for the trio while I'm there. It's the perfect opportunity. I head for the door—

"Pesto!" he blurts from behind me. "Chicken and pesto. Knew the word."

I laugh, then promise him and the cat, "I'll be right back."

Outside, I notice the clouds have pulled across the sky. Only the occasional car passes, and there's no one nearby, with the exception of an older woman walking a dog, which pauses to pee on every parking meter. I wonder what she thinks of Greenborough and its residents. But she's too far away to ask.

I walk inside Bean Street, and it instantly feels hours later. The weak light barely penetrates the windows, and one of the lights flickers on and off overhead. I scan the coffee shop and notice, to my disappointment, it's nearly empty. No trio. Not even the guitarist.

The barista smiles and waves as I come in. "Hey, you're back."

"First day of work." I wave in the direction of the Book Cellar. "Owen sent me for sandwiches. One chicken and pesto, and one . . ." I examine the sandwiches in the display case. Their lettuce droops like a frown, but the one with turkey looks fine. "Turkey and cheese?"

"It's Gouda."

Any kind of cheese is fine with me. "That's—"

"Sorry, that was an extremely bad pun. It *is* Gouda, but it's also good. I definitely shouldn't try to pun."

I think it's cute—who doesn't like a good cheese pun?—but before I can reassure her, she changes the subject.

"How's business at the Book Cellar?" she asks.

"Great." I work up the nerve to ask a question: "How long as Owen been looking to hire someone?" *How long has he wanted to leave?*

"Months? Years? I don't know." She wraps up the sandwiches neatly and efficiently. "He's been talking about all the trips he wants to take for a while. Meanwhile, he's open seven days a week without a break. It's not healthy. We're all happy he hired you."

"Oh?" All? I'm surprised people have been talking about me.

"You could be just what he needs." She winks at me, and suddenly I want to be done with this conversation, even though there are a dozen more questions I know I should ask. I pay for the sandwiches and scoot out of the coffee shop.

I am a coward when faced with a determined matchmaker. Plus, I don't need any more attachments. Look how that turned out with Tyler.

After only a few long strides, I am back in the bookstore. Owen looks up from the book he has propped open. "That was quick."

I look at him for a moment, unable to explain why I was so uncomfortable with the barista's not-so-subtle attempts at matchmaking. That's *not* what I want out of Greenborough. The last thing I want is to be tied to this place. I'm already far too charmed by him, Charlie, the Book Cellar. "The barista says you don't get out enough, so here's the plan: you go eat your lunch in a park or somewhere in the sun"—I'm thankful he doesn't point out that it's cloudy—"and I'll watch the store again."

"I don't—"

I hand him the change and his sandwich and herd him toward the door. "I promise the Book Cellar will still be standing when you come back. Maybe I'll even sell all the books, and you'll return to discover you're a millionaire and can travel the world on your profits. Go, eat your sandwich, and decide where you'll travel to first. And when you come back, I'll tell you about the time my mother and I lived in a 'quiet community' in Florida, where the alligators outnumbered the senior citizens."

He leaves with minimal protest. Mostly, I think I confused him.

As the door closes, I turn back to see Charlie watching me with a judgmental expression. "I just . . . Never mind." *I don't need to justify myself.* Cats always seem to peer into your soul.

Sinking into one of the chairs, I plant my face in my hands. I don't know why this place has me so unsettled. Perhaps it's because it keeps surprising me. I'm used to being more in control of who I talk to and when, but between Allison and the so-called trio—

The bell chimes again.

As if my thoughts summoned them, the three blue-haired ladies enter the bookstore, one after another. It's so uncannily timed that I shiver. The world has space for coincidences, I know, but they still unnerve me.

The trio is dressed in vibrant, loose-fitting outfits: one in Hawaiian flower prints, another in geometric shapes, and the other in a red muumuu with bright-yellow lightning bolts. I admire how much they want to be noticed, or how much they don't care if they are.

"Hello, welcome to the Book Cellar," I say. "Can I help you?"

One of them, Sky Blue, elbows the other. "Here."

"She *said* she works here," Purple Blue says to her. "Of course she's here. She's only a liar to herself."

Well, that's a bit personal and also false—I lie to everyone, including myself, every damn day. I lean against the desk of books. "I didn't get a chance to properly introduce myself yesterday. I'm Elisa," I say, smiling. I hope they're in a chatty mood. There's a lot I want to know, and in my experience, older women know much more than anyone assumes.

Purple Blue points to herself. "Clotho." At the others: "Lachesis. Atropos."

"Oh no, my dear," Peacock says. "I'm Cordelia. She's Goneril, and she's Regan." She points to the others.

"Angelica, Eliza, and Peggy," Sky Blue sings.

I offer, "Blossom, Bubbles, and Buttercup?"

"Ooh, I like that," Peacock says. "Much more pronounceable than Moirai, Charites, and Erinyes. Or Alecto, Megaera, and Tisiphone. We were them last week."

"I was Lyssa last week," I say. "I'm Elisa today."

They smile as if we're sharing a joke, but I'm not sure which of us is joking. I'm also not sure why I told them the truth. That's the problem with conversation—sometimes what you don't mean to say slips out. Still, there's not much harm they can do with that information. It's not as if they know Tyler. Besides, I don't know if Tyler is looking for me, or, if he is, what he'd do if he found me. I can withstand yelling and tears; I'd just prefer not to. Besides, this is the most promising place I've been in a while, and I don't want to leave too quickly, at least not before I have my questions answered.

"You can call me Annie," Peacock says. The others are Barbara (Purple Blue) and Elaine (Sky Blue). Their oohs and aahs as they identify themselves make me think they're plucking the names out of the air, but I don't recognize Annie, Barbara, and Elaine as any famous fictional trio, and there's no point in questioning them. I'll call them whatever they want, especially if they'll answer my questions. "We wanted to properly welcome you to Greenborough," says Annie.

"Thanks," I say. "Have you lived here for long?"

"Feels like forever," Barbara says.

"Far too long," Elaine agrees.

Annie nods. "I remember when this place used to be a record store."

"I remember when it was a general store," Barbara says.

"I remember . . . emptiness." Elaine spreads her arms, and her sleeves flare out like wings. She sweeps her sleeves in a circular gesture. "Quiet." She says the word in a hushed voice, as if quiet means death. I can't help but shiver.

"It used to be farmland all around," Annie says. "This was a quiet town. A nice town."

I notice the past tense and wonder if it means anything, or if it's just a general everything-was-better-in-the-old-days kind of sentiment. What made it not nice anymore? Is it just a generic complaint or was there a specific incident? *Quiet.* But this isn't the mystery that I need to solve. I dig into my backpack and pull out my Ziploc with the two photos. The women watch me with interest.

"Does she look familiar?" I ask them, displaying the photo of my mother in her wedding dress. "You wouldn't have seen her recently, but maybe when she was younger? She could have passed this way?"

"Aw, she looks so happy," Barbara says.

"Young," Elaine sighs. "Beautiful."

"To be that young and beautiful again! Oh, how precious," Annie says.

"She was my mother," I say.

They pick up on the past tense. "We're sorry for your loss," they say in near unison. It's almost eerie, a rote response, but I see sympathy in their eyes—I don't want it. I want answers.

"She didn't talk much about her childhood. I'm looking for any family I might have left." Or anyone who might have information. I flip the bag over and show them the yellowed photo of my grandmother. I try to steel myself. It shouldn't hurt every time the answer is "No, I don't know her," but it chips away at me. It makes me feel a bit more invisible, like my family didn't exist and neither should I. "My grandmother."

"She looks like you," Barbara says.

Annie shakes her head. "No, dear, she looks like Rose."

Elaine touches the photo lightly. "Rose," she agrees.

Barbara squints at the photo of my grandmother. "You're right. It *is* Rose."

Rose.

I never knew her name. It feels as if a waterfall is tumbling over me. My hand holding the photo shakes so hard that I almost drop it. I hold its edges with both hands.

"Rose Grayson," Annie says. "Oh my, yes. We went to school together."

"She became Rose Ellert," Barbara reminds her.

It doesn't surprise me that she changed her name—Mom and I changed our names with every move. It was part of our routine, to disconnect us from the past. I *am* surprised they know about her name change.

I wait for them to say more. I want to drink in everything they know about my grandmother. And me. Ellert. Could it be my real last name? Elisa Ellert. It doesn't feel right, but that's because I've tried on dozens of names. Nothing would feel right.

When I was younger, I used to wonder if Mom even remembered my real name, if I was truly Elisa. She used to call me everything but whatever my "name" was that year: Pumpkin, Sugar, Honey, Muffin. She had a thousand, usually food-related, pet names. I was French Fry for about a week when I was supposed to be Bridget. I remember once accusing her of forgetting my newest name. She said she just wanted me to know I was loved, whatever my name. Hard to be annoyed after that, even at someone calling you Chicken Dumpling. By middle school, she'd dropped the pet names. Now I miss them.

"What's she like?" It shouldn't be my first question. I should ask if she's alive, where she is, and if I can meet her. I want to ask her . . . oh, a thousand questions, but of course only one matters. Still, I let the question float in the air and wait for them to answer.

"Fierce," Barbara says with a fond smile.

"Fiery." Annie.

"Fast." Elaine.

"Fast?" I ask, looking at Elaine's sky blue hair. It's a curious adjective to choose, even if she's just riding on alliteration.

"In high school, she was always hurrying somewhere," Barbara explains, a smile on her face as if reliving a memory. I wish I could snatch the memory out of her head and hoard it close to my heart. This stranger owns a piece of my past that I've never been able to access, and I want it so badly that I'm almost vibrating with need. It tastes coppery on my tongue. "She was on the school track team. I think. Or softball? Yes, I think softball. She played sports. I didn't. But we were friends, of a sort." She amends: "Friendly. At least on my part. She didn't seem to like many of us."

Annie nods. "Always looked down her nose at us. Thought we were small town."

"Small," Elaine agrees sadly.

Had she moved here from a city? Where? I open my mouth to ask—Barbara jumps in. "But it's a nice small town. Or it was. Everyone used to know each other. Look out for each other, at least as much as they were able within the scope of their understanding and the limits of their empathy. When we first arrived—"

"Rose Ellert." I have to know. It feels like a hunger—if they don't tell me, I'll devour them. That's how badly I need to know. "What happened to her?" It's unlikely they can answer that—she would have had to keep moving; the family curse wouldn't have allowed this to be more than a skip of a rock on a pond. At best, the trio knew her for one year in high school many decades ago. Some schools I attended for a full year, joined teams and clubs, and made friends that I hoped would remember me at least slightly, but none of them know where I went or where I am now or why I left. Even Jackie. Especially Jackie. Still, I have to try—perhaps they can at least point me in the right direction, give me a trail to follow. "Do you know where she went next?"

The trio looks at one another. Annie says gently, "She never left."

Then they give me directions to the cemetery.

CHAPTER THIRTEEN

ROSE

1973

"Today," Rose declared, "was perfect."

Spreading her arms, she spun in a circle. She tilted her head up toward the stars; it felt as if they were spinning with her. Her skirt flared out around her, and she turned until the ground wobbled. Glenn caught her hands, and she fell against him, laughing. He kissed the top of her head. "You were incredible," he told her.

"Yes, I was," she agreed.

She'd stepped up to that podium in front of the entire town council and presented, on behalf of her sorority, their plea that Greenborough designate the woods between the high school and cemetery a nature preserve. A developer was itching to buy it, but surely they could find another location to build their mall, one that didn't involve bulldozing trees that had been there since the town was founded, trees that contributed to the town's very name. She made an impassioned speech, and she felt her voice ringing to the rafters, or at least up to the fluorescent lights. It was glorious!

When the council had passed the resolution in her favor . . . "Ahh! That was the best!"

"You are the best," Glenn said. He was beaming at her, and it made her feel as if confetti and balloons were falling all around her.

"I know it's just a little thing—"

"It's *not* a little thing," Glenn said. "What you did is going to echo through generations—my dad said that. My parents think you hung the moon."

Rose laughed. She'd been so worried about winning them over. They hadn't been happy that Glenn had kept dating a girl who commuted to Farnsett State College, two towns over, and who wasn't going to one of the Seven Sisters. They wanted him to broaden, to find a girl who was his intellectual equal. That was not a conversation she'd enjoyed overhearing. Today, though, she'd impressed even them—that was a victory worth celebrating. *Not that I care what they think. I know what I'm capable of.*

"Marry me," Glenn said.

Rose laughed. "I do." She kissed him.

He kissed her back. "This is a perfect night. And I promise I will make you so happy. Deliriously happy. Anything you want. I just . . . You really want to marry me?"

"Yes, of course." She loved him. He loved her. Why not? Rose wanted to throw her arms around the entire world and squeeze. Everything felt possible.

He grabbed her hand. "Let's tell my parents. Unless you want to tell yours first."

What? But— Had they just gotten engaged? Like, officially engaged? She'd thought it was a hypothetical, future kind of question, *Will you marry me someday?* With the unspoken caveat: *After you see the world? After you've had your fill of adventures? After you've done it all?*

It's not like I don't want to marry him.

She certainly couldn't imagine being married to anyone else, and it was the logical next step in their relationship, the expected step. Just . . . already?

He was pulling her across the yard toward the house.

She was still in college. She'd imagined getting engaged a year or two after graduation. Until then, she'd explore the world. She'd backpack across Europe. Sail down the Amazon or the Nile. Stand on the Great Wall of China. She wanted to see Mount Fuji. Or even the Grand Canyon. How could she get married before seeing the Grand Canyon?

Granted, she hadn't worked out the logistics yet. She had zero savings. And there were her student loans, to pay for the tuition not covered by her scholarships. She had no idea how she was going to pay for her grand dreams—it wasn't as if her art history degree would make her employable, as her father frequently pointed out. But she always figured she had time. She was only a junior. She had over a full year to figure it out.

I don't need to marry him tomorrow. It could be a long engagement. She could have both her dreams and her future. *I have time to figure it all out.* Just because they were announcing their intentions didn't mean she was locked into a specific time frame.

Besides, he was so happy. And it had been a perfect day. She couldn't ruin it now.

Glenn will understand. He'll wait for me.

They reached the back porch of his parents' house. Light spilled out through the windows, and she saw his parents in the living room, his mother with a glass of wine and his father seated in an armchair. Glenn, pulling her behind him, burst inside.

1975

Rose tossed the bridal magazine onto the stack in the corner of her bedroom. She'd been engaged for over a year—she'd convinced Glenn that she needed to at least finish college first—and the stack was knee high. She flopped back on her bed and stared at the popcorn ceiling. Tentatively, she laid her hands across her stomach and spread her fingers.

Her period was late.

Downstairs she heard the clatter of her mom preparing dinner. Her father would be home from work soon. They'd sit at the table, and Dad would switch the news on. He'd ask her about her day while he chewed. *How were your classes?* he'd ask while his eyes slipped to the TV screen. Her grades had dipped last semester, and that wasn't acceptable. *Knuckle down and study hard,* he'd say. *Finish strong.* She was a senior, less than half a semester left at Farnsett State, two months before graduation. *I'm not paying for you to play,* he'd say. Never mind that between scholarships and her student loans, it was barely costing him a dime. Especially since she'd lived at home all four years. He'd refused to pay for her to live in a dorm when she had a perfectly nice bedroom in his house, and besides, what would her mother do without her?

But that was fine. She'd known they didn't have the money—her parents' money had to go toward the mortgage, their monthly bills, and their retirement savings, in that order. When she'd agreed to stay home and commute, she'd vowed to save whatever she could and travel after college.

But that hadn't worked out as well as she'd hoped. Rose had squirreled away some—maybe enough for a cross-country trip. Not around the world. Not the multiple-month-long adventures she'd dreamed of.

Miraculously, she'd convinced Glenn to honeymoon in Mexico, which his parents had been adamantly against—*Such a dangerous place*—right before insisting that they weren't racist, of course; it was simply that with all the poverty . . . She let Glenn tell them that she and Glenn had already decided, and that if his parents wanted to withdraw their offer to pay for the honeymoon, they were welcome to, which of course they insisted they didn't. Rose was cynical enough to believe it was because they'd already told all their friends they'd offered to pay, and they didn't want to look ungenerous. They'd softened considerably once they learned that JFK and Jackie had honeymooned there in the fifties. If it had been good enough for the Kennedys, then perhaps it was all right.

But a honeymoon wasn't the same as a wild adventure, at least not the kind she'd dreamed about since she was a kid. *Maybe those were a child's dreams.*

Rose had pushed the wedding and the honeymoon off as far as she could. Not the summer before senior year. And not the summer after either. It was too close to graduation, and Glenn would just be starting his new job, at a company owned by his uncle, the following June.

It had felt distant, at the time, but now it wasn't far off enough. Not with her lack of savings. And now . . .

They'll want it sooner. They'll insist.

Unless it was a false alarm.

"Rose!" Mom's voice ricocheted up the stairs. "Come set the table!"

Rose peeled herself off the bed. She thumped downstairs and tried to ignore the spider of fear crawling into her mind. When Glenn proposed, she thought she could still control the trajectory of her life, but since then it had felt as if everything was careening forward without waiting for her to express an opinion. *It has to be a false alarm. Stress can do this.*

She set the table as her mother stabbed the pot roast with a meat thermometer. "Carrots aren't as tender as I'd like," Mom sniffed, "but it will do."

"Do you ever feel like time is moving too fast?"

Mom flashed her a smile. "Absolutely, sweetie. To me, you're still eight years old in pigtails. When did you become such a beautiful young woman?"

Yes, yes, very nice. "I mean, out-of-your-control fast. You think you have time for everything you want to do, and then suddenly there's no more time."

Mom pulled on her oven mitts and lifted the pot roast out of the oven. Meaty steam rose and filled the kitchen. Rose inhaled the familiar aroma of the beef and vegetables that her mother had cooked a hundred times. "Honey, you're describing being an adult."

"I don't want to be on my deathbed with a hundred regrets."

"Regrets aren't a thing you can avoid," Mom said. "They're just a part of life. Every time you say yes, you're saying no to a dozen other things you could be doing." She then put down the oven mitts, turned, and sighed heavily. "Rose. Is this about Glenn? You aren't cheating on him, are you?"

"What? No!"

"I understand you didn't have much opportunity to date in college, but just because you met Glenn early doesn't mean he's not the one for you. You don't have to experiment with other options—or whatever you want to call it—to know that. He isn't cheating on you, is he?"

"Of course not." She had no idea where all of this was coming from. Glenn was not the type to cheat. She didn't think it would even occur to him. If he walked into his own bedroom and a naked woman lay on his bed, he'd assume she was waiting for someone else. Or that she'd lost her clothes in some kind of bizarre laundry accident. He was her fiancé, and thankfully, in Glenn's mind, a fiancé didn't cheat. He wouldn't have even entertained the idea. As for her, no, she loved Glenn, and she had absolutely no interest in sneaking around and complicating her life. It was already stressful enough between classes and worrying about how she was going to fund all the travel she wanted to do, and now with her late period . . . Why would her mother even suggest—

She heard keys rattle as the front door opened. Her father called, "I'm home!"

"Welcome back!" Mom answered. "Fifteen minutes to dinner." She trotted into the hallway, and Rose heard her ask Dad about his day and his commute, all the typical questions. Rose drifted over to the stove and looked at the pot roast. She dipped a finger into the sauce and tasted it, then added more pepper.

Behind her, Mom said, "Rose Grayson, you leave that alone. You know your father doesn't like spice."

"Pepper isn't spice. It's just . . . seasoning."

"It's seasoned enough." She shooed Rose away from the stove. "And it is indeed a spice, the most famous of spices."

Dad stuck his head into the kitchen. "I don't like spicy. Don't make it spicy."

"See?" Mom smacked her lightly with the tip of the oven mitt, as if she were knocking away a fly. "You can cook as spicy as you like when you have your own kitchen. Well, depending on Glenn's tastes."

Rose backed away from the stove and instead filled water glasses in the sink. Forks on the left, knives (blade toward the plate) on the right, spoon beside them, even though there was nothing in the meal that required a spoon. She didn't bother to question it. She set a bottle of ketchup next to her father's plate. He liked extra ketchup. That wasn't a spice.

"Are you happy?" Rose asked. She didn't know why the words came out just then, but it suddenly felt like the most important question in the world.

Mom didn't answer immediately, and Rose looked at her.

"Why ask that?" Mom asked. "Of course, I am. A little tired. I had to reschedule my hair appointment, which wreaks havoc on the rest of my schedule because exactly when am I supposed to fit it in now? Also, the gas prices rose again, and the washing machine is making a *glumphing* noise that I don't know if your father is going to be able to fix. We may need a new one." She chattered on, a litany of little complaints, before she took a breath. "What is this about, Rose? You're not acting like yourself." She placed the back of her hand on Rose's forehead. "Do you feel all right?"

"Keep your germs to yourself," Dad said, coming into the kitchen. He'd changed out of his button-down and into a T-shirt with the faded logo of a seafood restaurant they liked. "I've got a meeting on Friday that I don't want to sniffle through."

"I'm not sick." *I just may be pregnant.*

He turned on the TV and sat down in his chair at the kitchen table. "How were your classes?" he asked as the news anchor filled the screen, shots of helicopters leaving Vietnam behind him. "Studying hard?"

Rose sat down next to him and placed her napkin in her lap. "Yes, of course." She watched her mom serve the pot roast and listened to her dad praise her cooking and then tell her that her hair looked beautiful. She laughed and insisted it didn't because she hadn't been to the salon. Rose added more pepper to her slab of pot roast while the TV switched to local news. She thought of what her mother said: every yes is a no to a dozen other things.

But she didn't think it was that simple.

What if yes was the only answer because no was unthinkable? Or impractical? Or unacceptable? If she'd said no to marrying Glenn, she'd have lost him. If she'd said no to living at home for college, she wouldn't have been able to go at all. If she said no to staying in Greenborough after graduation and getting a job and marrying Glenn and instead traveled the world, what would she lose? And how would she afford it? And if she said no to what could, potentially, be growing inside her . . .

No one would forgive me.

She looked at her parents, who loved each other, who loved her, who had such dreams and expectations for her. She thought of Glenn, of what he would say. How happy he'd be to have a family, to have everything he ever wanted. She had the opportunity for the perfect picture-frame life.

I have to say yes.

It's time to grow up.

CHAPTER FOURTEEN

LORI

2000

Lori leaned her head against the bus window and watched the fence posts flicker by. She'd lost track of where in Indiana they were, and it didn't really matter. All that mattered was that she'd scrounged up enough money for two bus tickets and gotten out. She could breathe again. As she gazed out at the fields, every minute another mile away, she felt the muscles in her back unknot just a little more.

In her arms, two-year-old Elisa squirmed. She burrowed her face into Lori's neck and made a little sleepy smacking noise with her lips, which was so adorable that Lori couldn't help but smile. She leaned her head over Elisa's and inhaled the strawberry scent of her shampoo mixed with sweet toddler sweat. Her pudgy knee was digging into Lori's thigh, but Lori wasn't about to make her sit in her own seat. Soon, she'd be too big to be held all the time. Until then, Lori wasn't going to give up a minute of sleepy-toddler time.

"Aw, it passes so fast," a woman said from across the aisle. "Enjoy it while you can."

Lori tensed, her arms tightening around Elisa, but she forced her lips to smile pleasantly. "I will. Thanks." She hoped that ended the conversation and that it wouldn't lead to—

"You know, you shouldn't let her suck her thumb like that," the woman said.

—unsolicited advice.

The advice giver looked to be about sixty, with dyed black hair and caked-on foundation that didn't reach the wrinkles on her neck. She held a pink purse on her lap. "It'll lead to braces. Oh my, those orthodontist bills! You don't want to see those. I swear I put my orthodontist's kids through college all on my own."

"She only does it when she's asleep." Lori wished she could suck the words back in. It never paid to engage with someone who was determined to be "helpful."

"Ah, that's the worst. She can't break an unconscious habit on her own. You have to do it for her. You know, they sell this peppery nail polish—it's supposed to discourage thumb-sucking."

She wasn't doing that. If Elisa was comforted enough to sleep wherever they were, that was enough. Frankly, Lori would suck her own thumb if it would help her fall asleep. But all she said was "Thanks. I'll think about it." That was always the safest response. Be polite, then disengage.

"She needs to learn to self-soothe."

Lori pressed her lips together. *That's precisely what thumb-sucking is, and she'll outgrow it. Or she won't, and she'll be wonderful either way.* She opened her mouth to thank the woman again, more firmly, but the stranger was on a roll.

"When mine were that age, I only let them in their beds at nap time and bedtime. If they weren't tired, they had to lie there anyway. Otherwise, they never find a schedule. Up all night." As she chattered on, Lori looked out the window at the fields. Why did strangers feel the urge to share their judgment—all dolled up as advice? Some people just couldn't help themselves.

Maybe it's jealousy.

It was clear the woman's children were grown, and she was missing when they were warm, squirming, sweet, delicious armfuls that clung to you as if you were a tree and they were a vine.

Or it's guilt. Maybe people like her needed to justify their mistakes and convince themselves they weren't terrible parents. They'd insist to everyone that they'd done what was best for their child. Lori imagined her mother would have been like that, if she'd lived. She'd have broadcasted how selfless she'd been—

Lori cut off that thought. She'd sworn never to think about her mother.

At last, the woman fell silent. Perhaps she'd exhausted her supply of advice, or perhaps she'd tired of dispensing it to someone who had lost interest.

Lori wondered what she'd say if she knew how she and Elisa really lived; that there weren't any orthodontists in her future; that Elisa didn't have a proper bed to learn proper sleep habits in; that Lori didn't know where they were going to sleep tonight, but it could easily be in the bus depot if luck wasn't on their side. The woman with the pink purse would not have approved.

And Lori didn't care.

We're doing fine.

Elisa stirred in Lori's arms, lifting her head. Her hair was matted to her cheek, and her eyes were swollen from sleep. "Cow," she said, pointing at a field.

Lori glanced out the window. "Yes. Cow. Do you want to hear a story about a cow?"

"Moo," Elisa said.

"Once upon a time, there was a cow who loved to watch buses drive by his field—"

"No. Moon."

Lori laughed. "That one again? Okay, once upon a time, there was a cow who loved to jump over the moon. His best friend was a—"

"Rabbit!"

We're doing better than fine. "That's right. A rabbit! And one night . . ."

◆ ◆ ◆

2003

Lori waited outside of Rose Street Elementary School. It felt as if her heart had lodged in her throat and was beating so hard that it was difficult to breathe. She squeezed her hands into fists, then released them, over and over.

"Kindergarten pickup?" a woman asked beside her.

Without glancing at her, Lori said, "Yes."

"First kid?"

"Yes." Was that Elisa by the front window? No, it could have been anyone. The children in the halls looked warped through the speckled glass. She searched for Elisa's pigtails, for the backpack that she'd scored at a thrift shop . . .

"By the third child, it's a relief," the woman said. "And by the fourth, you just hand them the car keys and tell them to drive themselves."

Lori couldn't even muster a polite laugh. What if Elisa was miserable? What if she didn't make any friends? What if she was so far behind her peers that they'd laughed at her? On their many bus rides, Lori had taught her the alphabet. She could read simple sentences. And she knew how to read a map very well. But they hadn't done much with numbers. Or history. What was a kindergartner supposed to know already?

"Hey, take a breath," the woman said. "They'll be fine."

She blinked hard at the kindness in her voice and was about to thank her when the school doors swung open, and kindergartners poured out. They stampeded like wild bison across the plains, and Lori craned her neck, looking for—

Elisa!

Elisa spotted her at the same moment and came running toward her. Her smile was huge, her pigtails lopsided and flopping as she ran, and she was clutching something in her left hand. "Mommy! Mommy!"

Kneeling, Lori scooped Elisa into her arms. She felt as though the two ripped-apart halves of her soul had been smushed back together, and her rib cage loosened. Elisa squirmed out of her arms again and opened her hand.

On her palm lay a green crayon.

"I have a best friend," Elisa said proudly.

For a moment, Lori thought she meant the crayon.

Elisa began chattering: her new friend's name was Emma Sanchez, she had a pet turtle named Mr. Mouse, and she had shared her green crayon because Elisa wanted to draw a tree and didn't want to make it a tree in autumn with red leaves because they were sad.

"Why are red leaves sad?" Lori asked.

"Because they have to say goodbye to their branches," Elisa said, as if this were the most obvious thing in the world. She took Lori's hand and began pulling her down the sidewalk. They walked away from the school, while Elisa gushed about kindergarten: she loved her teacher, she loved the classroom, she loved the desks ("My size!"), she loved the rocking chair that Ms. Scali told stories from, she loved the Red Light, Green Light sign on the bathroom, she loved the alphabet rug ("I sat on the *E*!").

She chattered the whole walk, taking gulping breaths before launching into the next anecdote. Lori felt her heart lift higher and higher until she thought it might pull her off the ground and she'd float all the way back to the tiny over-the-garage apartment she'd rented. All the paperwork, all the lies she'd written to get Elisa into school were worth it.

Lori hadn't had much choice. Her new job wouldn't allow her to bring Elisa with her, no matter how quiet and well behaved she promised her daughter would be. She was working at the Pickle Café, and they didn't want a child underfoot, especially in the kitchen. Lori didn't blame them—it was tight enough back there, between the counter, the sink, and the stove. But she hadn't imagined school would be such a success!

She pulled out her key and opened the garage. One car, an old Buick, was parked on the right side, and there were piles of boxes on the other. They skirted between them, and Lori pulled down the ladder to the attic apartment.

Elisa scrambled up, her backpack bouncing on her back.

It wasn't much of a place: the house itself was one strong wind away from blowing down, and the attached garage was in even worse shape. But the tiny apartment in the eaves above the garage had a mini fridge, a sink, and a toilet in a closet. A bathtub sat in one corner of the main room, next to the sink, with a hose hooked up in case you wanted to pretend it was a shower; though, there wasn't enough water pressure to stand. Elisa called it a "sit and splash." The owners used to let their adult son live here "until he got his feet under him," they said, and it was just sitting there unused. Lori was happy to hand over a portion of her paycheck to have a place of their own, at least for a little while. She'd spent a solid weekend scrubbing until it was as clean as possible, stains excluded, and now it was almost homey.

She was careful not to think of it as home.

"Homelike" was okay.

Elisa dumped her backpack by the door and flopped onto the "couch," which was three sofa cushions Lori had rescued from the curb on trash day. They smelled faintly of mildew but were otherwise fine. "It was *amazing*, Mommy."

"I'm so happy you had a good day, Lovey Dove."

"It was the *best* day."

Lori grinned and plopped down next to her on the cushions. "Well, then you'll be happy to hear that you have three more days this week and then *five* next week and then five the week after that and the week after that . . ."

Elisa gasped. "Forever!"

"Until the end of the school year, in June, and then we'll pick the next town we want to live in. But you can go to kindergarten from start to finish. Does that sound good?"

"I don't want another town. I like this one."

"I know, but we can't stay. At the end of the school year, we have to leave."

"But why?"

She knew this moment was coming: the day Elisa asked *why*. She was now meeting people who stayed in one place. It was natural that she'd wonder why the two of them had such different lives. Lori lifted her arm, and Elisa curled into her side, snug under her armpit. Lori had hoped to have a little longer, but this was fine. It was better that Elisa knew the truth. Lori hugged her daughter closer. "Do you remember that story about the cow and the rabbit and the moon?"

"Ooh! Yes! The rabbit says to the moon, 'You can't catch me! You're stuck in the sky!' And then the moon says, 'You can't reach me! You're stuck on the ground!' And then the cow jumps so high—"

"Yes, that one." It was one of the more ridiculous stories she'd ever told, but Elisa loved it and made her tell it over and over again. In it, the moon doesn't think the cow should keep jumping over her, so she curses the cow. If the cow doesn't stop jumping, she'll be transformed into a mushroom, the curse says. And so, the cow is stuck on the ground, because she's afraid of the curse. In some variants, the rabbit then learns how to jump over the moon in the cow's stead, but in most the rabbit and cow become best friends, sharing the grassy field under the light of the moon. "Well, the women in our family . . . we're like the cow."

"We don't moo."

"We are cursed," Lori said. "A secret curse that only we know is there. Like the cow. Except we aren't cursed to stay; we're cursed to always leave."

Elisa frowned, which made her nose crinkle adorably. Lori had told her plenty of stories about curses—to prepare Elisa for their reality. "Why? Does the moon not like us?"

"She loves us," Lori said, "but she thinks she knows what's best for us. Cows aren't supposed to jump over the moon, and we aren't supposed to stay in one place." She touched the tip of Elisa's nose with her finger. "That's what the moon believed."

"Other people can stay or leave—they get to choose."

"We aren't other people."

"But what if we try to be?"

"That's the curse," Lori said. "If we try, we transform." She hesitated over how much to say. She didn't want to frighten Elisa, but she also wanted her to understand. "The moon did it out of love for her daughter and her daughter's future daughter and her daughter's daughter's future daughter. She was afraid that if we stayed in one place, we'd get stuck and lose who we are. So the curse says we can't stay, or we *will* get stuck and lose who we are. Our skin will turn to bark, our hair to leaves, and our blood to sap. We'll become trees."

Elisa's eyes went wide, and her mouth formed a little *O*.

"But I've figured out rules to keep us safe. One: don't stay anywhere for longer than ten months. Two: don't return to any place you've ever been. That's it. Can you say that back to me?"

"Don't stay for longer than ten months," Elisa parroted. "Don't return to any place we've ever been."

"Good! So long as we're careful, we'll be safe from the curse," Lori said. "And being careful means we don't leave anything behind, and we don't take anything that ties us to where we were. No pictures. No mementos. Not even our names. When we leave, we fully leave. Do you understand, Pumpkin? We don't want the curse to catch us."

Elisa sat quietly, clutching the green crayon. She opened her hand and looked at it. "I'll give the crayon back to Emma."

"Eventually, that would be best," Lori said. "But you can keep it for now."

"For ten months," Elisa said, and Lori felt pride flutter in her chest. Elisa hadn't burst into tears. She hadn't argued or fussed or reacted in any of the ways Lori had feared. The pride helped counteract the ache—her daughter shouldn't have to think about any of this, especially at such a young age. Other kids got to have normal lives, normal worries, and normal fates.

"Yes, that's right." *I love this girl so much.* Lori wasn't certain the limit was ten months—the curse hadn't come with a rule book—but it seemed like a safe amount of time, and it would allow Elisa to complete kindergarten at Rose Street Elementary. As much as she'd determined, the important thing wasn't the amount of time; it was that a place didn't begin to feel like home. They couldn't put down roots. Ever. "A place can't become our home."

"That's okay," Elisa said, closing her little hand around the crayon and snuggling closer to Lori on the mildewed cushions. "*You're* my home."

CHAPTER FIFTEEN

ELISA

Now

It's my first day, so I can't rush out and leave the bookstore unattended while I hunt down my grandmother's grave, despite how desperately I want to. I'll have to wait for Owen to return. She is, quite literally, not going anywhere.

After the trio leaves—Annie (Peacock) bought a cookbook of muffin recipes, Barbara (Purple Blue) bought a poetry book with a shouting woman on the cover, and Elaine (Sky Blue) bought a ribbon bookmark that she tied in her hair—I flutter around the bookstore, trying to squeeze stray books onto shelves, failing, giving up, and returning to the desk, which is, I've determined definitively, actually made of books. I wonder what would happen if anyone wanted to buy any of the books that make up the desk. It must be like a game of Jenga on busy days, if the store ever has busy days. And then I think about my grandmother, Rose Ellert, who never left (which is impossible—of course she left; what they meant is that she can't leave anymore). I flit around, wondering where she went after her year in Greenborough and why she came back at the end of her life, while the cat watches judgmentally from the front window, as if he wants to say he would never be so undignified as to fidget in a bookstore.

No one else enters the shop before Owen returns. He ducks under the bell, absently pats Charlie's cheek, and then looks startled to see me. I can't tell if he expected me to leave or if he's forgotten he hired me. Either way, a smile quickly swallows the expression. "Any excitement?" he asks.

"A bus full of speed readers stopped by, bought every book in the shop, read them, and returned them," I tell him. "It was tragic."

"Did they at least leave reviews?"

"They gave everything two stars, except the cat. He got five stars."

"Obviously. He's a cat."

I take a breath. "Actually, Barbara, Annie, and Elaine stopped by—"

He frowns. "Who?"

Maybe he doesn't know all his customers' names. "The three ladies with blue hair? They seem like regulars?" I gesture next door. "They were at the coffee shop yesterday."

"Ah, they told me they were Anne, Emily, and Charlotte Brontë the first time I met them," Owen says, "and Athos, Porthos, and Aramis the second time. Stu, who runs the diner at the end of the street, calls them Larry, Curly, and Moe."

"Huh." I wonder if they told me their real names or if they plucked them out of thin air.

"You should try one of Stu's omelets while you're in town. Really excellent. I think he adds a secret mix of cheeses."

I blurt out, "I need to go to the cemetery."

Owen blinks at me. "Sorry?"

I tell Owen the key facts, the ones that don't involve impossibilities: I don't know much about my family history, and I've been searching for clues as to where my mother's family came from; when I showed the three blue-haired ladies the photo of my grandmother, they recognized her as Rose Ellert and said she's buried in North Hill Cemetery; I'd like to visit her. It's a reasonable enough story, with the added benefit of being true.

"That's fantastic!" he says. "Not that she passed away. I'm sorry for your loss. Deeply sorry. I didn't mean it was fantastic that she died without you meeting her, but I meant—"

"I feel the same way. It's more than I hoped to find."

"Naturally, now you want to see her grave," Owen said. "You need to." He bustles around the book desk and shoos me toward the door. "Do you want me to go with you? I'd be happy to, if you want company, but if you don't, I, of course, understand. You might want a private moment."

I laugh. There's something so sweet and comforting about his awkwardness, how he has no idea what to say or do. He will be hard to leave behind. I wonder why Allison left him. "I'll be fine. Thanks."

"Do you know where to find it?" he asks.

After he shows me three maps of town (including one from the 1800s, because he thought it was interesting), I hurry out of the Book Cellar. It takes a lot of self-restraint not to run. As I hurry through the downtown, barely registering the stores or cars or anyone else, I wonder if I should bring flowers. Isn't that what one does? I've never visited the grave of anyone I knew—or, more accurately, could have known. That would require returning to a place where I'd formed bonds, which is far too dangerous.

I feel as though my body is humming. After so long, to have a connection. All these years, all these towns, all the times I've shown those photos, no one has ever recognized them before.

Rose Grayson.

Rose Ellert.

It couldn't be her married name, could it? She *did* have a child, but marriage requires a more permanent commitment. Unless it was a short-lived marriage? I wish I'd asked the trio. It wasn't at all odd for a woman in my family to change her name, but it was unusual that she did it so openly, for others to know about.

She ran track for the local high school the year she lived here. Or played softball. Or both. She was fierce, fiery, and fast. I want to know more. More memories. More stories. I want to build a history out of the crumbs of memories, anything I can get from those who knew her. I want to devour every bit of knowledge I can beg, borrow, or steal. I want to soak it in from the air she breathed and the ground where she lies.

Thanks to Owen's maps, I have a good sense of where the cemetery is—behind one of the town's New England–style churches, at the edge of the woods. Ahead of me, the church's spire rises up, framed by blue sky. It looks like a postcard: white clapboard, red doors, and a dogwood tree in front of it, white blooms bright against green leaves. But I'm only interested in what's behind it: North Hill Cemetery.

It's a small cemetery, and the first thing I notice is how quiet it is. Even the wind feels hushed. I let myself in the gate and note that the grass hasn't been mowed in a few weeks. It waves like wheat in the breeze as I scan the stones. Closer to the church, the stones are older, worn away by wind and time, eroding the words. Orange lichen crawls over them in lacy flowerlike blooms. I read the last names: a lot of Strongs, Bartletts, and Weldons. As I weave through the stones, I wonder where it's okay to walk. Am I stepping over someone? Is it better to walk in front of or behind the stones? How long do the actual graves extend? I've never been to a funeral—well, only one. It requires staying in a place long enough to honor a death. I've never known anyone well enough.

Except for Mom.

There was a funeral for her, with a service. She had a casket, and he'd filled the funeral home with so many white roses that I thought I'd choke from the scent. I had to walk outside. And then I kept walking all the way to the willow tree by the water.

I didn't move until the sun went down and the sky was too dark to see anything but shadows. When I finally went inside, I stayed in that house—that sad, silent house, *his* house—another day or two, long enough to figure out how Mom had taken care of me: she'd ensured I'd always have money. She'd gifted me with my own bank account, under a name that matched one of my many IDs: Elisa Tuileries. It was a security net, the kind she'd never had, to make sure I never had to do what she did. If I were careful and smart and frugal—all of which she'd taught me to be—I'd never starve, and I'd always have a roof over my head. I am well aware that I should be grateful for her extraordinary gift. But I would, without question, rather have my mother back. I haven't touched the money, and I don't intend to.

There aren't any recent graves in this cemetery. The most recent deaths are from about a decade ago. There must be another cemetery in town; certainly no one else is visiting this one. It's only me and the stones.

I slowly study the names and dates until:

ROSE LORELEI ELLERT.

Born 1953. Died 1994. She was forty-one years old when she died. Young. Kneeling in front of the grave, I touch the etched letters and wonder why she came back here. Did Mom know why? A breeze blows, and I hear a few birds calling to one another from the trees. It's peaceful, the way a cemetery is supposed to be, but I feel anything but peaceful inside.

I wonder if Mom was here when her casket was buried. She might have been. But would she have risked it? She may have never visited. I know Mom didn't return in recent memory, since I've never been here before.

Of course not. That would have been returning home. And being home—that was the one thing that was absolutely forbidden. Once a place became a home, we never returned. Mom was very, very clear about that rule.

I wonder if she ever wanted to come back here. Mom didn't talk much about what she wanted. Just about what we had to do. She tried to make the best of it, at least when I was younger. Later . . . At least I have a lot of memories of the two of us, laughing together as we rode a bus out of a town, as we explored a new place.

I remember a little rest stop outside of Phoenix. Mom pulled into the parking lot—she had a yellow Toyota with side view mirrors duct-taped on, a dent in the rear fender that looked as if it had been rammed by a bull, and one back window that was stuck halfway up. It hadn't passed inspection in three years, but she was careful to park where no one would notice. She grinned at me. "Ready to choose our next destination?"

"My turn this time?" I think I was ten. Eleven?

"Your turn."

"Coin flip? Alphabet game?"

"I've got a new idea." She plucked a sock out of the backseat, one of her knee-high ones. "Come on. First one in gets a vending machine treat."

I leapt out of the car and raced into the rest stop.

It had, like many rest stops, a row of vending machines, a bathroom of variable cleanliness, and a map on a wall. This one was painted, with flowers and birds to depict the state flowers and birds.

She wrapped the sock around my eyes like a blindfold. "Okay? Can you see?"

"It's good."

"No cheating."

"I'd never cheat." Unless it meant extra french fries. But I never cheated at this kind of game.

"Spin." Mom put her hands on my shoulders and guided me as I spun until I was laughing and stumbling. Then she gave me a gentle shove forward. I held my finger out as I weave-walked toward the map on the wall. I halted when my finger hit it.

Mom applauded behind me. "Excellent choice!"

With my finger still on the map, I pulled off the sock. "Midway, New Mexico?"

She dragged my finger north, up the highway.

"That's cheating," I said.

"That's Roswell. Come on. I've always wanted to see a place with people weirder than we are." She bought me Fritos from the vending machine, and we set off for Roswell.

We loved all the tourist traps. Once, shortly after our Roswell stint, she found a book about odd tourist traps in the United States. We spent a few months visiting as many as possible, viewing them from a distance if there was a fee to enter. Often, you could see the giant metal chicken or the rock that looks like a cowboy without any fee at all. I can still picture her, inventing stories about how the huge metal chicken saved civilization by laying a giant metal egg that hatched into the Empire State Building. I'd try to top it with a fake legend about the giant ball of twine that had been lost by a cat the size of an 18-wheeler. We even visited the oldest piece of taffy, which was exactly as unimpressive as advertised.

We marveled at all of it.

Until nothing seemed to amaze her anymore. But again, that was later, before she chose to stay and die. I wish I knew why my grandmother chose to return here—and I wonder where she is right now.

I stand and turn in a slow circle. The rolling grounds of the cemetery lead toward the woods—*there*. I walk toward the trees. Around me, the birds sing, and I can hear a faraway lawn mower, like the faint buzz of a bee. There's a muffled sound of cars from the town, but I can't see the road from here. And by the time I reach the edge of the woods, that sound fades.

I know the trees, each of them by name:

Oak.

Sugar maple.

Eastern white pine.

Beech.

I greet them as I enter the woods. Dead leaves from past autumns crunch beneath my feet, and the mossy ground gives like a soft carpet.

There's lichen on the bark, curled around the crevasses, and lily of the valley tucked into the shade. Their white bells have shriveled into brown husks, but I still recognize them.

I didn't know her, so how can I guess what she's become? Laying my hand on each tree that I pass, I try to picture what she might have looked like when she'd died. The photo is my only clue, but it was taken far earlier. I can only picture my mother. They both died too young, and I wonder if they would have lived longer if they hadn't been cursed. I wonder how many years I can do this, how many goodbyes I can say before I would rather stay and face the consequences.

I am going to break the curse.

Somehow. Somewhere.

But first, I am going to find my grandmother.

She's in these woods. I am certain of it; though, far less so that I can find her.

And so, I simply start talking, as if my grandmother can hear, telling her about my life with Mom, always on the move. I don't tell her about the nights I waited in our barely functional car while Mom went into a motel for a while, or how she'd come out looking as if she wanted to cry but couldn't. I don't tell her about the petty thefts, the shoplifting, the dumpster diving. I don't tell her about squatting in abandoned buildings. I don't tell her about the shelters where we slept with all our belongings under our heads. Instead, I detail the summer houses we lived in while their owners were away and the gourmet meals we were gifted for a few hours of washing dishes. I go on about the times Mom tried on different personas that made me laugh—to me, it was all a game we played. Could she fool these people out of a meal? Could she find out about a lakeside cabin that wasn't occupied for a whole week? Or one up in the mountains? She was resourceful, Mom was. She was clever. She taught me everything I know.

I leave out that my mother hated herself for what she'd done. I tried to tell her how much I admired her, how resourceful she was, how strong, but I don't know if she ever understood how I saw her.

"You're strong, Cupcake," she'd tell me. "I'm only strong for you."

I didn't like hearing that, to feel I was responsible for keeping her going—because then it meant I was responsible for her decision to stop, that I hadn't been enough to prevent that.

At last, I run out of words.

Silent, I stand in front of a sugar maple. It's in a grove beside the remnants of a shack. There is a breath of space between the glorious maple and the pines and oaks around it. It has flourished in that open area—widened by the demise of the old building—its branches spread wide and symmetrical as if trying to embrace the sky. The shack's roof has collapsed, and ivy trails over the windows and door. It almost looks like the maple kept it company as it died.

I approach the tree and lay my hand on the bark. Looking up through the branches, I see slivers of blue sky between the interwoven leaves.

"Hello, Grandma," I say.

I'm answered by silence, which is all I expect, for now. Answers will come—somewhere in town there will be a scrap of a clue that will lead me to Rose Ellert's past, to what happened to her daughter, and what will happen to me. But for the first time in all my years searching, I finally have a place to begin.

CHAPTER SIXTEEN

I duck into the coffee shop, looking for the blue ladies.

"Want a table?" the barista offers.

"Have you seen Barbara, Elaine, and Annie?"

"Who?"

Not their real names then. I'm not surprised, especially since Owen didn't recognize the names either. "Goneril, Regan, and Cordelia? Alecto, Megaera, and Tisiphone? The three women with blue hair."

The barista grins at me. "Ah, yes. They should be around here—"

Twisting, she looks at the wall behind her, which is filled with clocks, each one a novelty: one made of LEGOs, one that appears to be melting like a Salvador Dalí painting, one in the shape of a cat with a swinging tail, one with constellations instead of numbers, one with pictures of chickens. All of them are set to a slightly different time, three minutes off here and six minutes off there. One has hands that move backward.

"—soon."

"I'll wait." I shouldn't. I haven't even worked a full day, which means I'm not off to a spectacular start. "A few minutes at least."

"Great! What can I get you?" She hovers, pen poised over a notepad.

There aren't many customers in the coffee shop at this time either. There's a woman hunched over a laptop in the corner. Her lips are moving silently, and she isn't typing—a writer, not unusual. There's at least one in every coffee shop in every town. At the counter, an older man in a tattered hat is stirring his coffee. Shadowed by the brim of his hat, his eyes are fixed on the wall, and he continues to stir and stir and stir.

"How long have you been in Greenborough?" I ask the barista.

Her pen is still poised.

Glancing at the menu board, I select the cheapest item. "Lemon tea? Small?"

She scribbles it down, beams at me, and then darts behind the counter. She dumps a tea bag into a cup and pours in hot water. I lean against the counter and try a different-yet-similar question, "So, Greenborough . . . what brought you here?" She's tossed her notepad on the counter, and I peek at it. Instead of a lemon-tea order, she's drawn a picture of a bird. Its beak is open as if about to sing, and she's managed to capture the puff of feathers on its inhale. "You're an artist?"

She snatches the notepad back and stuffs it under the counter. "Not much of one."

"That looks really good to me." I add, "I didn't mean to snoop. It was just—"

"It's a warbler," she says. "It's why I'm here, in Greenborough. You asked."

It isn't much of an answer. I wait for more, and she doesn't disappoint. I've noticed that: sometimes if you're silent, other people fill the void. I wonder why there's such a preoccupation with birds in this town. First Cora and Allison, and now the barista.

"I had a boyfriend who was a bird-watcher," she says. "Not professionally, but he had a list, and every weekend, we'd hike a different trail—sometimes in the mountains, sometimes through a marsh—and he'd try to check off another bird on his list. We came to Greenborough to find a golden-winged warbler." She hands me the tea, and I add sugar as she talks. "Stayed in a bed-and-breakfast, now closed, but it was . . . nice." She smiles a bittersweet smile, and I can tell there are a thousand other words behind that adjective.

I know that smile. It's the one you make when you had something fleeting that you didn't appreciate enough before it was gone. It hurts to remember, but it would hurt more to forget. I've worn that smile more times than I can count, but I don't know that anyone has ever smiled that way for me. Perhaps Tyler will, someday, if he ever forgives me.

"I'd been laid off from my job. It wasn't much of a job anyway. I was 'office manager' for a graphic design firm, but my boss had me do whatever errands or chores she didn't want to do. I was this close"— she pinches two fingers together—"to leaving voluntarily when she out-of-the-blue told me she was moving to Florida. My boyfriend worked remotely, and . . . I don't even remember the moment we decided to stay here. Feels like one morning I woke up and suddenly I owned a coffee shop." She laughs. "Any rate, you asked a simple question, and I bore you with the long version." She shakes her head. "Can I get you a cookie? The oatmeal M&Ms are freshest. Secret ingredient is honey."

I don't point out that it's not much of a secret ingredient if she announces it. "You aren't boring me." I note that she didn't answer my first question, but it doesn't matter. If she moved here as an adult, then she hasn't been around long enough to have known my grandmother. "Did your boyfriend find his bird?"

"He must have," the barista said. "He checked it off his list, and the next day he was gone." Her eyes flick to the door, and then back to me. "It's a sad story, and I don't know why I told you. Usually, people tell me their sob stories, not the other way around. So, how about you? What brought you to Greenborough?"

I sift through several stories in my head and settle on the one closest to the truth: "Family. My grandmother lived here for a time, and I'm trying to retrace her footsteps." *Gone where? "Gone" dead, or "gone" left her?* I wonder if the barista's boyfriend had to leave because he couldn't stay, like me, but I don't know how to ask that. So far as I know, I've never met anyone, other than my mother, with my affliction. On the other hand, would I know? How many are cursed and never say so? How many of us never even know?

The old man stirs his coffee. He doesn't speak.

The writer's lips move. She doesn't type.

As I stare at her, the writer turns her head and meets my eyes. I can't read her expression. I look away and notice the old man watching me as well.

The minute hand on one of the clocks stutters before ticking forward, and I shudder. I *know* there are answers here, if I could only come up with the right questions to ask.

"Ooh! You're interested in genealogy," the barista gushes. "You know, one of my relatives had eight kids with his first wife and then six kids with his second. My family tree has more branches than a . . . well, whatever kind of tree has a lot of branches."

"There's a banyan tree in India known to have over three thousand branches," I say.

She whistles. "That seems excessive."

I glance at the many clocks on the wall. I don't know how long I can wait for the three blue-haired ladies to stroll in, and I doubt I am going to learn anything about Rose Ellert from the barista. Glancing at the old man, I wonder how long he has been in Greenborough. He's stirring his coffee again, his eyes fixed on the swirling brown as if it holds answers. Maybe it's my wishful thinking. I bite the bullet and ask him, "Have you lived in Greenborough long?"

He stirs, not raising his eyes. *"I have known them all already, known them all—have known the evenings, mornings, afternoons."*

That isn't an answer, is it? I push on. "Can I . . . show you a photo of my grandmother? I think she lived here . . ." I pull out the photograph and hold it up.

He lifts his spoon in the air. *"I have measured out my life . . ."*

I know this poem. "T. S. Eliot."

He looks at the photo and quotes, *"I have known the eyes already, known them all—the eyes that fix you in a formulated phrase."*

"Do you recognize my grandmother?" I ask.

Looking down and stirring again, he mumbles, *"I have measured out my life with coffee spoons . . ."* He rocks slightly on his stool. *"I grow old . . . I grow old . . ."*

I glance at the barista, and she shrugs. Her eyes are full of pity, but I can't tell if it's for him or for me. I ask her, "How much for the tea?"

"On the house, for listening to my story," she says.

"Thanks . . . um . . . I'm Elisa, by the way. If you see Artemis, Athena, and Aphrodite, could you tell them that I stopped by and would love to chat again? I'll be at the Book Cellar, next door."

She chuckles. "Artemis, Athena . . . Love it. I'm Monica. Monica Ramirez."

I pick up my tea and turn to leave, but something stops me. I again try the question she never answered. "How long have you been in Greenborough?"

Monica looks at the clocks again, as if they hold the answer. "You know, I've lost track of when I came here. Guess time flies when you're having fun." She laughs again, but it's strained this time.

The man stirring his coffee says, *"And indeed there will be time to wonder, 'Do I dare?' and, 'Do I dare?'"*

I shiver.

"Certainly seems like forever," Monica says cheerfully, as if he hadn't spoken. "You'll see, this is a place that makes you feel at home. Lots of friendly people. You're going to like it here."

"That is not it at all, that is not what I meant," says the old man. I can't tell if he's still quoting poetry or not. He doesn't look at me or at Monica. He just keeps stirring, and I feel prickles continue up my spine. "You won't ever want to leave. Never leave. Never dare. *I have heard the mermaids singing, each to each. I do not think that they will sing to me.*"

I begin to ask, "Why do you—"

Monica lays a hand on my wrist and shakes her head.

I don't finish my question, and she releases.

"If my three favorite blue-haired regulars pop in, I'll be sure to mention that you were looking for them," Monica says. She refills the stirring man's coffee, although I haven't seen him take a single sip since I stepped inside.

Backing toward the door, I glance at the writer in the corner, then at the myriad clocks, before I retreat onto the sidewalk. Charlie is pressed against the bookshop window, watching as I exit the coffee shop and return to the Book Cellar.

The bell rings, and Owen looks up.

He smiles, a genuine happy-to-see-me smile, and it stops me for a moment. I'm not used to being liked so quickly. If he were trying to get me in bed, yes, but that would be a different kind of smile. This . . . this is a friend's smile, and it usually takes a few months to achieve. It's rare to win one so quickly, and I find myself smiling back. "I found her," I tell him. "She was really here. Thank you for being okay with me going off like that. I know it's my first day—"

He waves his hand in dismissal. "I'm glad you found closure."

That is so the opposite of what I found that I let out a surprised laugh. "I'm not looking for closure. I'm looking for . . ." I don't know how to explain. "I've been searching for years for any hint of my family's history. My mom . . . I don't know where she came from. She didn't talk about her childhood, and I never met my grandparents."

Once, when I was in . . . maybe second grade? . . . I had to draw a family tree as a school assignment. Mom fetched an old phone book that she'd stuffed into a crack in the wall—"to keep the wind out," she'd said.

"Pick a number," she said.

"Forty-three," I responded.

She flipped to page forty-three. "Another number?"

"Nine." I peered over her shoulder as she counted down to line nine. She read off the name: "Edward Fulton. That's your grandfather."

I remember giggling and shouting out a new number. We filled in the entire family tree chart that way, and then I drew pictures of cousins that didn't exist (with sticks for arms and circles for hands) and pets we'd never owned. I presented it proudly to my teacher the next day—I can't remember her name, but I do remember she hung mine next to all the other family trees, and I laughed inside every time I saw it.

In those early years, Mom was so good at making it all a game.

To Owen I say, "I now know that my grandmother died here, which is more information than I've uncovered in . . . well, ever, but all that means is that I'm on the right track. I don't know what her life was like. I want to know . . . oh, so much more! Who was she? Where did she go? Why did she come back? So this . . . this isn't closure. This is hope!" I'm so excited that I realize I'm flailing my arms for emphasis.

He nods. "I can see that."

I lower my arms. "You can?"

"Of course." Gently, he asks, "When did your mother die?"

The question shocks the breath out of me for a moment, and all I can see is the deep mahogany of her casket, the smooth grain in the wood. All I can hear is the wind through the willow branches and the endless tumble of water over rocks. I run through the conversations we've had, and I can't remember if I told him that she died. "How did you know she did?"

"Because when I lost my parents, I was desperate to reconnect with them any way I could." He bends behind the desk, disappearing for a moment. I rise on my tiptoes to see what he's doing, and Charlie rubs his head against my elbow. Owen pops up with what looks like a scrapbook. It has a frayed cloth cover with an embroidered bluebird. Ribbons decorate the spine. The pages within are mismatched, faded by sunlight and crinkled at the corners. "I had all of their friends and whatever relatives were around send me little stories about them. Bits of memories, anecdotes, even jokes that my parents liked, and I collected them in this book."

He shifts to a stool closer to the window, and I sit on a stool next to him. On the first page, there's a printed email from someone named Gladys, in all caps: I REMEMBER WHEN YOUR FATHER WAS BORN. HE WAS AN UGLY BABY.

"Love that one," he said.

"I'm hoping that wasn't your dad's mother."

"His aunt, my great-aunt Gladys. She prided herself on telling it like it is, which just means she was rude whenever she felt like it. I'm told it wasn't charming when she was younger, but I thought she was hilarious. Thanksgiving was always filled with her off-color jokes, usually centered on different ways to baste a turkey."

"I'm torn between wanting to know and not wanting to know at all."

He grins. "It's not the kind of thing you can unhear. Keep your innocence." He turns the pages. There are mostly email printouts, plus a few hand-scrawled notes. On later pages, he's pasted newspaper clippings. There's a woman who must be his mother standing on a ladder beside an apple tree. There's a handkerchief wrapped around her hair, and she's smiling at the camera, with an apple in one hand. "She worked at a local orchard."

I tap the clipping with a finger. "That's what I need."

"An apple?"

"A newspaper. As local as possible. I know my grandmother went to high school here." I could find her obituary as well, now that I know the name on her grave. If I can find out where she came from and trace back the curse to where it began . . . It's a place to start at least.

"You need a library, not a bookstore," Owen says. "Luckily, Greenborough has both. Unluckily, our library closes early on Tuesdays. But it will open at nine tomorrow."

The Book Cellar opens at ten. I can research my family, uncover the secret of my fate, and still be on time for work. "Thanks," I say.

Shuffling behind his desk, Owen stares at his scrapbook, at the window, at his cat—anywhere but at me. "Would you . . . ah, if you don't have other plans . . . would you like to meet for breakfast before the library opens? I can drive you there and introduce you to the librarian."

Usually librarians don't require introductions, but I'd appreciate the drive. And breakfast. He still isn't meeting my eyes. Did he just invite me on a date? I'm going to choose to believe this is a friendly proposition. I don't have time for this kind of complication, and who picks breakfast and the library for a first date anyway?

Actually, that sounds like an incredible first date.

"I'd love that," I tell him.

CHAPTER SEVENTEEN

ROSE

1975

Rose wished she'd picked a wedding dress one size larger. She felt as if she couldn't breathe. Every time she inhaled, her rib cage was arrested by a lace prison. She wanted to run as far and fast as she could. She hated feeling like a cliché on her wedding day.

You said yes, she reminded herself.

Yes to his proposal. Yes to a June wedding, immediately after graduation. And yes to the baby.

Glenn had originally let her pick the date: after college, after a year out in the world. It felt far enough in the future—time to do all the adventuring she wanted. Except she had student loans and next-to-zero savings. Except he was starting a new job, his first out of college. Except she got pregnant, during her last semester, even though they were careful. And then there was really no other option but to move up the date of the wedding, cancel the honeymoon to Mexico, and prepare for their lives as a soon-to-be family of three. None of their parents would even consider any other alternative. The fallout when she and Glenn had announced the news . . . It hadn't been pretty, and the unyielding consensus was that the wedding had to happen as soon as possible.

As a side effect, Rose hadn't had to decide anything about today. In the wake of the "disaster" (as both her and Glenn's parents called it) of the unplanned pregnancy, their mothers had chummed up, even though they'd never had anything in common before other than a love of blonde hair dye. Every single detail, down to the saw napkin folds, had been discussed, dissected, and decided. Rose had no doubt the result would rival the bridal magazine spreads that her mother loved to pour over.

She knew it was going to be beautiful. Memorable, even, despite the sudden date change to a year earlier. But was it what she wanted? Of course it was. It had to be. She didn't want to have a child while she was unmarried, and she didn't want to have a wedding where she waddled down the aisle. Luckily, she was one of those women who didn't show much. At four months, there was barely a curve to her stomach, and it was hidden beneath the boning and lace of the bodice. She (and, more importantly, their families and friends and neighbors and parents' coworkers) could pretend it was all planned this way.

Their mothers were determined to drown all disapproval with buttercream, tulle, and far too many roses.

Cora bounced into the room in her cupcake-like maid of honor dress. She was wearing coral lipstick that matched both the dress and her pumps, and she'd teased her hair into a halo of curls. "Oh, Rose! You look perfect!"

"I look like whipped marshmallow." Rose fluffed her skirts out. In the bridal shop, it had felt lavishly elegant and her mother had cooed over her, but now she felt as if she were wearing a Halloween costume. Back in her elementary school days, she'd been a ghost, a ninja, a witch, and a superhero. Once, an M&M. Never a princess. Especially a pregnant princess. "This isn't me."

Cora, on the other hand, had been a princess every single year, only varying her tiara. One year, she wove every fake flower in her grandmother's apartment to create a flower crown. She broke a few plastic petals, but she looked so charming that her grandma forgave her, or at least that's how she told the story.

"Of course not," Cora said. "You're not supposed to be yourself today. You're supposed to be the ultimate version of yourself. After all, it's not an ordinary day; you can't be ordinary Rose on your wedding day."

Rose raised her eyebrows. "What's so wrong with ordinary Rose?"

"That didn't come out right. What I meant is: it's a special day. You need to look special. And you do! You look like a princess. And I"—Cora spun in her dress, and the shiny fabric tangled instead of twirled—"am your lady-in-waiting. Come on, don't tell me you're getting cold feet. You know you love Glenn."

She did love him.

Usually.

Mostly.

He had a few habits that grated on her nerves. Like the way he refused to eat anything new. He was strictly a *burgers, steak, chicken, and the occasional meatloaf* kind of guy. She'd once suggested they go out for Chinese food, as a change from the Steak Loft, and he'd acted like she wanted to poison him. But the fact that she'd had an unrequited craving for moo shu was hardly a reason to end a multiyear relationship. They'd lasted from high school through college, with all the ups and downs. They'd cried together when his cousin had been drafted and then cried again when his cousin hadn't come home—she'd promised never to tell each time. The men in his family didn't do tears. She'd helped him study for his exams and cleaned him up when he'd celebrated too much after. If she'd said "no" or "wait" or "I'm not ready yet," especially once she had a ticking clock in her stomach . . . no one would understand.

She'd tried to explain it to Cora shortly after he'd proposed, when she was pushing for a long engagement, but even her best friend had utterly failed to comprehend. "If you plan to marry him someday, why not now?" Cora had asked. "You have any idea how lucky you are to have found 'The One' already? Why risk losing him when you could start your forever right now?"

Cora was still searching for "The One," or even, as she said, the "You'll Do." She'd made it abundantly clear she thought Rose was foolish for even considering throwing away something so special with Glenn.

I'm not foolish. I'm here, aren't I? Looking ridiculous. She plucked at her puffy sleeve. Maybe she should have taken a little more interest in wedding planning. Maybe then this would have felt more like her day. But it had all been such a whirlwind with finishing college and graduating and trying not to feel as if everyone was staring at her and judging her for being pregnant before she was married.

Mom had insisted they'd forget once she was married. By the time the baby was born, no one would even so much as blink. She'd be Rose Ellert, wife and mother.

"It's normal to be nervous," Cora said. "But remember: it's only a day. What's important is what comes after—you'll be married! With a family on the way! You're securing your happily ever after under the law and God and everyone you love, and no one will be able to take that away." Her eyes were bright, and Rose wondered if tears were about to tumble down her cheeks.

"Don't," Rose said. "Your mascara will smear."

"At least then I won't outshine the bride." Cora managed a smile.

Rose knew what Cora needed to hear. As sincerely as she could, she said, "Your day to shine will come soon. I'll throw you the bouquet."

"You'd better," Cora sniffed.

"Best pitching arm in three counties, remember?" Rose wound up her arm in a circle, but stopped when she heard the rip of delicate stitches. She hadn't played softball since high school. Her parents had encouraged her to focus on her studies in college. Insisted, really, because they couldn't afford for her to lose her scholarships. Besides, it wasn't an appropriate activity at her age, they'd said. She shouldn't be spending her free time showing off her legs and sweating. But she was certain she could still pitch. "I'll bean you with the bouquet."

"You're the best friend anyone could wish for," Cora said.

Rose plucked a Kleenex and handed it to her. Cora dabbed her eyes. They fell silent for a while. The sounds from the church vestibule had risen from a distant buzz to a pleasant hum. Most of the guests had probably arrived. Her mother and future mother-in-law had hired a harpist instead of the usual organist. They thought it would make the day "extra special," but Rose couldn't hear it over the voices of her nearest and dearest (and everyone else their parents had added to the guest list). It sounded as if the entire town were squeezed into the church. She wished there were more oxygen in the waiting room. She glanced at the window, but it was already open. A breeze wafted inside, and she tried to ignore the urge to climb out. She wondered if anyone else ever had thoughts like this on their wedding day. Certainly no one like Cora.

"Cora?"

"Yes?"

"What if I'm not happy? A year from now. Five. Ten."

Cora crumpled the tissue in her hand. "You will be."

"This is the first day of the rest of my life," Rose said. "Everyone keeps saying that, but what if it's a mistake? I mean, I love Glenn now, but what if—Look, every time you make a choice, there's a million other choices you aren't making, right? I don't know what I'm giving up. I've never even lived anywhere else. I haven't *done* anything." *Except get knocked up.* That she'd done. Was this her punishment?

Not a punishment. I love him. I said yes.

Cora was silent for a moment. "You don't have to do this. There's a reason the vows are in question form. You can say no and walk away. Yes, your mother would have a heart attack, and you'd break Glenn's heart and he'd probably never recover, and you might regret throwing away your chance at future happiness, and yes, you'd be a single mother with no support from your husband or your family, and you'd have to figure out where to live and get a job, and then there is the whole problem of childcare, but—"

"Exactly. It's not really a question." It had never really been a choice, had it? When could she have taken a different path? She couldn't see it. She'd met Glenn at a friend's house—he'd rescued a bowl of potato chips from crashing on her lap, and he'd made her laugh. They'd begun talking between classes at school. Everything after that had unfolded easily, so easily. A few dates. A few kisses. And they were official. No one was surprised when he'd asked her to their senior prom, and after that, they'd never had any reason to quit dating. She'd lived at home for college, and he'd visited every weekend and called every day. Sometimes he brought her flowers; though, she'd always suspected his mother had prodded him to do that. There were never fireworks—he was too easy-going for that. Stubborn, yes. He liked what he liked, and he went through life with the easy assurance of someone who believed they were always right. He never second-guessed a decision. He liked her; he asked her out. Rose was certain he'd never had cold feet. He certainly wouldn't understand hers. For him, it had all been a natural, obvious progression—you date for long enough, you get married. You spend your lives together. Get a house. Have kids. He had it all mapped out, and unlike their parents, he'd barely been ruffled when she'd told him the order would be reversed. A kid first, then all the rest. No point in arguing about any of it, he figured; it was just the way life proceeded. Really, not much ruffled him. It was actually one aspect of him that she fell in love with—his certainty that every decision he made would turn out just fine. She couldn't help seeing the future splintered in a dozen different directions—every yes was also a no to a hundred other futures, a hundred other Roses. How did she know one of them wouldn't fit her better?

"Let me ask you something," Cora said. "How would you feel if you never saw Glenn again? If he wasn't a part of your life? Don't think about the baby or money or any of that. Just Glenn."

She tried to picture it and couldn't. He'd been a fixture of her life since she'd met him. He called her when she woke up and called her again before she fell asleep. He was as comfortable as her old pillow. "I don't want to lose him. I just . . ."

"Then grab on with both hands," Cora pleaded. "Everything else will work itself out. Just . . . You don't want to be alone, do you?"

"But how do I know—"

"You don't," Cora said. "You can't. Just be happy for what you have now. A full family at twenty-two, without really trying! Don't do something stupid that makes you lose it because the grass looks greener in your daydreams."

She was right. Of course. But . . .

Cora grasped her hands. Squeezed a little too tight. "Rose . . . if Glenn made you unhappy, I'd tell you to walk out right now. Heck, I'd drive you as far as you wanted. Help you burn this wedding dress. Dance around a bonfire made of your wedding dress. I'll even, God help me, babysit whenever you want. Within reason."

Despite herself, Rose had to laugh.

"Does he make you unhappy?" Cora asked.

"Of course not," Rose said. "But—"

"No 'buts,'" Cora said. "You have someone who makes you happy. Hold onto him with both hands and don't let him go." She squeezed harder, as if to emphasize her words. "He'll be a good husband and a good father—how can you ask for more than that?"

Not unhappy isn't precisely the same as happy. If this was really what she should be doing, shouldn't she feel overjoyed?

Maybe not.

Maybe cold feet were cliché for a reason. Maybe all brides felt this way, and she just had to get through today. There was a lot of pressure on this one day to be perfect. That could be what she was feeling. So many people that she could disappoint—*It's just wedding day nerves. Or pregnancy hormones. Or both.* Once all this nonsense was over, then she'd be happy.

"We aren't kids anymore," Cora said. "It's time to stop living in what-ifs and appreciate what you have now. There's no certainty in life. If it helps, I'll tell you a secret."

Rose couldn't help but smile, even if it felt weak. Cora was never going to learn how to keep a secret. "All right. Tell."

"You can't let Glenn know that I told you, but . . . he's wanted to marry you since prom. Remember that weird statue we found in the woods that night, on our way to the Kissing Shack? Of the three witches of the woods, or whatever that creepy statue was? Remember how he made a wish?"

He'd wished to be with her that night, and she'd granted him that wish. It had been . . . nice. Nice enough that she'd wanted to do it again, pretty much every time she saw him. She smiled at the memory. "I remember."

"He wished to marry you. Have a family with you."

Rose felt prickles walk up her spine. "That's not what he said—"

"And now look! It's coming true! So, that should make you feel better, right? You're his deepest wish. I'd say that tilts the odds of having a lifetime of happiness in your favor. He's loved you for years. How can you feel anything but happy, knowing that?"

She's right. That should make her feel happy.

Why, then, did it make her feel caught in a cage?

CHAPTER EIGHTEEN

LORI

2014

On the stripped bed behind her, Lori felt her daughter's mutinous glare, hot and itchy as a sunburn between her shoulder blades. She ignored it, continuing to pack methodically. She'd done it a dozen times and knew exactly what they'd need and what they could find.

"Why do we have to move *now*?" Elisa asked. She'd been Alyssa here, and Lori had been Laura—they'd need to think about new names, once Elisa quit arguing and started packing.

A year ago, Elisa wouldn't have questioned their need to move when Lori said so. Two years ago, she would have been excited—a new adventure!—but Elisa was a teenager. She'd somehow sprouted her own opinions, which was wonderful and age appropriate and oh-so-inconvenient. It meant that Lori couldn't predict whether or not she'd cooperate. In fact, sometimes it was near impossible to guess what her daughter was thinking and feeling; though, right now Elisa was broadcasting her emotions as clearly as a Times Square billboard.

"Because we have no choice," Lori said. "It's time."

"Mom, I'm on yearbook. I'm doing fine in my classes—you said so. You said you were proud of me. I have friends! A best friend! Can't we at least stay until the end of the school year? I don't want to start over again, especially midyear. Please. All I'm asking is to stretch it until summer."

Lori couldn't meet her daughter's eyes. Her heart burned inside her like a hot pepper on her tongue. She wished more than anything that they could stay. She knew if she did, then Elisa would smile so brightly that she'd feel as if she'd stepped into sunshine. Elisa had no idea the power her smile wielded, or how desperately Lori ached to see it. She wanted to say "yes, yes, yes" to her and give her everything in the world that she wanted. Usually, she tried to wait until summer, when the move wouldn't be as disruptive. But last year they'd lost the apartment midyear and had to move, which meant that this year . . . *We have no choice.* "I'm sorry. It's been ten months."

"We don't know that's the limit," Elisa said.

Lori shook her head. "We can't risk—"

"Why not? Why can't we risk it and see? A few more months, not a lifetime, that's all I'm asking—see how far we can push it before we hit the limit, and then we go."

Lori wanted to say yes so badly that her words tasted sour, but this was her daughter's life, not an experiment. "You can't ask me to endanger—"

"You can't ask me to give up everything when you don't even know I'd be at risk. Don't you want me to be happy? No, I know why—you want me to need you, only you. You can't stand that I actually have other people who care about me. You want me totally dependent so you can control—"

She was so stunningly wrong that Lori let out a choked sound, almost a laugh.

"Are you *laughing* at me?" Elisa stomped over to the window, and Lori heard her take several deep breaths. "You don't understand. Every time we move, it's harder. Every year, I'm the new kid in school, and the older I get, the worse it is. All the friend groups have already formed. They don't need anyone new. They don't want anyone, except as a scapegoat. Yeah, it's really fun when you get to be the new victim for whoever is feeling insecure." The sarcasm practically dripped off Elisa's tongue. "But here—Mom, it's different here! People are nice! I fit in! I belong here! This place, for whatever reason, let me in."

Lori knew. Oh how she knew! She hated uprooting her. She knew how difficult it was for Elisa. *It's not like it's easy for me either.* Keeping a roof over their heads and keeping them fed when she couldn't keep a job for even a full year was a near-impossible task, and forget about any social life. She'd sacrificed any hope of that when she'd chosen to keep Elisa. She had to dedicate every second of her time and energy into securing her daughter's basic needs, ensuring she wouldn't starve or be taken from her—and she didn't regret any of it. Elisa was 100 percent worth it, but that didn't make it easy. But how could Lori explain any of that? How hard it was to keep them safe, warm, and fed? Elisa already knew how much of their food came from skimming through restaurant trash, from food banks and church giveaways. She didn't need to know how hard it was to resist theft, but if she were caught, Elisa would be left alone. Elisa didn't know how badly Lori feared every sniffle and cough because they couldn't afford doctors or medicines. She was terrified of illness, injury, and run-of-the-mill bad luck. It kept her up at night, imagining all the scenarios that could upend them into the floodwaters, drown them and sweep them away like debris in a storm. She'd swallowed her pride and abandoned her dreams so many times that doing so was as familiar as breathing, and she'd done things that she would never confess to anyone, ever, especially Elisa. No. Elisa didn't need to know. She deserved to grow up as free from worries as possible . . . *She'll know soon enough, when I'm no longer here.* She had to keep going. How else could she protect her daughter? Even when she did her best . . . It was hard to come to a new town, with no place to live, no way to make money. She had to rely on the kindness of strangers. And luck. Sometimes it didn't work.

This town had been relatively easy—she'd lucked into a job at a garden store. She loved flowers. Had always wanted a garden, even though it was the least practical hobby for someone who moved around. She got to water the plants, prune them, occasionally interact with customers. It was the best job she'd had in a long time. Her boss was nice, too—never a guarantee; she baked cookies for the staff every weekend. Supplied them with lunch whenever the store had a new shipment. She was prompt with payment and hadn't even blinked when Lori asked for cash. Never tried to stiff her either. Lori liked and respected her, which was rare. And their apartment here—it was not the worst by any means. It was a room over the garage of an elderly couple who asked no questions and were grateful for the help Lori and Elisa provided in taking out the trash, mowing the lawn, bringing in groceries—all of which had gotten more difficult for them. It delayed their having to move into assisted living, they said, which their kids were pressuring them to do. If Lori and Elisa left, the couple would miss them too. "I don't want to leave either," Lori confessed.

"Then let's not! Stop packing! Stay!"

"Elisa . . ." Lori sank heavily onto the bed. It had been easier before . . . *Had it? When had it ever been easy?* Never. But it certainly wasn't getting easier. Lori felt frayed. With each move, she left a part of herself behind. She was a sweater unraveling, yarn crisscrossing the country. A piece of her shed in every place they'd ever stayed.

She wanted to be the old couple, clinging to their home of fifty years. It was a mishmash of items they'd picked up over time: a new microwave sparkling next to an old teal green refrigerator, a plasticky couch in front of a flat-screen TV, a china cabinet filled with knickknacks that ranged from a "#1 Teacher" mug to teacups they'd inherited from their grandparents. Lori had nothing like that and never would. She wanted it all. Right down to the chipped teacup. But she couldn't let Elisa see that. It wouldn't help if she knew how deeply unhappy she was. "We can go any place you want. Pick the state. Pick the town."

"Here."

"Anywhere new. You know the rules."

"Maybe it's time we break the rules." Elisa crossed her arms.

"Elisa, you know we can't."

"Do I? Do you? Maybe the curse has worn off. Maybe it was just waiting for us to find the right place—and now that we found it, we can stay."

Lori shook her head. She wished that were true.

"How do you *know*? You don't! You don't even know if the curse is real. Remember when I was little? You told me the moon cursed us."

"I was trying to explain the unexplainable to a child . . ." It made sense to use a story. A myth, even a made-up one, was a lot easier to accept than the truth.

"And then later you said it's in our blood. Passed down like our height and our hair. You said it's the way it's always been, the way it will always be."

"That's the truth."

"Is it? What if it's not real at all? What if we've been moving all this time for no reason? Because you believed something you were told years ago. Maybe the curse never existed."

She'd pushed the limits hard enough when Elisa was a baby. She'd wanted her child to grow up in a home. And she'd suffered for it. She'd felt the sluggishness in her veins as her blood shifted to sap. She'd found the leaves in her hair. She'd felt her skin begin to harden. Plus, there were the nightmares . . . they'd start every time they pushed their limits, shouting at her in unsubtle metaphor that she had to leave now. There was no question in Lori's mind that the curse was real. "You need to trust me. Please, Elisa, pack what you need."

"How can I trust you when it's absurd? A curse? I don't believe in Santa Claus or the Easter Bunny, but you want me to believe we're cursed."

"What else would you call it?" It wasn't a gift. That was for damn sure.

"A lie," Elisa said.

Lori felt her breath lodge in her throat. "Why would I lie to you?"

"I don't know. Because you hate me. Because you want me to be as miserable as you are. Or because someone once lied to you and you're afraid to face it. You're scared that everything you've done, everything you've been through—all the terrible stuff, all the nights we had nowhere to sleep, all the days we had nothing to eat—were for no reason. If you admit that the curse isn't real, then you have to admit that we went through it all for no reason."

Lori had never heard Elisa like this. Had she come up with these ideas on her own, or had she been talking to someone? About her? About the curse? She had a vision of Child Protective Services showing up at their door, taking Elisa away from her. Putting her in a foster home. Not understanding that they had to keep moving, that Elisa wouldn't be safe if she wasn't with Lori. *If I'm ever not around to protect her . . .*

She had nightmares about that too, her worst fear. If an accident happened, an illness, then what would Elisa do? There wasn't anyone who'd understand, and she wasn't old enough to take care of herself. Lori didn't have any money to leave her. She tried to save, but it was impossible when every cent was needed for survival.

"It's called 'sunk cost fallacy,'" Elisa said.

"Who have you told?" Lori asked. She heard her voice rising louder and didn't know how to stop it. "Elisa, did you tell anyone about us?" She knew it had to be kept secret. No one else would understand. She'd be labeled an unfit mother. Someone would try to "help" and make things a thousand times worse.

Elisa took a step back. For the first time this afternoon, she looked uncertain. "There's a counselor at school—"

"You can't tell anyone! You know that! They won't understand!" Lori wanted to shake her, but instead she stood trembling. Perhaps Lori had shielded her too well. Elisa didn't understand the consequences. "They'll separate us. They'll endanger you! They won't mean to, but—"

"You don't know that! There's no evidence. Just an ordinary scab, the nurse said—"

She felt the breath stop in her throat. She managed a word: "Where?"

"My arm, but—"

Lori took a step forward, grabbed Elisa's wrist, and shoved her sleeve up to her elbow. She twisted her arm to reveal the underside.

There, in the center of her pink, young skin, was a scab.

Elisa tugged the sleeve back down. "I fell."

"You didn't."

"It's a scab. The school nurse said so, after I *fell*."

"It's beginning," Lori said. A patch of bark: that was how it started. To the outside world, it looked like a scab, but she knew the truth. Hard and brown like the flesh of a tree. She could see in Elisa's eyes that she believed her, even though she didn't want to.

"She said it's just a scab and everyone gets them. She said there's no such thing as a curse." But doubt threaded through her voice. Elisa knew what it meant as well as Lori. This had happened before, a scab-like hardness on uncut skin, and it only healed after they moved.

She said she fell. It could *be an ordinary scab.*

"Jackie thought—"

Jackie, Elisa's best friend. *I should have known she'd be at the heart of this.* She should never have let Elisa form such a close friendship, but she'd wanted so badly for her to have friends, for her to be happy, for her to have a normal life . . . *If it is just an ordinary scab, and I take her away . . .*

But what if it wasn't? How could she risk it? Especially given how attached Elisa was to this place. *Jackie was a mistake. They'd gotten too close.* It was clear: this was a warning sign, and they had to heed it. "We aren't leaving because of me this time," Lori said quietly. "This place feels like home to you, and the curse is reacting to that. We have to leave." She didn't blame Jackie to Elisa. She knew that would be a mistake.

Elisa pulled to remove her wrist from Lori's grip, and Lori released. Elisa's lips were trembling, and Lori wanted to gather her into a hug like she used to. She used to be able to comfort her. It used to be enough that they had each other. When had she stopped being enough for her daughter?

"What if it is because of you?" Elisa asked in a quiet voice. "What if I'm only cursed because I'm with you? What if you . . ." She trailed off without finishing.

"What if I left you here, without me?" Lori asked. She pointed toward Elisa's arm, covered again by her sleeve. "Do you really want to risk that? It'll keep spreading, you know. In another day, you could have patches of bark on your legs, your back, your stomach. A few more days, it could become difficult to walk. Hard to breathe. Your body will betray you. It will eat you from the inside as your blood turns to sap, and chlorophyll infuses your cells. You'll sprout leaves instead of hair, and your feet will root in the earth." She'd imagined it a thousand times. Dreamed it. Woken up screaming. She never wanted to experience it in the waking world, and she never, ever wanted to witness it happen to her daughter. It wasn't worth the risk. They had to keep moving— and they had to stick together. "How understanding will your school counselor be then? You'll be sent to a hospital. They won't know how to help. How will Jackie feel then? Your friend will visit you as your body slowly hardens until you can't breathe. You'll hear her voice as wind in your branches."

She believes me, thank God. Lori could see it in Elisa's eyes. She'd succeeded in truly frightening her, which was necessary, but Lori wished she could take back every word. She hadn't meant to scare her so badly. She just wanted to keep her safe.

"You have to come with me," Lori said softly, pleading with everything in her. "Please, Elisa. I've lost so much. I can't lose you too. I can't."

Elisa didn't say another word. Silently, she packed.

CHAPTER NINETEEN

ELISA

Now

It isn't stealing if it doesn't belong to anyone. And it isn't illegal if you aren't caught. At least that's what my mother said when she first taught me to dumpster dive. I linger by the Book Cellar after hours, waiting for the coffee shop to close. It's surprisingly difficult to go unnoticed in a small town. You'd think it would be easier than in a city, but in cities, with their constant bustle, people are devoted to not noticing, while in a town it's obvious when someone's out of place. But I've borrowed a book from the store (with Owen's permission, so long as I review it later and don't dog-ear the pages. I would never), and it's not odd at all to sit outside a bookstore and read, especially at the end of a blue-sky afternoon.

Charlie watches me through the window.

I am flipping through the pages. It's impossible to focus with my thoughts batting around. For the first time ever, I have a scrap of proof that my family existed. Before, we were a breath of wind, blowing through a place, never leaving so much as a footprint, but now . . . there's a gravestone with a name on it, three women with a memory of a girl in high school, and two names for the same person: Rose Grayson and Rose Ellert. I say the names over and over in my head, as if they're a kind of talisman that will grant me luck or keep me safe.

Half watching the door to Bean Street, I note when customers enter and leave. I imagine the many clocks inside ticking down to closing. I haven't seen the three blue-haired ladies, but I have seen:

One woman with a heart drawn in red Sharpie on her cheek.

A man with a small boy who walks with his eyes closed.

Maddie and Emma, the girls from the Greyhound bus, hand in hand and oblivious to me. They enter and exit without any coffee or tea, their heads tilted toward each other as if deep in conversation, although it's clear they aren't speaking.

The writer from earlier exits with a single lemon in her hand, but without her laptop. Her lips move like she's speaking to someone, but she makes no sound. I watch each of them as they pass by, as if I'm Charlie in the bookstore window.

Eventually, Monica twists the sign on the door to CLOSED, and I see the lights begin to shut off: over the counter, by the tables, in the front window. I'm lucky it's a weeknight. On weekends, they're open late, but on weekdays they close before dinner. If all goes smoothly, I'll be back at the house before it's fully dark.

I flip a page and listen for the squeak of the side door . . . and yes, there it is. Casually, I tuck a leaf in as a bookmark and slip it into my bag. I stretch and then stroll down the sidewalk, away from both the bookstore and the coffee shop. Behind me, I hear the jangle of the front door, but I don't turn around. I don't want Monica to talk to me. In fact, I'd rather she not notice me at all, but if she does, she'll see me walking away, hardly remarkable.

When I reach the next street, I turn with purpose. Another left and then another left, until I've come full circle around the block. When I reach the coffee shop again, I veer into the alley—casual, purposeful. With the sun low, it can't reach between the buildings, and the streetlamps haven't flickered on yet. Shadows embrace me, as they always do.

The trash cans are beside the side door, exactly where I expect them to be—yay for the convenience of predictability. Now I move swiftly: lift the lid of the first can, lay it on the ground, pull a brown Bean Street bag out, set it aside—that's my insurance. If I'm spotted, I'll toss it in as if I'm here only to dispose of my trash. I can hear my mother's voice: *Always have a reason to be where you are. It doesn't need to be a true reason. It's better if it isn't. Aim for plausible.* Other people's parents taught them how to ride a bike or mow a lawn or . . . I don't know what other kids learned, but my mother taught me this.

With an eye for anything unopened, uneaten, and unspoiled, I rifle through the can and shove into my pack three spotted bananas, a few bagels, a squashed muffin, and several other baked goods that I'll examine later. After a quick glance toward the street, I tackle the second can. Anything close enough to edible goes into the bag. Speed is key—you don't want to answer the question of what you're doing and why, or else the location is spoiled. I'll sort through the haul later. As soon as I've half filled my pack, I replace the lids and exit the alley.

Stroll.

That's key: stroll.

As I pass the bookshop, the cat watches me. I hold a finger to my lips. *Keep my secret, Charlie.* He raises his hind leg and licks it—such a banal action that the tightness around my rib cage loosens. I don't know whether Owen would judge me, but it's always a risk to dumpster dive so close to where I work. Still, I don't have much choice—I won't have a paycheck until the end of the week, which reminds me that I have to talk to Owen about paying me in cash. I *can* deposit checks in the account my mother left me, but I don't like how traceable that is. Cash is always simpler. Owen might be open to a cash-under-the-table arrangement. He hasn't had me fill out a W-9 yet, which means he either has no idea how to hire an employee or has no idea he's supposed to file taxes—or he knows and simply has no intention of filing them; though, he didn't strike me as that kind of person.

On my walk back to 125 East Oak Road, I try to focus on minutiae. It's dusk, and everything is swathed in gray. Shadows soften the trees, and the town has that end-of-day subdued feeling. I deliberately push thoughts of my grandmother Rose away. There's nothing I can do until morning, so I should focus on how I'll keep myself fed, at least in the short term. I have a job, which is phenomenally lucky, and a perfect place to sleep—again lucky. After breakfast tomorrow, I'll check out the diner's dumpster situation. And at some point, I'll scout the local grocery store. All grocery stores are required to dispose of expired food, which can be a gold mine if you're careful and quick (or a terrible trap of botulism and salmonella if you're not)—more lessons I learned from Mom.

She would have hated that I am using those lessons now, when she gave so much to ensure I wouldn't have to. But touching those savings would be like saying I'm fine with the fact that she's gone. I'd rather dumpster dive.

For my entire existence, the purpose of my mom's life was to ensure I was okay. She allowed no room for anything else. Her sole goal was to keep a roof over my head. Keep food in my stomach. Keep me warm enough or cool enough. Keep me healthy enough. Keep me whole. She used food banks and thrift stores as much as possible. She worked in hole-in-the-wall restaurants whenever she could, accepting lower pay in exchange for the lack of a paper trail, and sneaked home leftovers that would have been thrown away. I wish I had told her how much I admired her, how strong she was, how clever and resourceful. But when I was a kid, I didn't know how lucky I was, what extraordinary lengths she went to. In a way, I was more privileged and sheltered than many of the kids I envied. To this day, I don't know everything she did to keep us alive.

But I *do* know that she died for me.

As much as I love and admire her for all the rest, I'm not sure I'll ever forgive that.

The sounds of the town fade as I walk down the long driveway. I find myself listening harder to the trees around me. Shadows lurk between the trunks, and even though everything is still, I watch for hints of movement.

Mom taught me to be careful, and one rule was to never be alone in a secluded area. Before she died, I was rarely ever alone. Any time I wasn't at school or an after-school job, I was with her. We were a team. "Two peas in a pod," she used to call us.

Once, when I was about eight years old, in a town with an unmemorable name, I saw a pillow with a picture of two smiling cartoon peas in a pea pod. I wanted, more than anything, to buy it for her. We never gave each other gifts, unless they were practical. We had to limit what we moved with us. But I knew the pillow was perfect. I saved for it, shaving bits of change off every time she sent me on an errand, every time I spotted a spare coin on the ground. That was the same year I discovered that people make wishes by tossing coins into fountains. It didn't take me long to save enough—it was a cheap, poorly made novelty pillow, useless as a pillow, which made it useless to us. But I bought it and wrapped it in old newspaper. I twisted the edges of the paper to make a pseudo bow, and I presented it to her on a Saturday. I never knew when her birthday was, so there was no need to wait for a particular day.

I remember how proud I was and how she cried. Happy tears, she said, though even then I wasn't quite sure I believed her. She kept it on her bed, and when she'd slip out early to go to work, she'd tuck it in with me until it was time for me to wake. But right before our next move, I found it in the trash. I plucked it out and told her she'd made a mistake—this was us, two peas in a pod; we couldn't leave it behind. She told me it was too tied to this place, to her memories of our life here. It had to stay in the past. "In the past, but not in the trash!" I insisted.

We left it on a swing set in hopes that it would find a new home, and I tried to tell myself that it was okay. It was the last time I ever gave my mom a gift.

I reach Allison's house and notice the lights on downstairs, as well as one upstairs. Behind the shades, I see a figure move, but I can't tell if it's Allison or her mother. A few of the birds hop from perch to perch as I walk past, but most are silent and still in their cages. Their beady eyes follow me.

The front light gleams at the caretaker's house, although I'm certain I didn't turn it on. I know better than to waste electricity, even if it's included in my rental. We didn't discuss utilities—she didn't mention them, and I didn't ask. It's plain that Allison has never been a landlord before. And while I should feel guilt for essentially cheating her, I don't. I can't. I need a place to sleep. It's just survival.

A lot of the tricks I've learned would never work if I needed to stay in one place. You can't dumpster dive long term without being caught. You can't cheat a landlord or squat in an unoccupied house or skim leftovers from a restaurant or con anyone if you aren't willing to abandon it all the moment things turn sour. You can't accumulate things. Or give gifts. Or make connections. You can't build a life.

I wonder sometimes what it would be like to stay. Just stay. It's not a thought I allow often. Opening the door to the caretaker's house, I imagine what it would feel like if this were my home. I've seen plenty, filled with knickknacks, pictures, mementos, in addition to more practical items. I would have liked to own a pair of kitchen scissors and have a junk drawer that's filled with spare cables and twist ties and rubber bands. And one drawer that's just full of extra pencils. I'd also have a jar of peanut butter that I don't have to ration.

If I had my own place, I'd fill it with memories: a jar full of sand from the Pacific coast beach where Mom and I lived in an abandoned RV for a week, a rock from the waterfall in Vermont where we tossed sticks to see how far they'd travel, a shell from Long Island that Tyler found for me, a set of crayons that I didn't have to leave behind in my kindergarten classroom. Every item I left took a fleck of my soul with it. "You can keep the memories," Mom used to say, but she never said what to do when they fade and fray.

Will my memories of her fade someday?

I hate the thought.

To distract myself, I dump the contents of my pack onto the table and begin to sort with an intensity usually reserved for surgeons. A few items are clearly inedible—you don't mess with cream cheese from a trash can. Or meat, if you can't determine with certainty how long it's been out of the refrigerator. If you're starving, sure, take a risk, but not when I've been promised a fresh diner breakfast in the morning. I don't want to miss that because my stomach is turning inside out to rid my innards of rancid ham. But blueberry muffins can be kept. Ooh, a scone. As I sort, I hear my mother, mixed with the whistle of wind through the leaves of a willow tree. She's often the voice inside of me, reminding me of what I can and can't do. She's my guide.

She's my home.

Or she was, before she left me.

Finished sorting through the coffee shop remnants, I dump the garbage into the trash, tie off the bag, and haul it out of the house. Another of Mom's rules: don't leave trash where you live, unless you want roommates with beady eyes or too many legs. I remember spotting cans strapped to a shed by the house, the kind with raccoon-resistant lids. In the morning, I'll ask Allison if I can throw my garbage in the bins, but I can't imagine she'd say no. Everyone likes to know that their tenants are neat and tidy.

It's darker now than when I entered the guest house. The bushes look like squatting goblins and the trees frozen giants. Across the yard, the statues near the vegetable garden appear twisted into monsters, with limbs that reach toward the sky. Light spills through the window shades. There aren't any outside lights, other than on the porch around the front—I can see a stretch of amber-hued grass by the corner of the house—but the cans are by the kitchen door.

One of the birds squawks, then falls silent.

I lift a trash lid, and from within the house, I hear Allison raise her voice. "That's precisely my point: it isn't your decision!"

"You're claiming it was fate?" Cora's voice is brittle. A shard of glass, held like a weapon.

"That truck should have been my fate. Yes."

She does remember the truck.

Gently, I place my trash in the bin, but I'm hesitant to lower the lid. It will make a sound, and I want to hear what they say next, if it's confirmation that they're talking about the accident I witnessed. If they are . . . I don't know what it means if they are, but it means that Allison remembers and pretended she didn't and that Cora knows and pretended she didn't. Unless she only recently remembered? Or she's talking about a different truck altogether.

A bird squawks at me, and I freeze. *Keep talking. Don't notice me.*

"You think you know what's best for everyone," Allison says. "But you don't. You can't! You haven't lived my life. You don't know what I think, what I feel, what I want."

"You don't know what you want," Cora says. "If you did, you'd be—"

"Married? A mother? Rich? *You* wanted all that. Never me."

"—happy," Cora finishes.

There's silence.

"I don't want to lose you," Cora says.

"I'm not yours to lose. This is exactly what I mean: it's my life."

"You don't live your life in a vacuum," Cora says. "What you do affects everyone who cares about you. When you're my age—"

"I will never be your age," Allison says.

A crow lets out a loud, *"Caw!"* He batters the cage with his wings and screams. This sets off the nearby birds, crescendoing into a cacophony of cries and trills. I close the trash lid and begin to back away, quickly. Not quickly enough.

The kitchen door slams open, and Allison stalks outside. "Your birds—" She sees me and halts. I stare at her like a rabbit sighted by a hawk.

"What is it?" Cora calls.

"Neighbor's dog again," Allison says, eyes fixed on mine. "It took off into the woods. The birds will calm down soon. I'm just going around the house to make sure it doesn't come back." She ignores the birds and walks down to the darkened lawn.

I point to the trash cans. "Just throwing out garbage."

She glances at the bins. "Ahh."

Cautiously, I ask, "Is everything all right?"

Allison smiles and says in a chipper voice, "Of course. Why wouldn't it be? Let me walk you back. It can get pretty dark out here at night. We're so far from the main road." She accompanies me as we cross the yard.

A firefly flashes yellow like a tiny lighthouse. It's followed by another. Crickets are chirping loudly in the grass, a steady buzz. It's a pleasant night, or it would be if the birds weren't screaming like they were being murdered.

"My mother is . . ." Allison searches for the word.

"Mine was too," I say.

"Oh?"

"She meant well, but she never liked when I made my own decisions. My mom always believed that she was the only one who could keep me safe."

Allison nods and then takes a deep breath in and exhales. "I used to like to take walks at night. Before . . . Well, when I was younger. It was peaceful, the way the crickets chirp, the way the wind sounds in the trees. There are bullfrogs in the pond that make the most amazing *galumph* sound. Like a rubber ball bouncing on a cement floor. But she hated it. Put a stop to it. All the guilt trips—it was easier to stop the walks than handle the fallout, even if it meant giving up the crickets and the wind and the frogs."

She's sharing, and I'm not sure whether I want her to or not. I don't want to feel responsible for her emotions. It was enough to shoulder Owen's. On the other hand, she could have answers for me. There's enough mystery to her; she deserves my curiosity. It's not an avenue that I can afford to ignore. "Frogs are amazing," I say. "Wood frogs can freeze up to sixty-five percent of their body in the winter. They thaw in the spring."

"I wonder what happens to the wood frog that doesn't want to freeze. Do the other frogs pressure her to live the life they want for her, or is she allowed to move to a warmer forest?" Allison halts in front of the guest house. "I'm lucky she cares so much about me. It's been her and me for a long time, since my dad and brother died."

"I'm sorry."

She waves her hand. "It was a long time ago."

I wonder if she's forgotten the sounds of their voices. She could have recordings and photos and mementos. She could have others around who share the same memories. It isn't all on her to preserve them.

How long will it take before I can say "It was a long time ago" about Mom with such a casual kind of pain? "I'm sorry for overhearing a private conversation," I tell her. "I wasn't intentionally eavesdropping. But if you do ever want to talk, I've been told I'm an excellent listener."

"That's kind of you, but it's a family thing. I don't want to involve you in our mess."

I want to say I'm already involved and have been since she flung herself into my arms on the sidewalk, but I don't. I've already over-stepped enough for one evening—if I push harder now, she'll pull away, and I want her to continue talking. I know this dance. "Thanks for the walk back." I open the door, about to head inside.

Behind me, Allison asks, "Did she?"

"Did who what?"

"Your mother. You said she believed she was the only one who could keep you safe. Did she keep you safe?"

I think of the willow tree by the brook. "Yes."

"And who keeps you safe now?"

It's an obvious answer. "Me."

She looks back at the house. The birds have mostly settled; only a few are still hopping from perch to perch, letting out the occasional trill. "If you want that to stay true, then you shouldn't be here."

"Oh? Why's that?" *Tell me something.* What makes this place special? Why did my grandmother come back here to die? Why did you run in front of that truck and then deny it?

But she doesn't. Instead, Allison smiles as if she hadn't said anything the least bit ominous. "Let me know if you'd like me to wash any towels. I'll be putting a load in in the morning, and I'm happy to toss in a few more."

"Uh, thanks." I'm unsure whether I've just been threatened or warned.

With a wave and a jaunty "good night," Allison heads back toward the house. As she reaches the porch, the crow caws again, loud against the night silence.

CHAPTER TWENTY

Stu's Diner is cheerful and clean. I have to blink several times before my brain accepts that three out of the four walls are mirrored rather than an endless expanse of teal faux-leather booths. The tables are peppered with fake flowers in multicolored vases.

I didn't sleep well, and it wasn't due to the coffee shop scraps. The conversation with Allison kept running through my head—how quickly she snapped from threats to towels. In the shadows of the guest house, I deconstructed every nuance, and I still can't determine whether she meant to warn or scare me. Even though I should be focusing on my grandmother, the puzzle of Allison worries me.

At the front of the diner, we spot a waiter with a caterpillar-like mustache. He's wiping down a pastry display and doesn't react when Owen asks for a table in the corner. "It has the best view," he explains.

"Ah," I say. It clearly doesn't have any kind of view. It's not by a single window, and even if it were, the diner overlooks a street with an auto body shop, not any sort of scenic nature vista.

"One moment," the mustached waiter mumbles, still not looking at us. He rubs at a spot on the display case featuring a slice of coconut pie. I wonder how long the pie has been there. Its innards are drooping onto the side of the plate.

"I like to people watch," Owen says, and I realize he's still talking about his table choice. "My favorite game is to match diner patrons with a book I think they should read." He points to a man in a suit with his cell phone pressed to his ear, scrawling on a lined yellow pad, and ignoring the omelet next to him. "He needs *Winnie the Pooh*."

"That is not where I thought you were going with that."

"It's not about matching what they think they need," Owen says. "He'd probably ask for the latest legal thriller or a biography of a World War Two hero, but what he really needs is to spend a day in the Hundred Acre Woods and play Poohsticks."

Very familiar with that reference, I grin. "My mom and I used to toss sticks into a waterfall in Vermont and see whether they'd sink, break, or shoot down the river. It was a slightly more violent version of Poohsticks."

He grins back at me. "Still counts. When I was a kid, I spent an entire summer trying to skip rocks in a pond, as if that was a life skill I needed to master, along with the ability to identify quicksand and dodge lava."

Before I can ask whether he succeeded, a waitress pops up from behind the counter, and I jump—I hadn't realized there was anyone else working but the mustached waiter. She is very, very blonde and very, very pale and dressed entirely in teal—teal dress, teal scarf around her neck, teal apron around her waist. She holds two plastic menus and guides us to Owen's favorite corner table, while the waiter continues to meticulously clean the pastry display. We sit in front of paper place mats, and she pours us water.

"Is Stu around this morning?" Owen asks.

"It's Stu's diner," she says.

"I didn't know if he took a morning off . . ."

She shrugs and repeats, "It's Stu's diner. Juice?"

"Ah, just a decaf coffee," Owen says. He glances at me. "What do you want? It's my treat, so feel free to add bacon to everything."

His treat. I jump on that. "Orange juice." Fresh orange juice is a treat that I rarely have. It sours fast and costs more than gas, so I didn't have it much growing up. Tyler used to make me fresh-squeezed orange juice on Saturday mornings. "Wait, apple." I don't want to dwell on memories of Tyler this morning.

The waitress disappears, and Owen resumes his game. "See that couple? She thinks she should read the latest Elin Hilderbrand, and he wants the fattest science fiction novel he can find, but what she really needs is Margaret Atwood, ideally *The Edible Woman*, and he secretly craves a Meg Cabot, but he doesn't know it."

I love this game. It's simultaneously charming and vicious, depending on how you play it. "You should make this a Book Cellar promotion. Arranged marriages but with books. You pair them."

He lights up. "Clever. I could wrap the books in brown paper. I've seen other stores do that, as a sort of don't-judge-a-book-by-its-cover, blind-dating promotion."

The blonde-and-teal waitress returns with his decaf.

I glance across the diner. The mustached waiter is still scrubbing the display case with the determination of Lady Macbeth. "I think it's clean enough," I say, and then I immediately want to take the words back. If he can't help his actions, he doesn't need anyone's commentary. I know better than anyone what it's like to have to do what no one else understands.

"That's Tony," Owen says. "Funny thing is, he was a slob in high school. Locker spilling out into the hallway. Leftover sandwiches shoved under his bed. His mom used to despair of him. I would have given him Marie Kondo's *Tidying Up* back then. Now . . . hmm . . . I think Emily Wilson's translation of *The Odyssey*."

I am startled by the title's mention—it was my mother's favorite. She once said she was Odysseus, failing to reach home. "Why *The Odyssey*?"

"It has both structure and wildness."

I sip the apple juice and wish I'd ordered orange. In my mother's mind, every day she had to outwit another cyclops and counted herself lucky if she escaped with her life. Once, she nicknamed our landlords

Scylla and Charybdis. She claimed the Fates liked to laugh at her. "Has Allison always lived with her mother?"

He startles, and coffee spills over the edge of the mug.

Wincing, I apologize and hand him my napkin. He wipes up his hand and the table. The waitress rematerializes to pour more coffee. He adds cream and sugar again and stirs, reminding me of the stirring man in the coffee shop.

"Okay, a different question: what book would you give yourself?"

He relaxes minutely. "*Travels with Charley* by John Steinbeck, primarily for the title, but I also love Steinbeck and the punch he packs in his sentences. I'm more of a babbler, or so Allison once told me, though she meant it fondly, I think." He answers so easily that I know he's given it thought.

"And me?"

"A blank book."

I don't know how I feel about that answer, especially given how quickly he said it. I'm about to ask why when the waitress appears again beside us, expressionless, and taps her pencil on her pad. "What do you want?" she asks.

"An omelet with asparagus, mushrooms, and cheese," Owen says.

"Type of cheese?"

"Tell Stu to surprise me."

The waitress blinks at him. "You?" she asks me.

Owen recommended the omelet, and he said he was paying. As tempting as french toast is, especially with challah, I can't turn down protein, especially after a dinner of muffins and scones. "An omelet also, with cheese and tomatoes, and can I have bacon on the side?"

Grunting as if I've disappointed her, she scrawls a note on her pad. "You want a few strips like you're trying to look elegant, or you want a giant mountain of pig?"

I glance at Owen.

"Whatever you want," he says.

"I'd like an unreasonable amount of bacon, please," I tell the waitress.

She almost smiles for the first time since we've come in, and then disappears through the teal swinging doors into the kitchen, revealing a brief glimpse of who I assume is Stu by the way he commands the stove. He's a large Black man with a pink "kiss me, I'm the chef" apron, and he wields two spatulas. Before the doors swing back, I think I see one of the blue-haired ladies beside him, but I'm not certain. Why would one of them be in Stu's kitchen? I stare at the door, willing it to swing open again, but it doesn't. Could I have imagined the blue hair? "Do any of the blue-haired women work here?" I ask.

"So far as I know, they all retired years ago from whatever they used to do."

"But you aren't sure?"

"You've met them," Owen says. "Would you be sure?"

I laugh. "Okay, back to this blank book of mine. Why blank? Why not poetry or a thriller or a cozy mystery or some mind-bending, life-altering experimental work of literary fiction that will alter the course of my existence?"

He shakes his head. "You need a blank book with a beautiful cover, thick white pages, and a ribbon to mark your place, and you need a set of multicolored pens to write in it."

"You think I'm a writer?" He had no way of knowing how much my mother would have hated the idea of me recording my thoughts in a book. "Or, no, you think I keep a diary?"

"I think you have stories in you," Owen says, his eyes serious.

"Ah." It's a lovely thought, but there's only one story I'm interested in: my family story, and it's a tale that I don't know. "What time does the library open?"

"In a half hour," he says. "Don't worry. Stu's quick."

He's correct. It's only another minute or two before Stu himself carries two plates over and presents the omelets with a flourish. The ultrablonde waitress is behind him, and she lays a plate with a heap of bacon next to me. The distinctive greasy smell makes my mouth water. Wow, I haven't had bacon in . . . I shove down the memory of my last breakfast with Mom and focus on the mound in front of me.

"You're new to Greenborough," Stu said, his voice so low that it sounds like the rumble of a train. "Welcome."

"How do you know I'm new?" I ask, letting the omelet distract me from the bacon. It's fluffy and shaped in a perfect crescent, and cheese oozes out the ends. "This looks like it should be in a magazine. Omelet perfection right there."

"Told you," Owen says. He's already eating.

Stu grins at us, a smile so wide it feels like a hug. "Everyone in Greenborough comes to Stu's sooner or later. Never met a customer who didn't return."

It sounds like hyperbole, but the diner door opens, and Maddie and Emma stroll inside. When they see me, one of them whispers to the other, who nods. Both of them stare openly at me, with pity in their eyes. It's such an unexpected look that I miss Stu ducking back into the kitchen and fail to see if one of the blue-haired ladies is here. Are they sorry I stayed? Sorry that I'm eating all the bacon? What test have I failed?

"Maple syrup?" Owen offers. "It's fresh. Tastes amazing on the bacon."

Ignoring the two girls, I take the syrup and pour it over the heap of bacon. It oozes between the crinkles and onto the plate. "I love maple syrup on bacon. First time I ever tried it was in Vermont, only a couple of moves ago, and it was like a revelation." After Mom . . . was gone, I headed north. A trucker felt sorry for me. She bought me breakfast at a truck stop I'd wandered into, looking for a job or an answer or . . . I didn't know what. I had already decided I wasn't going to touch the account that Mom established for me, knowing what the cost was. I must have stared at that truck stop menu for a solid fifteen minutes before the trucker told me to come eat some bacon. She'd slathered it with maple syrup before remembering she was supposed to watch her sugar intake, she said, so I might as well eat it. Better than wasting it. Strangely, it was the maple syrup that helped me take the next step. Tasting syrup over bacon, I decided to keep going.

Owen and I eat in silence, but it's a nice kind of silence. Forks clink on the dishes. If I did have a blank book, I'd put an omelet recipe in it, with maple bacon on the side.

After breakfast, Owen comes with me to the library, which is nice, though it derails my plan to check out the diner's dumpster. Instead of merely dropping me off, he escorts me. We're greeted by two statues of lounging cats, domestic versions of the New York Public Library lions. "Just so you know, the librarian and I . . . We've had a few conversations that weren't"—he opens the door while he searches for the right adjective—"warm."

The librarian, an Asian American woman in her fifties, looks up from a massive desk that resembles the front of a ship. It boasts a wooden banner that says, "Sail into reading." She's wearing a blouse with wide lapels that loosely resembles a sailor's outfit, except the fabric has a pineapple pattern in a vivid yellow with a pink background. She scowls as soon as she spots Owen. "You again. I thought I told you your library card expired after you said my taste was pedestrian?"

"I didn't say pedestrian," Owen objects. "I said it was predictable."

She huffs. "That's worse." Grumbling under her breath, she appears on the verge of throwing him out, which seems counter to the whole nature of libraries. I've lurked in many over the years, especially in the dead of winter and summer heat. As a kid, I'd participate in every library program available, from crafts with yarn to CPR to "read with the librarian's dog." I've zigzagged across this entire country, and I can definitely say that libraries are its finest wonder.

He bravely steps behind me. "I've brought a new patron who has a research project."

The librarian's face lights up. "Ah!"

"Angelique, this is Elisa. Elisa, this is Angelique, the most brilliant researcher that Greenborough has ever seen. She can locate any tidbit of information faster than a pig can find a truffle."

Partially mollified, Angelique sniffs. "That was almost a nice compliment. What kind of information do you want, my dear? Science? History? Music theory? Popular culture? Climate change? Biology? Genetics? An update on the current debates in literary criticism?"

"Local history," I say.

"Ah, delightful!"

"My family history, to be specific." I explain about my grandmother and how I believe she attended Greenborough High School for a year in the sixties. "I know very little about her, but I thought maybe local newspapers . . ."

She beams at me as if I've presented her with a bow-laden present. "Oh! You'll be wanting the microfiche." Chortling, she beckons to me as she rounds her desk and leads us into the next room. "I don't get much call for records on microfiche anymore, but it does come up. Not everything's been digitized, you see. That's the problem that plagues archivists: when technology becomes obsolete, information can be lost, and there isn't the money or the time to save all of it. We're going to have massive gaps in our records if we're not careful." She continues to chatter about how we'll lose a slice of ourselves when we lose our history, and it's a shame stone tablets fell out of favor because at least those bad boys didn't need to be upgraded. She uses that precise phrase: "bad boys."

The microfiche machines are tucked beneath an oil painting of a scowling library donor with lace at her throat. There's a window out to the library's backyard, which has a cherry tree beside a bench. It looks lovely and peaceful, and I think if I were to have a choice, that's what I would become. Taking a breath, I sit down at one of the two microfiche readers. Owen sits beside me at the second machine.

"What year are you looking for?" Angelique asks.

"Late 1960s. I believe her name was Rose Grayson at the time, and she would have been here for a year of high school. She was on a sports team, either softball or track." I wonder how accurate the three women's memories are.

"All right then, let's start with the local newspaper—the *Greenborough Gazette*—at 1967 and work forward." Angelique darts to the shelves and returns with three boxes. She then demonstrates how to use the microfiche readers: pull a tray out until the glass over top lifts up, place the film on the tray, and then slide the tray back in. The film will display on the screen, and you can turn a dial to focus, if you need to. "Also, if you hear voices in the stacks, don't be alarmed. We've been having a problem with that."

With that odd statement, she sweeps back toward the circulation desk.

I look at Owen. He's already placing the first film on the reader. It lights up on the screen. Opening the box beside me, I lay the first one on my machine. It's the *Greenborough Gazette*, as promised, dated March 1, 1967. I skim through it—nothing of note—and then replace it with the next film. Owen works beside me.

"Voices?" I ask.

"It's an old building with a sordid history," he says, as if that explains it.

"Mmm?" I hope that will encourage him to say more. No luck. Checking the next film, I glance over the headlines and wonder how long this will take and what sort of voices we're talking about. Indistinct chatter? Ominous moaning? Cryptic commands? In eastern Michigan, I met a woman who claimed her chickens spoke to her. She heard voices from their roosts that later turned out to be her neighbor's kids smoking weed behind her henhouse. I joined them once, but the rooster was too ornery for it to be enjoyable.

"It was built in the 1800s for a woman whose husband's family owned most of the land in Greenborough. Story goes that, after he died, she and her two sisters became recluses, locking themselves inside these walls." As he talks, I am aware of how hushed the library stacks feel. While the front was bright and cheery, the light here is subdued, almost gray. The stacks are layered in shadows. "Meals were delivered to the front door, but no one was allowed inside until one of the sisters took sick. Emergency workers were called in for a burst water pipe or a fire? I don't know the exact details—stories vary—but they discovered the women had been living in squalor. One of them was taken to the hospital immediately, and another spent the rest of her life in a mental institution."

"What about the third?" Glancing at the shadowy stacks, I scan another film. Aha, I was right that local high school sports would be highlighted in the paper. There's also an entire column devoted to how the Anderson family, whoever they were, refused to move their beehives. Despite the date, there is no mention of the Vietnam War except for one obituary of a boy in uniform, nestled next to an advertisement for fresh eggs and a camper for sale. The police report is an equal mix of actual crime—a house break-in, in which jewelry and a TV were stolen—and not-quite-crime, specifically a traffic violation and a complaint about a misbehaved dog on school property.

Owen reaches for another film and positions it on his screen. "According to town legend, she wandered into the woods on a cold night and died of exposure. She was found not far from a stream that would have led her out, if she'd followed it. Of course, everyone said that grove was haunted after that."

"Oh?" Haunted wasn't the same as cursed, but all oddities are suspect. I've met paranormal investigators, and they become very excited around old shacks, attics, and basements, and especially the woods at night. Such relics don't have the same pull for me, although I do appreciate the ambiance of this library—it has the quiet of unspoken words and fleeting memories. But it's unlikely that the ghosts here have anything to do with me. I just hope they stay silent until I'm finished. I'd rather not be distracted.

"The grove was filled a few years later," he says, continuing to work through the films. "Deemed a hazard, which it was. And since then, no reports of ghosts."

"And the library?"

"There are lots of stories about the sisters who haunt the stacks, dismayed that their old sanctuary has become a public place," Owen says. "I've never seen them, but the library hosts overnight events for local teens. The next day, there are always a few kids in the shop, talking about how so-and-so swears they saw a hazy figure in the nonfiction section or that they heard voices in the bathroom." He flashes a grin. "I put out a display of ghost stories whenever there's going to be an event."

Local ghost stories aren't what I need, but I like thinking that my grandmother may have been in this library as a teenager, giggling about a ghost in the stacks. I wonder if the shadows were as thick then as they are now. Continuing to scan through the old newspapers, I ask, "When did it become a library?"

"It was inherited by a cousin after some kind of vicious property dispute, and he later donated it to avoid a messy tax situation. The ugliest part is that the people who decided that the sisters weren't fit to make decisions about the property were the same people who stood to inherit. Major conflict of interest there."

"Let me guess: they were male relatives?"

"Yes," he says.

"And could they have also called in the 'emergency' that led to the sisters' eviction?"

"It's possible."

I have a lot of sympathy for the sisters. They tried to live on their own terms, away from society. And then the world punished them for it, taking everything they cared about, labeling them and judging them and condemning them. They may have been better off turning into cherry trees.

We work in silence for a while.

I listen to the hush in the stacks—I know that it's only the heating system, but there's a whoosh to the silence, almost like a muffled whisper. It feels as if I should be able to parse words.

"Ah, hey, look at this," Owen says. He scoots back his chair so I can see. "High school softball team champions, 1968." On the screen is a clump of girls in white shimmery shorts and collared shirts. All of them are smiling. Those in the front row kneel on either side of an older woman, most likely their coach. Names are listed below the photo, and I scan through them until—

Rose Grayson.

Owen taps the screen. "Could that be her? Third from the left in the back row?"

He swaps seats with me so that I can see her directly. I can't tear my eyes away. It's a grainy photo, but there she is, with brown hair curled around her face, a wide smile with dark lipstick, and a face that looks eerily like my mom's. She has the same cheekbones, the same eyebrows. Only the smile is different, but that could be because I rarely saw my mother smile. I take the photos out of my pack to compare. First my mother, then my grandmother. "It's her."

It's like I've been punched in the sternum.

I found you.

CHAPTER TWENTY-ONE

Owen and I race through the microfiche after our discovery.

Rose went to Greenborough High School and was on the softball team. I find other mentions of softball wins, but nothing specific about Rose Grayson. After the initial elation of finding her, I fear it may be a dead end. She wasn't a star player, and there are no interviews with any of the players anyway. Just score reports and other stats.

The hum from the library air vents sounds like a murmur. I keep flipping through the microfiche and select yet another one and place it on the machine.

"Look, they won the next year too. Here's Rose," Owen says, waving at a photo.

"Okay, so I didn't inherit her athletic skills . . . Wait, what do you mean 'the next year'?" I lean toward his screen and see a newspaper from the following spring. That doesn't make any sense. My grandmother shouldn't have been at the same school for two seasons. She would have had to move on, with her mother—the curse is passed from mother to daughter. She couldn't just . . . stay. No one in my family could ever stay. It was a clear, unbreakable rule, if we wanted to avoid the consequences of the curse. "That's not possible."

"You win enough games, you win the championship," Owen says. "It's not as if teams take turns. They must have had a good coach, as well as decent players."

No, no, no.

My heart beats faster as I grab the next box of film. I rifle through it and find microfiche from what would be her junior year—if she were here. With shaky hands, I slide them onto the machine.

In the stacks, the shadows shift, as if they're curious.

"Want me to see if I can find her wedding announcement?" Owen offers. "You said her married name was Ellert, right? I'll see if it's in here. Any idea what year she was married?"

Such a thing shouldn't exist. Even if she managed to stay for two years of high school, she *couldn't* have been married here. Surely, that occurred somewhere else, if at all. It is absurd to even consider. More important is discovering where she went next, after Greenborough High. But I nod. Let him look while I try to corral my thoughts.

My hands shake as I position the next film, from a year later. The dates of the spring championship are approximately the same each year, and each year she's there, through senior year in the same town.

Ten months is the maximum Mom and I ever stayed in one place. Given that my grandmother carried the same curse—it affects all the women in our family—there is no conceivable way her face could be beaming from these softball photos every year of high school. How long had she lived here? Since elementary school? Junior high? Was she born here? Marry here? Die here? *Impossible.*

She never left, Peacock Blue had said.

Could it be true? How?

Mom always said we bore our family curse, passed from mother to daughter, but here is evidence right before my eyes that it didn't touch my grandmother. I feel as though a fist has been rammed into my rib cage. It's hard to breathe, and I hear a ringing in my ears.

This has been my truth since the day I was born. We are cursed. It's the way it's always been. My mother believed it would always be—that was the one thing we disagreed on—but I never once questioned whether it was the way it's always been.

Did she lie to me?

She had to have known that her mother had a home.

Unless Rose lied to her?

Or maybe the curse wasn't as vicious in earlier generations? Perhaps Rose could stay for a few years with no ramifications. Maybe her parents weren't as risk averse as my mother. She could have spent high school here, moved elsewhere, and returned to Greenborough for her death. I used to question whether ten months was too extreme, but Mom never wanted to gamble with our lives, especially with mine. Could this be proof that the curse is more flexible than we believed?

"Aha! Look!" Owen beams at me as he gestures toward the screen. "*Rose Lorelei Ellert of Greenborough, Massachusetts, and Glenn Aaron Ellert of Greenborough were united in marriage at three p.m., June 16, 1975.*"

All oxygen depletes as my "maybe" shatters.

She never left.

The library is silent, like a held breath.

"Elisa?" His voice sounds distant, as if he's under water. I want to reply that I'm fine, but I can't seem to force the oxygen out.

Curling over my knees, I hang my head low. I feel Owen's hand on my back and hear him call for help. There are other voices, women's, weaving together in the background. The librarian and other patrons or the library ghosts. I don't care who's there. All that matters is that my mother lied to me.

I finally suck in air. I can't panic in front of my new boss and, currently, my only friend. *Get a grip, Elisa.* I inhale and exhale. I can handle this.

I can't.

All my life, it was my mother and me. She shielded me from plenty; I know that. I'd be a fool to think I knew everything my mother did to keep us fed and safe, but she didn't lie to me about anything truly important. She had always very clearly laid out our limitations, the invisible bars of our cages. Our fate was bound by who we were—our inherited burden, passed from mother to daughter through the generations, that tied us together and bound us to a certain future.

But apparently our fates weren't bound.

Here is proof that my grandmother wasn't cursed. I don't know what to make of this information. What does it say about my mother? About me?

"I'm fine," I tell Owen. Slowly, I sit up. "Just a little lightheaded."

Angelique shoves a cup of water under my chin. "I have peanut butter crackers. Are you allergic to peanut butter?" She unwraps the pack and holds one out to me. I don't say no. *Never say no to free food,* my mom whispers to me.

"I'm just . . ." I fake a weak smile that undoubtedly looks worse than not smiling. "It's overwhelming. I've looked for my family for a long time." It's true and also a plausible explanation, if an incomplete one.

Owen asks, "Do you want to lie down?"

I shake my head. "I want to keep looking."

I wish I could confront my mother and demand answers. How could Rose Grayson-Ellert have lived and died here? What does it mean for me? I want to ask her why she never told me the truth, that the curse began with her. It wasn't a family inheritance passed down through generations of women. I want to know why she lied. Was it to keep me from looking for our home? Was it to keep me from false hope? She was always concerned about that. That I not look for ways to end the curse, that instead I find happiness while living with it—especially at the end, she said that over and over. She'd wasted years seeking a cure, when it was far better to make peace with your fate.

But what if it isn't fate? What if . . . I don't know what to ask or who to ask or what to do, but I know I am a swirl of questions. I eat the peanut butter cracker without tasting it and scroll through more microfiche. My eyes are glued to the screen, and my skin feels as if it's prickling all over. I'm desperate for more crumbs of information about Rose.

As the shadows shift in the stacks, I lose track of time. Occasionally there are footsteps and voices behind me, patrons that come and go, but I don't look anywhere but the screen. My eyes feel dry, and I am aware every time I blink.

At last, I find another clue: a casual shot of two softball players. My grandmother holds up a trophy in one hand, and another girl has her arm flung around Rose's shoulder. Maybe this friend is still alive. I could talk to her, find out if Rose always lived here, find out what she knows about my mother.

Over my shoulder, Owen says, "Hey, that's Cora, Allison's mother."

"You mean her grandmother." I know that Allison introduced the elderly Cora as her mother, but the math and biology don't add up. The girl in the photo is with my grandmother, and Allison is about my age. I peer at the caption.

Rose Grayson and Cora Halloran.

"Her mother," Owen corrects. "Allison always said she was a miracle baby, born after the doctors said her mother was too old to conceive."

I'm not as surprised as I should be. *I'd guessed that.* If Allison's birth was improbable enough to make it into tabloids, then Allison could be the reason that Greenborough made it onto my list of places to visit. I wish I could remember for sure. *A lucky coincidence.* I'm grateful for her miracle. Without Allison, I could have sailed past this town entirely and never have known that it held, if not answers, then at least a hundred more questions.

"Looks like Cora knew your grandmother," Owen says, pleased with this discovery.

I would be pleased too, except that Cora had looked at my photo of Rose and flat-out denied recognizing her. Either she forgot her, or she lied.

I don't know what to think of any of this, but I know I need air. I stand and turn to Owen and say, "We should open the Book Cellar. It's time, right?" Glancing around the reading room, I spot a clock. We've been here for nearly two hours. "Doesn't the bookstore open at ten?"

He stands too. "This was important."

He knew and just let me keep looking through old microfiche? What kind of business owner is he? God, no one has ever been this kind to me. Who is this man, and why did the universe deliver him to me now? *It knows I need him.* "Your store is important to you. You could have interrupted me. Or left. I could have joined you later."

Owen smiles. "You found a piece of your story. I wasn't going to miss that."

I help him open the Book Cellar—it's after noon by now, but Owen doesn't seem disturbed that he missed any morning customers. Charlie greets us by the front door. Owen scratches him by the collar, and Charlie leans into his hand.

I'm relieved to be back in the bookstore. I need a breath to think. Or maybe to *not* think. I don't know how to absorb what I've seen and learned.

"Is he by himself all night?" I ask. He's a cat. I'm sure he's fine, but I never realized that a bookstore cat might never leave the bookstore.

"He's not by himself. I live upstairs." Owen waves at the back of the shop.

I hadn't noticed stairs. Perhaps they're behind a shelf of books? It doesn't surprise me that Owen lives with the books. In fact, it wouldn't surprise me if he burrowed into the stacks, like a squirrel surrounded by acorns. It would do him good, I think, to see more of the world.

"Are you okay?" He interrupts my thoughts. "You seemed a little shook up back in there. I'd have thought you'd be happy to find pictures of your family."

"It was great," I say automatically.

He waits for me to really answer.

"It didn't match what I thought I knew about my family history," I explain. "My mother . . ." How much can I tell him? How much will he believe? I can't risk scaring him off. I'm dependent on him and his help and this job. Plus, he's nice, extraordinarily so. I don't *want* to scare him off. "She told me she'd always moved around a lot. Maybe she did." There was nothing at the library that said Rose didn't leave Greenborough to raise Mom. Her father could have moved with them—Glenn, that was his name. As far as I know, he wasn't cursed—my mom was very clear that only women in our family were affected, unless she lied about that too? He could have gone with them, though, to help Mom evade the curse. I feel like I'm twisting myself into knots, trying to make it all make sense. Trying to make it so my mother wasn't a liar. "But she'd said the same was true of my grandmother. Rose shouldn't have been here." Was she truly here through all of high school? Earlier? Later? Did she come back for her wedding, or had she been here all along? Did she leave afterward? Perhaps she'd only been in Greenborough for pockets of time, never long enough for it to be home. *No, if she married and died here, she considered this her home.* If this truly was her home . . . it defies everything I thought I knew about the curse. "I wish the library had school yearbooks." I need to know more. I am leaping to conclusions, and it is making me feel as if I am leaping off a cliff, rocks below me.

"They might have them at the high school," he says.

The bell at the Book Cellar door rings, and in walk Maddie and her girlfriend, Emma. Owen greets them, and they nod without saying anything. Sticking together, they begin walking down the aisles and murmur to one another in low voices.

Owen unfolds a map of the town. "If you want to visit the high school . . ."

Maddie sticks her head out from between the stacks. "Don't recommend that."

"Why not?" I ask.

"It's full of high schoolers." She retreats.

"I don't know if anyone will be there in the summer," Owen says with a smile. "In fact, I can pretty much guarantee that it's locked up and empty. But I can see if I have a friend who might let us in, if you like."

"Why are you being so nice?" I ask.

"He's bored," Maddie utters from behind the bookshelves.

Owen laughs, though it's a brittle kind of laugh. "She's right. You're the first bit of drama that this town has seen in . . ." His voice fades, and I know he's thinking about Allison. Guilt? Regret? I can't read what he's feeling. "Well, it's usually a quiet town."

"If you don't want quiet, why don't you leave?" I ask. He could at least venture out for a weekend, now that he's hired me. That's enough time for a mini adventure. I wonder if he has his own mysteries to unravel, unanswered questions. Or am I the only one who walks around feeling as if I've swallowed a tornado?

Emma peeks out from behind the books. In the shadow of the shelves, with her kohl eyeliner and pale cheeks, she looks ghostly. "We told you. It's the kind of place you get stuck."

She seems so serious that I ask, "Are you stuck?"

She ducks away without answering.

I follow their voices but don't interrupt them. I wonder what their story is, why they think they're stuck. A few books have been shelved out of order, and I reshelve them, squeezing them into their new homes. The word sticks in my throat like an unswallowed bite:

Home.

I can't believe I found my grandmother's home. Mom never said a word about Greenborough. I wish I could remember for certain why I added Greenborough to my list. Luck, coincidence, fate? I must have run across an anecdote about Allison's miraculous birth, one of those doctors-scratch-their-heads stories; though, that couldn't have been the only reason. For a while, I've been tracking down locations with more than one miracle. A single miracle is likely to be an anomaly or a medical mistake, but multiple miracles . . . There's more to this town than one improbable birth—I think of the man who quotes Prufrock as he endlessly stirs, the writer who never types, the guitarist with the stringless guitar, and of course, Allison. I need to understand what role this town played in my family's story.

But first . . . I need a breath. And I owe it to Owen to at least try to do my job, after all the time he spent with me in the library. I poke my head out from between the stacks. "Hey, want to try that blind date book idea? Do you have brown paper?"

He lights up. "Yes, I do."

Ducking down, he disappears for a moment, and I hear rustling before he emerges with a stack of brown paper bags.

I examine one of the bags. He hasn't stamped them with the store logo yet, so they're just brown paper. Cut them open and we can use them to wrap the books.

Owen grins at me. "Let's do this."

I pick up a copy of *Family of Liars* as Owen cuts apart one of the bags. He produces a roll of tape from beneath the desk—how many supplies are down there? I wrap the book, tape it closed, and then write on the outside:

Looking for a reader who loves . . .
Dysfunctional families.
Rich people with problems.
An island off of Cape Cod.

"Add 'betrayal and mistakes,'" Owen suggests.

"How about 'scandal and tragedy'?"

I add the words and set it aside to wrap the next book.

By the time we've wrapped and labeled five, Emma has drifted out of the stacks and picked one up: *Ghostly mystery, for a reader who wants to shiver.*

Emma frowns. "What's in this one?"

"It's a surprise," I say.

"But how do I know if I'll like it?"

"You don't," I say. "That's the fun of it. You're choosing it just on the description, not the author or the cover or what the packaging tells you it's supposed to be. It's a blind date with a book—all you know is what's written on the outside."

She looks at it dubiously.

The bell chimes, and I glance over to see the old man from the coffee shop, the one who quotes poetry. He doesn't meet my eyes, just wanders in between the stacks.

"Wrap this one," Owen says, thrusting a book of poetry toward me. It's Mary Oliver's *Devotions.* "He needs it."

I wrap it quickly while Owen rings up Emma's purchase—she's bought the ghostly book. I label the poetry book: *For the reader who has run out of coffee spoons.*

He buys it.

In between customers, Owen and I choose books to wrap and label. He suggests "for the reader who loves long walks" for *The Two Towers,* which makes me laugh, and I offer up "for the picky eater" for *The Very Hungry Caterpillar.* We label *Coraline* as "for the reader who doesn't fear buttons (but would like to)."

My left arm itches.

Absently, I scratch it and then resume wrapping.

It's the most fun that I've had in ages, since before it was time to leave Tyler, back when everything was shiny and new and the months felt plump with possibility.

Over the course of the afternoon, there's a steady stream of customers. I don't recognize most of them, but Owen greets them all by name. He offers up a book labeled *For the reader who wants nonstop action, with dragons and spice* to one woman I do recognize from the coffee shop—the one with a snake around her neck.

My fingernail catches a scab on my arm.

I don't remember getting a cut.

Not now. Not yet.

I don't want to look. I know I have to look.

I twist my arm until I can see it.

It isn't a cut.

I touch the patch of hard brown with my fingertip. Dread squeezes my throat, and I feel as though I can't breathe. I've seen this before.

It's a spot of bark.

I squeeze my eyes shut and then open them again, and it isn't bark. It's an ordinary scab, as if I scraped myself on a sharp edge, except I know I didn't.

No. It's too soon. I've only just arrived! I should have months and months before I'm in danger, before this place begins to feel like home . . .

Except that this is already home.

My grandmother lived and died here.

This is my family's home.

I can't stay.

But I'm so close to finding answers. I have to talk to Cora. I have to talk to the three blue-haired ladies again. I have to visit the high school and find the old yearbooks. I need to uncover when the curse began, how, and why. If it wasn't the moon, if it's not in my blood . . .

I stare at the scab. From a cut that I don't remember. From a cut that may never have existed, fused to my skin like bark on a tree. My heart beats hard and fast in my chest, and my mouth tastes coppery. I hear my mother's warnings echo in my mind. Once, I voiced my doubts to her—I was fifteen or sixteen and finally happy; encouraged by my best friend, Jackie, I'd talked to the school counselor about how to convince my mom to let me stay—and Mom detailed precisely what would happen if I defied the curse. I haven't forgotten a single word. For an instant, I think I can feel the sap in my blood.

"Elisa, are you okay?" Owen asks as the bell over the door rings again—the latest customer has left, and we're alone in the bookshop.

"Of course."

I can't stay.

But I can't leave.

Not yet.

CHAPTER TWENTY-TWO

ROSE

1989

Rose leaned against the kitchen counter. She balled her hands up and ground them into her stomach to keep from screaming. Out the window, she could see the lawn had been mowed into parallel strips. She'd weeded the flower beds on either side of the lawn yesterday and had washed the patio this morning. But the work didn't stop, and it was never enough. Outside was perfect, but the windows needed to be cleaned. The kitchen floor was perpetually streaked with whatever was tracked in from outside. Every time the sun shone, it lit up the dust on the bookshelves, even though she'd dusted on Monday. The bathrooms never stayed clean more than a day, with Lori sprawling her hair products and makeup everywhere. If Rose saw one more towel bleached by makeup stains . . .

Ugh, I don't care. Why did it matter if the house sparkled and the lawn matched home-and-garden magazines? It seemed to matter to other people so very much. She hated those pursed-lip looks when she didn't pull the trash bins back right after the garbage trucks rumbled through. She hated the mix of pity and disapproval in her in-laws' eyes and, worse, her parents' if Lori left the contents of her backpack strewn on the couch or Rose hadn't finished scrubbing a pot. Of course, they never warned her they were coming, no matter how many times she asked. And of course, they'd never blame Glenn. He couldn't be expected to worry about the house when he had his job, even though he worked nine to six and the housework was nonstop, even though he had two hands and weekends free, even though he had time to bowl with the boys on Thursdays and meet at the coffee shop on Saturdays and watch the game in someone's backyard on Sundays—there was always a game.

She didn't know why they even needed a house this size. Three bathrooms for three people when Glenn was at work and Lori was at school most of the time? Couldn't someone just wait their turn? Also, why a lawn? Why did lawns exist at all? There was no point to growing a plant just so you could lop it off once a week so it looked like a carpet. So what if it had a few dandelions? Dandelions were bright and cheery! So what if there wasn't a thick mat of mulch in the flower beds? Mulch smelled like manure anyway. Most importantly, why did she have to cook for Glenn's dinner party? He'd conceived it, planned it, and invited his coworkers without involving her. Why was it on her to play perfect hostess when she barely knew them? Why couldn't she just leave for the night and let him handle the logistics for his colleagues? She could take herself out to dinner or to the movies or to see Cora. He could manage a meal on his own if it mattered that much to him.

Except that he had asked, and she had said yes, with a smile. It wasn't his fault that this knot of resentment kept twisting and growing inside of her. She never told him it was there. He always asked how he could help. Whenever she needed an errand run, he'd cheerfully do it. Oh, he wouldn't think of it himself. If the toilet paper was low, he wouldn't think to add it to the grocery list that she kept on the fridge with the bumblebee **BEE HAPPY** magnet. He wouldn't volunteer to scrub a pot in the sink, but he would if she asked. Sometimes, he'd call

Lori in with a cheerful lecture about how she was fourteen and should be pitching in around the house more, to help out her mother. Lori would roll her eyes and half-heartedly scrub a pot before returning to her room to hop back on the phone. They were both helpers, but it was clear that it was all Rose's responsibility in the end. *Of course it is, and of course it should be.* Glenn had work, and Lori would have high school. Rose felt like a cliché even complaining. She had a doting husband, a well-behaved daughter, and a beautiful home—everything she'd been told by every friend, every family member, every commercial, every magazine, every movie that she was supposed to want. Yet, she wanted to scream. All the time.

Rose opened the drawer beneath the utensils and took out the envelope she kept there. She unfolded the brochure and looked at the photos for the thousandth time: rolling green hills dropping into a rocky seashore, a thatched-roof cottage beside the rocks, and a bike path winding between them.

The doorbell chimed, and Rose laid the brochure on the table. Cora, holding a brownie tin and a paper bag with flowers poking out the top, waited on the steps. She beamed at Rose.

"Ready for tonight?" Cora asked.

Rose stared at her. "Tonight . . . oh, tonight!" The book club! She'd forgotten. "Cora, I am so sorry. Glenn invited some of his coworkers for dinner, and book club went right out of my head. Come in. I'm sorry. We'll have to call everyone . . ." How could she have forgotten? She'd written it on the calendar, but she hadn't thought to look, in the swirl of Glenn's impromptu party. Usually, she was on top of every appointment, every errand, every chore.

Shaking off the brief flash of disappointment, Cora rallied. "It happens. We can reschedule." In an even brighter voice, she said, "You're hosting a dinner party! I'm proud of you!"

"Well, that's a bit condescending, but thanks?" She tried to dodge the stab of guilt, but it was too well aimed—she'd disappointed Cora and undoubtedly her other friends who looked forward to the respite that was their monthly book club meeting. It was the only event where it was okay to let the husband and kids fend for themselves, so long as you left them a casserole to heat up or a number for takeout.

Cora carried her bag and the brownies inside. "I'm donating the flowers and brownies to your efforts, but you should hide the wine somewhere. Likely one of your guests will bring a bottle, and that way we can keep this one for the next book club meeting." She scanned the kitchen. "You haven't started. What time are they coming?"

"Six o'clock."

"All right. What are we making?"

"Lasagna," Rose said. Everyone liked lasagna, and she could claim the sauce was homemade if she added enough basil and garlic and crap to it. "Salad on the side."

"Bread?" Cora asked. "You have to have bread, to sop up the sauce."

Rose checked the bread basket. The supermarket loaf she'd bought on Saturday would be fine if she cut it into slices. She should stick a note on it so Lori wouldn't eat it after school. "Thanks for the brownies." She'd thought she'd have to bake a dessert, but Cora's brownies were legendary. No one ever said no to her brownies. "Would you hate me if I took credit for your brownies? I'll tell everyone it's your recipe."

"Of course. They're all yours," Cora said with a wink. She picked up the Ireland brochure. "Ooh, planning a trip?"

An escape. "Not officially."

"You deserve a vacation. Can Glenn get the time off work? Didn't you already plan for that lake house in New Hampshire, the one with canoeing and the hiking and"—she fakes a shudder—"camping? Honestly, it's the bugs that would do me in. And the leeches in the lake. Didn't you have to pull leeches off of Lori's legs last year?"

"She's going to be a lifeguard there this summer," Rose said. "We're supposed to stay for three weeks." God, the packing for that trip! She didn't even want to think about it. The idea was to bring in everything they'd need so they wouldn't have to interrupt their idyllic time-away-from-the-modern-world for any reason—all the supplies, all the food, the tent, the sleeping bags, the grill, the little cook plate that never worked, the pots and pans, the folding chairs, the life vests, the towels, the swimsuits, the bug spray, the sunscreen. Ugh, the organization it required—the lists, the errands, the loads of laundry, the precooking of meals. "It's crossed my mind that they could do it without me this year."

"Ooh, that is a brilliant idea! Bill it as father-daughter time for them and take yourself to Europe!"

Buoyed by her approval, Rose brought out the other brochure. "I was thinking of possibly staying there for longer." There was a program to become a tour guide in Europe, she explained. You went on a thirty-day tour of fifteen countries, with lectures on how to lead your own tours and how to handle various situations, as well as history and culture classes. At the end, you got a certificate that allowed you to apply for jobs at a range of companies.

"You want to be a tour guide? In Europe?"

"It's the perfect way to see it all." Rose flipped open the pages. "Look at how many countries! I know getting certified isn't cheap, and if I had any relevant experience, it wouldn't be necessary. But PTA president isn't exactly a qualification for an expectant tour guide of Ireland. Or Greece. Look at the pictures of Greece."

"You want a *job* in *Europe*? I have to point out, Rose, that you don't live in Europe."

"But I could! For a time."

"You mean, when you and Glenn retire, right? Is this what he wants for his retirement?" Cora's voice was laced with doubt. She'd known Glenn as long as Rose had, and he'd never expressed any interest in living outside of Greenborough. He didn't even like traveling to new places all that much. He liked New Hampshire because his family had gone there for decades. He liked vacation, but always to familiar places. He'd always pushed her ideas for more adventurous travel down the road—Lori was too young, work was too busy, and wasn't it nice around here for the summer? It would be a shame to miss out on enjoying their beautiful home in the summer weather. Plus, there was the cost and the hassle. He didn't want to go somewhere you needed to change money, where he couldn't order what he wanted from a menu because he couldn't read it, or where he'd feel helpless. Even when she'd told him she'd do all the planning and preparing . . . Even when she *did* lay it all out, eliminate any spontaneity, and plan every hotel and restaurant, he didn't like that Europe didn't have the same kind of chain hotels, the food he was familiar with. *How do you know what you're getting?* Besides, he didn't want to be on a plane that long. *So uncomfortable!* And Lori . . . she was the same. You asked her where in the world she wanted to go, if she could travel anywhere she wanted, and she'd shrug and say "my room." On an exciting day, she'd say "Boston," but only if her friends could come.

Rose was sick of it. How long did she have to wait for what *she* wanted? When did she get to be the priority? It was always later, later, later. Why couldn't someday be now? Lori was fourteen. She could do her own laundry, cook a few basic meals, certainly make herself a sandwich. She took the bus to school, and she could get rides for anything else she wanted to do, if it wasn't close enough to bike. She didn't need to be watched or entertained the way she had when she was little. She'd be fine. A fourteen-year-old needed some space from her mother anyway, didn't she? And Glenn. He was an adult. He'd manage. Besides, she wasn't going to leave permanently. Just . . . until she could breathe again without wanting to scream. "I was thinking of it more as a sabbatical. You know, like professors at a university take. I'd go for a season. One season a year. Glenn and Lori will be fine."

"She's fourteen," Cora said. "She needs you now more than ever."

Rose snorted. "She needs me out of her hair."

"She only thinks that. You remember being fourteen. We thought we were so mature. Ready to take on the world!" She chuckles as she opens the fridge and begins taking out salad ingredients: tomatoes, cucumbers, onions. "Spinach or iceberg? You eat iceberg? Voluntarily?"

"Glenn likes it," Rose said, putting the iceberg lettuce back. She missed that take-on-the-world feeling. It wasn't a part of herself she'd wanted to outgrow. "I thought you'd be supportive."

Cora sighed. "If I thought you meant it—"

"I do!"

"Oh, and that's why you've discussed it with Glenn and Lori? You've had family discussions about how you'll afford this, how they'll manage without you, and why it's important to you?" Cora shook her head. "I know you. You haven't talked to them. You've just kept the brochure in—let me guess—one of the kitchen drawers?—and you take it out whenever you're feeling overwhelmed or sad."

Ouch. "I think it's doable."

"I think you like knowing the possibility exists. But you know it's not actually feasible, which is why you don't bring it up with them, because you know how they'd react." Cora waved her hand at the stainless steel sink, the spotless backsplash, the yard. "This is your life, and you can't just abandon it. What kind of mother walks out on her family to jaunt around Europe 'for a season'? What kind of wife? You know that's what they'll all say. You'll ruin your marriage and your relationship with your daughter." She pulls the bottle of wine out of the bag. "Okay, we're having this now, and you're going to get all this"—she pointed at the brochure—"out of your system before Glenn and his coworkers get here."

Rose picked up the brochure and caressed it with her fingertips. "Or I could finally take the plunge and chase my dreams. You know I've always wanted to see the world."

Cora softened, getting out two wine glasses and the corkscrew from Rose's drawer. "All right then, say you do it: What's your first step? Just pack and walk out the door, or have an actual conversation with Glenn and tell him what you want? Because I tell you right now that if the former is your plan, it's stupid and selfish. But if it's the latter, then yes, I'll support you, and I'll help you talk through what you're going to say. I'll even help pay for your plane ticket, if you need it. And I'll sign up for your first tour. But you need to decide if you want it badly enough to give up what you have."

"What am I giving up?" Rose asked. "Another year of PTA president? Another year of driving Lori to lessons, of packing for an annual camping trip that I hate, of keeping the house and the yard spotless? For what? So the neighbors don't glare at me? What's the point of it all? What's the point of my life?"

Cora uncorked the wine and poured two glasses half full, then topped them each off with another splash. "You just described my life, except I'm PTA secretary. And I don't camp." Her voice was light, but Rose knew her well enough to know she was hurt.

Rose winced. She hadn't meant to insult Cora. Usually, she was more careful, but today . . . *Today isn't different from any other day.* And that was exactly the problem. "The lawn service mowed this morning. Glenn is talking about how we should do it ourselves because it's wasteful to pay someone to do it, and he has his uncle's mower that he's sure he could fix up one of these weekends. Of course, we all know who will end up mowing every weekend that he's called into the office or wants to go to a barbecue or has to visit his mom."

"So you want to leave your life, your gorgeous house, and your family because you don't want to mow the lawn?" Cora asked. "Jesus, Rose, that is the epitome of 'the grass is always greener.' You realize that going to Europe won't solve whatever problems you think you have, right? *Wherever you go, you bring yourself with you.* I can't remember who said that. If you're unhappy, *fix* things. Walking out on your family isn't the kind of thing that people forgive. You can't just run away."

"It's not running away. It's making a change."

Cora sipped her wine and sighed. It was a we've-had-this-conversation-too-many-times-to-count kind of sigh, even though Rose hadn't shown her the brochure before. "If you really wanted a different life, you would have chosen one."

"You think I don't mean it?" She'd wanted to travel for forever. She'd never intended to become trapped in this town. She hadn't even imagined herself married with a kid. That had all just . . . happened.

"I think you don't mean it."

"Ouch." Rose flopped into a chair. "It wasn't that I chose this life. I kept taking step after step, and somehow I ended up here. There were always expectations and never an exit ramp. There was no point where the road forked."

Cora groaned. "You are the least passive person I know. Don't pretend anyone did this to you. You fell in love. You got married. You are the one that went on all those real estate tours and turned down house after house until you found this one. It was perfect, you told me. You loved the yard and the perfect flowers. You loved the skylights. You loved the garage. It was the house you were supposed to have, you said. You're the one who ran for PTA president, who made flyers and phone calls. I wasn't even going to join, but you talked me into it. You started our book club. You baked cupcakes for Lori's birthday every year. You had the idea for the flower sale. You campaigned for the library renovation, remember? You organized all the fundraising. You badgered the town officials. Ugh, all the phone calls we made! And the signatures we had to get—you're the one who insisted we go door to door and stand outside the supermarket. Point is: you weren't swept along by any tide. You dove into this ocean yourself."

All of it was true. She was proud of the library renovation. She'd even helped with the design, a nautical theme. The circulation desk was going to look like the hull of a ship once it was all finished. She'd been the one to start their town's Girl Scout troop as well, after she learned the boys had two Boy Scout troops. She'd insisted the girls earn interesting badges, like in world culture and carpentry and international foods. Lori had been a Girl Scout until this year. *How can I leave?*

Lori was about to start high school. She'd want to date, and Glenn wouldn't be around to help with any of that. He'd be home in time for dinner, and if Rose left, who would make that dinner? She liked to think he'd do what she did and learn to cook. All it required was reading recipe books and planning ahead a bit, which he was more than capable of. But she could see how it would unfold. Whether he meant for her to or not, Lori would step in with the chores and dinners and the laundry.

She'd make the appointments and ensure the lawn was mowed and that the mail was taken in and the fridge was stocked. He'd feel bad, but he'd be busy, and Lori would be good at it, because she was clever and liked to be helpful. Everyone would praise her about how she was stepping up, filling in for her absentee mother, and she'd fall for the praise. She wouldn't question it. *She'd fall into the same trap I did, made by other people's expectations.* How could Rose do that to her daughter? "I know it wouldn't be fair to Lori, but . . ."

"Once she's off to college. Or married. Or whatever she wants to do, that's when you can flit off to Europe if you want," Cora said. "I'll even go with you."

Rose laughed. "You shouldn't make promises you don't mean."

"You shouldn't make plans you don't intend to follow," Cora said. "Rose, I don't mean to be harsh or to shoot down your dreams, but are you really willing to give all of this up, your life here? Because that's what this means. You can't guarantee Glenn will stay with you if you traipse off to Europe for a season every year. And I know you—you'll want nice hotels and nice meals. Unless being a tour guide pays a lot more than I think it does, Glenn won't be able to support your lifestyle and keep the house. Would you want him to sell it? And how would you explain your plan to Lori? She's not going to understand why her mother wants to live another life. She will be hurt in ways that can't be fixed. If you do this, everything will change, and I'm just not convinced you want that."

Each sentence felt like a slap, especially since she knew all of it was true. Rose folded the brochure and put it back in the envelope. "It's not that I don't want what I have; it's that I want *more*."

"You've always wanted everything," Cora said. "And I've always loved that about you. But we get one life and the same set of hours in a day. Choosing one path means not choosing another. You can't have both."

"I'll find a way," Rose said. And then she sighed heavily. *Cora's right.* How could she walk away from the life she'd made. "Maybe not now, but someday."

Cora held up her glass. "To someday."

Rose clinked it. "To someday."

They both drank, and she tucked the brochure into the drawer. She wasn't going to toss it. There was still a possibility—she just couldn't go right now. Not without jeopardizing the life she had. But someday . . .

"Hey, what if you made a wish?" Cora suggested. "Like a promise to your future self. You'd be putting out into the universe that you want this in your future. We could make a pilgrimage out to that statue in the woods—you remember the one, from prom night—if it's still there."

Rose laughed. It was something her old self would have done, back before . . . well, all of this. She placed her glass down. "I'm sure it's still there. Who would take it? That ugly thing? Besides, who else but us even knows it exists?" She wiggled her glass in the air. "We could bless it with wine. It needs a sacrifice to work properly."

Cora grinned and took another sip of wine. "You're totally making that up. Glenn didn't sacrifice anything, and he got his wish. You just want to get drunk in the woods like we're kids again."

"If I wanted to recreate that night, I'd be wearing a lot more chiffon." Rose sighed as reality settled on her shoulders again. "I love the idea, but I've a lasagna to bake." She sipped more wine before standing up. "You could stay for dinner. Unless Mike needs you home?"

"He's late at the hospital again," Cora said. "I'd love to stay." Standing, she looped her arm through Rose's, and they strolled across the kitchen. "You want to know a secret? I'm glad you aren't going anywhere. I'd miss you too much."

Rose laughed again as she turned on the oven and began pulling ingredients from the cabinets. "You are truly terrible at keeping secrets."

Cora laughed. "I just need more practice."

CHAPTER TWENTY-THREE

LORI

2022

Lori shivered in the hospital gown. The worst part about doctor visits was how exposed the robe made you feel, even if you wrapped it as close as you could and tucked it under your thighs. She fidgeted, feeling like she was eight instead of forty-seven, and the paper crinkled beneath her. She felt as if anyone who walked in would see all her mistakes, all her lies, and all her flaws, in addition to her flesh.

She checked the clock, wondering if Elisa had heard about the garden-store job, which would never in a million years pay the cost of the blood work and the ultrasound, never mind the CT scan that the doctors insisted she needed. But it would buy a few meals and pay the overdue electric bill. Lori felt a flash of guilt. She'd borrowed a woman's identity to get these tests. Rena Hamilton was going to have a hell of a time unraveling the confusion that Lori was about to leave in her wake. She consoled herself knowing it would be over soon. The results from the earlier tests were in, and this was her final appointment, to discuss what they said. After, she'd drop Rena's purse in the hospital parking lot and never use it again. She'd promised Elisa she'd see a doctor—she just hadn't expected it to snowball into this circus.

It had started with a cough that never quite seemed to go away. Plus a little indigestion, but that could be explained by her inconsistent diet. She'd started having trouble swallowing a year ago, and she'd hid it from Elisa. It was hard, though, to hide how tired she felt or the weight she'd lost. Sometimes she'd wake up in the middle of the night and just *hurt*, with no explanation as to why. For a while, she thought it could be long COVID, but the symptoms didn't fit. Elisa had begun to nag her to see a doctor, but Lori knew what that would lead to: appointment after appointment, test after test, none of which they could afford, all so some doctor could tell her that she needed to get more sleep, eat better food, and eliminate stress. It was the constant worry of their lives that made her feel this way. She was always calculating their next move, how they'd afford it, what jobs they could find, where they would live, how they would eat, how she would need to degrade herself so that her daughter wouldn't have to. Every day was a steady stream of tasks just to avoid disaster. And yes, it was simpler now that Elisa was an adult and fully capable of shouldering half the burden, but Lori hadn't been so perpetually tired back then.

I've been living like this far too long. That's all that's wrong with me.

She'd lied to herself so much over the years that when the doctor delivered the news that it was cancer and had metastasized, she filed it away as another story, belonging to a life that wasn't hers.

There were more words that didn't feel like hers: "fourth stage" and "spread to lymph nodes, bones, liver, lungs." It had started in her stomach, he believed, but unfortunately had spread. She stared down at her clenched hands while the doctor's voice washed over her. Her body didn't feel like hers. She wondered if she could leave it behind for Rena, along with her purse and ID and helpful health insurance cards.

He was a kindly man. Later, she wouldn't remember his name or what he looked like, but she could remember the soothing sound of his soft voice as he laid out her options. There weren't many. They might grant her a few months more, but they would be painful and exhausting and intrusive.

"And expensive?" she asked.

He attempted a kind smile. "Health insurance should cover the vast majority, after the deductible is met, but yes, you will need to dip into your savings if you choose to proceed with treatment. We can set you up with a conversation with our financial people to discuss—"

It's not my health insurance. And of course, she had no savings. It had never been possible to save anything more than leftovers from a stolen breakfast.

Most of what he said next was a blur, but she did hear him say she should think carefully about the quality of life she'd have in exchange for a possible few months. Given the low probability of success and the toll that it would take on her body, he didn't advise treatment.

"What would you recommend I do then?" Lori asked, in a voice she thought sounded calm and rational, not as if her mind was fleeing a thousand miles away, to the top of the Eiffel Tower. All she could hear was the wind, the elevator, the chatter of tourists. All she could feel was the memory of a kiss.

She could be made more comfortable, he said.

A nurse joined them.

There were more words. An official diagnosis. More info sheets for her to read. More tests they should run. More appointments to be made. It was her choice whether to pursue treatment or not; he merely wanted to be honest about the likelihood of success and the quality of her life in the interim. Did she have someone to call? It might be simpler to navigate with an ally by her side. It was a lot to take in at once. Take some time to absorb and come back with questions.

She wasn't coming back.

She only had one question: "How much time?"

A year. Maybe less. More if she was lucky.

"Ten months?" she asked.

The doctor hesitated. "There are no guarantees . . ." He continued, discussing statistics and probability and the influence of other variables such as lifestyle choices . . . But yes, he could reasonably approximate that amount of time.

Ten months.

I can work with that.

◆ ◆ ◆

Lori deposited Rena's purse with her keys, license, lipstick, and cancer-free life on a bench in the hospital parking lot. She'd planned to take the bus home, but the thought of being crammed in with all those bodies and their smells . . . *I'll walk. And I'll rest when I need to.*

It took her four hours to reach home, and it felt as if she walked through just about every possible emotion. By the time she reached the beat-up garage they were living above this month, Lori felt something unexpected:

Relief.

There was a name for what was wrong with her, even if she'd forgotten the exact term for her diagnosis, and she had a timeline. Even more, she had a purpose. She had approximately ten months to make sure Elisa never had to live the kind of life she'd lived, that she wouldn't ever experience the kind of fear she had, make the choices and sacrifices, or feel the hunger and unending exhaustion.

Circling around the back of Speedy Repairs Garage, Lori climbed the steps up to the door. She had to stop halfway and rest. It was, she considered, most likely a mistake to walk home from the hospital, given her diagnosis. She doubted the doctor with the soft voice would have approved, but she didn't need his approval. In fact, she didn't need anyone's. All she needed was ten months, and she had that.

There was a lot of living she could do in ten months, if she tried.

Inside, Lori called, "Elisa? Are you home?" She saw immediately that the answer was no. The apartment had only two rooms: a kitchen and living space, with a tiny bathroom in the corner, and a flimsy wall to block off a bedroom area. She slept there, and Elisa used the old couch with the sagging cushions in the primary room. It smelled heavily of oil, gas, and rancid car fluids that she couldn't name. But the perk was that it had a working phone, hers so long as she answered for the garage owners when it rang off-hours. Speedy Repairs was the only garage in town that promised twenty-four-hour tow service. She just had to take a message and then call down a list of employees and see who was awake and sober enough to take the job, and in return, the owners sliced their rent in half.

Until now, she hadn't had much need for the phone.

She had a rule against mementos: you didn't take a piece of any place with you to the next locale. It was too dangerous to be tied to a potential home. But she did bring a small book of useful information: notes on future places to live, tips on where to find jobs, and one special phone number that she had been carrying for eight years. She'd looked it up on a library computer one afternoon while Elisa was at school and had been carrying it with her ever since. She'd never let Elisa know she carried this book or what it contained.

Lori pulled it out from beneath the couch cushion and opened to the number. No name. No address. She let her fingers run over the digits that she'd sworn she would never call. She hadn't allowed herself to memorize it, hoping someday she'd have the strength to tear out the page and leave it behind. She carried the book over to the phone.

Cancer.

Ten months.

She wasn't going to tell him any of that. She was simply going to do what she'd never allowed herself to do before. Lori dialed the number.

It rang once, twice . . . *Do I leave a message?*

No, what would I say?

If he didn't answer, that was fate.

If he—

"Hello."

His voice sounded the same. She felt lightheaded, and her breath lodged in her throat. "Mark?" she managed.

"Yes. Who is this?"

Lori closed her eyes. "You probably don't even remember me, and I know I shouldn't have called out of the blue like this, but—"

"Lori?"

Her breath caught once again. "Yes."

He remembered, even recognized her voice. She hadn't expected that. She was gripping the phone so hard that her hand started to sweat. She forced her fingers to loosen before she broke the plastic. It had been years since anyone had said her real name. Back then, it was all she used. She hadn't begun cycling through her various identities with their attendant stories—why she had come to town, why she had no paperwork, why she couldn't provide references, why she had to be paid in cash, why she could only pay rent in cash. Usually, she said she was escaping an abusive husband. It had been such a convincing cover that he almost seemed real, which made Mark feel like a dream. "You remember me."

"Of course. How . . . ? Where . . . ? No, I don't know what to ask."

She didn't know what to say. That made them a pair.

"Okay. This is . . . Yeah. Um, don't . . . hang up. Don't go. It's . . . ah, good to hear your voice. How did you find me? Why are you calling?" He didn't sound hostile. He sounded shaken.

Lori didn't know how to answer the second question. "I looked you up. Online. A while back, but I just . . . I didn't know what to say."

"So, you're calling to say hi? After twenty-five years?"

Yes. And to say she was sorry and that she'd thought about him every single day and wondered about the life she might have had, that Elisa might have had. How would she tell him about Elisa? She tried to gauge whether he was angry or curious or something altogether different. She couldn't tell over the phone. "Do you still like smelly cheese?"

He laughed as if she'd startled him. "Do you still like Munster?"

Tears leaked from the corners of her eyes. And from there, they began talking as if years hadn't passed, as if they were at a little café in Paris. If she closed her eyes, she could smell the wine and cigarettes from the other tables, and she could hear a street violinist playing near the metro station.

He told her he was divorced, and she tried not to hope.

She told him she had a daughter but no husband.

She didn't tell him Elisa was his.

"Her father hasn't been in our lives," Lori said. Not a lie, at least not entirely.

"I'd love to meet her," Mark said. Even though he didn't know the whole truth. Perhaps because he didn't know? She clutched the phone tighter.

She didn't tell him about the cancer or the ten months or the many lives she'd led or the many things she'd done to keep her daughter—their daughter—fed and warm and safe, but she told him about the best pizza she'd eaten in a little dive, surprisingly, in Illinois. He told her that he was taking care of his mom now, after his dad had died. He told her that he'd taken up beekeeping, and she laughed at the image of him in a beekeeper's outfit.

He invited her to visit, and Elisa, if they wanted to come.

Lori said yes. She could feel the sap in her veins, moving sluggishly within her bloodstream, and she could feel the leaves just beneath her skin, waiting. But she said yes anyway. And she hoped Elisa would someday understand. Maybe even forgive her.

CHAPTER TWENTY-FOUR

ELISA

Now

I dart out of the Book Cellar right at closing time, anxious to speak with Cora. It's nearly dinner time, so she should be home, perhaps feeding her birds. I wonder what I'll say to her. *She knew my grandmother.* As I walk through town, I wonder: Did Rose and Cora visit this post office? Did they walk on this sidewalk and avoid that tree root? Did they shop in Second Chances, the thrift shop on the corner of Main and Edison? Or in that flower store? How about the pharmacy? Was that here when they were in high school? Was this bench here, and did they ever sit on it? Did Cora live in the same house, and did my grandmother visit her there? Did they walk down the driveway together, beneath the same trees? Did they watch the shadows?

The caged birds are quiet as I approach the house, despite the advent of evening, and I tug on my sleeves, grateful they cover the bark scab. I don't know how quickly it will spread. I've never tested its limits.

I don't know when Mom's symptoms began. Unlike me, she considered Mark's house home from day one. For all I know, it could have taken root then. Or perhaps it was earlier, the moment she decided to return to him, her one true love, my father, and never leave again. Mark claimed she must have been sick for a while, for it to have progressed so far so quickly. She hid it from me, from Mark, from everyone. As soon as he suspected she wasn't well, he'd pushed her to see doctors, just as I had when her cough first appeared, but there was nothing they could do—the cancer had spread too far, they said.

At first, it bothered me they called it that. "Cancer." Not "curse." They tossed around the words "tumors" and "malignant cells," and she let them, while she felt bark and chlorophyll spreading within her. She told me it didn't matter who called it what. This was her fate, and it couldn't be stopped, regardless of how others saw it.

Let them think it a metaphor. Cancer or curse, I lost her regardless of the cause. But while I couldn't change her fate, I still hold out hope that I can change mine.

As I step onto the porch, the nearest songbird trills at me. It's yellow with a rust-colored streak on its belly, yellow-and-black-streaked wings and tail feathers, and black beady eyes, and its song is quick and pure: *"Sweet sweet sweet sweet!"*

I walk along the porch, and the nearest birds burst into chaotic song. *"Jejeje jeet jeet!"* A jumble of notes that explodes into a trill from a tiny brown bird.

A gray-and-white bird fluffs its feathers. *"Teela woo!"*

Bright red with black wings and a black tail: *"Hurry hurry hurry!"*

Another whistles, and one of the porch doors swings open. "Now hush, my dears. Dinner's coming soon," Cora says as she toddles outside. She sees me and halts. "Ah, that explains it. Elisa, is it?"

"Sorry to disturb them," I say. "They're beautiful."

"Oh, and don't they know it." She chuckles.

They're all cry-singing now, and it's a cacophony of chirps, trills, whistles, and calls. I have to raise my voice to be heard over them. "I was hoping to talk to you, Cora, if you're not too busy."

Cora opens her mouth to speak, then shakes her head at the clamor of birds and beckons to me. Carefully, she descends the porch steps onto the lawn. She walks as if a breeze could knock her over. I follow her to a bench by the sculpture garden. It's in disrepair, like the rest of the yard, with vines growing over the various granite statues. There's a Greek theme: Perseus with a sword in one hand and a Medusa head in the other, nymphs dancing in a circle, and an old pockmarked statue of the three Fates that hasn't weathered time well. It's off kilter, stuck at an angle in the lawn, as if it's broken off its pedestal, and the faces of the three women are chipped and worn. This garden was probably a beautiful spot years ago, the kind of place where you'd have a wedding, with flowers and sculptures peppering the lawn. I think of my mother's wedding, shortly before she died. It had been outside and lovely.

Cora sits with a sigh, and I sit beside her. "Sometimes those birds are more trouble than they're worth," she says. "But then I think of the alternative . . . I can't part with them. They'll settle down once the sun sets."

Above, the sky is tinted orange. "How long have you been collecting birds?" It isn't the question I want to ask, of course, but it's an easier transition than *Why did you lie? What do you know?*

"Eh, years and years. Since my Allison was about your age."

Allison *is* about my age. But I don't correct her. "What made you start?"

Cora fixes me with a look that I can't quite discern, and I wish I'd led with another topic. She's seen through me. "That's not what you want to ask me, is it? You aren't really interested in an old lady and her feathered friends."

I exhale. This is going to be one of *those* conversations. It's so much easier to sneak up on what I want. Like dumpster diving. You stroll up to the subject, never let them see your desperation, and dance around the key questions so that they don't realize they've told you as much as they have. But Cora is too alert for that, so I plunge in. "I've discovered that my grandmother used to live here, at least for a time. She went to Greenborough High School. Played on the softball team. With you."

"Oh?"

"She went by Rose Grayson and later became Rose Ellert." I pull out my photo and show it to her a second time. I try to keep my voice steady so I don't scare her off. "I don't know if you knew her after high school, but the photo—it's from her wedding day, which apparently took place here in Greenborough."

Cora stares at the picture, and I think she is going to deny it again. Perhaps she doesn't remember. It was many decades ago, and it could have been just a moment where teammates celebrate a win. It's possible that they didn't know one another well, and my grandmother didn't make a lasting impact—but Cora nods at the photo and looks out at the trees.

"Glenn's family had quite a bit of money, especially for around here. She had her photos taken on their lawn. She did look beautiful that day. I told her she did, even though she hated that dress."

"You remember her?" I file each tidbit away.

"Of course."

"Then why did you . . ." I catch myself before I say the word "lie." People tend to clam up when you call them liars. *Soft and casual. Stroll.* She has more to say, but I have to coax it out of her. "Why didn't you tell me before?"

"She was my best friend," Cora says, "and I miss her every day." Tears wet the puffy skin under her eyes. "I couldn't make her stay, as hard as I tried."

Of course she couldn't. Not my family. We don't stay. I breathe easier. Rose *was* cursed, and my mom hadn't lied to me. There must be another explanation for why Rose was able to live here through multiple years of high school, possibly even until marriage. Perhaps a weakening of the curse? Or a technicality she was able to exploit? Maybe Rose knew more about the curse and its rules than we did. Mom and I did the best we could, always erring on the side of caution. "It's not your fault. Some people just have to keep moving, even if they don't want to."

"She wanted to see the world, and I should have let her." She smiles at me with such intensity that it's clear she wants me to understand what she felt for my grandmother, though it isn't clear why, when she denied knowing her earlier. "I was just so afraid that if she left, if she left *me*, she'd never come back. I didn't understand . . . Anyway, you didn't come here to hear about an old lady's regrets. You want to learn about your grandmother."

Yes! This is what I want! I feel as though my heart is going to explode within me. I've never been with anyone who possessed answers before. What did she mean, *I should have let her*? It wasn't up to Cora. I hope she hasn't been feeling guilt for something she couldn't have prevented—the women in our family have to move on. "Please, anything you can tell me. I know she graduated high school here. And she married Glenn Ellert." I don't know if she left between high school and marriage, but I know she returned. Mom and I—we never returned to a place. Never dared. Changed our names so we wouldn't be found and made to return.

"They were high school sweethearts."

"How long did she stay in Greenborough after that? I especially want to know: Where did she go next?" And why did she come back? And at what point was my mother born? Did Mom ever live in Greenborough? Did Cora ever meet her? No, that's not the most important question. *I need to trace the curse back to its origin, if I'm to understand it.* "Wait, let me back up. Where was Rose born? Do you know? Where did she live before she came to Greenborough?" If I can figure out the curse's beginning, perhaps I can find the key to its end.

Cora looks at me as if I'm confused about obvious facts, and I want to scream, *Tell me what I'm missing,* but I wait until she speaks. "She was born here, same as me," Cora says. "Our mothers used to push our strollers together, side by side down Main Street. I don't remember a time before I knew Rose. We were inseparable from before we could walk and talk. There are stories of us as babies." She chuckles at her memories. "Rose learned to walk before I did, and she was cruising around the park while I would crawl around. Until one day, apparently, she got so far ahead of me that I just stood right up and *ran* after her! Yes, that was Rose and me. She was always running somewhere, and I was always the tether that kept her from getting lost."

"So she lived here. Birth through . . ."

"Birth until the day she died," Cora says with conviction. "She never did see the world, as much as she wanted to. She'd wanted to, after high school, but there wasn't enough money—she did attend college, but she lived at home and commuted, to save. And then . . . she was married and then Lori was born . . . She always thought—*I* always thought—there would be more time. She could see it later, when her family didn't need her so much, when it wouldn't upset Glenn, when Lori didn't need her, and later when her parents weren't sick . . . It just wasn't done back then, for a mother to leave."

But Cora had said that she couldn't make Rose stay. Did she mean she couldn't make her stay *alive*? I feel as though I've plunged into murky water, and I can't tell which way is up. I know it shouldn't throw me as badly as it does—I suspected all of this from the microfiche, but hearing it confirmed unsettles me like a wave hitting a ship. I cling to my mother's name. "Lori. What happened to her?"

"Ah, sweet Lorelei. Our little Lori." Cora sighs. "She was the sweetest child. So kind and polite. Always a good girl. She never acted out. Rose just couldn't understand her. But Lori took after Glenn. Even tempered, a little bit scared. She liked things the way she liked them, and she'd get anxious if anything changed."

That . . . doesn't sound like Mom at all.

What if Cora's memories are mixed up? What if she's not remembering Rose and Mom at all? What if none of this is true? *She has no reason to lie.* She's speaking with too much certainty for these to be false memories.

"She was engaged to a nice boy. Real sweet boy. Can't remember his name or his face, but I think he was handsome? She was going to get married when Rose took sick."

I nod, knowing what it's like to leave a real sweet boy, and then it hits me . . . "Wait. My mother lived here too? Until she was old enough to be engaged?"

"Oh yes. She went to Greenborough High also, with my Allison."

I shake my head. She couldn't have. It was hard enough to comprehend that my grandmother hadn't been struck by the curse—the one Mom had said over and over was inherited, nothing to be done—but my mom as well . . .

She had a childhood. Here.

She went to high school here. She was engaged here.

"She was crushed by Rose's death," Cora said. "Broke off her engagement with barely an explanation. I heard she mailed that poor boy his ring—it was a family heirloom. He's lucky it wasn't lost in the mail. She never came back. She didn't even stay for a week beyond the funeral." She sighs. "I never knew what happened to her."

I do.

But I don't say a word. Behind us, a crow's caw cuts through the songbirds' trills. It silences them for a moment, and then they start up again. "Ugh, never a moment's peace." Cora pushes herself up. I want to follow and ask more questions, but I feel the weight of it all grounding me to the bench. "Would you like some lemonade? Allison made a fresh batch this morning. She knows it's my favorite."

"That would be lovely, thank you," I say automatically, because my mother taught me never to say no to free food or drink. My mother, who had a childhood in one place, who left when her own mother died, and who never came back. I don't know what to believe.

It can't be true. It makes no sense.

There are things one knows about how the world works. Certainties. Foundational facts. If you drop a toy, it falls to the ground, and sometimes it breaks. If you turn the shower on too hot, it will scald you.

If the sun is just right, you can see the moon during the day. You learn very quickly that people are capable of random acts of kindness and random acts of cruelty, and that people who are cruel are usually hurting themselves. Not that that makes the cruelty okay. Also, people will judge you by your appearance—and by how you speak, how you stand, how you smile, and how you dress—but you can sometimes slip by invisibly, unjudged, if you mimic what they expect. I know a dozen ways to ask for a job, a hundred ways to scavenge for food, and at least as many ways to say goodbye.

I hear the porch door behind me, and I realize I have to get a grip. I have this opportunity to ask as many questions as I can, before the curse forces me to move on. At least I have an explanation for why the scabs are forming after such a brief time here—this town was home for both my grandmother and my mother, which makes it feel like it could be mine too.

Why was my mother able to have a home?

And what made her leave?

If the curse began with her, what caused it? Was it something to do with this town? Does Cora know? Hearing the creak of a door and the chirp of the birds, I look for her, but it's Allison coming across the lawn. She's smiling, gripping two glasses of lemonade so hard that her knuckles look like fat pearls. "Mother said you'd stopped by."

She hands me one of the glasses, and I thank her.

"Just got back from work," I explain. The words feel thick in my mouth. It's hard to have a normal conversation in the wake of all these revelations. "Is your mother—"

"She'll be back soon," Allison says. "She's tending to her birds." She looks over her shoulder at the house, and then says, "I heard you're working at the Book Cellar with Owen."

"Yes." I wonder who told her. "I'm sorry for not telling you myself, but I knew you two have a history, and I didn't want it to—" I cut myself off. My brain latches onto something that Cora said: she claimed my mother went to Greenborough High with Allison. She must have meant they both graduated from the same school, not that they were classmates. Allison is loosely my age, not my mother's, so of course they couldn't have been in high school together. What else was Cora mistaken about? Shaking my head, I focus on the conversation at hand. "I'm sorry for not telling you that I'm working with your ex."

"You can't go back there," Allison says. "It's not safe. You need to leave."

I feel my arm itch where the bark has burrowed into my skin. I'm grateful Allison can't see it through my shirt. "I don't plan to stay long. But what do you mean, it's not safe? It's a bookshop."

"Owen is not what he seems."

Okay, this is an alarming turn. "What do you mean?" He seems very nice. Awkward but sweet. Plus, he owns a bookshop, which counts for a lot. Then again, I know full well that people can have many sides and many secrets. I rarely trust anyone with mine.

She drops her voice to a whisper. "I tried to leave."

"I'm sorry?" I remember how she looked at me. What she said. *Help me leave.*

"So many times, I've tried to leave." Another glance back at the house. "Mom doesn't like me to talk about it. Other people don't understand, you see. But I can't . . . I can't sit by and let the same thing happen to you. I saw you and Owen the other day. I saw how he looked at you, like you were new and shiny, like he could cling to you. He'll cling to you, if you don't get away."

I stand up. "Do you remember? The other day? You were in pink—"

She nods. "Yes. I ran into the street."

"You were hurt."

"I knew the truck was there. I thought—" She sucks in air, cutting herself off, as the porch door squeaks open again. "Stay away from Owen."

"Why? What did he do?" He hadn't been outside when she ran.

Cora calls to us as she wobbles her way down the porch stairs, "You should let that girl rest, Allison. No talking her ear off. She's got a job, and she's earned an evening of peace. You know, you could get yourself a job, Allison. It would be good for you."

Allison smiles at her. "I have a job, looking after you."

Cora tuts as she crosses the lawn. "A job out in the world, with other people. At your age, you should be seeing friends. You should find a new boyfriend, or reconnect with an old one. What about that nice boy, Owen?"

"Mother, don't start again. You know I can't. That piece of me—I can't."

"Elisa, you should talk to him—tell him he should get back with my Allison." Cora's halfway across the lawn. She's smiling so cheerfully. It's unnerving.

In a low voice, I say to Allison, "Tell me what he did. What's wrong with him?"

Allison shakes her head. "That's not the question."

I know what to ask: "What's wrong with you?"

Before Cora reaches us, Allison whispers. "I'm cursed. And it's his fault." She then raises her voice. "You should drink your lemonade before the ice melts. My mother and I need to feed her birds."

CHAPTER TWENTY-FIVE

Stars sprinkle the sky as I stand in front of the Book Cellar. It's dark inside, and the silhouette of the stacks form a cityscape—a peaceful view at odds with the way my skin feels, as if it wants to leap off my bones.

Charlie is a moving shadow within. He pauses by the window, and I see the reflection of his eyes from the streetlight. He stares at me, and I stare back.

"Where's Owen?" I ask.

He licks his front paw.

I try the door. Locked, of course. I wonder if there's a separate external door to his upstairs apartment, or perhaps a doorbell. Yes, there's a doorbell and a mail slot tucked behind a vine. I ring the bell, wishing I knew what I'm going to say. Do I begin with pleasantries or blurt out Allison's accusation? He's been friendly to me so far, but the friendliest cat can scratch when it feels cornered. What if he's dangerous? People often hide who they truly are; I know better than anyone. I've been so many different people over the years, tried on personalities and histories as if they were shirts in a store. I've been the carefree cool girl who glides into a bar like a breeze. I've slunk into coffee shops, nursed a latte and a grudge, and moved on. I've been the manic pixie dream girl, the hermit, and the con woman. I've been desperate and confident, chatty and withdrawn, full of secrets and an open book. I'm not even certain I know who the real me is anymore, or if there is one.

Still, I can't imagine I could have misjudged Owen so badly.

Far more likely that Allison is mistaken. Or lying. If so, maybe Owen can explain.

And if he did curse her . . . Why? Why would he? But if he did . . . maybe he can explain how, and if it can be reversed—and how, by extension, I can apply that knowledge. To me. Now.

Footsteps echo within, and a light switches on, illuminating one aisle of books as Owen shuffles to the door. He looks the same as when I left him less than an hour ago—hair slightly disheveled as if he's just woken from a nap, lips on the brink of a smile, penetrating eyes, as if he can see the shape of your soul. How do I ask him if he doomed his ex-fiancé? How do I ask him if he knows how to save me? I should have prepared for this conversation better.

Owen opens the door, and Charlie curls around his ankles and looks up at me. "Elisa, are you okay? Is anything wrong?"

Wrong? I'm not certain. My heart is beating so hard it feels as if it's echoing in my skull. This man, my almost friend, could hold the answers I've been seeking my entire life, or this could be another dead end. I don't know whether to hope or scream, and I feel like I could do both simultaneously. "Can we talk?"

He winces. "Ooh, those are terrible words. Come in."

"Sorry," I say, entering as he opens the door wider for me. "I didn't mean it to sound that way. You're right, it's an ominous phrase." My voice is light. I've had years of practice lying, disguising what I'm really feeling. Every time I moved with Mom: *Oh yes, this is a fine place to live.* Or: *School is fine. I'm making friends.* Or simply: *I understand.* But still, I should have used a different opening question with Owen. Those words. They're what I said to Tyler, before I tried to explain that I was leaving, that it wasn't because of him. He didn't believe me, of course. No one ever did. I wouldn't have bothered, except that without that conversation, I knew he'd look harder for me. With my explanation, perhaps he'd have a chance to move on.

Move on. What a phrase. As if we can ever really move on. Mom claimed it was possible, but look at where she ended up. All her lessons on how to let go, how to sever ties, how to cut off your heart, how to package your memories and lock them away. And she returned to die in the arms of a man she'd supposedly let go of over two decades earlier. Even she, the expert at leaving, couldn't "move on." How can anyone move on when you carry your past with you? I carry Tyler with me. In fact, I carry all of them, everyone I've ever cared about—Tyler and Jackie and Ruben and Destiny and Carlo and Evelyn, and my best friend, Suzie, from the third grade, who I pinky swore would always be my forever friend and then never saw again, the first promise I knowingly broke.

I have no photos of Suzie, but I can picture her perfectly: belly flat on the grass, the ribbon her mother had so carefully tied in her hair now serving as a tightrope for imaginary circus performers. We used pencil toppers with googly eyes as the actors in our recess dramas. The blue one was the acrobat, and the red one was the ringmaster. Their home was the big top, and they never left it.

He shuffles behind the desk and turns on an electric kettle. "Tea?"

Now that I know the truth, at least according to Allison, will he poison me? *Ah, now that's melodramatic.* First, Owen doesn't seem the type. Second, he doesn't know that I know.

Third, I don't know if it's true.

"No tea, thanks." I move a stack of books from a chair and sit, as if we're about to have an ordinary conversation, and wonder how on earth to begin. Charlie hops onto my lap, kneads my thighs with his claws, and then jumps down. Perhaps he can sense how tense I am and wants no part of it. He jumps onto the windowsill and curls up on a cushion.

"Do you need more hours? Fewer?" Owen pulls a stool out from behind the desk and sits while the electric kettle hums. "I can't pay you more."

"This isn't about work."

"Ah." He selects a tea bag and pours water. His mug says, "I'd rather be reading." He returns to his stool with the mug, looks at it. "Allison?"

I flinch.

"You're living in the caretaker house behind her mother's," Owen says. "At least that's what I heard—the ladies in the coffee shop thought I should know. I understand you felt it was awkward to tell me, given my past with her. Is she . . . okay?"

"Okay." Now that is a loaded word. Is she okay? She tried to run in front of a truck and then pretended she didn't. She whispers ominous warnings to her new tenant when she thinks her mother can't hear.

"She believes she's cursed." There. I spit it out.

The word floats in the air between us. I'm aware of the hum of the kettle, the rattle of the pipes in the wall, the wheeze of the cat's breath. Outside, a car passes, and its headlights sweep the bookshelves.

Owen emits a laugh. "She thinks *she's* cursed?"

He's going to deny it, which is expected whether he's guilty or not. I didn't expect this conversation to be easy, and I brace myself. "She didn't want to tell me more in front of her mother." Or perhaps she simply didn't want to tell me more. "I was hoping you could."

He frowns at the mug and stands up again to stir in sugar. Returns to his stool.

"She's the one who cursed *me*."

I blink.

I don't know what to say to *that*.

He sips the tea and grimaces before setting the mug aside. "After Allison broke off our engagement, I wanted a change. I wanted space—to think, to adjust, to grieve—and I wanted to give that to her as well. I thought she'd appreciate it." He sighs heavily. "I had a buyer for the bookstore, as well as a plan for where I would go. I've always wanted to do a cross-country road trip, see every state from Atlantic to Pacific, and visit the corniest tourist traps possible, like the world's largest ball of twine, Carhenge, the Gum Wall . . ."

I've been to all of those places, but I don't interrupt. Mom and I once visited as many tourist traps and roadside wonders as we could—they're surprisingly ideal for our kind of life. Many tourist traps hire people passing through without questioning their qualifications or requiring any tax documentation. In New Mexico, we worked at an Area 51 pop-up that offered "proof" of alien visits. One of my tasks was to paint scuff marks on the remains of a "spaceship" that had crash-landed in the desert. The fact that it consisted of parts of a Chevy truck wasn't as well hidden as the owner believed. Actually, that was part of its charm.

"I intended to crawl across the country until I found a place I wanted to settle for a while," Owen says. "I didn't have an end destination in mind, just that it wouldn't be here. Unfortunately, the buyer fell through. The bank couldn't contact him, and he never showed up to sign the paperwork. It was as if he disappeared. Fine, so he got cold feet. I could understand that. I found another solution: not a buyer, but a woman who wanted to run a bookshop. I'd still own it, collect a percentage of the profits, but I'd be free to leave Greenborough. She even wanted to rent my apartment. It was the perfect solution."

So far, all normal. I wait, as patient as a tree.

Another car passing outside throws light onto the shelves, then plunges them back into the shadows.

"My car broke down just outside of town, and I couldn't pay to either fix or replace it. But I was still determined to see my plan through." He smiles sadly. "I bought bus tickets. An even better idea, I thought. It would be an adventure, me and Charlie seeing the country, surrounded by strangers—off we went before I could change my mind. Halfway through Ohio, I fell asleep, and I woke as the bus was pulling back into the Greenborough station."

A shiver catapults up my spine.

He shakes his head. "I know what everyone said happened, when I tried to tell them: half-asleep, I boarded a bus in the wrong direction, and my subconscious took me and Charlie home."

I know the question I want to ask next, because I know what I would have done. "How many more times did you try?"

"Twice. On the next try, the bus broke down just over the town border. On my final try, I woke in the hospital with a concussion. Apparently, I blacked out while trying to board and hit my head on the pavement—I was dehydrated, they told me at the hospital, but I knew that wasn't it. I also knew I couldn't risk another attempt."

"Because you're cursed."

He nods. "I can't leave."

I want to laugh, but not because it's funny. He can't leave; I can't stay. *Aren't we a pair?* He could be lying, of course, or mistaken. All that he's experienced has a rational explanation, but then the same could be said about me—who better than me to understand when the truth is irrational? I've asked myself the forbidden question: Am I cursed, or does it just feel like I am? It's pointless when the end result is the same.

My mother is a willow tree who stands by a stream.

My mother is buried in a cemetery where not a single weed grows and all the flowers die in vases.

Which is true? Does it matter, when I'm alone either way?

"How do you know that Allison did this to you?" I ask.

"Once I recovered, I went to see her at her mother's place. She opened the door but didn't let me inside. She told me I was cursed to stay, and that was the last time in three years she's spoken to me. She wouldn't explain why or how or what she meant. I kept trying to talk to her, but she wouldn't answer the phone or my messages, wouldn't come to the door. I'd lurk around the supermarket and the post office, try to intercept her when she came to town. Her mother would encourage me to keep trying. She wanted us to get back together, I think. She'd invite me in, offer me a sandwich, dinner, but Allison refused to see me."

"What did her mother say about your curse?"

He laughs hollowly. "You can't go around telling an old woman you think their daughter cursed you. No, I told her mother that I wanted to talk to Allison, to resolve things and understand why . . ." He takes a deep, shaky breath. "You're the first person I've ever told all of this. Why aren't you saying it's all in my head?"

Because I'm cursed too. I wonder if this is how others feel when I tell them I can't stay, as if a hundred questions and doubts are vying to pass from my lips, but I can't let them all tumble out. *Stay focused on what's important.* Now isn't the time for my story. First, I need to understand what's happening here. I can't shake the feeling that it's bigger than Owen, than Allison, than me, and I need to know all of it. "Why would Allison claim that you cursed her, if you think she cursed you?"

He spreads his hands. "I have no idea. As I said, she won't talk to me."

"And you haven't told anyone else?" Maddie and Emma—they warned me on the bus, before I even arrived. A dead-end town, I thought, but is it more than that? A terrible suspicion creeps through me, and I very much hope I'm wrong.

It's a place people get stuck.

Owen shakes his head. "How? You can hear how it sounds. I can see in your eyes that you don't believe me, and you're the one who said the word 'cursed.'"

Oh no, that isn't it. "I *do* believe you. I just think you're wrong about the cause." It feels like I don't have enough pieces yet to understand how they connect. Or enough time to explain. *Come on, focus. You can figure this out.* I scratch at the bark on my arm. The skin around it itches, and I want to dig the hard lump out of my skin. It goes deeper than I can reach though, and I force myself to stop and to lay my hands on my lap. "When I took the bus here, I met Maddie and Emma . . ." I describe them and our conversation.

"You think Allison cursed Maddie and Emma too? But why would she? I don't think she even knows them. I only know them because they come into the bookstore and they're always at Bean Street."

"I think this is larger than a broken engagement. I think Allison is a victim too, that this touches more people than you know." Me. My mother. Our curses must be connected. It's too much of a coincidence. But *how?* He can't leave; I can't stay. What about the other coffee shop regulars? Monica, waiting for her bird-watcher who never returned. *I have measured out my life with coffee spoons.* And what about the waiter at Stu's Diner, endlessly cleaning the pie display case? I think, too, of the supposed ghosts in the library. "How many people want to leave but haven't?" I don't ask about the people who want to stay but can't; I'm not ready to go there yet.

"It's not something I talk about . . ."

Not a satisfying answer, but it doesn't matter. I'm on the edge of a cliff, the sea below me. It's dizzying to be so close to the answer but not be able to quite see it yet. I ask the next important question. "What have you done to try to break the curse?"

"Allison won't talk to me . . ." He trails off, and Charlie stretches, saunters across the books, and jumps onto Owen's lap. Owen scratches him between his ears, and Charlie leans against his fingers. His purr starts, a lawn mower rumble. "I suppose I never thought to try. I didn't think of it as something that could be changed. It's just how it is. I can't leave. Once I accepted that, well, I love my bookstore. I love this town, the people in it—and I can't help feeling that what happened with Allison, it has to be my fault. I don't know why she'd turn on me if I hadn't hurt her in some way. So, I suppose I think of this as my penance. I wasn't able to help her when she needed it. I wasn't able to see what she needed. Or to understand . . ." His voice catches, and he blinks down at Charlie. "Besides, what's so terrible about staying here? It's a much more rational choice than walking away from my life with no itinerary, no destination, merely wanting to see the country. How is that a life plan? That was just an escape. No, my life is here, in Greenborough, in my bookshop. It's not a terrible life."

"If you could leave," I ask, "would you?"

He doesn't hesitate. "Yes."

There's a hunger in his voice, and I know I have an ally. But will that be enough? "I think it has to do with the town itself."

"You think the *town* won't let me leave?"

It's a place people get stuck.

My heart starts to beat harder, and I stand up. There is a way to test my theory—that the curse is broader than Allison and Owen, that it's somehow to do with the town and not them.

And if I'm right about this, then I have a very serious problem. "That's exactly what I think. And I know a way to test it."

He shakes his head. "I told you. I can't leave."

"I believe you," I say. "But what I don't know yet is: Can I?"

CHAPTER TWENTY-SIX

There's only one bus leaving Greenborough tonight—right now. I have no time to return to the caretaker's house to reclaim my backpack, but it doesn't matter. I always keep the essentials on me—cash in my socks, IDs in my pockets, a travel toothbrush and a half-squeezed mini tube of toothpaste, and a granola bar.

This isn't the first time I've had to run; though, the reason is unique. Owen waits with me at the bus station.

"You'll come back, won't you?" Owen asks.

"Only if I fail."

"But . . ."

"I'll call the bookstore," I say. "You can research things here while I . . ." *While I escape my fate.* The bark itches my arm, and I have never felt more eager to leave, even though I know this place might hold answers or even *the* answer. "I'm sorry. I have to leave."

Maybe because my mother left, none of her descendants can safely stay? Maybe because my grandmother didn't, none of her descendants can safely leave? What if Mom never told me about this place because she never wanted me to risk being trapped here? I have no idea how the curse works, especially given all the new variables.

But I know that I have to be on this bus.

"Where will you go?" Owen asks. "What will you do?" He offered to buy the ticket, which I agreed to. He owes me for the handful of hours that I worked, and I owe him an explanation that I don't provide.

Instead, I shrug. "What I always do: keep moving."

Headlights splash across the station as the bus pulls around the corner, and its brakes squeal to a stop. The bus makes a whooshing sound as it settles, and the door opens. No one gets off. I don't know whether it's a good thing or a bad thing or totally meaningless. It is difficult not to read into every detail, as if each is a sign. I feel on edge, every bit of my skin aware of the prickle of the night breeze.

I can do this.

It's the one thing I'm good at: leaving.

I have done this thousands of times. This won't be any different, and once I'm safely away, then . . . I don't know what comes next, but I know this is the first step.

"Take care of Charlie," I tell Owen.

"Take care of yourself, Elisa."

"I always do."

I board the bus before either of us can say anything that we'll wish we didn't. My heart constricts, and I want to cry. I don't know Owen well, and it's abundantly clear that I can't stay in Greenborough without endangering myself. Perhaps he'll be able to uncover answers on his own. Perhaps I can assist from afar.

Still, he's different. He helped when he didn't have to. He listened when few others do. He smiles like his heart is open, like he's gifting it to you. I've never met anyone like him, and I doubt I ever will again.

I'll miss him.

I barely know him, but I'll miss him and his ridiculous book desk and his charming bookstore and his adorable cat and his kindness. Using the same technique I've used a thousand times, I try to fold my feelings into a neat little package, shove it into a box, and seal it. I know how to say goodbye. *I can do this.*

The smell of the bus—exhaust, fake leather, faint urine—settles me in its familiarity. I wonder how the curse would react if I decided that home was the open road, and then I push that thought far down, hoping that I haven't caused further complications.

I don't look out the window as the bus pulls away, but I know Owen is there, waiting in anticipation as the bus rattles down Main Street and out of Greenborough.

It doesn't break down.

There's no accident.

But I don't relax until we're an hour out of town.

◆ ◆ ◆

I am dreaming.

It's one of those dreams where I'm conscious of my state but have no clarity. It feels as though a metal tube has been placed around my rib cage, keeping my lungs from fully filling. I can only suck in a whisper of air at a time—enough to breathe, but I flail and thrash, needing to inhale an ocean-size amount of oxygen.

Wake up.

Maybe something fell on me. I try to picture the caretaker's cottage and imagine what could be pinning me in place. Perhaps a bookcase? Or I've fallen off the bed and rolled beneath it? The roof caved in?

But I don't wake. My eyes feel both open and shut, like my shallow breath that leaves me wanting more oxygen. Then darkness feels layered, shadows on top of shadows, and I try desperately to identify shapes in the black and gray.

It's just a dream. You'll wake soon.

I can feel my heart racing, and I wish I could take a deep breath to calm down—one damn breath! Am I drowning? The silence is pressing in on me. I want to scream, but nothing comes out. It's as if a fist has been rammed into my vocal cords.

I can't scream.

I can't wake.

I'm dying.

No, I'm not dying—I'm caught in a nightmare, and eventually I'll wake. All I have to do is stay calm and wait. Soon. I hope.

Staring at the darkness, willing it to take shape, I think I see a hint of movement. "Hello? Is anyone there?" I try to call, but no words come out. Instead, a cascade of notes—birdsong—echoes around me, and then suddenly that's all I hear, shattering the silence, the calls of a hundred birds. Caws, tweets, warbles. Screams.

I am screaming in birdcalls.

And there is a hand, pale and huge, reaching through the darkness. It looms over me, and I back away until I hit a metal bar. I try to move around it, but there is another. I feel it cold against my feathers.

The pale hand scatters seeds in front of me, and I see them illuminated by a circle of amber light—the moon? No, a light above, but I can't see who the hand belongs to. It withdraws, leaving the seeds behind, and I hop forward.

I want to laugh because it is such an obvious dream. The cries of Cora's birds echo day and night. Of course they'd enter my dreams. When I wake, I will hear them.

If I wake.

I must wake.

Why won't I wake?

A metallic screech shatters the birdcalls, and at last I jolt from my slumber. I'm curled up in the bus seat, cheek pressed against the filthy window. My tongue tastes of peanut butter, thick and sticky. It's morning, just barely, and I blink open my crusty eyes to focus on the station.

I am back in Greenborough.

CHAPTER
TWENTY-SEVEN

ROSE

1994

Rose thought it was absurd to be dying at forty-one. She'd ping-ponged among denial and anger and depression and had now settled on outrage: she felt cheated and a bit offended. She had done everything that everyone had expected of her, and in return her life should have followed a predictable path.

She'd been a good wife. A passable mother. An excellent friend. All through it, she'd waited patiently (and sometimes less than patiently) for her turn.

Now, when Lori was at last an adult, and Rose and Glenn were officially empty nesters . . . *this* was what happened?

It had started as mere exhaustion, which she was no stranger to after years of PTA and school board duties, work with the environmental board, volunteering at the library, and a stint at the local historical society, plus the gardening club, her book club, and . . . Oh, it made her tired to think of everything she said yes to just to feel like she was using her days for something important, to fill a void. *Ugh, I don't know why I did any of it.*

Because they asked. Because they expected her to. Because she expected herself to? Yes, that too. She hadn't built the cage, but she'd walked into it. Rose gazed up at the ceiling tiles from her hospital bed as the machines whirred beside her. She'd never pictured herself dying with regrets. That wasn't supposed to be her fate.

When she'd finally gone for a checkup, the doctor told her it was stress. She should eat more fruits and vegetables, take a walk, and try to eliminate worries—he'd essentially patted her on the head and dismissed her symptoms. She had believed him. He had an MD, after all, and she'd been vulnerable in her hospital gown, and agreed that, yes, her weight loss was desirable, the tiredness explainable, and the aches and pains were her body telling her she wasn't twenty anymore.

It was Glenn who'd insisted she make another appointment when the fatigue didn't subside no matter how much she seemed to sleep. This time, he went with her, and the doctor had grudgingly offered a few blood tests because her husband insisted. He'd directed all his questions to Glenn, as if she weren't capable of reporting her own symptoms, which had been irritating, but at least he'd ordered a slew of tests.

After that, things moved quickly.

Chemo had been even more unpleasant than promised. She'd purchased a wig that closely resembled her natural hair, thinking the worst of it would be the hair loss. It wasn't. It was the endless nausea and the feeling that her body was at war with itself. And both sides were losing.

Cora had been right beside her for all of it. She'd bought Rose two more wigs: one with Dolly Parton hair and the other apple red. Rose loved them both far more than the sensible one she'd picked. She was wearing her apple red one now and was fully aware of how ghoulish she looked, with her sunken cheeks and eye circles. She took delight in that, and there was precious little to delight in these days.

The rap of a knock reverberated at the door, and a nurse stuck her head in with a bright smile. "You have a visitor," she trilled, as if to a child.

Rose resisted the urge to throw a pillow at her, mostly because she doubted she had the strength to throw it farther than her own feet. What was it about your body failing that made people treat you like your brain was failing too? "Thank you," she said sweetly, because that was what the nurse expected her to say.

She hated that she worried about what the nurse thought of her. She shouldn't care about any of it—what people thought, what they expected, what she was supposed to do.

The nurse, whose name Rose hadn't bothered to learn, opened the door wider, and Lori bustled in. "Hello, Mom!" she said, beaming.

Lori's reaction to Rose's cancer had been overwhelming optimism. It was, frankly, exhausting. Lori had convinced herself that this was a blip, a bump in the road, not the great stop sign at the end of Rose's journey. Only Rose seemed to see the cliff on the other side of the stop sign—*Well, me and the doctors.*

"I have some news that will cheer you up," Lori said.

Did her smile seem brighter today? *She's going to wear herself out.* Rose wondered if Lori had allowed herself to cry. It wasn't that Rose *wanted* Lori to weep in her hospital room, but this steadfast denial was only going to hurt her more in the end. "Oh? Did the Red Sox win the Super Bowl?"

Lori laughed as if that was the funniest thing Rose had ever said. "You should ask Dad that. No, wait, don't—he'll spend all of visiting hours explaining the names of championships for all the different sports."

"He would do that," Rose agreed. "Is he coming today?" A little traitorous part of her hoped the answer was no. He required Rose to be brave and strong, believing there was no illness that couldn't be defeated by a positive outlook and willpower, and she wasn't certain she felt up to that nonsense today. She'd rather be irritable and sleep.

"Later on," Lori said. "He agreed to let me have a little time alone with you first, to share my news."

Rose felt a clench in the pit of her stomach that had nothing to do with her illness or the medication. Given how much she was on, she shouldn't be feeling much of anything. "Oh?"

Lori beamed and shoved her hand toward Rose. "Ryan proposed! I'm getting married!" She let out a little squeal, like a piglet.

Smile, Rose ordered herself. *Say "congratulations."* Her cheeks wouldn't cooperate. "Oh. He did? That's . . ." A dozen adjectives bubbled up in her mind, and none of them were appropriate, but Lori didn't seem to notice.

Lori plopped into the visitor's chair next to the hospital bed and held her ring up toward the fluorescent lights. "It's princess cut, because he says I'm his princess, and I know it's not as impressive as yours, but I think that's fine. I don't want a ring that will catch on my sweaters anyway." She shoved the ring toward Rose's face again, and Rose resisted the urge to swat her hand away. "Don't you think it's beautiful?" Lori gushed.

It looked exactly like every wedding ring in every diamond commercial on TV. Nothing special. And too large to be sensible. "Yes, it's lovely, but Lori, don't you think you're rushing this?" She regretted the words as soon as they were out of her mouth, but she knew she'd regret it more if she didn't say anything.

Lori's smile dipped, and she sank into herself like a deflating balloon. "He's the one. How can it be a rush once you've found the person you want to spend the rest of your life with?"

"But you're so young." Rose couldn't seem to stop.

"I'm nineteen, not a child bride," Lori said.

"Younger than I was, and I was too young." If she hadn't married so soon, perhaps she could have traveled. She could have adventured before she had a house to take care of. She could have experienced being in a country where you didn't understand a single word or walked a city that was thousands of years old. If she hadn't been so certain that she had no choice . . . "You don't have to do this, sweetheart."

"Mom, I want to marry Ryan!"

"You think you do because you've been conditioned to see this as the only path," Rose said. "But you have so many more options, if you'd give yourself a chance! You should explore the world. Spend some time on your own. Get to know who you are as a person."

Lori emitted a little half laugh and shook her head. "You want me to 'broaden my horizons'? That's your reaction?" She gazed at her hands. "This is the best thing to ever happen to me. Ryan loves me, and I love him. We're going to be happy together."

"You think that, but you don't know what else is out there," Rose said. She knew that Lori wanted her to stop talking, but she couldn't. There was so much that she wished someone had said to her. Lori just needed to know there were options, that her life wouldn't be ruined if she waited, that there was a big beautiful world out there that she'd never even seen and wouldn't see if she continued on this path. One day led to the next, and before you knew it, you were forty-one and unlikely to live to forty-two. Life wasn't going to wait for her. She had to seize it now, before it was too late. "You're young! Let yourself be young! You should be out having adventures, seeing the world!"

"Ryan and I will have adventures," Lori said. "We're going to start our lives together. Mom, can't you see this is a good thing? You like Ryan. You said so yourself."

"As your boyfriend, yes," Rose said. *He is a perfectly nice boy,* she thought. He was polite, quiet, a little meek, but she recognized that Lori had a strong personality. *He's perfectly fine. It's only that he's a bit dull,* Rose reflected. No sparkle. Her daughter deserved sparkle. "But not as your future. Lori, listen to me, sweetheart, you have so much potential, and you've only just begun to taste the world. I want you to go out there and set the world on fire! I want you to drink down all that it has to offer! Climb the Great Pyramids! Race dogsleds in Alaska! Go on an African safari! Walk on the Great Wall of China!" A cough stole her breath, and her whole body shook as she hacked and gasped and choked.

Lori rushed to her side. "Mom?"

As the fit subsided, Rose waved her off. She concentrated on breathing in and out, reminding her lungs what they were supposed to be doing.

After a moment, Lori said, "We're going to have the wedding as soon as possible. I want you there, and Ryan agrees. There's a chapel in the hospital. He has a cousin who's a florist, and she's agreed to do the flowers for half price, so we're going to fill the room with so many flowers that you'll think you've entered a greenhouse. It'll be awash with color."

Rose shook her head and tried to speak again. It came out as a croak.

"Do you need me to get the nurse?"

She shook her head. "You aren't getting married in a hospital."

"Mom, I want you there more than I want a gaudy over-the-top wedding and reception," Lori said. "This is what's important to me."

"You're rushing because of me," Rose said. "I won't let you do that. You have your whole life ahead of you—"

"And I want to spend it with Ryan," Lori said.

"You don't know what you want," Rose said. "You've barely been outside Massachusetts. This is such a tiny piece of the world. Don't you want to see what else is out there? Don't you want to learn who you could be, away from your parents' house? You've never lived on your own. You should experience that before you become someone's wife."

"Mom . . ." Lori took a breath. "I didn't come here to fight with you. I thought . . . I thought you'd be happy for me."

Rose reached her hand toward Lori and then let it fall onto the metal bar of the hospital bed. "I just want you to take a breath and think about this. The world tells us this is what we should want: be a daughter, be a wife, be a mother. But you deserve to be *you* as well."

"I *am* me," Lori said.

She's not hearing me. Rose closed her eyes. She didn't know how to make Lori understand. "It's insidious, the way the world cages us. We don't realize it's happening. We don't see the bars as we blithely walk into the cage. All the expectations . . . on TV, in books, in commercials, the damn baby-doll toys we give our children, the house-and-picket-fence dream, as if it's what everyone should have. You can say it's the men, it's the patriarchy, and it *is*. Of course it is. But it's not only the voices outside you that cage you. It's the voices that you let inside: *This is just the way it is, this is the life you should lead, this is what you want, this is who you should be . . .*"

I walked into my cage.

"Mom?" There was a note in Lori's voice. *Fear?*

Rose stopped. She wasn't certain how many of those words she'd said out loud. "I've been thinking a lot lately about choices."

"You've made good choices," Lori said. *It was fear.* Rose could taste it in the air. "You're a great mom. And you have a great marriage. That's what I want—what you had. *Have.* I want what you have: a happy marriage and a happy family."

It was hard to keep her eyes open, but there was more that had to be said. Lori had to hear her, before it was too late, before she walked blithely into her own cage, just like Rose did. "I wasn't a good mother."

"You were! I mean, you *are*!"

Rose felt Lori's hand on hers. She pressed too hard, and Rose let out a little hiss. Lori didn't notice. She clutched her mother's hand as if her grip would keep her here, alive. "I could have been more," Rose said. Or maybe she only thought it. She was so very tired.

She didn't hear when Lori left.

When Rose woke again, Cora had replaced Lori in the plastic-leather chair beside the hospital bed. Cora had her latest crochet project on her lap: a plush parrot that she hoped would eventually go to her future grandchild, if her daughter Allison ever decided to marry and have children, which was not on the immediate horizon. Seeing Cora, Rose thought about going back to sleep.

"You're awake," Cora said. "I see you."

"What time is it?" Rose asked. Her mouth felt woolly. "Water?"

Cora helped her drink from the blue plastic cup. Rose hated how weak her hands were. It was hard to hold the cup steady without Cora's help. "It's four o'clock. Glenn was here, but you slept through it."

"Lori was here earlier," Rose said.

"I heard," Cora said brightly.

"She was out in the waiting room crying," Rose guessed.

"Yes, she was. It seems you lost your tact along with your hair. What did you say to that poor girl?"

"What I wanted to say was she's far too young to get married," Rose said, "and she's making a terrible mistake by rushing in just because she wants me at the ceremony. What came out of my mouth . . . I'm not quite sure, but I hope it was what she needed to hear."

Cora snorted. "You can't blame her for wanting her mother at her wedding."

"Did you hear the first part?" Rose said. Ugh, Cora was exhausting. Rose loved her, but she never listened. "She shouldn't be getting married at all."

"And my best friend shouldn't be dying," Cora said. "We don't all get what we wish for." She sighed and looked down at the crocheted lump in her hands. "I should have picked socks instead of a parrot. Ugh, what was I thinking?"

Rose managed a smile, but even that felt tiring. "I have no idea."

They fell into silence for a while. Rose listened to the soft sound of yarn whispering as it passed over the crochet hook, the hum of the hospital air filter, the steady whoosh and buzz and beep of the various machines that had become the soundtrack of her life. She thought she might welcome silence, when it came. All the little sounds of the hospital, from the faded voices of the nurses and patients, to the phones that rang in other rooms, to the constant opening and closing doors—they never stopped. She used to think she wanted to travel to see cities like Tokyo and Paris and Cairo and Rome. Now she wished she'd seen quiet lakes on mountaintops and seashores with waves so gentle they were like a parent's kiss.

"You said 'wish,'" Rose said. "Not 'want.'"

Cora was silent. Then: "I did?"

With an effort, Rose turned her head to look at her friend. "You found it, didn't you. In the woods. You went looking for it, and you found it."

Cora looked up at the ceiling tiles. "It was a while ago."

"What did you wish for?"

"It didn't work."

Louder, Rose said, "What did you wish for?" And then she coughed, and her body shook like she'd swallowed an earthquake. When she got control of her breathing again, she eyed Cora. "Don't try to lie. You know you can't keep anything from me."

"It was years ago," Cora said. "You showed me this brochure—you had this wild idea to become a tour guide in Europe, as if that was a reasonable thing to do. I . . . I made a wish that you'd stay. I didn't want to be left here without you."

Rose began to laugh, but it hurt as it shook her torso, and she fell into a fit of gasping. "Oh my, well, you got your wish. I'll never leave Greenborough now."

Cora looked stricken. "That's not . . . It didn't work."

"But it did!" She giggled, which didn't hurt quite as much—it felt like needles in her flesh rather than daggers in her sides. "You just weren't specific enough." Even though Cora was glaring at her, Rose still felt like laughing. It was the best she'd felt in days. She enjoyed the feeling for a while, until it faded and she was left thinking about Lori.

As Cora crocheted another row, Rose thought about the statue in the woods, the three witches. "I want you to make a wish for me," Rose said. "Specifically, for Lori, to keep her from making a terrible mistake."

"No. It won't work."

"Every wish has come true," Rose pointed out.

Cora lowered her crocheted bird. "Damn you, Rose. I won't do it."

"I can't do it myself."

"She wants to be married," Cora said. "You can't deny her a chance at future happiness."

"Please," Rose said. "I don't want my daughter to become stuck. She can't see what's happening, but I know. She's walking into a cage. Like I did. Don't you see, Cora? I don't want her to repeat my mistakes."

"Then talk to your daughter," Cora said. "Heart to heart. Don't ask your best friend to traipse through the woods in search of a miracle. It won't work. Believe me, if I thought that stupid statue . . ." The words clogged in her throat.

Of course, it was absurd. Rose wasn't sure what she'd been think-ing. *Must be the medication.* An old statue wasn't any kind of answer, obviously. "Rants of a dying woman," Rose said as lightly as she could. "Cora, I'm sorry."

Cora snorted. "Apology accepted."

CHAPTER TWENTY-EIGHT

LORI

2022

Lori was surprised at how easy it was to slip into the life she'd always wanted: two hours on the phone, and she and Elisa were on their way. A few days of caution: coffee first. A walk by the local duck pond. He cooked them dinner, chicken parmigiana with garlic bread. At the start, she and Elisa stayed in Mark's guest room, with downy hotel-like pillows and lavender towels, but after three weeks, Lori was sharing Mark's room, and Elisa had the guest room to herself.

She padded into the living room in the slippers Mark had bought for her. Elisa was curled up on the couch with a bowl of popcorn. Mark was on the opposite side.

"How can you not like popcorn?" Elisa was asking him.

He shrugged. "It sticks in my teeth."

"Then you have more popcorn for later."

Lori halted in the doorway and watched them. Mark was every bit as handsome as in her memory. Older, of course. But his eyes were the same: intensely kind. When he looked at Lori, it felt as if he saw right inside her and thought her messed-up tangle was beautiful.

"Okay, fine, so what movie snacks do you like?" Elisa asked.

"Carrots?"

"You're either lying or you're a rabbit."

Mark tucked his lower lip in to make rabbit teeth, and Elisa laughed.

I have to tell them. Not everything, not yet—she wasn't ready—but the most important thing. *They deserve to know who they are to each other. Who we all are.*

A family.

She'd wanted this for so long, even though she hadn't dared let the wish rise to the surface. It almost hurt, like a fist inside her heart, to think how close she was to everything she'd ever dreamed of having— and to know how little time she had left to hold it close.

But how would she tell them? What would she say? Would she just blurt it out, or softly lead into it? There was no graceful way to do this. *Look at them*: the two people she loved most in the world, side by side, on the same couch.

Mark spotted her dithering in the doorway. He patted the cushion between them. "Come sit. We were debating the best movie snacks."

"There's no debate," Elisa said. "It's not carrots."

"She's right," Lori said. "It's fried chicken."

Both Elisa and Mark jumped in simultaneously: "What? No. How is that a snack?" (Elisa) "How would you sneak fried chicken into a movie theater? The logistics alone . . ." (Mark) "In no universe is fried chicken a movie snack. Great, yes. Snack, no." (Elisa)

Lori grinned at them. "I like what I like."

"Then next movie night we'll have fried chicken," Mark promised. "Okay, we need to decide what to watch—who's in the mood for what?"

Lori took a deep breath. "First, there's something I need to talk to you about, both of you." Butterflies lodged in her throat. She wished she'd planned this out. She felt their eyes on her, curious, concerned.

"It's not . . ." She swallowed. "I should have told you before . . ." *Why is this so hard? It's a* good *thing.* Or at least she hoped they'd consider it a good thing. "Please understand . . . I wanted to tell you . . ."

"Mom. If you don't spit it out, I will pelt you with popcorn."

Lori turned to Elisa. "Did I ever tell you about Paris?"

Elisa studied her face, and Lori could tell she wanted to ask questions, but she just said, "No. When were you in Paris?" The two of them had never left the country. There had never been enough money for that. Add in the complication of obtaining a passport, especially with their frequent name changes . . .

"It's where Mark and I met," Lori said. "Before you were born." She closed her eyes so she could say it without seeing Elisa's expression. "Nine months before you were born. Well, eight months and two weeks—you were a little earlier than expected." Lori opened her eyes. She was facing Elisa and very aware that Mark was behind her, on the couch. She'd have to turn around to see his expression.

Elisa's face twisted, as if she'd tasted a lemon.

Lori turned toward Mark. "I should have told you. Years ago. I'm so sorry. That word doesn't go far enough. I . . . You deserved to know. And I know you must be angry. You have every right to be furious, and I accept that."

He wasn't looking at her. He was staring at Elisa. "I have a daughter."

As if her vocal cords were being squeezed, Elisa said, "So this is why you used our real names with Mark. This is why we're here."

Yes and no. "It was time," Lori said.

Mark ran his fingers through his hair. "I don't know what to say."

"You don't need to say anything," Elisa said. Her voice was firm, and she was clasping her hands together hard. "I don't expect anything from you. I don't need anything. I'm not looking for a father, and I never missed having one. We were fine, Mom and me, and we'll be fine."

It meant a lot to hear those words: *We were fine.* But Elisa's knee-jerk rejection of Mark also stung. Lori reached toward Elisa and squeezed her hand. Elisa squeezed back. "I wanted you two to have a chance to get to know each other," Lori said. "I think . . ." She didn't want to say how she felt about it. Her eyes already felt hot, and she didn't want tears to follow. "That's important to me."

Mark swallowed hard, and she watched the emotions play across his face. "I . . . I would have loved to have been a part of your childhood, Elisa. I . . . am glad to have the chance to get to know you now, if you'll let me."

"I . . ." Elisa began. She stopped.

Lori held her breath.

"Yes," Elisa said. "I think . . . that's fine. For a while. For as long as we're here." She sat up straighter and smoothed her face. "But first you have to admit that popcorn is the superior movie snack."

He smiled. "I can do that."

And Lori could breathe again.

CHAPTER TWENTY-NINE

ELISA

Now

I stumble off the bus.

It's shortly after dawn, and a murder of crows in a nearby tree are screaming at one another. Only a few cars pass by. The downtown is quiet, except for the crows and the crickets and the rumble of the bus engine. My thoughts careen into each other, crashing and exploding like waves hitting the shore, and I can't calm them.

My feet carry me directly to the Book Cellar. I don't know if Owen is awake yet, and I don't know what I'll say to him if he is, but I don't know what else to do.

I am relieved to see the bookshop lights are on. *He's awake.* Seeing me, Charlie strolls in front of the book display. "Yes, I'm back," I tell the cat as I knock on the shop door. "Miss me?" My voice is shrill, and I want to laugh or cry or scream.

There's movement inside. Owen's not alone. Another man is in the shop, but I can't see his face. Who? *I don't have time for this.* His back is to the door, and he's gesturing as he talks, his voice too muffled for me to hear words, only the angry tone. *I should retreat.*

Owen pulls open the door. "Elisa, are you all right?"

No. "I can't leave, and I can't stay." Very shrill.

He opens the door wider and shoos Charlie back with one hand. "Did the bus—"

"Fine. Just fell asleep, and here I was, like you said." I hold out my hand toward Charlie, and he butts it with his forehead. I pet his cheeks, and he leans against my palm, as if he can sense my chaos swirling and wants to soothe me. Breathing in, I try to steady myself. *I can handle this.* I've handled everything else: all the goodbyes, all the fear, all the running, all the starting over, all the heartbreak, as well as when my mother—

"Lyssa." The other man turns and steps toward me.

Everything inside me freezes. I don't breathe, I don't think, and it feels as if the blood in my veins has ceased to flow, suspended in shock.

At last, I manage one word, his name: "Tyler."

He rushes forward as if to embrace me, and I instinctively step away, back against the door, as if he were a stranger. Or a ghost. He halts, and his eyes flick from me to Owen and back again. On the counter, Charlie bristles, his tail fluffed, and he lets out a rumble deep in his throat.

"I'm still asleep." I've sunk deeper into the nightmare, and I don't know how to wake myself up. I feel the panic bubble in my throat, and it's hard to breathe. I squeeze my eyes shut. He can't be here.

Hands grip my arms, and it feels so real that I open my eyes. I'm not on the bus; I'm in the bookshop, but how do I know I'm awake? Just because it feels real doesn't mean it is real. All of this could be in my head.

Tyler releases me and backs away. He's wearing the teal polo shirt he had on when I met him, but he hasn't shaved in a couple days. *He's not a memory.* "Sorry, I thought—you looked like you were about to pass out. Lyssa, I—"

I shake my head. "You aren't here."

"I am! I found you."

"How?"

I've been found before by ex-lovers who wanted a better explanation than I could give and by former friends who worried about me and by a few people I'd scammed who demanded their money back, but I had learned to be careful by the time I left Tyler. I had left no clues. No breadcrumbs. I only used cash. He'd never seen my list of odd places, and he couldn't have guessed I switched buses before Springfield. Granted, there were witnesses, and if he talked to the right person, someone who happened to remember me from the bus depot—

"A woman called and told me where you were," Tyler says, "and that you were in danger and needed to leave town right away. Lyssa, what kind of trouble are you in?" His eyes flick again to Owen. He's tense, his fists clenched and his muscles tight. I wish I could tell him everything's fine. Go home. Forget me.

"What woman?" *Allison.* But how would she know how to call Tyler, and why would she? Since I set foot in Greenborough, his name hasn't passed my lips, not once. Even if she'd searched my backpack, I carry no photos, no letters, no mementos. I don't know who or how—

"She said her name was Athena, and that she's an acquaintance of yours," Tyler says, and I instantly know—one of the blue-haired ladies. But how? And why? "She said you didn't intend to stay here, but that you needed extra incentive to leave. Lyssa . . ." Another glance at Owen. I don't know what Tyler expects him to do, but all he does it stroke Charlie, who continues his low growl. ". . . I want you to come back. I know I"—he rakes his fingers through his hair, a nervous habit that I used to love, just as I loved how he'd peel an apple in shard-like flakes with no finesse at all—"I know I'm too needy, and I know I haven't given you space, but I can change. We had something real, Lyssa, and I don't want to throw it away."

Tears spring to my eyes, and I feel a tightness in my throat. It was real, but it was temporary, and it was always going to be temporary. I wish I didn't know I'd hurt him, that I could pretend he was content to treasure my memory and not care that we'd ended. Everything ends, especially with me. "Tyler—"

"If you want me to beg, I will. If you want me to back off and take it slow . . . I can do that. Whatever you need, but you need to give us a chance. You need to come home."

Home.

A sad laugh bubbles in my throat, but I don't let it escape. "I told you: I can't stay, not with you, not here, not anywhere. I'm cursed." I push the sleeve of my shirt up to reveal the patch of bark. "It's already happening. I have to move on, or it will spread."

He shakes his head. "You cut yourself?"

Owen steps forward. "What happened?"

"Can't you see?" I shove my arm into the light so the hard brown patch is visible. "It's not a cut. It's a *change*. The bark is already started to spread. There will be more each day, each *hour*. It will swallow me, and I will root in this town, unable to leave ever again."

Tyler looks confused. "It's a scab, Lyssa. You cut yourself, and it's healing. I don't understand what you're trying to say."

"My blood will thicken to sap."

"Lyssa . . ."

"I will sprout leaves."

He's shaking his head, and I wonder why people do that. Denying it won't make it any less true. "You aren't . . ." He shakes his head harder. "People don't . . . I can't believe you're continuing this absurdity. I thought . . . You need to stop this."

Owen steps in. "If it's true for her, that's enough."

"Who the hell are you?" Tyler snaps. "I'm trying to talk to my—" He halts, rakes his fingers through his hair again, and then continues in a softer voice. "Lyssa, we were good together. I don't understand why you're doing this. Come home with me, and we can talk it all out. We can see a couples therapist, if you'd like. In fact, I think that's a great idea."

"I am trying to tell you the truth," I say. My truth. "You aren't listening."

Owen answers his question. "I'm a friend."

But I have my own questions. "How did 'Athena' know to call you? And why?" I already said goodbye to him. Unless . . . Did the blue-haired lady know that I wouldn't be able to leave? How? Never mind that now—could she have sent me an alternate way out? I switch my question: "Did you drive here?"

Of course he did. He has a car, and no one who owns a car ever thinks to take a bus.

Could he be here to save me?

"Yes, I drove, but—"

I grab his hand. "Yes, let's go. Right now. I'll go with you. Take me away from this town, and we'll talk." I yank him out the door to the sidewalk and scan the parked cars.

Ah, yes, there's Tyler's little white car, with the dent in the back fender. He hits unlock, and I open the passenger door. My heart is beating fast—blood or sap? I can't tell. I want to shout at Tyler to move faster.

Owen has followed us. "Elisa . . ." Shifting from foot to foot, he looks anxious. I think of what he told me about his car breaking down and, worse, the concussion he sustained on his final attempt. This will be my second attempt—but how can I not try? It could work.

"I'll be okay," I tell him.

Tyler was sent to save me. Somehow, the blue-haired lady knew: she knew what I'd need, and she sent this answer to my problem. Later, I can figure out how and who and all the millions of other questions, but now it's time to act, while I have this one chance.

Charlie watches through the bookstore window. I notice there's a small crowd by the coffee shop—the two from the bus, the barista, and the guitarist who plays without strings—despite the early hour. It's another mystery: What drew them here so early, and why do they care what I'm doing?

"Good luck," Owen says.

Tyler is already in the driver's seat.

I sit beside him. Buckle my seatbelt. Look straight ahead. I feel as if my veins are humming, and I try not to dig my fingernails into my palms. "Go."

"I don't understand why you—"

"Just go."

He starts the car. Or tries. It revs and then sputters.

No.

My heart sinks, and I feel as though all the air in my lungs has drained with it, pooling by my feet. My shoulders sag, and I stare at the dashboard, willing the car to start as Tyler tries again. He taps on the gas, but it coughs, sputters, and silences. "It was fine a few minutes ago," he says. "It shouldn't be stalling like this. I don't know why now it—"

"I do." Or I think I do. It could be a coincidence.

Hoping I'm wrong, I unclip my belt, open the door, and step onto the sidewalk.

"Lyssa—"

"Try it without me," I say.

He tries, and the engine purrs to life. "Okay, great, it's working," he says. "Hop in."

I know what will happen, but still I climb in and snap the seatbelt. My stomach is a rock, and my limbs feel leaden. The car engine dies.

"What the—" Tyler thumps the dashboard, as if that will help. He swears at the car, apologizes to me, and tries yet again. After the third attempt, I put my hand over his on the steering wheel.

"You need to leave before you can't," I tell him.

"We'll call AAA, get it towed. It could be the battery—"

"It's not the car. Tyler, listen to me." I look at him, my beautiful Tyler, who's so certain he's not worthy of me when it's really me who isn't worthy of him. He doesn't deserve this tangled mess, and I know he isn't capable of understanding; it barely makes sense to me. "I need to know you're safe and that"—I swallow hard—"and that you will think of me sometimes, fondly, maybe when you're drinking orange juice in the morning, or when you look at one of the seashells on your mantle, or just for no particular reason at all."

Tyler doesn't like this, of course. I don't expect him to. I have hit the limits of his trust and perhaps his imagination—or is it empathy? His world is not the same as mine. In his, bark cannot grow on skin. In mine, my mother is a willow by a stream. "Lyssa, I didn't come all this way to just—"

"What we had was real, but it was temporary. And this"—I don't want to mention the curse again; it feels too heavy to drag out into the morning light, especially in front of an audience, especially since it will do no good to explain again—"is the universe saying that I can't go home with you."

"It's an old car. Probably needs a new battery. It doesn't have anything to do with the universe talking to anyone. You're not acting rationally, and it's freaking me out." He tries again, and once again I lay my hand over his when the engine sputters.

"I'm sorry, Tyler. I thought for a brief moment—but I can't." The blue-haired lady, whichever one called him, might not have known it was already too late for me. Perhaps she thought I could be saved. If I ever see her again, I'll thank her for caring enough to try. "I'm sorry you got involved in any of this."

"There's no 'this,'" Tyler says. "I'll have someone jump-start it—"

I can't let him stay and keep trying. Either he'll become trapped too, or worse, something will happen to him when he tries to save me. I think of Owen's car, totaled, when he tried to leave again and again. "We were always meant to be temporary."

"You don't know that—"

"I've seen forever love." My mother and Mark. I saw how they looked at one another, how they fit into each other's lives, how they expanded each other, made each other more whole. "My parents. They had it. It made my mother incandescently happy at the end, and it was why she didn't leave, even though she might have lived if she hadn't . . ." My voice breaks. "I can't be what you need me to be, what you deserve. You need to move on."

"I came here—"

"I know. It was a beautiful, grand, romantic gesture. But I'll never love you enough to risk everything." I can already feel the sap, sluggish in my veins. The blood and sap are intermixing now, and I don't know what I would see if I pierced my skin and let it flow. "And I . . . have unfinished business here." I look out the car window at Owen and the clump of people by the coffee shop. Whatever is happening here, it isn't only me. And if I leave without answers, even if I could leave, that won't solve anything.

Tyler looks at me with such a crushed expression. I wonder if he'd have been better off never meeting me, even if it meant I'd never have the memories of our months together. It's rare that I get a second chance to say goodbye, and I am making it worse rather than better.

I get out of the car, and immediately the engine starts, without him even touching the ignition. Tyler is momentarily taken aback, but he leans over the passenger seat and pleads, "It's a coincidence, not a sign, Lyssa. Come with me." But there's a hint of doubt in his eyes, and I wonder if he's beginning to suspect there's truth to what I've been saying, if he could be trapped here too, or if it's all in my head.

"You need to leave," I tell him as kindly as I can. "Please, leave."

I know he cares about me, but I also know he doesn't love me as much as he thinks he does. There's a cost he won't pay. He might not understand why he has to leave, but there is a part of him that is whispering to him to save himself.

"Lyssa—"

"You came, you tried, and it isn't going to work. We aren't meant to be, and it's not because the car won't start and I think it's a sign." He wants to argue, but I plow over his words. "But the truth is that I don't love you enough, and I never will. And you . . . you don't really even know me."

"You're wrong," he says quietly.

"It doesn't matter if I am or not," I say. "It's what I believe."

"I could have loved you forever," he tells me.

I doubt that. But all I say is, "Goodbye, Tyler."

He wants to stay and argue more. I can see it in his eyes. But I can also see it's unsettled him, the way his car behaved. His eyes flicker toward the coffee shop and the crowd that's gathered, and I see the moment he decides I'm not worth the risk, even if he can't explain what that risk is. A piece of him believes me, which should feel like a victory but instead feels like a little death.

I watch as he drives away.

I'm alone again.

◆　◆　◆

Or not alone?

Squaring my shoulders, I turn back to the Book Cellar. The other onlookers have ducked into the coffee shop, and Owen remains alone on the sidewalk, with the cat peering through the bookshop window behind him. Before he can speak, I say, "I need to break the curse."

He nods.

He doesn't question or doubt me, and I stare at him for a moment. He's the first person I've met who understands what it's like not to be free to choose your fate. "How?" he asks.

"I need to talk to the blue-haired ladies."

Owen steps into the bookshop, switches off the lights, and checks that the sign says "closed." He pets Charlie before coming outside and locking the door. *He's going to help me.* I find myself smiling even though there's nothing to smile about. Tyler is gone, forever, but I'm not completely alone—that's a little bright light in all this. "They're often in the coffee shop," he says. "Maybe the owner, Monica, knows where they live? She knows all her regulars."

Together we enter Bean Street, and a hush envelops us. It's dim inside, and I don't know why the morning sun doesn't pierce the windows. No one is smoking, yet the entire room feels saturated with haze.

The blue-haired ladies aren't here, but Monica is at the counter, and Maddie and Emma are seated in a shadowy corner. The guitarist is on a stool, strumming air with his right hand as his left forms chords on the bare neck of the guitar.

I gather my voice to cut through the haze and gloom. "Can any of you leave?"

No one answers me, each seemingly waiting for another to speak first.

I pause for a moment, even though I have a dozen more questions: Is it everyone in the town? When did it begin? How long has this been going on? Who noticed first? Has anyone ever left? Soft music begins to play, simple guitar chords. Addressing Maddie and Emma, I say, "You were on the bus. Did you go somewhere, or did you come straight back here?"

"We went to New York City," Maddie says.

"But we came back," Emma adds quietly. She's drawn the kohl thick around her eyes, and it makes the whites look even whiter. More frightened.

Could a curse sense intent? Did it understand round-trip tickets and return trips? In the background, the simple chords become more complex, developing a gentle melody. "When did you first notice that you couldn't leave?"

They look at each other.

"I got into UCLA," Emma says quietly, looking down.

"She was supposed to start last September," Maddie says. "I helped her pack. We said our goodbyes, promised to stay together. But her parents regretted letting her go so far away. Her mom, especially."

"The tuition fell through."

"Her enrollment was canceled," Maddie says. "Our guidance counselor tried to get it fixed. Her parents tried. It was a massive fuckup that somehow couldn't be fixed. She had to postpone enrollment until spring semester."

"Spring semester, it was the plane," Emma says in her soft, shaky voice. "Flights kept getting delayed, then canceled. And I just didn't want to keep trying. At that point, it felt like fate. I'm supposed to stay. At least we can be together." The two young women share a somber, yet tender, look.

The guitar turns melancholy, a sweet but sad sound. I think about dreams, those I was never allowed to have. I could never dream about college. Unlike high school, you can't hop from college to college every year. Sure, you can transfer, but not every ten months. Even an accelerated program was beyond my reach.

"But I'm not sure I *can't* leave," Emma says. "Not the way you mean. Just that life changed. My mother, she became sick, and I had to help take care of her. So it's . . . that's the way it turned out, that's all."

"It's more than that," her girlfriend argues.

"I know, you think it's some grand conspiracy, but it's just life. It doesn't always go the way you plan. Other people . . . Family . . . I *have* to stay. They need me."

"I need you, but I was willing to let you go so you could have your own life. Your parents . . . Well, you know what I think. I don't think it was an accident. They wanted this."

Emma looks down. "I don't want to argue."

I turn to the barista. "Monica? Are you trapped here?"

"I . . ."

I don't want to pressure her, but I can feel the bark; I can't afford to be nice and patient anymore. I need to know the scope of the curse: how it began and how it can end, even if it doesn't have anything to do with my family curse. I am caught between two opposite fates.

I will be a willow tree.

Or a pear tree.

A linden tree, with symmetrical shade.

A pine tree, brittle, with cones in every branch, welcoming woodpeckers and squirrels, dropping needles to coat the forest floor below me.

I won't let it happen.

In a voice heavy with memories and regret, Monica says, "In a way, yes, but it's my own fault. When my boyfriend left, I didn't try to leave. I was already here, with an apartment and a job. I didn't have any place better to go, so I just stayed."

From the back corner, the guitarist pipes up, "I can leave whenever I want, but there's no one who will hear me, so why bother?" He bends over his guitar and picks out another melody—and I suddenly realize that I *can* hear him. In fact, I've been hearing his music since I walked into Bean Street, since Tyler drove away. It's a sweet, soft melody that lifts the shadows of the coffee shop.

Something has changed.

I don't know what or when or how, but somehow, I went from being a visitor to a permanent resident, and now I can hear his music. Turning to Owen, I push up my sleeve. "What do you see? Skin or bark?"

He looks into my eyes, not at my arm. "What do you want me to see?"

"That's not the question." He sees skin and a scab. He wouldn't have asked that otherwise. I roll down my sleeve and try not to think about what that means. Can he hear the music? Am I imagining it? Is this all in my head—the bark, the sap, the stalled car? Is it all just a string of actions that I've let myself believe is fate? Coincidence, as Tyler said?

I fell asleep on a bus.

A car wouldn't start.

My mother had cancer.

As for Emma, her parents could have sabotaged her attempts to go to college across the country. They could have had second thoughts, canceled her enrollment and her flights, and then lied to her. Or perhaps it was all a set of coincidences, and she simply decided it wasn't worth the effort to overcome it all. Either way, it didn't have to be a curse. Owen's attempts to leave could be excused in the same way. I wonder, if Tyler and I had taken the car to a mechanic, would they have discovered a faulty battery?

"Monica, can I borrow a knife?" I ask.

"Why?" she asks, retrieving a cheese knife from the counter.

"I want to know if I bleed sap or blood."

Without prompting, the guitarist says, "I see bark."

All of us look at him. He just shrugs and continues to play. It's an even more complex melody, weaving in and out with the harmonies, increasing in speed as he plucks the strings faster and faster. I've never heard music like this, not from one single instrument.

"Where did you learn to play like that? It's beautiful," I say. That isn't the right word. Enchanting, perhaps. Sad. Lovely. There is no one word to describe the sounds emanating from his stringless guitar; the music fills the coffee shop, and it fills me. It echoes inside my bones, within my skin. It haunts me.

"I am the best player who was ever born," he says simply. "That was what I wished, to be the best, when I found the three women."

Owen startles beside me. "You mean the blue-haired ladies?"

He shakes his head and stops playing. Silence settles around us, and I hear the tick of the clocks, syncopated. "Nah, not three real women. It was a statue. I found it in the woods between the school and the cemetery. I went there with my guitar, told the statue what I wanted . . . and after that, I could play. Really play. But only a few could hear me, and no one outside of Greenborough. So I don't think I'm trapped in this town, but how can I leave when it's the only place I'm heard?"

I've never heard such a story before, such a curse, but it's clear what I need to do.

He resumes playing.

"Can you take me to this statue?" I ask.

CHAPTER THIRTY

LORI

2022

Three months in, Lori cracked an egg into a mug. She hummed to herself as she stirred it with a whisk, its handle a plastic egg with eyes. A skillet was already heating up on the stove, and she had ham, cheese, and chopped tomatoes ready in little glass bowls. Mark had nearly every kitchen utensil anyone could imagine, plus copper pots and a food processor, and his stainless steel fridge produced three different shapes of ice. It was heavenly.

Eighties music played on the speaker, and Lori swayed as Elisa came out of her room, tying her wet hair back with a hair tie. "Off to work," Elisa said. She'd gotten a job at a local art gallery, answering phones and sweeping up—a friend of Mark's had needed the help, and Mark had been happy to arrange, no job application or references needed.

He had been so amazing with Elisa since learning the truth. *And so amazing with me.* Not that he wasn't amazing before. But he genuinely embraced the news. He made Elisa feel as if no time had passed, as if she'd never made any mistakes, as if she was *more* than she ever thought she was.

"I'm making omelets," Lori said. "Stay for one?"

"Can't. I promised I'd be early to help set up for an opening reception. Did you know that people pay money to be the first to look at art that they could see less than twenty-four hours later for free? And to eat sandwiches that cost more *because* they're smaller than normal sandwiches?"

Lori smiled. "I'll plan a substantial dinner. What time will you be home?" She turned back to the stove and poured the whisked egg into the skillet. It sizzled, and the edges whitened satisfyingly.

When Elisa didn't reply, Lori twisted around to look at her.

Elisa had frozen, like a mouse, cornered.

"What is it?" Lori asked.

"You shouldn't use that word."

The egg sizzled. "What word?"

"'Home.' How many times have you warned me not to use that word?"

Oh. Yes. *That* word. Lori rolled the word around in her mind. It should have terrified her—it had slipped out so naturally, but it simply felt right. She added a handful of shredded cheese and slid the spatula under the edges to check if it was ready to flip. She wasn't certain whether she should apologize or explain. *Not explain. Not yet.* She'd tell her everything when the time was right, but that wasn't now. *For now, all she needs to know is that we're a family. And we're happy.* "Yes. I know. You're right."

"You *are* clear this is temporary, right?" Elisa asked. "Mark is great and all—"

"He said you could call him Dad."

Elisa fell silent again.

"But he isn't going to push. He only wanted you to know that he's open to building a relationship with you. He always wanted a daughter, and he wants to make up for lost time." Lori didn't think she had to point out that it wasn't Mark's fault he'd been an absent father. She'd made that clear. He hadn't known Elisa existed, and that was entirely on Lori. And the curse, of course.

"I'm not . . ." Elisa stopped and gulped in air. "Unless he's going to uproot his life and start traveling with us, then this is temporary. I'm not going to start calling him Dad only to say goodbye in seven months. You know that, right? You know we both have to leave, no matter how much you like him and his kitchen? You can't . . ." She stopped again. "I don't know what we're doing here. You're just going to break your own heart. Not to mention his. Have you thought about how he'll feel when you have to walk away from him again? You know he won't understand why."

"I'm living in the moment," Lori said. "I'm happy right now, and that's enough. It could be enough for you too." She added tomatoes and ham to the egg, and used the spatula to ease half of it over. She smiled down at the egg—it hadn't reverted to scrambled. The first few omelets she'd tried had been a disaster. "Hey, I'm getting better at this."

"Happy for you," Elisa said, in a tone dripping with sarcasm. Her concern sizzled through her voice like heat through the eggs. "You're the one who taught me to protect my heart. Are you . . . You can't be falling in love. Mom, you know the rules. You taught me the rules."

Lori slid the omelet onto a plate. She stared at the perfect half-moon of egg and cheese, with little bits of ham and tomato poking through, and she tried to find the words to explain without actually explaining. "Life is fleeting."

"Are you falling in love with Mark?" Elisa demanded.

Falling? Lori almost laughed. Oh no, she'd been in love with Mark since the day she met him, over twenty years ago. She'd never stopped loving him; she'd merely paused. Last weekend, at a cocktail party they'd hosted on Mark's patio, she'd overheard one of Mark's friends asking him if he thought this was moving too quickly, and Mark had replied that two-plus decades was too slow—that was exactly how she felt. She'd waited for so long, never thinking she'd be able to have it, even for as brief a time as she had left. She was going to treasure every second, hoard her moments of happiness.

"Mom, listen to me. Do whatever you want. Love him as much as you want. Play happy housewife as much as you want. But don't make the mistake of thinking this is forever. It can't be. You know that. Please tell me you know that."

Elisa's arms were crossed, and Lori took one of her hands. "I know it's not forever." God, she knew. Every cell in her body reminded her of that. "But I want to be happy while I can, and being with Mark . . . He makes me happy." That was such an understatement. She felt as if she'd been wrapped up like a mummy for years and he'd come along and unwrapped her—everything was brighter. This omelet, perfect. The smoothness of the tile beneath her bare feet, perfect. The morning sun through the window, perfect.

Elisa rubbed her temples. "I want you to be happy, but I also want you to be careful. You could trigger the curse early, if you're not."

It was far too late to worry about that, but Lori said nothing to Elisa. Releasing her hand, Lori returned to the table and waved for Elisa to sit. She sliced the omelet and scooted half onto a second plate. "Eat before work. You'll starve with only tiny sandwiches."

Elisa picked up a fork and ate a few bites of the omelet, which was enough to say that the conversation was over, for now. Lori ate her half and blew Elisa a kiss when she headed out the door. It banged shut behind her, and Lori laid down her fork.

She looked out the window at Mark's backyard. He liked to mow and weed and take care of the lawn, because of course he did. A peach tree grew in the back corner, near a row of cypress. She wished she would still be here when the peaches were ripe.

From the doorway, Mark quietly asked, "Is this temporary?"

She wasn't surprised he'd heard. She'd known he was home; though, she'd hoped he was working in his office. "Everything's temporary. But I will stay until my last breath." She was more honest than she'd meant to be. Perhaps the omelet made her brave.

At any moment, he could decide that she wasn't worth it. He could remember to be angry about the way she'd walked away from him, about the fact that she'd never reached out to tell him he had a daughter. She'd stolen the chance to be a father from him, and she'd stolen his dream for the future. He could, at any moment, tell her she was too much. Or too little, that she didn't match up to the dream version he'd built up in his head.

"Why didn't you move on?" Lori asked.

"I did," Mark said. "You know I did." He crossed to the coffee machine and poured himself a cup. "I was married, briefly—you've seen the photos. I haven't hidden that from you."

"You divorced."

"I did."

"Why?"

He adds milk and sugar to his coffee and stirs.

"Do you want an omelet?" Lori offered. "I can make you one."

"She met someone else," Mark said. "It's in the past. I don't want to talk about it right now. I want to talk about us, the present, the future. *Our* future. Do we have a future, or am I going to wake up one morning with a note on my pillow? Because if that's our future . . . I have been trying very hard to do as you said to Elisa, to be happy in the moment, but I'm not built like that. I have to know if we have a future."

She looked down at her plate; the eggs sat heavy in her stomach. She could lie. She could reply with a whole range of platitudes, of promises, of intentions, but she was so very tired of lying and running and hurting. Lori closed her eyes and then reopened them.

It wasn't a dream. He didn't vanish. Her hands rested on the table, and she could feel the wood solid and warm and comforting under her palms. The kitchen smelled like her omelet and cleaning spray. A window was open, and she could hear birds outside.

Maybe I'm already dead, and this is heaven.

"Lori. I know it's a mistake to pressure you, but . . . I have to know. Is this temporary? Am I just a stop on your travels?"

"You're the final stop," she said.

He sat beside her and took her hand. "You mean that, Lori? Because I can't—"

"I'm dying," Lori said abruptly.

He opened his mouth and then shut it. She had an urge to sweep the hair back from his eyes. He looked so very much like the boy in her memories, a little stockier, his face more weathered, his hair thinner, but his eyes, even with a few extra creases, were the same. His heart shone through them.

"When I left you before, it was because I was afraid of dying," Lori said, trying to find the right words. She'd been so afraid back then—the consequences had felt so final and overwhelming. "But now that it's unavoidable, I'm not afraid anymore, and I can at last live."

He reached across the table and took her hand. "Lori . . ."

"Let me tell you everything. You see, I'm cursed."

He didn't believe the curse.

But he did believe she had cancer.

After Lori cleaned up breakfast, they walked to the back of his property. A stream burbled over rocks beside a meadow that had once been a farmer's field, a century ago. He'd thought about planting a vegetable garden there but hadn't found the time.

"We can marry," Mark said.

Lori quit walking.

"I know you ran the last time I asked, and I wasn't going to mention it because I don't want to scare you off again. But if we marry, you can be on my health insurance. We'll get you the best treatment possible."

"I didn't come to you for health insurance."

"Why did you come?"

For happiness. For love. And for Elisa. She only wanted to say the first two. But she knew she had to tell him the third. Lori lowered herself onto a rock and watched water dance over the pebbles. "Where does the stream go?"

"Into a duck pond downtown." He sat next to her. "You know, that's part of why I bought this place? Because it reminded me of those Monets."

"We only had a few days together," Lori said. She'd relived those days in her memory a thousand times until every moment was woven into her mind like the lyrics to a song. "I didn't know if you'd even remember me, but I had to try. For me, but also for Elisa. She bears the same curse."

He nodded. "Some cancers are genetic. After your mother—you should have been tested earlier. We can make sure that Elisa is and that she receives regular checkups."

"She won't stay long enough to be monitored," Lori said. "I've taught her that. She'll be here seven months more, never more than ten in all, and then . . . I won't be able to protect her anymore. That's why I came. I hoped that after I'm gone . . ." *You'll help her.* She couldn't make herself form the words. It was far too much to ask. He was only starting to know Elisa, to see how amazing she was, to care for her, to be with her, to love her. How could she ask this of him? It was too much to ask after all that she'd done.

She wanted to say she was sorry, she never should have come, she never should have told him the truth, and she never should have asked this of him, but she had to ask it.

"I don't want her to have to do what I've had to," Lori said. "I know how this all sounds. Mercenary. You must think that I'm only here because you have money, because I want you to give my daughter what I couldn't, and you'd be right. I know that makes me a despicable person—"

He took her hands. "It doesn't."

Lori looked down, gathering herself, then back up at Mark's face. "I wasn't fishing for compliments. But now you know the ugly truth: I came to you in hopes that you would help me protect our daughter."

"Tell me how."

She fell in love with him all over again. He should walk away from her in disgust. He shouldn't be looking at her with such sympathy and pain. She'd hurt him. She'd prevented him from knowing his daughter. "How can you forgive me?"

"You've punished yourself so much in the years since Paris," Mark said. "You did what you thought you had to. The person who I cannot forgive is your mother, for making you leave your home in the first place, for making you believe you had to keep running when you don't—you never did."

"My mother—"

"I don't blame you. You did what you believed you had to, for Elisa, for our daughter." His voice caught in his throat. "You did a phenomenal job with her. She's strong and smart and kind. You can see the strength in her—she's resilient."

"She shouldn't have had to be." Lori waved her hand at the burbling brook and the meadow filled with wildflowers. Crickets chirped between the grasses. "She should have had all this. A peaceful childhood, where she could run around and get to know the stones in the brook like they're her family. She should have had a proper family."

"She had you."

"I'm sorry, Mark. For all of it."

He smiled, and it was as if the sun shone for the first time. She wouldn't have been surprised if a hundred birds burst into song, deer started frolicking in the meadow, and rainbows appeared—it was that kind of smile. It made her feel like dawn was rising inside her, golden light and warmth flooding through her.

"She'll need money," Mark said. "An account in her name that she can draw on whenever she struggles to find a place to stay or food to eat."

Tears pricked her eyes. How did she meet someone so wonderful? With such a great heart? She didn't deserve him, but she was never, ever going to walk away from him again. She was going to love him with every second she had left.

"And an open invitation to come home whenever she's ready."

"I don't know if she'll return. She can't." *He doesn't understand. She can't stay.* He hadn't believed her about the curse. But he did understand that *she* believed it was true, and maybe that was enough? "But yes, that's what I want her to have: a safety net." Someone who cares, who can catch her if she falls. Lori never had that. "I don't want her to ever be afraid. Or to feel alone. Even if she never returns. Can you give her that?"

"Yes," Mark said.

Yes. It was a beautiful word. Lori felt tears slip down her cheeks.

"But I need something in return."

"Anything," Lori said. She meant it. There were no limits to what she would give to keep Elisa safe. *All that I have and all that I am.*

"I'll establish a trust for her, all the money that would have gone into her child support, if I'd known, and the money I would've saved for her for her college education—it's hers anyway, or it should have been," Mark said, growing more enthusiastic with every word. "The guest room will be hers, whether she chooses to sleep there. She will always have a home with me, whether she wants it or not."

Lori was crying openly now, the brook and the meadow blurring through her tears.

"And in return, you will try."

"Try what?" Lori asked, her voice quivering.

"Try to *live,*" Mark said. "You will go to the doctor, and any specialist they send you to. You'll take whatever tests they recommend, take whatever medicine they prescribe, and you will try, for the first time as I understand it—and I do admit I don't understand it—to *stay.*"

CHAPTER THIRTY-ONE

ELISA

Now

The guitarist won't take me to the statue.

But he will tell me how to find it.

Owen scurries back to his bookstore and returns with a topographical map that shows the town, including the woods, in detail. The girl with kohl eyes peers over his shoulder as he spreads it out on a table. "You know, you can use maps on your phone," she says.

"I like my maps larger than the palm of my hand," Owen says as he smooths the seams. "Now, Devon, where did you enter the woods?"

Devon, the guitarist. I file the name away. It's easier to gain trust if you know a person's name; it's easier to leave if you don't. He's Devon; she's Monica; they're Maddie and Emma. And I am connected to them now. Perhaps I always was. The guitarist, Devon, studies the map for a moment. It's quiet in the coffee shop without his playing, and I listen to the hum of the espresso machine, the drip of the coffee, the click-click-click of the many slightly out-of-sync clocks on the wall, and the breath of the people around me. He points near a turn in the road. "There. That's where I started."

"Great. Where did you go from there?"

"In between the trees." He waved his hand vaguely northward.

"Which direction?" Owen asks. He points to the curved lines on the map. "These mark changes in elevation—do you remember if you went uphill?"

"Was there a trail?" I ask.

"Mmm, better question," Owen approves.

"Yes. I walked on a deer trail." Sitting on a stool next to the map, he runs his fingers over the neck of the guitar, as if trying out new chords, and I wonder what it must be like to have an incredible talent that you can't share.

"For how long?" I ask.

He shrugs, and then he whistles like a birdcall, a few notes descending. He pauses, then repeats it. "I heard that, and it reminded me of that song, 'Hotel California.'" Plucking harmony on his guitar, he sings a few bars. His voice is pleasant, soft and furry, and the added guitar makes it sound even sweeter and heartachingly sad. Out of the corner of my eye, I see Monica wipe away a tear with the back of her hand. *She hears it too.* He stops singing, but his fingers keep plucking the air above the guitar. "I reached the lyric about *some dance to remember* and *some to forget*, and that's when I heard the stream."

Owen purses his lips as he studies the map, looking for a stream. My finger traces the curves of the hills around town. It rolls like the unsettled sea.

"Left the trail and headed for that because it sounded musical, and I was there for inspiration, you know? I hadn't written music in weeks, and I was . . . Well, let's say if I couldn't come back from the woods with a song, then I would've been fine not coming back at all."

Monica lays a hand on his shoulder. He doesn't look at her, but the chords he plays are all minor, as if his guitar mourns.

Tapping the map, Owen says, "Here's the stream. Which way did you go from there?"

"Followed the stream this way." Pausing his playing, Devon reaches over and traces the squiggly blue line. "Not sure for how long, but I remember there was a huge tree. Yeah, like really huge, with branches that blocked the stream, so that was cool. And I went around it—"

"Which direction?" Owen asks.

He shrugs. Plays again. "I don't know. Around it. And that's when I saw the clearing. That's where the statue was. At least, I think. It's not like I was keeping notes."

"You did great," Owen reassures him.

I fold up the map. "Can I take this with me?"

Owen looks startled. "I thought . . . I mean, that is, if you don't mind . . . This isn't just about you and your family history. It affects all of us."

I gawk at him. "You want to come?"

He took me to breakfast and helped me research in the library. He's been kind and supportive since I walked into the Book Cellar. But I didn't think it would extend to tramping through the woods in search of a potentially wish-granting statue. I'm so used to being on my own with all of this absurdity and horror, even when it was Mom and me, but I suppose this isn't just my strange little quest anymore. *Huh.* I find I'm smiling, so wide that I know I look ridiculous, but I can't stop. "Monica, do you want to join us?" I ask the barista and then turn to the two girls. Maybe it'll be a party. "Maddie, Emma, how about you? Do you want to come?" Come to the woods to find a statue, come to break the curse, come to change your fate. Unless I'm being foolish and grasping at straws.

The two girls exchange a look, the kind you can only share if you know one another's thoughts, hopes, dreams, and fears. Emma shakes her head almost imperceptibly, and Maddie squeezes her hand, a full conversation in silence.

"You don't need to." I wonder if they're afraid of what I might find, or afraid of what I might *not* find. Which do I fear? I wonder what rests in those woods, what secrets the statue has absorbed, and what secrets it will tell. I try not to dwell on the possibility that this is all a wild-goose chase, that I'm wasting time I don't have—it *has* to be the right path. Too much had to align to lead me here. Sheer chance can't account for it. *It's fate.*

"I just can't see how a statue could be responsible for my choices," Emma says in a whisper. It feels like a blow. I remind myself that no one has ever accepted the truth about my family's curse before. Why should these people? Just because Owen believes doesn't mean they all do.

Or perhaps they know they're cursed and don't want to do anything about it. That's not an option for me.

"Monica?" I'm tense, but I try not to show it.

Monica shakes her head. "Go on ahead. I have to run Bean Street. And you"—she wags her finger at Owen, as if he's a puppy out of his pen—"should open the Book Cellar."

He frowns, as if he'd forgotten that he's a shop owner with responsibilities. I know I should feel guilty. He opened late yesterday to help me at the library. I shouldn't be asking this of him, but the idea that I don't have to face it all alone . . .

When my mother lay in the hospital, I asked her yet again why she hadn't left. She smiled, a rare smile in those final days. *If you have the choice,* she said, *don't face your fate alone.* I yelled at her then, saying she hadn't been alone, she'd had me, and now she was leaving me alone. She cried, which made me feel far worse. She'd done her best, she said, and she was sorry it wasn't enough. I wish I could leave that memory tied up, but it leaches out. "It's your store," I tell Owen. "You control the 'open' sign. You can close it just as easily." *I don't want to be alone anymore.*

As if I've just insulted her, Monica argues, "You don't know what it's like to be responsible for a business. Your customers expect—"

"That's how the curse wins," I say. "Expectations cage us. What other people expect. What we think they expect. What we expect of ourselves. The rules that we think are unbreakable." I used to beg Mom to try to break the rules. She never once allowed it, until the end, when she chose . . . *She chose to be happy.* She paid the cost, but she relished her happiness.

But I can see that Monica doesn't understand. I look at Emma, Maddie, and Devon—none of them are convinced either. It's only Owen and me.

"I'll put a note on the door," Owen says as he darts out of the coffee shop.

Without a backward glance, I follow him outside.

Behind me, Devon plays his stringless guitar, sad and sweet.

We walk into the woods together, first side by side then single file as the forest folds around us. It smells like pine and wet earth, and I hear rustling through the leaves and a stray birdcall. It's peaceful, contrasting how I feel, my insides churning.

Behind me, Owen asks, "Was he your boyfriend? Your ex? I know it's not my business, but it sounded like it was serious. Are you . . . That is, what I'm trying to ask is: Are you okay?"

"He was the latest person I loved and left. I've left a lot of people." I shrug as if it doesn't hurt. I don't know why it does. After all, it wasn't a surprise that I had to end the relationship—I knew from the second I met Tyler that it couldn't last. You'd think that would make me emotionally prepared. It was Tyler who was blindsided. He was the one who ignored my hints. He was the one who was hurt. Worse, I'd known he would be. I wonder if I'm a monster for loving and leaving again and again.

Owen is quiet behind me.

The trail is packed with dirt and thick with brambles on either side. We have to walk single file and duck under branches. A spray of pine snags my hair, and I pause to detangle it. I keep my eyes forward as I ask, "Are you going to judge me for this?"

He barks a short laugh. "Judge? I'm impressed. I've never left; I've only been left, and I've made a mess of that, enough of one that it does seem plausible that I'm cursed—though, if I'm cursed, does that absolve me of responsibility? It shouldn't. I've made my own choices, except where I've butted up against the universe, which I suppose is your point."

"Do you *want* to feel guilty for what happened with Allison?" I don't ask to be cruel. I genuinely want to know. If I felt guilt for everyone I left, it would wear me down more than the sap penetrating my veins. There was a stretch where I tried not to form any bonds, but that's no way to live. I do try to leave gently. It's never easy, but what choice do I have?

"I want to feel that what we had mattered," he says after a moment. "I want to own whatever mistakes I made, even if I'm not entirely sure what they are. But this isn't about Allison—I wanted to say that I understand why Tyler followed you here. You're worth following."

That's the nicest compliment that anyone has ever given me. Glancing over my shoulder, I see he's blushing, which is how I know he means it. His shoe catches on a root, and he steadies himself. "Did you ever ask him to come with you?"

"He wouldn't." Frankly, it never occurred to me to ask. Tyler has his own life, and I know from years of experience that most people want a home. It's ingrained—everything around us, all of society, reinforces it. "He wouldn't want to be untethered."

"Lots of people dream about a nomadic kind of lifestyle."

I think about how hungry he was for stories of my travels. "Sure, there are people who like life on the road. Plenty choose to live like snails, traveling with their homes, a car or a van or even a motorcycle. I've even met a woman who lived on a boat." I once thought Mom and I could have that kind of life, travel by choice.

"'Vanlife,' I think it's called."

"Unfortunately, that particular lifestyle requires money." Less than owning a house, of course, but there is initial expenditure, as well as gas and maintenance. It isn't just taking a bus to a new town. *Granted, that wasn't the only reason we didn't do it.* "We tried to join that community once, my mom and me. I loved it. Some of the vanlife folks had kids, which was great. Even better, some of them wanted them and were happy to treat me like the child they never had. For about six months, we traveled with this older couple, Ben and Steven. I'm not even sure how my mom convinced them to let us join. It was crowded in their van, but nice. My mom and I slept in this little attic they'd built. The roof of the van was maybe six inches from your nose when flat on your back. We'd cook over a campfire or on their mini grill. I think they'd had a lot of money before taking to the road. They used to talk about their house on the lake and how it got to be too much to maintain." I try to picture the two of them, but the memory is fuzzy. Ben had a white mustache and a laugh that rolled right out of him, and Steven was skinny and tall with a quiet voice. But he used to tell the best stories.

"What happened?" Owen asks.

"With that lifestyle, you go from campground to campground, and you often see a lot of the same people. It's a whole nomadic community, which you'd think would be perfect for us. But it hurt too much because they *chose* it. We didn't. And besides, we had no way to maintain that kind of life on our own—as I said, it does require some money, even if you already have a vehicle, for maintenance, gas, food, supplies, campground fees. Eventually, Ben and Steven decided they couldn't keep moving, and that was it. Their daughter had kids, and they wanted to live near them, help out. Plus, Ben's health deteriorated, and they needed to be closer to a hospital. It's not always easy on the road, even with the cutest van in the world. Engines break down. Weather doesn't cooperate. When they said goodbye, we moved on, back to dingy apartments and overcrowded shelters and abandoned houses until we were kicked out." I haven't thought about that slice of my life in a while. I wonder where Ben and Steven are now. We'd promised to keep in touch, but of course we didn't. How could we? No phone. No email. No address. Even if we wrote to them, they wouldn't have been able to write back. It was too dangerous to visit, Mom said. They'd felt too much like family, for a time at least. Any place with them would feel like home.

"If you could afford that kind of life, would you do it? Carry your home with you?"

I could, I realize, if I use the money that Mom arranged for me; Mark's money, really. In fact, he encouraged me to buy an RV or a tiny house on wheels or a van before I left. He said he'd help me any way I'd let him, but I took my backpack and the bus, like always, without even considering it in any serious way.

Why didn't I seize the chance at that lifestyle once I could afford it? Why do I keep clinging to the kind of life I can never have? Why did it seem so important to leave the money untouched? Was it anger? Pride? Sadness? All three? As I turn the questions over, "Hotel California" loops through my mind. "You know, song lyrics are something we never leave behind," I say. "We carry them with us even when other memories fade."

Owen seems thrown by the change of subject. "Ahh . . . ?"

"I didn't want to share this part of me with Tyler," I admit. "He was separate. He was Lyssa's boyfriend. I know I wasn't fair to him—he didn't get all of me. Or even the true me. He had a version that I created and then left behind. You probably think I'm despicable."

Owen ducks under a pine branch. Loose needles sprinkle the forest floor. "It makes you brave. You found a way to keep your heart intact through all of this—the fact that you can still care, that you're still a good person . . . It's remarkable. I wish you could see that, Elisa."

Remarkable. No one has ever called me that before, and I want to say that he's the remarkable one, coming out here, trusting me, believing me, but I've reached the lyric that Devon mentioned in my head. I wait to hear a stream bubbling. When Owen starts to speak again, I hold up my hand.

Water burbles in the distance. It sounds like an unkind laugh, and I realize we are deep enough into the woods that I can't hear the road anymore. Suddenly, it doesn't seem so peaceful. Overhead, I hear a rustle and flinch—it's a squirrel, racing across a branch. Reaching the end of the limb, it hurls itself across the expanse. The next branch sags as it lands, heavy with the creature's weight, and I tell myself not to be ridiculous. *This is a nice forest. The trees aren't watching us.* They don't care.

Following Devon's directions, we head toward the water. As we tramp through the woods, our steps disrupt the relative quiet: the crunch of dead leaves beneath our feet, the snap of branches, the heaviness of our breath, but the burble of the stream draws us farther in.

"Are you still in love with Allison?" I don't know why I ask. It's not my business.

After a moment, he says, "I miss who she was. I guess I still grieve what our future could have been, if that makes sense. But no, I'm not in love with her anymore. She's not who she was, and neither am I." He lifts a branch to pass beneath. "I read once that every person's cells are replaced, on average, every seven years, so maybe it was inevitable that we'd grow apart, become different people. Maybe her cells changed faster than mine."

I think of my mother, who remained in love with Mark for a quarter century and he with her, but I don't say a word. If it makes him feel better to think it was inevitable, I'm not going to tell him it isn't.

"On the other hand, if you believe it's still the Ship of Theseus, even if every part has been replaced, then the number of years doesn't matter. Regardless, she changed, and that was it," Owen says. "I had to change too, if only for self-preservation."

We reach the stream, and it's as picturesque as I imagined: water dancing over stones, moss growing nearby, and the stream tumbling between the trees. It's a beautiful place, and I can see why someone would choose to call it home. *Like my grandmother. And my mother, until she left.*

I can't help thinking: *Cages can be beautiful.*

If I had the chance to choose, would I stay or go?

I ask Owen, "Where would you go, if you could leave?"

"I haven't let myself think about it in so long that I don't know. But I think I'd start with mountains. Lots of glorious mountains." There's so much longing in his voice that I can nearly see the peaks in his mind: topped with snow, blanketed with evergreen, etched against the bluest sky.

A sprawling tree blocks our way, its trunk wide like a squatting giant, and its branches dip low across the stream. This must be the tree that Devon mentioned. It's a monster of a tree, hulking as if waiting for prey. I look for the clearing. It should be nearby.

"If the curse breaks . . ." Owen says, "if we can all leave . . . would you like to . . . that is, if you wouldn't mind, I think we could . . ."

I reach for the closest branch and push against its trunk with my foot, trying to ignore that it feels like I'm climbing into the arms of a monster. "I'm going to climb it." It'll give me a better view of the clearing. *It can't hurt me. It's a tree, motionless.* I boost myself onto the first branch. "Sorry—what were you saying?"

Owen takes a deep breath. "Do you want to see mountains?"

"Right now, I just want to see the clearing."

I climb higher into the tree, and I feel its bark under my fingers. My heart beats faster, again feeling like sap is penetrating my veins. If I continue trying to leave, might that hold the curse at bay? If intent matters, will this buy me time? All I want is more time so I can figure it all out: why my grandmother stayed, why my mother left, and what I'm supposed to do about it all, if there's anything I can do.

I stand on a thick branch, holding on to the one above. Sunlight spatters the woods, lighting up a fern here and a patch of moss there. Between the pools of light, there's a softness to the shadows. I am grateful that it's midday. I wouldn't want to be in these woods at night. I wonder if my mother and grandmother ever came here and if they felt welcomed by the trees or if the trees hovered over them, watching.

Ahead, I see more light, a steady amber—that must be the clearing. I point toward it. "That way."

Owen reaches up to steady me as I jump from the last branch onto the moss-covered roots. I grab his hand and pull him toward the sunlight.

Overhead, birds chatter, and we barrel through the underbrush until we burst into the clearing. I realize that I'm still holding Owen's hand, a gentle touch, and he shows no sign of letting go.

I lift my face up to feel the sun on my cheeks and inhale. At last, it feels like the trees aren't pressing in on me and I can breathe. This is where Devon said he found the statue. Releasing Owen's hand, I walk forward. Instantly, my hand feels cold, and I wish I'd held on. I look back at him. "It should be here."

We search every inch of the clearing. The open grasses and yellow flowers cover rocks and branches. Devon didn't say how large the statue was, but I hadn't imagined it small. I wish I'd asked for a better description. He said one statue, three women.

Across the clearing, Owen says, "Elisa, you should come see this."

He found it! Rushing to him, I see he's kneeling beside a square piece of stone. It's clearly carved—no natural stone is shaped like a pedestal. In the center, it's rough, as if a piece has been broken off.

"It was here," Owen says.

I touch the broken pedestal and feel the sluggish sap replacing my blood. It's difficult to breathe. So close. It was here. *Was.* "Someone took it."

CHAPTER THIRTY-TWO

I circle the clearing, looking for any other clues. Maybe it was knocked aside by a storm? Maybe it fell off its pedestal and rolled elsewhere?

It clearly isn't here.

"Who . . ." I don't finish the question. There's no way to answer it. This is a dead end.

"What am I supposed to do, ask everyone in town if they took an old statue from the woods? I don't have time for that, and whoever took it would most likely lie anyway." I feel as though I am on the edge of a cliff and there is no way to retreat. "This was my only clue."

I have clung to optimism for so many years. Kept moving forward. Kept trying. I update my list of places to search whenever I hear of any possibility. I try to suck whatever joy I can out of my moments in between. Tyler—that was me trying to live, trying to steal little bits of happiness. But all this time, the world has been conspiring against me. My mom—she tried to find a way out with Mark, a way to be happy on her own terms.

I could have figured out how to be happy on the road. Created a life that she never had the resources to build. But I wanted to stay in one place, like other people, to have the life that I couldn't instead of making the most of the one I did. Why? Why stay anywhere? There's beauty in travel.

I think of Mom and me, looking out the bus window at endless fields, waking up under a rose-stained sky, walking into a new library in a new town, dipping our toes in the Pacific Ocean, wading through a mountain stream . . . We had so many wonderful moments. Why did I let the difficult ones overshadow them? I should have found a way to love them all.

Who really gets choice in their lives anyway? Other people's choices hem you in. Look at Owen. He didn't choose for Allison to leave him or for the sale of his bookstore to fall through. He was cornered by other people's decisions.

But I came here and trapped myself.

"We'll find another clue," Owen says.

Maybe. But would we find it quickly enough?

He said "we." It calms me. It isn't over just because this one wild-goose chase failed. I am still closer to answers than I've ever been. I simply have to keep going. "What if I focus on my original curse again? If I can figure out why I have to leave—"

"We," he says.

We.

"If we can undo your curse, then we'll have time to figure out why we must stay in this town." He looks pointedly at my arm, and I'm comforted that he believes me.

His plan makes sense. If we can eliminate the ticking clock, then I—*we*—will have time to track down whoever took the statue, learn why, and figure out how to free the rest of the town. "We know my grandmother's a dead end," I say. "She didn't have to leave. It began with my mother, just after high school."

"Can we find out more about your mother? What about your idea to look at yearbooks? We aren't far from the high school. Perhaps there's a clue in there?"

High school yearbooks won't tell me what happened after. They won't answer why she left or where she went, but there could be clues that I can't predict. It's a better idea than wandering around these unfriendly woods.

"Let's go," I say.

"I know the head custodian at the high school," Owen says as we retrace our steps. He seems oblivious to the way the woods surround us, but he keeps pace as I walk faster and faster. "He thrives on Eudora Welty short stories, and I'm the one who introduced him to them. He's come into the bookstore at least once a month since for new recommendations." He's already pulling out his cell phone and dialing. "He might be able to get us into the school library, even though it's closed for the summer."

As Owen chats with his custodian friend, we emerge, and I feel my muscles loosen—the woods have relinquished us. I check the scab. Has it thickened? Perhaps spread? I pick at it, then force myself to stop. I wonder what it feels like to have leaves for hair.

Owen drives. It's only a few miles to the school—a squat building made of brick. Silent. Still. Empty. A **Go Bears** banner flutters in the wind, and the parking lot is vacant. All the windows are dark. *It's summer. It's supposed to be abandoned.* But my skin prickles, and I don't know if it's my imagination, my nerves, or my curse.

As we walk inside, welcomed by the custodian, I try to imagine my mother here, but I can't. To me, she was never young. She was always an adult, the one taking care of me.

Our footfalls echo in the empty halls. It's impossible not to be barraged with my dozens of new-school memories, of trying to make friends, trying not to feel uncomfortable in my skin. It was tough to do well in school, when each one had different rules, both written and unwritten. I was invisible at some and far too visible at others.

Escorted by Joey, Owen's friend, who wears a Greenborough High hoodie and smells heavily of aftershave, we enter the school library. It's as empty as the rest of the school, and it feels as though our every inhale and exhale echoes through the stacks.

"Got any new recs for me?" Joey asks.

"Did you try Alice Walker?"

His head bobs. "Loved her."

"I have some collections by newer authors you could try . . ."

Tuning them out, I walk between the shelves and am flooded with memories of all the school libraries I took refuge in throughout my childhood. Librarians always welcomed me, especially as the new kid. Here sit old friends—I run my finger over the spines of a collection of Madeleine L'Engle books. Three shelves down, I see Louis Sachar's *Holes.* Across the aisle, Sharon Creech's *Walk Two Moons.* All the Harry Potter books are there with well-worn spines, as are the Percy Jackson books. John Green. Oh God, I cried over so many of his books, and I laughed at Meg Cabot's.

It doesn't take me long to locate the school yearbooks: filed by year behind the circulation desk, in a special section decorated with the school colors. I select a few, based on my mom's age, and sit down at a long empty table.

Joining me, Owen flips through too, scanning the names in each class. My fingers tremble as I turn the pages. For so many years, I've had so little information that I don't—

"Here," Owen says.

He slides a yearbook across the table, open to the senior photos. There, without the circles under her eyes or the thinness in her cheeks, is my mother. She's smiling at the photographer and wearing a blue blouse. She has a dusting of makeup on, with extra-pink lipstick. And her name:

Lori Ellert.

A photo and her name—her real name, in print.

It hits me so hard that I nearly can't breathe. All my life, as far back as I can remember, she avoided letting anyone take her picture. She certainly never would have allowed anyone to print her real name. Yet here she is, in black and white, as if she were just like everyone else.

She was on yearbook, as well as on the prom committee. Really? My mother? She was also involved with the literary magazine. That surprises me less. She always did love to read, and I'd seen scraps of poetry she'd written. She never kept them, always crumpled them up, but I'd fished a few out of the trash.

Under her photo, she's chosen a senior quote: *Hope is the thing with feathers—That perches in the soul—And sings the tune without the words—And never stops—at all.*

It doesn't suit her at all.

She gave up on hope. Until the end, at least.

I keep flipping, hungry for more of her, and the yearbook rewards me: there she is on the bleachers with friends. A football game? A pep rally? I drink in the images. Who are her friends? Do they know what happened to her? Can I find them?

Gently, Owen blots a drop, and I realize I am crying. He doesn't say a word; he just sits with me as I flip through the yearbook, staring at the photos as if they could speak to me.

"I should . . . take notes . . ." My voice sounds ragged, as if I haven't used it in years. "If there's anyone in a picture with her . . . if they're still in Greenborough, maybe they remember her? Maybe they know what happened to her."

Owen finds me paper and a pencil, one of those short eraser-less golf pencils. I flip back and forth between the group pictures and the seniors, noting anyone who is photographed near my mom. She's in a number of photos, perhaps because she was on the yearbook committee. I don't recognize a single name that I've written down.

Once I've compiled the list, I sit back. "Know anyone?" I ask Owen.

He studies my scrawl, then shakes his head. "I don't know everyone in town by name, though. Most I only know by their taste in books. We could look through the customer list at the Book Cellar, if you'd like. We might be able to pair people with addresses or phone numbers, if anyone has bought a book with a credit card recently. The system tracks that stuff, or it should, if I didn't mess up."

I open the next yearbook, this one from her junior year, and repeat the process, adding names to my list. I stop on one very familiar one, and my finger slides to the matching picture.

Allison smiles out at me.

Cora said my mother and her daughter had gone to school together, but I was certain that she'd misremembered. *This can't be possible.* The basic math doesn't work out. She's my age, Owen's age. She was engaged to him. Obviously she couldn't have gone to high school with my mother. Twisting the yearbook so Owen can see, I tap on the photo. "Is this Allison's mother, also named Allison?"

He stares at the photo. "Her mother is Cora. How is it possible? She's my age. We celebrated her birthday. It's in June. She can't . . ."

I agree. The math doesn't compute. "Did she have an aunt who looks like her with the same name?" This person has to be related. The resemblance is too exact, except for the dated haircut and makeup.

He shakes his head. "Not that I know of."

Allison.

Owen couldn't leave after she broke off their engagement. And here she is, in high school with my mother when she very much shouldn't be. Our curses could be connected after all, through her. Allison's the common denominator.

Maybe it's not this place that's at the heart of the curse. Maybe it's a person.

She's not the victim.

She's the cause.

"I have to talk with her," I say.

Owen nods. "I can't follow you there. She won't talk to you if she sees me."

Then I'll do it alone. I'm used to alone, so it really shouldn't bother me as much as it does. I close the yearbook and stand. I don't know what I'm going to say, but it feels as if everything is rushing forward.

On a whim, I lean over and kiss his cheek. "I'll find answers."

Without waiting to see his reaction, I hurry toward the door. Glancing back, I see his fingers lightly touching his cheek. He then jolts forward and calls out, "I'll drive you there."

◆ ◆ ◆

Owen leaves me at the start of the driveway, and I walk between the oaks toward the cacophony of birds. I feel like that inside, a swirl of voices and calls and screams, mixed with a cautious hope.

Allison could be the answer.

But will she help me? If that truly was her in the yearbook a generation ago, she's full of secrets and lies and impossibilities. She may deny it all or refuse to answer any questions. Oh, I have so very many questions.

I also feel the snarl of anger. If Allison holds the answer, then it means she's responsible. She did this to me, to Owen, to all of us. I walk faster, and the bird cries grow louder.

I see the house ahead. Battering the bars of their cages, the birds flap their wings as if they want to break free, reminding me of my nightmare on the bus.

We're all caged.

I knock. "Allison, are you home? We need to talk." When no one answers, I knock again and then prowl up and down the porch, peering into the windows, while the birds cry at me. Cora should be home at least, and she should be able to tell me where her daughter is. Unless she doesn't know? I wonder if Cora is one of Allison's victims as well and, if so, what kind of curse she is under. I never asked her if she's left Greenborough, if she's ever left this house. Perhaps her mother was Allison's first victim. *I should have asked.*

The birds are agitated as I pace beside their cages. The floorboards of the porch squeak as they bend beneath me. My hands clench and unclench into fists, and I try to calm my thoughts to figure out what I am going to say, what I am going to ask—no, what I'm going to demand.

Allison seemed so desperate, so sad, so innocent—was all of that a lie? Or is she unaware of what she's done? I halt at that thought. She could still be innocent. Or perhaps she doesn't know how to stop the curse? Or she could be unaware . . . That seems unlikely, given that she was in that yearbook. At the very least, Allison must know she is two decades older than she appears, older than Owen believed.

There could be another explanation. I'll ask, and I'll listen before I accuse.

A squawk sounds next to me, and it's so similar to a cry from my dream that I shiver. I look at the bird—a drab songbird in a cage that's been painted gold. I look into its eyes and feel a lurch of familiar sadness. Without thinking, I reach toward the latch and—

"Don't!" a sharp voice says behind me.

The bird is so close. Its feathers brush my fingertips through the bars.

A wrinkled hand catches mine and pulls it back from the door, and I turn. Cora. She's pale, as if I've frightened her, which I probably have. "I'm sorry. I . . ."

Her fingers are tight on mine, twisting my hand, and I let out a gasp.

She releases me and smiles shakily. "No harm done. I know it seems like they should be flying free—it probably seems cruel that I keep them caged. *They're birds! They should fly!* But not these birds. Each of them is in their cage for a reason; they wouldn't thrive outside. Believe me, this is a better life for them."

They're rescues, I remember. Most likely they don't remember how to live in the wild. Unable to hunt, they'd die without Cora there to feed them. I'm not even sure they know how to fly. Their wings could be damaged or too weak. I'd be condemning them if I opened the cages. "I'm sorry," I repeat, and Cora's expression softens. I keep my hands behind my back to show I mean no harm, either to her or her birds. "Is Allison home? I'm actually here to talk with her . . . about the caretaker's house . . . just a rental question."

"Is it the plumbing?" Cora asks with a sigh, as if it's always the plumbing.

"No." Then I think: that's a perfect excuse. "Yes. It's not an emergency, but I just wanted Allison to take a look at it. Is she home?"

"She is, but if it's plumbing, we have a fellow we call. I'll fetch the number." She hobbles toward the door and then pauses. "You'll leave the cages alone?"

"I will," I promise.

She eyes me for a moment and then steps inside.

I pace again, this time ignoring the birds. My hands are still behind my back, clenched so hard they hurt.

When Allison steps out, I spin to face her.

She sees the look on my face and closes the door behind her. "You know."

CHAPTER THIRTY-THREE

LORI

2022

On her wedding day, Lori had two thoughts:

I am incandescently happy.

And

I am dying.

The two truths battled inside her as she adjusted her veil. She stared in the mirror. The makeup couldn't hide the shadowy circles under her eyes. The satin sleeves of her wedding dress hid the bruises on the insides of her elbows, thanks to all the needles she'd been poked with over the past few months. Her skin felt as knotted as bark, and her breathing was tight, as if her lungs were stuffed with leaves. She expected to see hints of green in the whites of her eyes, but all she saw were the red veins of burst blood vessels.

Her head had only the soft peach fuzz that had grown in the past few weeks, since her final chemo treatment. She had opted for no wig, only the veil. She was tired of lying, even about her hair, and Mark didn't mind. He called her beautiful no matter what, even when she was on her knees in front of the toilet, vomiting from the latest treatment, even when she woke in a sweat, after a nightmare about Elisa, lost, alone, and scared.

Lori took a breath, coughed, and then breathed again. On paper, they were already married—at the courthouse on a random Tuesday. They'd needed the paperwork to add Lori to Mark's healthcare plan. They'd agreed then that they'd have a proper ceremony later, when the garden was in full bloom. It was going to be a small celebration. Only a few guests. No bridesmaids or groomsmen, only Elisa as her maid of honor. Mark's best man was a friend from law school, the only friend who hadn't questioned him about marrying a dying woman who had disappeared on him for years. Unlike Mark, she didn't blame his friends for their doubt, and she didn't let it bother her. It didn't matter what anyone thought of her, except for Mark and Elisa.

They are my world. No, they are my home. Yes, that word finally fit. Home. That word had been such an enemy for so many years, but now she welcomed it with all its meaning and burden and expectations.

The bedroom door opened behind her. "Mom?"

"Over here," she said.

"Wow, you look beautiful," Elisa said.

Lori saw her daughter reflected in the mirror behind her. Elisa was wearing a dress she'd chosen for herself: blue as the night sky, sleeveless, and beautiful. Her hair was in an intricate set of braids, but she'd refused all makeup except lipstick. She carried a spray of white roses. "So do you," Lori told her.

"Aw, this old thing?" Elisa twirled, and the skirt fluttered, as gentle as a butterfly's wings. Lori had never seen Elisa in a formal dress before. *It suits her.*

She felt a stab of guilt that this was the first nice dress Elisa had ever owned. They hadn't been able to afford prom, even if Elisa had wanted to go. *So much I was never able to give her. At least I can give her this: a happy family, for a little while, and security thereafter.*

Elisa's expression turned serious, and Lori tensed. "Are you certain—"

"Yes."

"You don't know what I was going to ask," Elisa said.

"I do know." She didn't, but she knew she wouldn't like it.

"It could have been about having mushrooms in the appetizers. Even stuffed with crab meat, they're barely edible. It's the texture. They're far too sluglike."

Lori smiled. Crossing to the window, she looked out at the backyard. She'd wanted a home wedding, and Mark had jumped on having it outdoors—he was still trying to keep her healthy, and she loved him for that. They'd had a white tent set up for the reception and white chairs in the garden for the ceremony. The trellis of roses in front of the lavender bushes would be their altar. Jars with candles had been set up around the garden for when the sun set. A violinist friend of Mark's was tuning in preparation for the ceremony. The stray notes drifted in through the window.

"Mark said you refused a honeymoon," Elisa said. "Why? It could delay . . . things, if you traveled for a while."

"I've traveled enough," Lori said.

"It's been eight months. You're done with the chemo. You could travel again. With Mark, if you want. And maybe . . . Mom, we could go back to my list of places with unexplained oddities. I know you think it's pointless, but we could try again, see if we can break—"

Lori cut her off. "Elisa. Let me have this day."

She heard Elisa sigh heavily behind her. "I'm thinking about the future."

"Don't," Lori suggested. "Enjoy today. Let tomorrow be. It's the only piece of all of this we get to choose."

"I can't do that."

"Then you're not trying hard enough," Lori said. "How we face what the world throws at us . . . that choice is the only thing that's truly ours." She saw Mark out in the garden, so handsome in his tuxedo. He ran his fingers through his hair, and one of his friends batted his hand away and brushed his hair back into place. She'd told him he didn't have to wear a tux—this was their wedding, and it was about doing what made them happy, not what other people thought they should do. He said he wanted to match her and, more importantly, match her image for the day. "I want it to be perfect," he'd said.

She'd told him it didn't need to be perfect; it just needed to be real.

"I don't understand why you're doing this," Elisa said, sinking down on the edge of the bed. She laid the white-rose bouquet next to her, and the petals drooped onto the quilt. "I do understand why you said yes. You thought you were dying, and leaving Mark was your greatest regret. You wanted some happiness at the end. Plus you needed his healthcare, his money. It makes sense. But now that you're okay . . . You have to know this can't last. Ten months anywhere, that's all we get. I didn't make the rules."

Oh.

Oh no. She thinks . . . Lori knew she should say the words out loud: the doctors didn't stop the chemo because it worked; they stopped it because it wasn't working. She'd thought Elisa understood. *Perhaps she doesn't* want *to understand.*

Outside, the violinist had finished tuning, and there was only the soft murmur of voices as the guests took their seats. *Later. I'll explain later.*

"Give me today," Lori said to Elisa.

"Sorry, yes, I can do that," Elisa said. She plastered a smile on her face, and though it was as fake as the painted smile on a plastic doll, Lori thought it was both kind and brave of her to try. She picked up her maid of honor bouquet. "I didn't mean to ruin today."

"You couldn't ruin anything," Lori told her.

Elisa made a face. "You haven't seen me try. I could face-plant into the cake. Start a food fight with the appetizers. Eat the flowers."

Laughing, Lori linked her arm through her daughter's and guided her toward the bedroom door. She picked up her bride's bouquet from the top of the dresser as they passed. "You know, when I was a little girl, I used to dream about my wedding day. I had it all planned out at age six, or so Aunt Cora says. The cake was going to be made of marshmallow fluff, with a vat of chocolate next to it, and I wanted tons and tons of calla lilies, because I thought they looked like a bride, with their white petals. My mother told me that marshmallow can't be made into a cake and calla lilies were only for funerals." They walked through the house and out the back door as Lori talked. She showed Elisa her bouquet. Mixed with the white roses and peonies were three calla lilies. "I compromised on the cake. Mark really loves chocolate."

"I know you think it's the other way around," Elisa said, "but he's lucky to have you."

She kissed her daughter on the cheek. "You walk first. I'll follow."

Holding the white roses in front of her, Elisa walked down the aisle between the array of Mark's friends. Lori had met a few of them, knew the names of the rest, but didn't particularly care. All that mattered was that Mark and Elisa were here. She smiled at him from her end of the aisle, and he smiled back, as radiant as the sun. After all these years, his smile was still free and innocent, as if joy flowed through him like a river. She felt like a stream where the water had to fight its way over branches and stones. She thought of the stream beyond the meadow at the edge of his property. Perhaps this was why she loved it so much. It was like her, fighting for every scrap of happiness she could seize and uncertain if she deserved any of it.

She was here, though, and whatever rocks and sticks and roots had been in her way, they didn't matter today. As the violin began to play, Lori felt herself smile, just as free and joyful as Mark.

I am here today. That's enough.

CHAPTER THIRTY-FOUR

ELISA

Now

"It all ties back to you," I say.

Glancing at the house, Allison moves off the porch, away from the birdcages. "My mother won't like us talking about this. She worries about me."

I want to yell at her, shake her, make her undo whatever she's done. Instead, I keep my voice level and soft, as if she herself were a frightened bird. Joining her on the lawn, I halt a few feet away from her, just beyond arm's reach. "You were there with my mom, in high school, and you were with Owen—two decades later but only a few years older, an impossibility. I saw the photos. I know the truth. You cursed us."

Allison stares at me a moment, then laughs. "*That's* what you think?"

"He can't leave, and now I can't leave, except I also can't stay. You see, you cursed me twice." I roll up my sleeve and show her the bark, which has spread to the size of my palm. "You need to fix this. Reverse your curses."

Stepping closer, she touches the scab lightly, but she doesn't reveal what she sees or what she thinks. Instead, she says, "I knew your mother. She was the daughter of my mom's best friend, but we weren't close."

Don't scream. Stay calm. "Then why did you curse her?"

"I didn't. I didn't even know she was cursed. She was supposed to be married, and then she just left, after Rose died. I knew her fiancé, and he was heartbroken."

There was so much about Mom's life I didn't know before coming to Greenborough. Cora had mentioned a fiancé, but Mom had never once talked about anyone before Mark. Then again, I hadn't even known about Mark until we moved in with him.

What else didn't she tell me?

"As far as I know, your mother never came back and never spoke with him or anyone from Greenborough again. It was the talk of the town for a while. Everyone said that grief makes you do crazy, unexplainable things, and they expected her to come home eventually, but she never did." Allison glances at the house, continuing to retreat from the porch, and I wonder what it is she's afraid of: her mother's anger or the truth.

Is she telling the truth?

I had been so sure she was the cause of the curses. At the very least, I thought she held the answers. But perhaps this isn't a dead end. Allison might not have caused my family's original curse, but she could still be responsible for my inability to leave Greenborough. "Okay, so what about Owen and me and the others from the coffee shop—Emma and Maddie and Monica—and how we can't leave—"

"*I* am the one who can't leave. That's *my* curse."

"Owen said—"

Allison cuts me off. "I died."

She what?

"I got sick. Very sick. The doctors didn't know what was wrong with me, but my mother told me not to worry, she'd take care of it, and then . . . I died. My heart stopped, and before you ask, no, they failed to restart it.

I was dead. Completely and utterly. And then, now, I'm here, but . . . less than I was, and I cannot leave no matter how hard I try."

She *died*? This is so far beyond what I expected her to say that all I can do is gawk. She's flapping her hands, birdlike, in agitation, and it's clear she believes every word she's saying. But . . . died? *Is that so much more unbelievable than my mother turning into a willow tree?*

Who am I to determine the truth? If Allison says she died, then that's her truth.

"My mother convinced me it was a second chance, a miracle, and eventually I did try to keep on, despite how I felt—despite how incomplete, how hollow, how empty I felt every second of every day. When I met Owen, I thought if I pretended everything was fine, it would be. I thought I could learn to feel again, to *be* in this skin again. Truly, I tried to make it work, my second life, if you can call it a life, but I already knew it wasn't working. I tried to pretend that I was still . . . here. Still me. Owen and I would go on dinner dates, and I would hide the food in my napkin, pretend I could still swallow. I'd slip out of bed after he fell asleep, and aimlessly roam, eternally awake. Then the car accident happened, and I died again. After that, I knew these miracles, these recurrent lives, were a curse."

She died twice. *Twice.* I think of the moment I met her, her galaxy-filled eyes and the U-Haul truck—was that her third death?

What did this mean for Owen? If she couldn't leave and was living a hollow half-life, what was he? I try to shape the question: "Owen . . ."

"I left him because I wasn't in love with him—I can't feel love for anyone or anything; that piece of me died long ago—and it wasn't fair to him. It took the car accident, my second death, before I realized that my life *did* end." She sighs and holds up her hands as if she can see through them. "I'm not supposed to be here. I can't feel what I'm supposed to feel. It's muffled, as if I'm underwater or far away. I can't cry. I can't feel joy. I don't sleep. I don't eat. Some days, my heart doesn't beat. I am a shadow of what I should be, not dead but not truly alive, either, in this endless limbo where nothing feels real or right. It's torture, not life; I'm constantly reminded of everything I've lost and can never have. I don't belong here, not anymore. I have tried everything I can think of, but I cannot leave."

Help me leave. I'm reminded of her first words to me.

"I'm dead," she says, "yet I cannot die."

"I'm so sorry." It doesn't feel like enough, but I don't know what else to say.

"The dead are supposed to rest in peace. I don't know what I did to deserve this endless agony."

There is no good response. No one deserves what she's been forced to endure. "Is Owen like you? Is he dead?" It feels wrong to suggest, especially about Owen. I think of his smile, his kind eyes, how warm and alive he feels. He doesn't seem like someone who can't feel joy. How could he be dead? How could she? What is she? A ghost? She seems substantial for a ghost, but if she can't eat, can't sleep, can't age, can't cry, can't feel . . . That's no kind of existence.

"Owen's alive, completely ordinary. He's just stuck. At first, I thought he was staying for me, but if you say he *can't* leave . . . I don't know if he's cursed or merely thinks he is, or if there's a difference. I doubt it's the same curse as mine since he isn't dead—he's able to feel and grow and change and *live*—and I know that I didn't curse him. Or you."

"Someone did." I tell her what happened with the bus and with Tyler's car, aware it could be coincidence but convinced it isn't. "I talked to people at the coffee shop, and Devon, the guy with the stringless guitar, said he made a wish on a statue of three women that he found in the woods. He thinks that's what changed him, a wish gone wrong. Owen and I went to find it, but all that was there was the pedestal. Someone took it, maybe whoever cast the curses over us."

Allison goes very still. "A statue?"

"Yes." That meant something to her. "Of three women."

"Like the Fates?"

"Yes, exactly like the . . ." There's a statue garden here at Allison's house, drowning in vines and weeds. I saw it when I first arrived and didn't think much of it. "Oh." She stares at me, and I stare back, and then we both walk fast across the lawn.

From the porch, the birds begin to squawk, and their cries escalate as the door swings open. "Allison?" Cora calls.

Allison doesn't answer. She breaks into a run. So do I.

Ahead are the sculptures, strangled by weeds. I remember all of them are Greek mythology themed—and there is one of the three Fates.

We see it at the same time.

It's half-buried in ivy, rammed into the ground at an angle—as if it were broken from its pedestal. Allison hurries toward it, and I grab her arm. My fingers close around her flesh. She doesn't feel like a ghost. "What do you plan to do?" I ask.

"Make a wish to break the curse."

I shake my head. "You could make it worse. Devon's wish turned out wrong, remember? What if all the wishes come out wrong, like monkey-paw wishes?"

"I have to try," Allison says. "I can't continue like this. Half-alive. Denied peace. You don't understand what it's—"

From the porch, Cora calls, "Best to leave it alone."

Both of us turn toward the house. Allison's mother is ringed in light, the cages flanking her on either side. Her face is shadowed, and I can't see her expression, but her voice rings out with certainty. *She knows about the statue. About the curses. She knows it's not safe to make a wish.*

"You did this," Allison says soberly.

Cora?

"You made a wish," Allison said. "You trapped me." Her voice grows louder, stronger. Her eyes blaze, and I imagine flames within her, trying to burst free.

"I saved you!" Cora says.

Backing away from Allison, from Cora, from all of it, I try to clear my mind to think. I only half believed it before, but Cora is acting as if it's true: this weatherworn statue grants wishes. Or curses.

If it's true, then it could be responsible for all the oddities in Greenborough.

It could be responsible for my curse.

For Mom. For everything we went through, all the goodbyes we were forced to say, all the hopes and dreams we had to leave behind. But who would have made a wish that made my mother so miserable?

Maybe that wasn't the intent.

They don't come out right.

It creates curses instead of granting wishes.

Allison is shouting at her mother, and her mother shouts back as she hobbles across the lawn. "You should have let me go!" "I couldn't lose you! You can't ask a mother to lose her child, not when there was something that I could do about it!" "You had no right!" "I'm your mother! I have every right!" "You've seen what I go through—the pain of every day. You didn't save me; you condemned me!"

Cautiously, as if it's a rattlesnake, I approach the statue. The three women's faces have weathered in the wind and rain. I can't tell their ages or get any sense of what they truly look like, but it doesn't matter. Here, at last, is the answer I've been looking for, a weatherworn lump of rock that's responsible for so much chaos and pain.

I can end this.

No more wishes.

No more curses.

Certainty settles into my bones, and I pivot toward the caretaker's house. I know where I left the tools, specifically a heavy-duty plumbing wrench. I pull it from the toolbox and then march back outside. Both Cora and Allison are crying and shouting at each other across the lawn. On the porch, the birds scream and squawk as if they're being torn apart.

I feel the weight of the wrench in my hand.

I have seen ample evidence of a wish going wrong: me, my mother, Owen, Maddie and Emma, Devon, and Allison. I can't make another wish. I don't have the right to mess with other people's lives like that, and no one has the right to mess with mine. But if I break the statue, will that reverse the curses? Certainly, it will prevent any new ones from being made. Without hesitation, I swing the wrench toward the statue. It hits with a clang, and a piece of rock flies off.

Cora and Allison turn toward me.

"What are you doing?" Cora shrieks. "Stop!"

"Don't stop," Allison orders.

I hit the statue again. One of the faces breaks in half. It feels right. But I pause. "Tell me what will reverse the curses," I say to Cora. "Or I'll destroy it." I am going to destroy it anyway, but she doesn't know that. "How did you discover the statue grants wishes?"

"Your grandmother found the statue, and your grandfather was the first to make a wish," Cora says. She smiles as if it's a fond memory. "It was the night of our prom, and we were joking around in the woods. On our way to the Kissing Shack."

"I've heard of the Kissing Shack," Allison says. "It burned or fell down years ago."

I remember the collapsed shack that I found in the woods when I was searching for signs of my grandmother. "Go on. What happened?"

"He made a wish for your grandmother to stay with him, and it came true. She always wanted to see the world, but he proposed, and she said yes. How could she say no? He loved her, and she loved him, at least as much as she could. It was a sensible match, a good marriage. They were as happy as two people can be. She just . . . didn't always see that. His wish kept her on the right path. When your mother was a teenager, Rose concocted this crazy plan: she wanted to go off to Europe without them, become a tour guide, have adventures. Well, it was absurd. She had a husband and a child. And me. I couldn't let her leave me. I remembered that night in the woods, after our prom, and I thought if it worked for Glenn . . ." She trails off.

"Then what happened?" I ask.

Cora takes a step toward the statue.

I heft the wrench. "I need to know all of it."

"I made a wish that she'd stay in Greenborough," Cora says. "But it didn't come out right. She got sick. Cancer. And she didn't get better. My wish wasn't specific enough. I kept her body in Greenborough—she never left, just like I asked—but her soul didn't stay."

Allison is no longer staring at the statue. She's staring at her mother, with a growing look of horror. "Tell me you didn't."

"I wasn't about to make that same mistake twice," Cora says. "When you died, I wasn't going to let your soul go."

"You trapped me," Allison says. "You caged me. It was you, and I didn't realize. All these years . . . I didn't see it."

I think of the birdcages, and my blood runs cold. Or is it the sap? I can feel my skin crinkling. Every minute I'm here is a minute too long. I am playing at the edge of a cliff, and I can feel the wind rushing around me. She caged Allison's soul like a bird.

"It worked beautifully," Cora says. "Here you are, with me. Still young. Still perfect. Still mine." She looks at me. "I'm only sorry that I couldn't do the same for Rose. But I have been trying to fix things as best I can. I've refined the wish for others—they'll live and die in their own time, no sense violating nature for everyone; who knows what that would do? And they don't all deserve it anyway—but you, my darling, you will always stay. I will never have to do without you, my sweet girl. I'll never be alone, and neither will you."

There are many, many caged birds on the porch.

Are they . . .

Could she have . . .

Yes, of course she did. "How often did you make wishes?" I demand.

"Only when necessary."

"Like with Owen," I say.

Allison flinches. "You didn't!"

"He should have become your husband," Cora says. "I thought if he stayed in Greenborough, you would eventually reconcile. He loves you, you know. You could make each other happy, like your father and me. If I'd known what to do before I lost your dad . . . But I didn't, and

I have done the best I can since then. I've done what people needed to be happy, even when they couldn't see it themselves."

She has no regret. Zero awareness that what she's done is wrong. She will keep making wish after wish, trapping soul after soul in her birdcages.

"Most don't even notice what they're missing," Cora says blithely, "though there was one—a nosy lad who was too interested in my birds. My wish for him transformed him entirely. It was quite remarkable."

"And the other people in town?" I think of the writer who can't write, the waiter who fastidiously cleans the pie case, the librarian who hears voices. "What did you do to them?"

She shakes her head. "Aside from saving my daughter, I did nothing beyond wish for a few friends to stay . . . and then a few more—with every wish, a bird would fly to my porch, dazed and confused. I'd place it in a cage, for its safety, for its own good, and the friend would stay. Simple, elegant, harmless. But I can't speak to what others did to themselves. Not everyone understands how to correctly make wishes. Of course, once I realized that others had found the statue, I moved it here, to protect those who don't know what they're doing, but I don't know how many made their own wishes before I intervened."

She's already confessed to transforming the "nosy lad." And to keeping Allison in a torturous kind of half-life. So her claims of "nothing beyond" are clearly a lie.

"You agree this can't be allowed to continue," I say to Allison. If I don't destroy it now, Cora could ruin yet another life. I can't allow that to happen. I know what her answer will be, but I need her to say it.

Allison presses her lips together. "Do it."

"No!" Cora yells.

Allison firmly places her hands on her mother's shoulders, pinning her in place, and I bash the statue with the wrench again and again until the rock crumbles beneath the metal.

CHAPTER THIRTY-FIVE

LORI

2022

Lying in the hospital bed, Lori listened to the beep and whir of the machines and dreamed that they were the babble of a stream by a meadow. She heard the nurses' voices in the hallway, mixed with the birds in the pine trees. She breathed in the stale hospital air as if it was a fresh spring breeze.

It was happening.

She felt a heaviness in her limbs. She was taking root. Her heart felt as if it was struggling to pump, and she knew it was because of the sap in her veins, sluggish compared to blood.

She drifted in and out of dreams, until she wasn't certain what was reality and what was a dream, but it didn't disturb her.

That day, Lori was by the stream that she loved, and she was sinking into the earth. The wind was in her hair, and she felt it stir her willow branches. She draped into the water, her leaves brushing the bubbles. They tickled her, and she laughed.

She couldn't hear the beeps and whirs and voices anymore. Only the breeze and the water and the birds. She couldn't feel her body. Only the bark and leaves and branches.

Lori wished she could speak to Elisa one more time, tell her that it wasn't so bad, that she'd be happy here.

I'll tell the wind as it blows through my leaves.

CHAPTER THIRTY-SIX

ELISA

Now

I hit the statue until it's a pile of rubble. My arms ache, but I don't feel any different. The bark still sinks its tendrils into my arm. I can feel it creeping over my skin, and my heart pounds harder.

"It didn't work," Allison says. "I'm still here."

"Which bird am I?" I ask Cora.

She's sobbing into her hands.

I don't need her to answer. I have dreamed of the cage that I'm in. Charging across the lawn, I run toward the porch. The caged birds are pounding their wings against the bars, and I wonder if they know what I'm here to do. My heart hammers in my chest as I race up the steps. I scan the cages, looking for one that—

It doesn't matter which one. They should all be free.

Opening the closest cage, I step back as the songbird, gray with a white breast and a tuft of gray feathers on its head, hops toward the door. "Go on. Fly." It pokes its head outside as I open the next cage.

This one looks like a small hawk, and it eagerly flies out the instant I open it.

I hurry along the porch, opening cage after cage. Sap oozes through my veins, and I feel leaves itch in my throat. As I release a crow, Allison reaches the porch. Cora is close behind her, yelling at me. "Stop! You don't understand! It's better for them this way!"

"You can't just decide you know best," Allison says. "It's not your decision to make." She begins opening cages too, heading in the opposite direction. One after another, the birds fly out, swooping away from the porch.

One bird, yellow and black and brown, hesitates on the rail. "Fly," I tell it. "Go home. Go to your person. Go wherever you want. Go to the sky." I open the next cage, and an owl waddles through the opening and then launches to soar soundlessly over the lawn.

Cora clings to my arm as tears pour down her cheeks. "Please, stop. Elisa, I'll show you your bird. You can free it and leave. You can save yourself. I'm sorry I trapped you. I thought you belonged here, a friend for my Allison. I thought this place would be good for you. You move around so much. I didn't realize . . . I didn't know Rose's gift would transfer to you."

Hand on a cage door, I freeze. "Rose's gift?"

"She was dying, and Lori thought it would be beautiful to marry her boyfriend before Rose died," Cora says. "Lori was grasping for anything. She had this scheme to have the wedding in the hospital so that her mother could be here. She wasn't thinking about her future happiness. She thought she was supposed to be married, supposed to have her mother there, but Rose knew she wouldn't be happy. She couldn't let it happen, but Lori wouldn't listen."

"My grandmother did this to her, to us?"

"She couldn't."

"Then who—you did it?"

"Rose asked me to make a wish."

I yank my arm away.

"It was her dying wish! And she was my best friend," Cora says. "I had to."

All that my mother suffered. All our goodbyes. All the times we were hungry and homeless and friendless and alone. The sacrifices that her mother had to make . . . She could have had years of happiness with Mark. *I could have had a father. A home. A childhood.*

"I gave her a gift," Cora says. "Rose didn't want to see her daughter make the same mistake she did. Her greatest regret was conforming to what society expected of her, doing what she was told would make her happy instead of seeking out her own version of happiness. I set your mother free."

"You . . ." My throat closes. I don't know how to describe how wrong she was. She clearly doesn't see it. She's smiling at me with tears in my eyes, as if she expects me to understand and forgive her—or thank her?

It wasn't the moon. It wasn't fate. It wasn't my blood. It was an ordinary person, a friend of the family, who decided she knew what was best, damn the consequences.

Grabbing me again with her bony fingers, Cora pulls me by the wrist to a cage halfway down the porch. It's the one from my dream, with the gold-painted bars. "This is yours. Open it. And you can resume your life, exploring the world, the life that Rose never got to have."

"You had no right—"

"Rose was meant to fly free," Cora says. "I didn't understand that. I thought she should want what I wanted. I was part of what kept her trapped here. I never understood . . . until it was too late. I had to set it right by granting her wish for her daughter."

"It wasn't Rose's choice," I say. "My mother's life, my life, our mistakes were ours to make. We should have been allowed to make them."

"She wanted her daughter free of society's constraints," Cora says. "She didn't want Lori to settle when she could have the world!"

"So instead she placed her own constraints on us? You don't know what our lives have been like. To never set down roots means to never have a home. To always have to say goodbye. To never have a family. A job. To always be scraping by. You have no idea what we've had to do just to survive, what we've given up. My mother—You took her life away. She wanted more than anything to have a home. To have what you have!"

"I didn't think it was right," Cora says, "but then I never understood why Rose yearned to fly away. Most would be happier with a home. That's why I caged you. I thought you would be happier if you learned that lesson. I didn't realize that you were already destined for another kind of life."

I peer at my caged bird. It's pale yellow with gray-and-white wings, an olive back, and a lightly speckled face.

Behind me, Cora says, "You're a warbler. Specifically, a pine warbler."

The warbler stares back at me with black, glassy eyes. I can't tell what it's thinking. I open the cage and step back, and the bird launches itself out through the opening.

It doesn't hesitate, trilling notes as it flies, and I rush to the railing and watch as my bird spirals up toward the blue. I feel a certainty that I can now leave. I push up my sleeve and look at the bark. "Now we free the others."

"But you can't—"

Allison approaches from behind. "Mother. Where's mine?"

Cora turns slowly, as if she's carrying a heavy weight. "Yours is special. It's not just holding you to this town like the other birds; it's tethering you to life."

Allison hesitates. "You aren't keeping the others from dying?"

"Oh no, for them I used the same wish as I did for Rose," Cora says, as if this is all reasonable. "I'm not here to play God."

Except that's what she tried to do.

"But that's what you did with me," Allison says, as if she heard my thought. "You interfered in the natural order of things. You stole my fate."

"You're my daughter. All I want is your happiness. Of course, I couldn't let you die. You deserve to have a full life."

Allison takes her mother's hands. "It's not a life anymore."

"You just aren't trying! Get out there and start making friendships and relationships. Find joy in the little things. You could love gardening, if you'd try it. Or books! Why not visit Owen's bookstore?"

I continue opening cages and encouraging the birds to fly free while Allison shakes her head. Her voice is gentle now, sorrowful. "My life ended a long time ago. This . . . it's a shadow of a life. I am a hollowed-out shell. You have to let me go."

Rivulets of tears show through Cora's wrinkles. "You can't ask me to say goodbye to you. A mother shouldn't outlive her child."

"You can't force your choices on everyone else," Allison says. "My life ended, twice. You have to let me go on to whatever comes next. I'm ready. I've been ready for a long time."

Cora touches Allison's face, her shoulder, her hand. "You're here! How can you ask me to—"

"I'm not asking," Allison says. "I'm telling you. It's time."

Turning her back on her mother, Allison helps me open more cages, and Cora lowers herself onto the porch swing. Her shoulders sag, and she sinks into herself. I don't feel pity. She has played with people's lives. I open the cage of a sparrow, and I wonder which one is Owen. I wonder if he can feel it, now that he's free.

Finishing with the porch, we move inside. Allison opens all the doors and windows as I release the birds within the house. They circle above us, until they each find their way out.

At last, we come to the final bird, a bluebird with a blue-gray back and rust-colored breast, the only bird in Cora's bedroom. Allison hesitates, her fingers on the cage.

"It's your choice," I tell her.

She smiles and opens the cage.

CHAPTER THIRTY-SEVEN

I walk away from the house.

Allison doesn't want me here. "One request," she said, as her bluebird fled its cage. "Leave now." None of us knows what will happen to her next. But if it is the end, she wants to say goodbye to her mother in private, and I respect that.

I don't look back as I return to the caretaker's house. I pack my things: socks rolled, underwear tucked into the cups of my bras, extra cash wedged into the bottom of my backpack. Only a few traces of me remain—the windows are clean, the rafters are free of dust, a few items (from the coffee shop trash cans) remain in the refrigerator. I make the bed and clean the dishes. I take a moment to look around. This is a place I will always remember; though, I can't say that I'll miss it. With my backpack stuffed, I head out—brisk pace, walk with purpose, don't look back. Never look back.

I can sense my bird flying overhead; I can sense it even if I can't see it. The wind is in my feathers, and the sun is on my back. There are birds all around, splashes of yellow and red and blue and black and brown. An owl glides silently between the trees. Many of the bird-souls have flown on, but some are perched as if unsure where to go. I'm sure they'll find their way. I stroll down the driveway between the pine trees. I don't know what time the next bus is, but I know I'll be on it.

My heart feels lighter, perhaps because of the birds. I didn't find the cure I wanted, but I found answers. Our lives were shaped by other people's expectations, other people's dreams, other people's choices. We are constrained by love—granted, it was misguided love, a belief that they knew best how our lives should take form. That doesn't make it better or forgivable, but it's an explanation, understandable. Even liberating. I don't have to search anymore. I can choose to live. Perhaps I'll use some of the money from my mother and Mark, buy myself a little camper, make it a roving home. Now that I know my fate is sealed, that I can never settle in a single place, perhaps I can at last find a way to make peace with it.

It feels as if there are possibilities now, which is strange since all I've done is restore the natural order.

Nothing has changed, yet it feels like everything has.

I walk down the sidewalks of town and admire the linden trees and their perfect symmetry. At the Book Cellar, Charlie lounges in the window. He doesn't budge when I come inside, the bell ringing over the door. Owen is at his desk.

"Can you feel it?" I ask him.

"Feathers in the wind," he says.

"Yes."

He follows me to the coffee shop. It's filled mostly with regulars, though Monica is behind the counter with a bearded man I haven't seen before. The writer who doesn't write is by the window, Devon is on his stool with his stringless guitar, Maddie and Emma are at a table with elaborate coffees with hearts made of cream, and the three blue-haired ladies are perched at a round table. I think they are waiting for me.

"I broke the statue," I tell them.

All three ladies stand up in the same smooth motion. I wonder what their real names are. "We knew you'd do it," Purple Blue says, and I blink. She looks the same, yet also young? As if she's all her ages at once. *It must be the lighting in the coffee shop. Or perhaps it isn't?*

All three of them look blurred, as if I'm viewing them through a haze, or as if the artist that painted them has smudged the paint. I shake my head, but my vision doesn't sharpen.

I notice that Devon is playing his guitar, a sweet melody that dances in the air. Like me, his curse wasn't broken when I shattered the statue—the guitar still has no strings.

I wonder about the man who quotes T. S. Eliot. What was his wish? And the writer who doesn't write? What about the waiter in Stu's Diner who can't stop cleaning the display case? Did they all make wishes? Or were they merely living their lives, measured with coffee spoons?

Had they been caged, or had they caged themselves?

"You knew about the statue?" I ask the three ladies.

"Us," Sky Blue says.

I want to ask about Tyler, how they knew about him. I want to ask about Rose and Cora. I want to ask if they knew my mother and what they knew about me. But her one-word answer throws me. *Us.* "Who are you?"

All three of them smile in unison, and I shiver. It's not an answer, and it's clear that they aren't going to give one, at least not one that magically explains it all, tied with a pink bow.

"We're free, my dear," Peacock says. "And now you are too."

I picture the birds in the cage and wonder if they were among them. Perhaps she was one of the brightly colored parrots—there were no peacocks. "Did Cora trap you as well?"

"Oh no, we were trapped long ago," Purple Blue says. "Another tale from another day."

"But we knew we could count on you." Peacock pats my hand. "We knew you were the one who'd change things as soon as you arrived here, back where it all began. We knew if you were pushed hard enough, you would do it."

"We'd hoped before," Purple Blue says. "We thought if only some-one wanted badly enough to be free, as badly as we did—but there was only so much we could do. Until you came and set yourself free, as well as this town."

I don't know if that's what I've done or not. But I do feel different, like my feathers are spreading out. I hope the others feel it too.

"Free," Sky Blue says with a happy sigh.

Peacock says, "You're right, my dear. It will be nice to see the world again."

"Oh yes, sisters, I think we should travel," Purple Blue says. She links arms with the other two ladies. "That was our mistake when we first came here—we withdrew from the world. We thought it would be a lovely way to pass the years, together, in a home of our own. But the world wouldn't let us alone."

"I wonder if the world has changed enough for us to be ourselves," Peacock says.

"I wonder if we care," Purple Blue says and laughs. "Shall we find out?"

"Yes," Sky Blue says.

"Yes," Peacock says.

"Yes," Purple Blue says, and they saunter arm in arm across the coffee shop. Everyone is watching them, unsure of what to say.

Over her shoulder, Purple Blue says to Owen, "Charlie can go with you. You'll find he's amenable to travel now."

Owen looks baffled. "Um, okay?"

To me, Peacock says, "The next bus leaves in a half hour. We suggest that you're on it, my dear."

I intend to be. "Will you be?"

Sky Blue giggles again. "Not necessary."

They exit the coffee shop. Those of us that remain look at each other. Devon puts down his guitar and follows them outside. Emma and Maddie hurry after him. I follow as well, with Owen and Monica, but when we all step outside, the three blue-haired ladies are gone.

"What just happened?" Owen asks.

I'm not certain.

"Maybe," Emma says tentatively, "they're just three ladies who like their coffee." She swallows, then continues. "Maybe they like to sound cryptic and mystical because it's easier than admitting that life doesn't always go the way you planned."

"Or they're leaving because the curse is broken," Maddie says.

"Is there any proof that any of you"—Emma pauses, then amends— "that any of *us* were truly cursed?"

There isn't. But I do notice that Monica is holding the hand of the bearded man, whom I've never seen yet she seems to know well, and it makes me wonder. Another coincidence? I don't believe in them. *The cages are open. We all fly free.* "Is this your bird-watcher?"

Monica smiles at the man.

He smiles back at her. "I never meant for so much time to pass," the bird-watcher says. "I don't understand how it did. But I'm going to spend the rest of my life making it up to her."

"We'll take it day by day," she tells him.

I think of all the different birds and wonder how many different wishes Cora made—only Allison was granted immortality. Perhaps Cora had experimented with many different variations on a theme. She'd mentioned a nosy lad. Perhaps in his search for the golden-winged warbler, Monica's bird-watcher showed too much interest in her collection. Or maybe he did leave town and decided to come back. Maybe his return is merely a coincidence.

I know only what I believe is true. And that's enough for me.

"I have a bus to catch," I say.

"May I come with you?" Owen asks. "With Charlie, of course." He seems as if he expects me to say no, but there's hope in his eyes. I don't know if I should say yes. He has a life here, a bookstore—all the excuses he gave me when I first asked why he didn't travel are true.

"What about your store?" I ask. "And your apartment? Your life here?"

"I'll figure it out as we go. Just . . . I'd like to come with you, if you want company."

No one has ever offered before, but I suppose no one has ever known the whole truth or seen the real Elisa before either. I'm not sure it will work. He's lived all his life in one place. He could miss his store and his home. He could still love Allison, for all he claims he doesn't. We don't know each other well. We might not have a future.

Then again, we might.

"Yes," I say. "I'd like that."

CHAPTER THIRTY-EIGHT

It takes several months, but eventually we buy a van: a bookmobile.

Owen sells his bookshop to the town librarian, who hires Maddie and Emma to run the shop during library hours. He transfers a portion of his stock to our van, which still leaves room for two Murphy beds and a cushion for Charlie. We string fairy lights inside and lay plush carpet.

Our plan is to travel to the nomads, those that have chosen life on the road in their vans and RVs. We'll move from campground to campground, stop at festivals and markets, and sell our books to the traveling community; they like to read too. There are details to figure out, and after I call and explain, Mark offers to assist with permits and such—in exchange for the occasional phone update and visit.

I think it's okay to visit, so long as I'm careful not to make it my home.

That's easier now that Owen and I have the van, which feels more like ours every day. Some mornings I wake up and marvel at the beauty of a technicality that makes my portable home possible—and at my mother and Mark, whose love made this possible.

As we drive toward Mark's house, I try not to feel nervous. In all my traveling, I have never come back to a place, and this one is particularly fraught with memories. Owen is at the wheel, and Charlie is asleep on my lap. I stroke his fur and try to keep calm.

As we pass the mailbox, I study Mark's home ahead. It was never my dream to have a house like this, with perfect flowers in manicured beds and windows adorning the door, but it was my mother's dream. Cora's actions didn't take her dream from her; they merely delayed it. She was true to herself in the end. As the car slows, I'm surprised to discover that I am proud of her. Mom died on her own terms.

I am crying when Owen parks in front of the house.

"Are you sure you want to do this?" he asks. "We can leave and keep driving. It doesn't matter where."

"I want to do this," I sniffle.

I was so angry when I left before. And scared. I used to think my mother's fate was the worst in the world, and I wanted to lash out at everything that forced her to walk the path that she did. Part of me was angry at Mark, for not understanding the lives we'd had to lead and the choices she'd made, but I'm not angry now. Not at my mother, who lied to protect me. Not at Cora, who tried to honor her dying friend's wish. Not even at Rose, who just wanted her daughter to experience what she never could.

Mark . . . *my father* emerges from the house with a nervous smile on his lips. I climb out of the van, gently depositing Charlie on the seat. He makes a *merp* sound in protest but curls up again and falls back to sleep.

Owen steps out of the driver's side and shakes my father's hand.

"The book van looks fantastic. Congratulations," Mark says.

"Thanks," I say.

There's an awkward silence.

"We appreciate your help getting it all started," Owen says. "It's going to be quite an adventure."

Mark smiles, looking less nervous. "I'm looking forward to hearing all about it." He leads us into the house, my mother's ultimate home. "I've started making dinner . . ."

After dinner, I walk alone down to the stream as twilight twinkles around me. The sun has already set, and the fireflies blink in yellow flashes. Crickets chirp, and a few birds cry out as they settle into their nests for the night.

I hear the burble of the stream before I reach it.

It's a short walk to the willow tree.

I sit beneath the branches and lean against her trunk. The evening breeze blows through her leaves, and they rustle around me—I imagine she's whispering to me, though I can't hear the words.

Laying my hand on her bark, I say, "Thank you. For everything you did. For everything you tried to do. Even if it wasn't . . ." My throat clogs. "It's okay. That's what I want to say. I understand, and it's okay."

As the shadows deepen, I sit for a while and listen to the wind through the willow leaves, the stream dancing over the stones, and the crickets in the grasses around us. I don't feel alone. I am aware of Mark and Owen back in the kitchen, cleaning the dishes from dinner, and our van waiting for us to begin the next part of our next journey.

"I have a story to tell you, Mom," I say. "It's not quite what you wanted for me, and it's not quite what I thought I wanted either. You wanted me to have a home, and I wanted answers. I kind of found both? Sort of?"

The branches whisper as the stream burbles at my feet. Above, stars begin to appear, scattered across the sky. The crescent moon watches through the willow leaves.

"It's the story of a girl who couldn't leave and a girl who couldn't stay—and the boy who loved them both. And it's the story of three blue-haired women who wouldn't let anyone else define them. And of one woman who didn't know how to let go. Oh, and there's also a cat and a coffee shop, an old crumbling statue, and the most beautiful guitar music I've ever heard . . ."

ACKNOWLEDGMENTS

One afternoon, I went for a walk, and as I reached the stump of the late great tree that splits my street, words whispered to me, *"My mother is a willow. She stands by a stream that burbles like a toddler's kisses, and her leaves dip into the water whenever the wind blows, to be nibbled by fish who don't know any better . . . perhaps I will be a pear tree."*

I kept repeating the sentences to myself for the rest of the walk so that I wouldn't forget them before I got home and could write them down. And then I went back to writing the book I was already in the middle of.

But I couldn't stop thinking about those words—or about my tree woman. I didn't know what her story was or why I kept coming back to those same few lines.

My friend Amy kept saying, "I think that means you should write it." She was right, of course. Thank you, Amy!

Sometimes stories come as whispers. And you just have to write them to see what they want to say. That's how it was with this book. Writing a book is an exercise in trust—trusting that whatever part of you whispered those words has something it wants to explore—in this case, about choices and curses, about how the dreams and hopes and heartbreaks of others shape our lives, and about how to find our own way forward.

Thank you to my phenomenal agent, Andrea Somberg; my incredible editor, Danielle Marshall; and my amazing developmental editor,

Laura Chasen; as well as all the tremendously awesome people at Lake Union! You have all been such a joy to work with!

And thank you to my husband, my children, my family, and my family-in-law! You have given me both roots and wings, and I love you more than words can say!

ABOUT THE AUTHOR

Sarah Beth Durst is the *New York Times* bestselling author of over twenty-five books for adults, teens, and kids, including *The Lies Among Us*, *The Spellshop*, *The Lake House*, and *Spark*. Her writing has won an American Library Association Alex Award and a Mythopoeic Fantasy Award, and Durst has been named a finalist for the Andre Norton Nebula Award three times. Several of her books have been optioned for film and television, including *Drink, Slay, Love*, which was made into a TV movie and became the subject of a *Jeopardy!* question. Sarah is a graduate of Princeton University and lives in Stony Brook, New York, with her husband, two children, and an ill-mannered cat. Learn more about the author, her work, and upcoming events by visiting her website at www.sarahbethdurst.com.